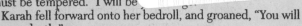

The old man whispered in the gods—but you are not y must be tempered. I will be

Karah fell forward onto her bedroll, and groaned, "You will be my death."

"Only if you prove unworthy.

Karah squinted up at the madman, who sat cross-legged, and stared blindly off into nothingness. As she watched, he became more translucent with every passing second.

She closed her eyes, and murmured. "Please, just kill me now."

First Captain Morkaarin's voice said, "If you aren't out of that tent in five seconds, I just might. You've slept through call."

Karah's whole body jerked, and she opened bleary eyes. Two legs in high boots stood framed by her tent opening. "Oh, godsall, no. I can't get up," she groaned. "I'm dying."

The First Captain's face peered into her tent. Karah noted that what had been an expression of annoyance on his face became one of—shock? Fear? Incredulity?

"What happened to you?" he asked.

"I couldn't sleep last night," she said. And then she considered what she had been through, and decided a lie would be safest. "Nightmares."

He cleared his throat. "Nightmares..."

She nodded.

He gnawed thoughtfully on one side of his bottom lip, then sighed. "We're packing and moving out today, but you can sleep for the moment. And go to the infirmary when you wake."

He walked away.

Karah rolled on her side, ready to let herself drift into sleep. However, she noticed an odd glow in her tent. She looked down at her legs, and then at her hands and arms

Then she rolled onto her belly and pressed her face into the coarse blanket of her bedroll. She started to cry.

Her body glowed with a soft, pale light.

Baen Books by S.M. Stirling

The Fifth Millennium
Snowbrother
Saber & Shadow with Shirley Meier
The Cage with Shirley Meier
Shadow's Son
with Shirley Meier & Karen Wehrstein

The Draka Series
Marching Through Georgia
Under the Yoke
The Stone Dogs

The General Series (with David Drake)
The Forge
The Hammer
The Anvil
The Steel
The Sword (forthcoming)

With Jerry Pournelle
The Children's Hour
Go Tell the Spartans
Prince of Sparta
Blood Feuds
with Susan Shwartz, Judith Tarr & Harry Turtledove
Blood Vengeance
with Susan Shwartz, Judith Tarr & Harry Turtledove

Baen Books by Holly Lisle

Fire in the Mist
Bones of the Past
Minerva Wakes
When the Bough Breaks with Mercedes Lackey

S.M. STIRLING
HOLLY LISLE
The RoseSea

BAEN

THE ROSE SEA

This is a work of fiction. All the characters and events portrayed in this book are fictional, and any resemblance to real people or incidents is purely coincidental.

A Baen Books Original

Baen Publishing Enterprises
P.O. Box 1403
Riverdale, NY 10471

ISBN: 0-671-87620-1

Cover art by Clyde Caldwell

First printing, September 1994

Distributed by Simon & Schuster
1230 Avenue of the Americas
New York, NY 10020

Printed in the United States of America

⊙ CHAPTER I

First Captain Sir Bren Morkaarin, Hereditary Guardian of Timlake, yawned enormously, leaned back against his saddle and pulled his cloak over his legs. The deck was hard, but better than mud, which was something he'd slept in often enough on campaign; summer nights in the clear dry air of the central provinces were just cool enough to make sleep comfortable.

The barge rocked, water chuckling against its bows. All three moons were up, silver coins in the sky—stately Falcon Father, Wolf Mother near Him and The Child moving below, in their eternal dance. The river was high as a result—no worry of sandbars for a while.

The towing cable curved away to the bank, black against the star-shot, moonlit water. The low-slung, pillar-legged shape of the twofork leaned into its harness with ponderous deliberation. The towing beast was a formless lump in the darkness until it threw up its head and showed the Y-shaped horn on its nose; it trumpeted a complaint through thick, blubbery lips.

Bren stretched and shifted position on the hard deck; it was the twenty-first hour, an hour past sundown in summertime. Nobody was awake save the watchstander at the tiller, leaning silently on the long pole. *Easy night for him,* Bren thought, and grinned. Behind his barge came ten more, equally quiet,

1

dark save for the great glass-globe lanterns that hung from the sternposts above the steering oar. Ten barges of men and women, pikes and halberds and muskets, barreled gunpowder and barreled salt pork and hardtack, tents and bandages and boot grease and the boxed Shrine of the Three that moved with the standards. The whole of the XIXth Imperial Regiment of Foot was on the move from garrison duty in the foothills of the North Shield Mountains to the seaport of Derkin in the far south, on the shores of the Shoban Yentror, the Imperial Sea.

Well, not quite the whole of it, he thought sourly. Lord Colonel Feliz Gonstad, Overlord of Maldard and commander-in-chief of the XIXth, was not along for the trip. He'd gone ahead in a well-sprung carriage, with his hangers-on and aides, leaving Bren to do the work.

Nothing new in that.

Lights were coming up ahead, as the canal curved southward through the great riverine plain of the Olmya. Villagers with lanterns, moving like fireflies amid the apricot trees of an orchard, getting in the early harvest and not stopping for sundown. For a few minutes the strong sweet smell of fruit filled the air, and then they were through into an endless rustling of barley, stretching white beneath the moons and table-flat to the horizon. Nearly ready for the reapers.

Nothing but corpses to be harvested where we're going, he thought, his head nodding back against the saddle he was using as a pillow.

A woman came screaming at him out of darkness and dank heat, running toward him. Running toward him with a sword in her hand, plastered with mud and sweat and blood, looking over her shoulder down a pathway through jungle deep and rank and alien. Closer and he could see details, that she was young and dark and probably pretty when she wasn't gasping with effort and terrified. She had Tykissian markings like his on her face, the tattoos on each cheek and between the brows, despite her southron looks. His heart knew her, and his heart leapt in recognition—she shouted for him to beware—and he roared an answer.

His shout woke him.

Waking, the knowledge faded, slipped through the fingers of his mind as he reached for it. So did the warning she shouted: only the desperate urgency in her voice remained.

"Not asleep, sor?" Sergeant Ddrad asked quietly.

"Dreaming," Bren said shortly, wrapping his cloak about him. After a moment: "Dreaming about women."

The noncom grinned and sketched a half-salute. "Good luck then, sor," he said, before moving back to his own bedroll.

Bren Morkaarin's eyes stayed open, long after his sergeant went from quiet repose to deep, resounding snores. He lay on the deck absently rubbing the medallion at his neck—old habit; the medallion was the only remembrance he had of his long-dead father. It was a soothing token and a soothing gesture, after that less-than-sweet dream.

Bren did not believe that all dreams were omens. Most were the mind scratching itself, or the result of a bit of bad sausage or too much wine the night before.

He wasn't sure about this one. The stink of hot jungle air hung in his nose even waking. And the girl . . .

He touched his markings, thumbs to the cheeks, index fingers pressed together between his brows, sending a wordless prayer to the Three Above.

Sleep, he told himself. *The work of the day won't wait on your dreams.*

"Twenty-two hundred forty-six silver crowns, drawn on Bemmah and Daughters of Derkin," the Imperial agent said, handing over the elaborately sealed parchment.

Karah Grenlaarin snatched the rolled document from him and looked at it closely. The stamp on the seal read "Shemro IV, of the Strekkhylfa line, Emperor by Grace of the Three" with the signature of the fisc's agent beneath it. *Good as a bag of silver coins,* she thought. *Better, since it's easier to carry and harder to steal.*

"Done," she said.

Godsall, but that was a lot of money. She'd gotten better than seven crowns per horse for the whole herd—and back home on the ranch in Farbluffs County, one crown was a good price for a saddle-broken four-year-old. Cash money especially. Prices had gone completely crazy with the war coming on.

Best go before the fisc comes to his senses, she told herself. *Get out of this office and out of this city.* Great-Uncle Jaiwan, the busybody, would get his report on conditions down here in Derkin, for what it was worth . . . and Ma and Pa would get the banker's draft. The Grenlaarins could finally get that dam built on Sungren Creek and refinish the roof—and pay off the back taxes besides.

"Father, Mother and Child witness it," she said, spitting on her hand and holding it out in the traditional deal-sealing gesture of the horse trade.

She grinned when she saw the clerk swallow—Derkin bankers were a citified bunch. *Fit to be geldings,* she thought. *Not much else.*

The clerk slapped palms with her, then surreptitiously wiped his hand on the hem of his frippish overtunic. Karah pressed her lips together to keep from laughing out loud, tucked the document into an inside pocket of her jacket and clattered out the door.

Konzin wasn't waiting where he said he'd be. Karah frowned. That wasn't like him at all. She unhitched her horse, swung into her saddle and looked over the heads of the crowd for him. She thought she saw him and his horse partly hidden down a side alley, but there was no sense yelling—or chasing after him, either. A military unit of some sort was thundering toward her down the narrow street, drums and pipes making a terrible racket, and everyone around her clambered up onto the raised walks and against the walls to get out of the way.

Karah urged Glorylad onto the walk, then watched with

interest as ten hitch of big platter-hoofed draught horses lugged a cannon down the cobblestone streets. The gun was a breechloader—a fancy new bit of craftwork her uncle had told her about. The big gun rumbled between the high, white-washed walls on its way to the docks. The huge northern horses dripped sweat and tossed their heads as they bent to the traces, and the nail-studded wheels of the field carriage clattered counterpoint to the drums.

Karah squinted into the glare. Behind the cannon, pikemen marched five abreast, heads straight forward and chins jutting; sweat ran off their noses and flushed faces and matted their hair to their heads. They looked almost as uncomfortable as the horses. Krevaulti yokels from up around Dire, she judged. She counted rows and guessed the length of the line; her estimate put their numbers at five-hundred strong. All in steel back-and-breastplates, helmets slung to their belts beside their swords, heavy packs on their backs.

Phew! Uncle would find *that* bit of gossip fascinating. He was always talking about what grand warriors the bloody mad Krevaulti mountaineers were. *Warriors and tinkers*, she thought. *In between revolts*.

Not everybody in the New Empire of Tykis liked playing second flute to the Tykissians, her own people. The Krevaulti were about the only ones who tried to do anything serious about it, though.

The soldiers' long pikes swayed to the rip-thrip-rip of the drums and the whine of sackpipes. Sergeants with half-pikes marched at their sides, snapping orders to them and the bystanders alike. The troops went by with a swing and the crash of hobnails, and then they were gone and the crowds closed in behind them.

Karah caught the flash of red out of the corner of her eye, and looked across the street. That was Konzin; Karah was almost certain. The man's back was to her and he was still dickering with one of the runty little Derkinoi over some piece of local tripe. But he wore a red hat. She knew no one else who would taunt the gods in such outlandish garb. Karah cupped her hands to her mouth and bellowed over the noise of the crowds, "Heya! Konzin! I'm ready t'get outta here!"

Konzin's head jerked up and around, and his eyes narrowed. "A moment, madine!" He turned back to the Derkinoi. Karah waited, watching him above the bustling crowds in the street. She'd never known Konzin to be much of a shopper—she wondered what a seedy backstreet vendor had to offer that would interest him.

The chief herdsman on the Grenlaarin ranch finished his dicker, swung into his saddle, and trotted down the street toward Karah's inn without so much as looking back at her. Karah had to fight her way through the crowds and hurry her mount over the damned cobbled road to catch up with him. She sighed. Konzin had carried a burr under his skin the whole trip—this was the first time Karah had done the trading instead of him. He wasn't happy. She knew it. But there wasn't a thing she could do about it.

At least he'd have to admit she got a good price.

She caught up with him. "I got seven crowns a head for the herd."

He raised his eyebrows, then shrugged. "War prices," he said, then looked straight ahead and kept riding.

Just be that way, then, Karah thought. *It's not like I don't know they're war prices—and not like I don't know you could have done the same thing.* She tried not to let him make her angry. He'd been in charge of trading the horses for the Grenlaarin ranch for a long time. She knew she had to understand it was hard for him to let go.

She and Konzin rode in silence. Karah forced herself not to rubberneck as they moved through Derkin's narrow back streets, breasting the crowds like water at a river-crossing. Derkin was big, full of twisting streets and alleys, nearly all paved. A person could ride all day and barely cross from the north gate to the south, and many of the buildings were four and even five stories high, all stone or brick-built.

They crossed the narrow wood bridge over an evil-smelling canal, passed one of the Temples of the Three—small, since most of the locals were still heathen—and turned off into the walled courtyard that fronted Karah's inn.

Karah said, "Well, then. Have everyone here first light." She touched cheeks and brow—a gesture of both courtesy and dismissal. Family dignity demanded that she stay under a roof in town. Konzin would be camping with the other herders out on the outskirts. "See you tomorrow."

"Madine," he said. He touched a finger to his brow and smiled—the first smile she'd seen on his face all day. Then he wheeled his horse around and cantered out of the courtyard.

For all that she liked Konzin, Karah was glad to see him go. He'd been damned prickly the whole trip, and kept giving her funny looks. If he'd said she was too young to be put in charge one time, he'd said it a hundred.

She'd shown him, though.

She swung down from the saddle and stood gratefully in the shade of the arcade that ran around three sides of the little square. There was a fountain in the center, running into a stone horse trough and shaded by a jacaranda. She scooped her broad-brimmed leather hat full of water and dumped it over her head. Then she rested her hand for just an instant on Glorylad's breast, checking to be sure he wasn't overheated before she let him drink. Not that she'd run him hard, but Tykis' southernmost province was hotter than either of them were used to.

He was fine. She checked his hooves, then sat on the edge of the fountain and watched him drink. The ostler peered out of the stables, and she waved him over. "Brush him good," she told the man. "Rub him down. Don't feed him till you're done, and when you do, it's to be bean mash and oats!" The man listened and nodded but didn't speak. He was one of those piebald thralls from across the sea. Karah had never been easy trusting a horse to a thrall. They were fairly common along the coast, so there was no avoiding them—still, she had little faith in work done by those who weren't freemen.

She studied Glorylad's gait as the thrall led him off; he walked easy and straight. No limps, no fumbles. She smiled. He was the better of the two horses she'd ridden this trip, though Windrush was a solid mount, too. With a sigh, she turned, and went inside looking for food.

Thick adobe made the common room of the inn almost cool, even in midafternoon. The room was nearly empty. In Karah's brief experience, it would stay that way until near dark, when the locals left off work to gather and drink and carouse until the early hours of the morning. Karah tossed her gear down onto one of the adobe benches, adjusted the tattered rug that covered it, and settled at a table near the wall.

"What's going?" she shouted.

One of the inn's workers ambled in, scratching her bare stomach. "Roast a' mutton, sliced, wit' greens," she said, speaking Tykissian with a thick Derkinoi accent; Derkin Province had only been added to the New Empire a century or so ago. "Or yestidday's roast a' pork, minced inna pie. Wit' t'same greens."

"Today's wit'—I mean, with—wine and water," Karah said, flipping a tenth-crown bronze coin. The local coffee smelled wonderful but they brewed it thick as stew and strong enough to melt a spoon. "Keep the change," she added expansively.

That speeded up the service considerably. Karah cut the too-sweet lowland wine with half water; more wine and less water was the rule down here in the coastal plains, unless you wanted a case of belly-fever or the runs and an expensive trip to the priest-healer. The mutton arrived, greasy and heavy with garlic and buried under tomatoes and onions.

Southron food would give me eternal heartburn, she thought, mopping the plate with a heel of loaf. With enough wine, even it wasn't unbearable, and now that everything was wrapped up—all but the boring journey home, anyway—she felt entitled. But she'd be glad to get back to real Tykissian cooking.

Twenty-two hundred crowns, she told herself again, pouring another slug of wine-and-water into her earthenware mug. The few others in the common room were a mixed crew. Small dark locals, mostly.

She wished she were tall and blonde like the classic Tykissians, instead of short and ruddy. A bit less enthusiasm on her ancestors' parts, she thought, and a damn sight more selectivity, and she would have been as lithe and fair and thin as she deserved. She slugged back a large draught of the wine and scowled at no one in particular. The migrations were five hundred years past, so there was nobody to complain to.

Two of the Derkinoi scowled back. Probably resentful of the upcoming war on their kinsmen in Tarin Tseld south over the Imperial Sea. Probably they'd rather be ruled from An Tiram than from Olmya.

Piss on them, then, she thought. *Heretic-lovers.*

Over in one corner, two enormously tall black men with glossy shaven heads and sweeping white robes played some foreign card game; Karah finally guessed them to be Shborin traders, who were notoriously standoffish. She glowered at them, as well.

The man at the next table was Tykissian. He had thinning red hair and freckles across his snub nose—she guessed him to be midding thirty. He dressed in citified clothes, but from the look of his hands, he'd done real work in his life. He was reading a little leather-bound book, peering down his nose at it through small spectacles and eating forkfuls of meat pie at the same time.

She noticed the man was wearing a ring with the totem head of the Running Wolves. "Evening, lodge-brother," she said.

"Ah?" He looked over at her, and then past her, his expression puzzled. Karah flushed—she had been embarrassingly mistaken for a native several times since arriving in Derkin. But he focused on her again, and she saw his eyes flick from her ring to the three blue dots tattooed on her face.

He touched thumb and forefinger to his own cheek marks and both together between his brows. "Good evening to you, lodge-sister; the Three be with you." He started to turn back to his book, but Karah, lighthearted from the success of her hard-driven bargain, and a bit giddy from the wine, suddenly didn't want to eat her meal alone.

"So, lodge-brother, what do they call you . . . and what brings you to this hot, stinking *mourye*-hole of a city?" she asked the man.

He closed his book with a faint air of regret, leaving one finger between the pages to hold his place. "I am Amourgin Thurdhad, a law-speaker of Olmya. I am here on . . . business."

He had a capital-city accent, slightly pedantic to her ears; the profession explained the book, at least.

Karah felt bold and successful at that moment. If she could outbargain the Imperial fisc, surely she could hold her own in conversation with a scholar from the capital.

"Yah—business." She winked and raised her glass to him. "Then here's to business. Karah Grenlaarin."

The law-speaker smiled politely, and raised his glass just off the table in recognition of her gesture, but he didn't drink. *So maybe,* she thought, *his business hasn't been as successful as mine.*

Well, Pa was always on at her to talk about something besides horses and County gossip. If it wasn't business, maybe it could be books.

"*Consolidated Analects of Mero Rimsin?*" she read from the spine of his book. He studied her with increased interest—this time his expression showed both surprise and respect. The book was printed in Tarinese, the classical tongue of the Old Empire. Few could read the old tongue anymore.

"Relevant to a case," he replied, with a smile that was slightly shy. "You've read Rimsin?"

"Some of the poetry." She winced a bit, remembering; the poetry was bad enough. Three spare her the legal philosophy. Actually the tutor had to whale Rimsin into her with a willow switch, she recalled. She picked up pitcher and plate and joined the law-speaker on his bench. "I can't drink this pitcher alone with a lodge-brother here," she said.

Bren Morkaarin drew his sword and whirled it in a complicated figure eight as he marched, before thrusting it straight up in salute.

"Eyes . . . *right!*" he snapped. Drums and trumpets relayed the order.

Behind him eight hundred booted feet struck the earth together as the XIXth gave a wordless shout of hail to the high officers on the reviewing stand. Pikemen and halberdiers in breastplate and tassets and helmet, musketeers in floppy hats and broad bandoliers with dangling wooden charge-tubes clicking as they marched, each screw-topped cylinder holding one shot worth of powder.

"Regiment—" The underofficers and noncoms echoed it to their units.

"Company—"

"Platoon—"

"Left . . . *face.*"

Snap-*stamp* as every soldier took a half-stride and turned ninety degrees to the left, marching on without breaking stride. What had been a column was now a broad line, eight files deep.

"Pikepoints . . . *down.*"

There was another deep shout as the sixteen-foot shafts swung down and bristled forward; first rank held low, next four at staggered heights, last three high but slanted forward. Out on the flanks of the formation the halberdiers brought the broad chopping blades of their six-foot weapons forward as well, the bright morning sun glinting on the honed edges, the dagger points, and the curved spikes on the reverse sides.

"Sound *prepare to receive cavalry.*"

A complex ruffle of drums and scream of brass. Two more steps and the XIXth halted, marching in place. A war shout as they stopped. The first rank of pikes squatted in unison, bracing the butts of their weapons in the earth and holding them slanting out. The second rank knelt behind them, and the rest stood, presenting a bristling row of points that any horse would turn from.

The musketeers halted as well, bringing their weapons to their lips and blowing sharply on their slowmatches. The first rank let the rests drop to the ground and levelled their muskets, the heavy barrels resting in the U-shaped fork at the top of each rest.

"Fire!" S-shaped serpentines snapped the burning end of the slowmatches down into the priming pans.

A long *baaaammmmm* sound punched at Bren's ears and face; billowing off-white smoke, smelling of brimstone, hid the front of the formation.

"Countermarch! Reload in nine times. March!"

The musketeers who'd fired turned smartly and each paced back to the rear of their file to reload; the one behind stepped forward into first place, planted their rests, levelled their muskets.

"Fire!"

Bren watched critically as the eight-trooper files of musketeers took turns to fire and retire, step forward and fire once more. *Smooth*, he thought. Of course, these were veterans, and he'd had the training of them for six years now—most of his military career, stuck off in the wilds doing garrison and patrol work. Plus enough action to see what they were made of; the North Shield foothills were imperfectly pacified.

"To attention! Prepare for review!"

Weapons came upright, and troops braced. Sweat runneled their faces; down here on the coastal plain near Derkin it was *hot*. Particularly compared to the northern hill country they'd been stationed in for so long. Uncomfortable, and hellish if you were wearing armor and padding.

Lord Colonel Gonstad came up, in his showy horseman's three-quarter armor inlaid with silver and electrum, a light cavalry cloak of leopardskin half off one shoulder. Bren sneered behind an impassive, square-jawed face. His own simple coat of buffel leather studded with thousands of steel nailheads was a good deal more practical for an infantry officer.

The officer beside Gonstad probably thought so too. His own breastplate and open-faced helmet were as plain as Bren's. He held a command baton in one gloved hand, and the wrinkled planes of his face were covered with the elaborate tattoos of a man from Old Tykis, north of the Shield range.

Bren bowed and saluted with his blade. "Lord Colonel." More deeply: "Count Mustermaster General Feughylfa."

The older officer nodded. "Good drill, First Captain." Checking on soldiers' ability to march in step, maneuver to the word of command and use their weapons with skill was a primary reason for parading before the mustermaster.

Feughylfa looked critically at the ranks. The XIXth's equipment was worn but sound, weapons clean, armor carefully browned to a shade close to the dark-green uniform coats. Stepping closer he checked the sharpness of edges, ran a finger into the barrel of a musket, made sure each musketeer had bullet mold and spare coils of slowmatch. A priest beside him checked the spells on the engraved copper amulet each trooper wore on the left wrist—the most expensive piece of equipment, and about as vital as the weapons. It cost to maintain the combination of antifever, contraceptive and anticurse enchantments, but without them an army could lose half its men to dysentery in a month, not to mention pregnancy, the whorepox, or an enemy's antiexplosive spells damping your powder.

Besides which, of course, it was impossible to take the amulet off—and a priest could track it down if the soldier deserted.

"All rifled muskets?" the old man asked.

"Yes, sir; rifled, with the new pointed hollowbase bullets."

The mustermaster nodded again. "Well, the XIXth're in better shape than some of the handless cows who've shown up from back country garrisons," he said. "But the rolls carry you at six hundred muskets, three hundred pikes, one hundred halberdiers, fifteen mounted scouts and couriers, and fifty skirmishers, with ancillaries in proportion. You're two hundred down."

Bren swallowed and looked straight ahead. That was the *other* reason for parading before the mustermaster; it showed whether the colonel of the regiment was carrying nonexistent troops on the rolls and pocketing their pay. Which was exactly what Gonstad had been doing, of course. Skirmishers and scouts commanded double pay, which was why the XIXth had none at all.

"We've had casualties, sir," Bren said doggedly. "Bandits attacked several convoys to the silver mines near Dire."

Feughylfa snorted. "Well, get your recruits in order, then," he said.

"Recruits?" Bren asked.

The wrinkled hawk face turned towards him, pale eyes narrowing. "You're authorized to offer a twenty-crown bonus for volunteers and conscript the eligible if that doesn't work," he snapped. "*That* went out to regimental commands with the general summons to the war levy. What, didn't you get it?"

"N—" Bren began. *General summons war levy?* he thought dazedly. That only happened in a *real* war.

"First Captain!" Gonstad broke in. "I'm shocked at your dereliction of duty!"

Bren swallowed again, feeling the blood of rage darken his cheeks. He had the true Tykissian coloring—ash-pale hair and fair skin. He knew the mustermaster would see him flush, and regretted that he could not hide his feelings better.

"My apologies, Lord Colonel," he said woodenly. *After this war I will sell out and move to the colonies*, he thought.

"Well, you can press recruits from around here," Gonstad said.

Bren saw glimmers of pink before his eyes; that was part of his heritage too, the rage that took him beyond himself. He breathed deeply, feeling his armor squeeze at him. Derkinoi

Province was conquered land, recently conquered at that—only a century ago. Most of the natives were non-Tykissian, and of the Empire's subject races only Krevaulti were allowed to serve in arms rather than pay double tax. If he'd been told to make up the numbers back in the central provinces he could have gotten any number of sturdy, freeborn peasants; volunteers, even. How was he supposed to find a hundred Children of Falcon and Wolf *here*?

"See to it, Colonel Gonstad," Feughylfa said dryly. "See to it *personally*, because I hold you personally responsible. Dismissed."

Feughylfa was not blind, then—he saw whose armor bore gold inlay. A little of Bren's rage turned to sour amusement as Gonstad paled. Enough remained to put a harsh edge in his voice as he turned on his heel and shouted orders.

Amourgin was almost grateful for the intrusion of the broad-faced country girl and her cheerful banter—even her bawdy discussions of horsebreeding and her strained analysis of Rimsin's poetry and Dhourchoud's histories. She was charming, in an uninhibited, countrified way—and she made good cover. He needed that.

So when she grinned at him and whispered, "I'm for the jakes," he gallantly stood and said, "Hurry back. The meal will suffer for lack of your presence."

She giggled and strode off, with the rolling walk of someone who rode more often than she went afoot.

Amourgin smiled to himself and settled back into his seat to read and await her return.

A sudden burst of loud, lewd banter at the doorway drew his attention to the group just entering the common room.

Usually he would not have given the gaggle of thrall-whores who sauntered in and took seats a second look. The Shborin half-breed and the blonde, squat Tseldene were both attractive, in a worn-and-weary fashion, while the two Shillraki piebalds looked terribly young and still carried an air of fear around them—although the brown-and-pink patchwork which made up their skin concealed their expressions a little. None of this, however, was new to the law-speaker. Whores always looked either young and scared or hard and tired.

They usually didn't have fangs.

He stared at the last of the whores who entered the room. Momentarily he forgot his weariness with the stinking city and his stinking mission in the fascination of unraveling the puzzle she presented. *Woman?* he wondered. Yes, he supposed she was a woman. Human, though? He didn't know about that.

Her body was a woman's, all fine bones and rounded angles. Her walk was a wonder. She moved with some of a woman's grace and some of a predator's stealth. When he caught himself wondering if the two weren't the same thing, he smiled.

Strange girl. The eyes were human enough in shape, but of an odd color. They were large, with heavy lashes, and they were amber. The face was—unnerving. It was a normal woman's face, but stretched forward at nose and mouth to form a lean, strong-jawed muzzle. The girl watched her owner's back, and when he wasn't looking, she smiled. Amourgin Thurdhad, looking at her long, sharp canines, and at the way her clipped-and-painted claws flexed and retracted, would not have been the willing target of that smile for the wealth of three kingdoms. From the bruises on her face and arms, and on her thighs where they showed beneath the short tunic, he judged she probably had reason.

He could not make himself stop staring. He'd traveled the length and breadth of the Empire and to points beyond, and never had he seen a creature like her. He tried to decide whether she was hideous or lovely.

The girl's owner noticed his interest and strolled over. Too late, Amourgin buried his nose in his book, but the pimp would not be ignored.

"H'uncommon bird, h'ain't she?" the big man asked. He clapped Amourgin on the back, and sat down at the table with him; his Tykissian had a breathy Tobor accent and carried considerable evidence of garlic and stale wine.

"I'm busy," the law-speaker said. "I'm reading."

" 'Elluva thing for a man t'do. Y'could be puttin' yer time to good use. Y'can call me Zeemos, bye the bye. Purveyor of rare and h'exotic goods." He looked back at the table where his "goods" sat, and snapped, "Ho, Eowlie! Get yer ass over here, girl!"

All the whores looked up except the one he called. She ignored him.

"Here, girl! Here, y'stupid bitch!" He snapped his fingers, and the girl finally glanced over at the pimp.

The long-muzzled woman gave Zeemos a glare that would have sent Amourgin fleeing for his life, but the pimp was unfazed. She rose and strode to the table—slowly. The law-speaker could feel her hatred, radiating like body heat, enveloping her pimp, and him, and everyone in the room. She was a slave by virtue of the collar around her neck—but nothing enslaved her spirit. Every movement of her body spoke eloquently of future death for Zeemos—and perhaps for himself, as well, should he be foolhardy enough to touch her. Her hands clenched and spread, making the short chain that linked them jingle and the heavy leather bracelets creak.

"I'm not interested," Amourgin told Zeemos.

"So y'say—but yer eyes say otherwise. Be a man."

The pimp grabbed the girl's wrist and pulled her to her knees beside the table. He jammed one thumb under her upper lip and one under her lower lip and pulled until the girl's mouth opened. Those long white teeth gleamed in the dim light of the common room, and Amourgin could easily imagine them buried in the pimp's throat.

Zeemos said, "She eats nothin' but meat, y'see. So y'll be mindin' where y' put yours, won't you, then? I'll not be payin' damages for a man who was thinkin' with the wrong head."

"I'm not interested," Amourgin said again.

The big man grinned. "Right, right—we'll get t'the price in

a moment. I want y' t'understand what yer in for first. She killed the first man who tried her—that's bad fer m'business, so this collar's spelled. Keep her from killing you. Nothin' else, unnerstand—just that. So y'still have to be damned careful. She's stronger than y'd think, she's mean—and she's stupid. She don't speak at all, and she only understands a few words, and those when she wants to. Y' got t'show her who's in charge, y'unnerstand? Beat her around a bit, get behind t'keep th'hell away from the teeth, an you'll have a fine time."

Stupid, the pimp said. But Amourgin Thurdhad stared into the whore's deep yellow eyes, and what he saw there made his palms sweat and the back of his neck itch. If he did not see intelligence in those eyes, he at least saw focused rage, and hatred as pure and unalloyed as good gold. He managed to break away from that intense, terrifying stare. He looked back to Zeemos and said forcefully, "I'm—not—interested."

Zeemos looked surprised. "Truly? Well, I can understand that. I'd sooner screw my worst enemy's watchdog, truth t'tell." He smacked the side of the girl's head and said, "Gi' back wi' ye, then, y'bitch." The pimp returned his attention to the law-speaker. "Still, she h'appeals to a certain type. So what'll y' have, then? The Shillrakis are nearly virgin—I can let y' have the Shborin and the Tseldene both for what it will cost y' fer either of them. Or—"

Amourgin cut him off. "Look, you. Get yourself away from my table, and stop interrupting my meal."

Zeemos stood, and glared down at the law-speaker. "Y'lace-panted bugger," he whispered. In a voice intended to carry, he said, "H'I don't deal h'in little boys." He stomped back to the table his whores occupied, calling over his shoulder, "H'I don't do that sort of business."

Amourgin felt the heat rush to his face, but he said nothing. He returned his attention to his book. He wished that the man he was supposed to meet would hurry up, or that Karah would get back.

❖   ❖   ❖

On his white throne of ivory and platinum in the hot, dry-bone white city of An Tiram, Darkist XXV, Lord First Speaker to He of the Thousand Faces, Yentror of All Men, Lord of Ten Thousand Years, sat watching his naked concubines dance in the flickering firelight.

The body grows old, he thought, *old and weary and full of pain. But the mind never wearies of the dance.*

The concubines stamped their feet, and the bracelets on their wrists and ankles jingled, and the bells in their nipples tinkled. Darkist longed for youthful flesh again. He longed to feel his loins stir with lust, longed to savor again passion and release in the bodies of the beauties he owned. But young flesh lacked the power of magic old flesh knew. And now, more than the lust, he needed that power. He would take back the Northlands first, while he controlled the monstrous magic inside of him. And then . . .

Out of the corner of an eye, he studied the graceful, youthful movements of his great-grandson, Colchob. Colchob was a robust youth, broad and sturdy and randy as a prime ram. Bred from good stock, the old man thought, with just those characteristics in mind.

Just like me when I was young.

The ancient Yentror of Tarin Tseld looked to his immediate right, and for a moment he couldn't remember why the chair there was empty. It was where his grandson, Mirs Honiv, Colchob's father, was supposed to sit.

But then the memories came back, and the old man clucked his tongue. Silly of him to forget—this was the night he announced his heir—and Mirs *was* the direct line heir. His grandson couldn't make anything less than a grand appearance.

The little memory lapses worried Darkist. They were coming more often, getting worse. *Wearing down,* he thought. *Everything about this damned body is wearing down.*

From a side door across the dark hall, a figure swathed in green from head to toe appeared, bowed briefly toward

Darkist, then vanished back into the labyrinthine corridors of
the palace. Darkist noted the gesture, and smiled gently. That
was the signal he'd been waiting for. The glorious banquet
was ready. He tapped his vizier's shoulder once, and the man
stood and walked to the burnished gong at the foot of the
table.

The vizier struck the gong. As the lone note swelled and
reverberated to fill the hall, the concubines scurried away.
Servants laid virgin silk covers over the long banqueting
tables—the covers would be used only once and then burned.
Nobles rose from their cushions and took their seats in an
order of precedence unchanged in three thousand years. Only
the warslaves along the walls remained motionless. They were
two-meter figures in heavy armor of steel and brass; the double-
handed scimitars over their shoulders could bisect a man from
helmet to crotch in less than a heartbeat. Their slit-pupiled
amber eyes stared unwinking from beneath the faceplates of
their helms, full of a fanatic loyalty set by training, magic and a
hundred generations of selective breeding. They were Darkist's
pets, and he loved them.

Then, over the music of the gong, Darkist could make out
the faint, high trills of the chariole pipes. That music grew
louder as drums and rillets filled in the low notes.

Colchob was finally unable to contain his curiosity. "High
Lord Grandfather of Us All," he said over the pipes, "the banquet is about to begin. Where is father?"

Darkist gifted his great-grandson with a kindly smile. "He
has to make a grand entrance. Patience, child. Have patience.
This is a great night for all of us."

The massive main doors at the far end of the hall swung
open, and the pipers and drummers filed in. Behind them
came the kitchen servants, weighted down with their vast covered dishes and their tall carafes of thick purple *havassh*. The
rich scents of the banquet feast filled the hall.

Darkist watched the slaves settling the lesser platters into
place along the lower tables, and studied with satisfaction the

larger ones that made their way up the hall toward him, each on the shoulders of four strong slaves. The great gold and silver covers gleamed in the firelight. The flowers around the platter bases were exquisite. It was all quite perfect, really. Servants were lifting away the covers on the farthest platters already, and Darkist smiled as he heard the cries of delight and appreciation. Down the hall he could make out whole boars, glazed and roasted to perfection; stuffed great swans; and at the table of the High Lords, an entire baked *yols*, done so artistically that every fang and every claw remained intact.

"This is glorious," Colchob said. "Magnificent. I have never seen a banquet to match it." He inhaled and licked his lips. "The smell of the roast pork alone is enough to drive a man mad."

"It is very fine, is it not?" Darkist agreed. The servants settled the greatest of the gleaming metal salvers between him and Colchob.

A trio of heralds entered through the great door, and blew the first bars of the royal march of the Yentrors. Colchob sat up straight. Darkist folded his hands across his lap. The servants standing at the head table cleared out of the way so those seated could get a clear view of the proceedings.

Beroquim, Lord Principal of the realm, scurried in behind the trumpeters, a scroll clutched in his hands. He waved his hands violently and shouted over the trumpeters, "Not yet, O Lord of Ten Thousand Years. We can't start yet."

Darkist stood, and waved at Beroquim. "Read, please, Lord Principal."

"But we can't—"

Darkist pointed a finger at Beroquim and interrupted him. "Read."

Beroquim looked over his shoulder, then turned back to the hall full of waiting people. He looked sick, Darkist thought. Possibly unsuited for his position. It would do to keep that in mind.

"By royal decree," the man read in his nasal voice, "We,

Darkist XXV, sovereign lord and master of all We survey, do hereby present Our heir, Mirs Honiv, to Our court, and make clear Our intentions for the carrying on of the royal line."

The trumpets blared again. Beroquim stepped to the side, and stared back at the opened doors. The lords of Darkist's court stopped eating and waited in silence, watching the empty opening.

The silence stretched, and the nobles began to shift restlessly. Darkist frowned. He hated to be kept waiting. Finally he tapped his vizier again and said, "Enough, already. Tell the servant to prepare my food. I'll not sit in my own banquet hall and starve."

All down the hall, Darkist heard the uncertain whispers. He knew they questioned the fitness of his mind, and his ability to continue to rule. He knew they'd welcomed the naming of his heir—that they hoped to see him step down. He hated those whispers. He would put an end to them once and forever.

His personal servant and food taster lifted the cover of the salver, and froze. For a moment, silence again filled the great hall. Then the servant dropped the cover to the ground with a crash, and pressed a hand over his eyes. He shrieked. Up and down the hall, then, Darkist heard the gasps and horrified whispers of his subjects.

Colchob threw one hand over his mouth and stood so quickly his massive chair crashed backwards.

Darkist thought the cooks had done an exceptional job with Mirs Honiv. His grandson was a lovely golden color all over, very finely glazed and strategically decorated with cloves and chili spikes. And, as Darkist had requested, the royal cooks had left the face untouched. The chief cook had captured and kept the most delightful expression—one of sheer, utter anguish. The old man laughed and turned to his great-grandson. "I name *you* my successor, Colchob son of Mirs Honiv son of Tighirl son of Darkist."

Colchob paled, and broke out in a fine sheen of sweat. The

young man said nothing. He still had the back of his fist stuffed into his mouth.

Darkist added, "Remember what a very poor idea it is to plot against me. You will do that, won't you?"

Colchob nodded, speechless, staring at his father on the platter.

"Well, good. I'm glad." Darkist shrugged and nodded to his taster. "I'll take a bit of the haunch, you," he said, pointing to a nice juicy spot on his grandson's thigh. "And perhaps a slice of shoulder. But only the lean, mind you. None of the fat."

Karah, well into her cups, leaned over and confided to Amourgin in a loud whisper, "You know, I think those women sitting across the room are *whores*, by gods and slap palms. I've seen the short, fat one leave with three dif—dif—" She shook her head as if to clear it. "—diff'rent men. An' she comes back, but th' men never do."

"Sh-h-h-h-h," Amourgin said.

"But don't you think they're *whores*?" The last she said very loudly, and the law-speaker winced.

"Karah," he whispered. "Dear girl, perhaps you and I could walk outside—just a bit, for the air. I think you've had too much wine. Maybe some black coffee would help, too."

Karah refused to be distracted from her sudden fascination with Zeemos' troupe. In a horribly loud whisper, she said, "I've never seen real protsi—ah, prostitutes. My pa tole me about them." She looked at him solemnly and announced in quite a loud voice, "Pa says they screw strangers for money. I always thought tha'd be a—a helluva job. Don't you think so?"

The people for whom Karah had been buying rounds elbowed each other and smirked. There were a few titters. The whores glared over at him and Karah, and Zeemos started to rise from his place at table.

"There are those," Amourgin said loudly, "who say law-speakers are in the same line of work."

Several of the regular patrons and one of the whores laughed at his comment, and Amourgin saw all of them relax. *Peace bought at a low price,* he thought.

Karah quit staring at the whores. "Oh, look at him," she said.

Amourgin turned in the direction she indicated.

An officer, tall and mustachioed, his beard trimmed to a point, stood stiffly in the entryway to the common room. He wore a red-lined leopard skin hanging off one shoulder and jewels on his fingers and in one ear. The cheek pieces of his high-combed helmet were pushed back, and the steel plates of his three-quarter armor were engraved with silver and gold tracery. He rested one hand on his basket-hilted broadsword and tapped a toe against the brown tiles of the common room's floor. His spurs jingled.

A sudden hush fell over the diners; there were more of them, now the moon was up. Most of them were merchants and travelers of modest means; they'd all been glad of the several rounds Karah bought. The evening had been getting fairly merry.

"Greetings, brethren of the Three," the officer said, pulling a scroll from his belt. "Hear the word of Her Majesty Shemro, fourth of that name, of the Strekkhylfa line, descendant of Beltra the Great, Emperor by the favor of the Three."

All the Tykissians present touched cheeks and brow; the Derkin natives bowed; the two Shborin, immune by treaty, watched with detached amusement.

The scroll unrolled with a crinkling sound. The officer began to read, and as he did, baffled silence filled the room. The entire document was in the antique Tarinese of the courts, a dead language nobody but scholars and law-speakers had used for a millennium. The officer finished reading, and rolled the scroll again, and with a smug smile, tucked it into his belt.

For a long instant, no one so much as whispered.

Then someone behind Amourgin asked, "What did that mean?"

Amourgin had listened with growing disbelief. He knew damned well what those ancient words meant. Above the growing stir of puzzled mutters that followed in the wake of the reading, he announced, "He just said we've all been pressed."

The man in armor tilted his head slightly toward Amourgin, and smiled whitely through his barley-colored beard.

Zeemos, the purveyor of rare and exotic delights, heaved himself off of his bench. He faced the officer and cleared his throat. "Pardons, pardons, m'lord, sir. H'I guess me and m' girls should be going now, so you can carry out your business with these citizens. H'I'm not precisely Tykissian, y'see," he said. "H'I was born Toboran . . ."

"You have Toboran papers?" The officer arched an eyebrow, and held out a hand to the huge, fat man. "Let me see them."

"Well, no." Zeemos flushed a brilliant red. "Not anymore, that is—ah, h'I had to get Tykissian papers h'in order to bring my, ah, girls into the Empire—h'I mean, with the h'additional taxes on foreign businessmen and all, h'I . . . well, h'I am Toboran in my heart." He flushed and nodded firmly, and crossed his arms over his broad belly.

"Your papers. Now," the officer said.

Zeemos, with obvious reluctance, fished through a pouch at his ample waist and pulled out a sheaf of parchment. He handed the papers to the officer, and cringed.

Amourgin watched this development with interest. He wasn't precisely a loyal Tykissian either—but he certainly wasn't going to make a point of that to the officer.

"Your papers say you have been granted Imperial citizenship—that must have taken a considerable bribe—and the papers you hold on your girls make them citizens also. That makes you Tykissians by legal status." The officer smiled, an ugly feral grin. "What's more, since your whores are citizens, they can't be your property anymore. Did you realize that?"

"It was only a technicality—because of the outrageous taxes on imported slaves—you can't possibly—I paid good money for every one of them!"

"Pity." The officer turned to one of his men and said, "Take the collars off the girls. They are the right age, and look sturdy enough. They and the rest of these sorry drunks will fill the last of our quota."

Zeemos began to look panicky. "If you must free the others, I suppose I can understand, but please let me keep Eowlie—she can't talk, she's stupid as a stone, and she isn't even human. She needs me to take care of her."

Amourgin saw the girl's yellow eyes narrow as she stared at her owner. When she grinned—that vicious, toothy grin—the hair stood on his arms and the back of his neck.

The officer looked at her with interest. "She doesn't look quite human, does she? But she has her citizenship papers—"

"I paid for them," Zeemos said. "I'll pay the extra tax on transporting strange beasts, and you can tear those papers up. I can stand to lose the citizenship fee on her—but she'd be helpless without me, sir. She needs me. Besides, there's a spell on that collar. She'd be dangerous without it."

"Well—" The officer gave the girl Zeemos called Eowlie another, more doubtful look. "If she really isn't human, perhaps we could consider her in the same class as the wolves some of our soldiers keep—"

"I'm human," the weird girl said. Every head in the common room jerked in her direction at the sound of her voice. "I can s-feak well enough, you vastard," she said to Zeemos. She had an odd accent, but her Tykissian was fluent. "And I can take care of myself." She turned to the officer, and her smile went wider, pulling back along that lean muzzle to show the first of the jagged molars behind her fangs. "If I am a citizen, then I volunteer to serve in this army. I can fight good for you."

All the color drained out of Zeemos' face. Amourgin thought, *Ho, mighty Three—what nightmares that pimp will suffer tonight.* He would have laughed, but the girl was about to become a free citizen of the Empire and, if he couldn't get out of this press, his comrade at arms—and he wasn't entirely sure how well he would sleep, either.

The room had been mostly quiet while the patrons observed the byplay. But realization dawned on the Imperial citizens, and the silence shattered as everyone spoke at once—all except for the Derkinoi locals. They, for once, looked glad they were subjects by conquest rather than citizens, and so immune from military service. The babble turned to an ugly growl.

The officer's aide stepped forward and fired a pistol into the ceiling; he was shorter and younger than the officer, thick-set and tow-haired. He wore the embarrassed air of a man set an unpleasant task. The hundreds of silvered steel nails in his leather tunic clinked against the plain bowl helmet tucked under his left arm as he thrust the wheel-lock back through his belt. For a moment his eyes met Karah's, and Amourgin saw the young man pale. That expression of recognition lasted only an instant. Then it vanished, and the officer shook his head, frowning around the room.

"The XIXth Foot needs soldiers to fill its roster," he said into the renewed quiet. "Those Tykissians present and of military age are hereby summoned to do their duty in the war levy."

He nodded toward a priest standing by him, a stout man dressed in the fringed buckskin of his trade, an inlaid toma-hawk through the back of his belt to show he followed an order which worshipped the Warrior Aspect of the Three.

"Father Solmin here will take your oaths."

Karah lurched to her feet, swaying slightly. "In a pig's arsehole!" she yelled, shaking off Amourgin's hand and the weight of the wine. "Ma will kill me if I don't get back," she yelled. "You can't press free citizens for land service 'cept through the County levy!"

"I not only can, I just have," the tall officer said with amuse-ment. "Father Solmin," he went on to the cleric, "proceed to administer the oaths, if you please."

The shorter officer ducked out into the courtyard; the priest scowled, but began to set up the tripod and censor. Somehow Amourgin got through the press of the crowd to the officer's side and gently plucked the scroll from the hand of the armored commander.

"This," he said, "appears to be an authorization from Grand Admiral Willek, for the exercise of the press gang. Which by long-established edict of Emperor Tarn I, Three hold him in Their Grace, applies only to sailors—which we are not—and within the docklands of a registered seaport—which this inn is not."

The officer snatched it back. "Hadn't you heard, recruit?" he sneered. "Grand Admiral Willek is made Grand Constable Willek also, Governor of Derkin with authority to rule by the law martial."

"I don't think—" Amourgin began.

"That's right, soldier; I do your thinking for you from now on," the officer snapped. He put a hand on Amourgin's face and pushed him backward. "The next word earns you fifty strokes."

Amourgin's stomach knotted and he bit back the words he wanted to say; he carefully removed the glasses hanging from one ear and tucked them into a wooden case at his belt.

This will not do at all, he thought.

Karah felt her wits break free of the wine. She looked to the law-speaker. "Hey—this lobsterback doesn't have the Emperor's writ to press us?"

Amourgin shook his head curtly. A low growl went up from the other Tykissians in the room. For the first time, the arrogance left the officer's face, replaced by incredulous anger.

Be damned if I'll obey a fake writ, Karah thought. She had to get home to her folks and the horses, and . . .

Somewhere behind Karah sounded the low rasping slither of a sword coming free of its scabbard.

Never draw unless you mean to kill, her parents had taught her. She kept her own hand away from her hilt; she picked up a small wooden table by one leg instead. "No steel!" she said sharply. Killing an Imperial officer got the killer sent to the galleys, or beheaded. On the other hand, treating free Tykissians like thralls was against the law, too. "Let's cool this goat-buggering turtle's head in the horse trough!" she yelled.

The priest looked over the crowd with the experience of a long military career and swept up his equipment. Karah charged forward and smashed the table down on the officer's armored forearm. It splintered—and its sound released the room's occupants from their stunned reverie. The "recruits" surged forward, roaring. A dozen hands gripped arms, legs, and body, and the whole mob of them ran the man forward out the door; his helmet went bong on the wooden slats, and the moving mass of drunken tavern-goers stumbled laughing towards the fountain.

Karah realized the law-speaker was pulling at her sleeve, shouting for her to stop. She tensed her arm to shake him off until she saw the line of lights and froze.

It was dark in the courtyard; at first she thought the lights were fireflies. Then her eyes adjusted. The flickering was far too regular and unmoving for that. Twenty lit slowmatches glowed red, firmly clipped in the S-shaped serpentines of twenty long matchlock muskets, ready to lower the ember into the priming powder. Each barrel braced in a U-forked rest in front of a musketeer, whose finger hooked around a trigger, and all the muzzles were pointing straight at her. A solid wall of halberdiers stood to either side of the muskets, and at a single command, their heavy chopping blades came down with a disciplined ripple. Moons' light sheened on edged metal, on helmets, and on the plumes in the floppy hats of the musketeers.

Amourgin coughed discreetly. "I really think," he said, "we'd better put our commander down."

◉ CHAPTER II

Grand Admiral Willek Tornsaarin barred the door behind her, and crept up the long, steep flight of stairs into the attic of the house she'd commandeered for her quarters. It was hot and dusty up under the eaves, thick with the scent of dry timber and the baked clay tiles of the roof. The low ceiling of the stairwell made her crouch; squat Derkinoi houses were not built for tall, lean Tykissians.

When she reached the top of the stairs, she stood in darkness for a long moment, breathing hard, but not from exertion. Then she closed the door and lit a slowmatch, and carried it in a circuit around the low-ceilinged room, lighting the sturdy hurricane lanterns bolted in place on each wall. The light flickered and threw long shadows across the beams.

In the center of the room sat a trunk, of the standard black-stained military-issue variety. Willek had kept it well-oiled over the years, but the dents and scars in its finish told of its hard duty. She'd placed a squat table with a round, polished-stone top beside the trunk, and bolted each thick, stubby, wooden table leg to the floor with a lag-bolt the size of a man's fist. The contents of the room might arouse suspicion, but they could not convict her. Willek was careful.

Willek went to the trunk and unlocked it, and from it removed more uniforms, all neatly folded. These she carried to one wall and dropped in a heap on the floor. Then she knelt beside the

30

trunk, and leaned in, and slid back a cunningly hidden panel that provided a tiny key. She removed the key, then moved the first panel back into place—necessary before she could move a second secret panel, which revealed a keyhole.

The carpenter who'd built the box and made it a perfect match for ordinary military trunks had been a wizard at joinery, though he'd proved less clever at concealing his curiosity. *Curiosity*, Willek thought, struggling with the tiny key, *is a pitiful thing to die of. But better him than me.*

The key slid into place, and the false bottom of the trunk lifted smoothly, to reveal a compartment lined in thin hammered sheets of gold. The seams were gummed—the compartment was, when closed, watertight. The watertightness was a matter of life and death—it had been for the carpenter, and it could be for Willek. She regummed the seams regularly, and with scrupulous attention.

She'd packed three silk-wrapped bundles together in the bottom. They were untouched, exactly as she'd left them. She couldn't imagine them being otherwise, but the danger inherent in her activities made her worry about many things. She pulled the bundles out one at a time and put them side by side on the tabletop.

She unwrapped the first bundle, tucked the silk wrapper into her belt, and pulled out a dagger—lean and double-edged, with a narrow blade that tapered to a needle point. The dagger's grip was featureless, the handguard smooth with gently swelled knobs at either end.

She slipped the knife through her belt next to the wrapper, then rolled up her left sleeve. She opened the second bundle. It held a delicate glass tube: one end of it a funnel perhaps two thumbs wide, the other end nothing more than a hollowed stem.

Willek nibbled the side of her lip, and took a deep breath before proceeding to the third bundle.

She handled it differently than she had the first two. She untied the silk ties with extreme gentleness, and peeled the wrappings away cautiously. The closer she got to the center of the bundle, the slower she moved. She stopped once, long enough to stare at her trembling fingers. They wouldn't stop trembling, no matter how hard she tried to calm herself. She pursed her lips and continued.

The object she unwrapped was a flat disk of unpolished black stone no bigger than the palm of Willek's hand. It lay in the center of a diamond of red silk whose points reached almost, but not quite, to the edge of the table.

She took the silk cord that had bound the wrapping to the disk and wound it tightly around her left bicep, so that below the cord, her veins began to bulge. "That's it, then," she muttered. She drew the dagger and winced, and lay the edge of the blade along the bare flesh of her forearm. Her muscles tensed, she averted her eyes and sucked in her breath, and quickly slashed across her flesh. Blood welled from the shallow wound and stained the blade.

Willek hissed from the pain, the shallow cut itself and the sting of sweat running into it. She kept moving—wiped the blade along the old uniform shirt, dropped that to the floor, and slid the dagger back into her belt. Then she took the glass funnel, and began scooping her blood into it. She worked quickly, catching the blood and letting it drip out onto the tabletop. She worked her way around the circle once, then a second time, this time dragging the narrow point through the red drops to connect them into a single, unbroken thread. When she'd closed the circle, she took the bloody funnel and placed it on the stone disk, then stepped quickly away from the table.

"One may come," Willek whispered. Her voice broke, but she managed to continue.

"One may come,
No more than one,
No less than one.
Who sees the past,
Who sees the now,
Who sees the next."

Keeping a wary eye on the disk, she picked up the soiled shirt and untied the cord from her arm. She had enough time to use the shirt to stanch the bleeding before the surface of the disk began to bubble.

Willek's right hand twitched near the dagger grip. She knew the dagger was worthless for anything but drawing her own blood. It didn't matter. Her instincts insisted she'd be better off with a weapon in hand, and her hand kept trying for the dagger. She hated what would happen next. Her voice went hoarse as she said:

"One to trade.

One to take the gift.

One to draw the mirror forth

And show the threads of time."

The blood in the funnel suddenly crawled off the glass and spread over the surface of the disk. There it bubbled and bulged, growing both up and out.

As it did, Willek grabbed her wounded arm and shrieked. She felt intense, horrible pain around the wound, as if the blood in her veins had suddenly started to bubble in tandem with the blood on the stone. The demon she'd summoned had taken its sacrifice, and was not satisfied with that. It was calling the blood that coursed through her veins to come to it—calling like to like. She fought back her fear, and forced herself to push the added pain out of her mind. She dared not lose her concentration.

"The one who comes," she said through clenched jaws, "May take no more than offered,

May not cross from the circle.

Must leave when I demand."

The churning, twisting blood-demon on the table began to grow more slowly. Willek concentrated her will against it as it fought to devour her. Sometimes those who came were weak. Sometimes, they weren't very hungry, and would be satisfied with their little dollop of blood; they would give her what she wanted without much of a fight. This one was powerful.

Hungry. Evil. It was doing all it could to weaken her will, to bring out her fear—and it would take her if it could.

Willek began to feel light-headed from the blood loss. Across from her, the blood-demon reached out tentacles and lifted itself up on them.

Like calls to like, she thought. *I call back what is mine*. She willed her blood to return to her. The demon resisted the loss— Willek fought harder—and at last, she saw the first indication that she was in control again. The demon's tentacles slipped out from under it, and it flopped back to the tabletop with a squish. She felt stronger, and fought harder.

"Enough!" she snarled at last. "Show me what may be!"

The demon yielded to her. The air above it grew hazy as droplets of her blood streamed off its body and swirled into the air to form a red cloud. Within that cloud, vague shapes formed, and took on substance and definition.

Willek moved closer, and tried to make sense of what she saw.

There was a huge feast—and a man on a platter, carved and eaten by other men. The Grand Admiral wrinkled her nose in disgust. She recognized Darkist as one of the banqueters easily enough—it was through him that she'd gotten her bloodstone.

"I know about him," she told the demon. "Show me things I don't know."

The images in the bloodmist changed.

She saw an officer leading an Imperial regiment of pikemen and musketeers—saw men falling and dying all around this officer. But the regiment never faltered. The officer led, and it followed.

"A good man," she murmured. "The soldiers trust him."

The images shifted.

The same officer again, now up a rank—a commander, not a second, Willek noted, and this time *she* was with him—no, she knelt before him. He made a stiff, chopping motion with one hand, and Willek saw her own image sag forward. An executioner stepped up to her side, and lifted his sword.

"No!" Willek screamed, as the executioner's blade fell, and severed the Willek-image's head from her shoulders.

The living Willek stared into the bloodmist, unseeing, with her hands grasped to her neck. "One of *my* officers," she whispered. "He would betray me if he could. I have to find him before it's too late."

The face tugged at her memory. The Grand Admiral had climbed the greasy pole of military rank on far more than her excellent birth and considerable wealth; one tool of her trade was a good head for faces and names. *First Captain Sir Bren Morkaarin.* The name explained it—that clan had been at feud with hers since Beltra the Great unified the squabbling Tykissian tribes who'd overrun the Old Empire. In fact, there weren't many Morkaarins left, and with the Tornsaarins so powerful they had scant hope of any advancement these days.

Put it aside. The demon would show her more.

The images had moved on again. Willek caught a glimpse of a woman whose deformed face was made notable by a lean muzzle and fangs; then of a brawny squireen girl on horseback wielding a sword. The bloodmist thinned, and Willek strained her eyes to see the final image. A jungle—trees towering toward the heavens. A river. And stepping out of the jungle, a god.

As the last of her blood dried on the table, the mist and the visions vanished and the demon returned to whatever hell it came from.

Willek stepped back and sagged against the wall, weakened by loss of blood and the life force that went with it. It was over—and once again, she'd survived.

She must not let herself get too distressed about the visions in the bloodmist, she reminded herself. They were the footprints of the could-be, not necessarily of the would-be. Armed with foreknowledge, an intelligent woman such as herself could easily bypass potential disasters—the one with the young officer coming immediately to mind. That was easily fixed, she thought.

I'll have him inconspicuously killed. Although it might not be as easy as that. The future was mutable, but trying to avert a vision might be the very factor that caused it to come true. If—if—the visions were linked, it might not be possible to kill this Morkaarin before the other figures crossed the world-line of her destiny.

There was a man Willek knew who specialized in finding people—and in eliminating them once they were found. If the usual means didn't work, he could handle it . . . and the others.

The other images held no real meaning yet. She would hold onto them. The bloodmist showed visions that were frequently confusing, and often deceptive—but in Willek's experience, never unimportant. Those other people, the jungle, the god— they would all come to mean something essential to the Grand Admiral. She was certain of that.

Willek took a few deep breaths and gave herself a mental shake. It was time to be getting on with other things.

The recruits finished saying the oath, and Karah lowered her clenched fist. She wished there were some way she could believe what was happening was all a nightmare. But there wasn't. Not even in her worst nightmares could she smell the stink of piss and cookfires that permeated Derkin—and citystink hung in the damp salt-sea air and wrapped itself around her like a blanket. She could also smell the other recruits; the dozen or so swept up at the tavern, and a round hundred who must have been gathered earlier that night.

"Form a line," the second-in-command ordered. He marched past her, and she suppressed the urge to trip him and smash his round, bland face under her boot. Instead, she got into line with the rest of the poor, half-drunk souls, and wished to hell she'd gone to bed early.

Someone nudged her solidly from behind. She turned,

ready to strike out in the darkness, and found Konzin's face close to hers.

Konzin! He looked like salvation in human form to her.

"Ai, am I glad to see you," Karah whispered. "Get me out of here. These buggers have pressed me, by the Three. They're plannin' to make me a soldier." The line of unwilling recruits moved forward, and the sound of the master sergeant questioning a recruit for name and origin, and listing his inventory carried down the line.

"Get you out?" Konzin whispered. "I *can't* get you out. It took all I had to bribe my way into this courtyard for a moment, and that so I could take word to your ma and pa of what happened to you."

Of course. She should have known better than to expect a miracle. Karah gave him a quick hug. Dear Konzin—he was prickly and difficult but there when she needed him. "I'm scared," she whispered. "I'm no soldier."

"Tell 'em you train horses—they'll keep you back o' the lines that way." Konzin looked back at the entryway to the courtyard, and frowned. "The guard is giving me the sign already. There anything you want me to take home to your ma and da?"

"Godsall, yes! How could I have forgotten?" Karah dug through her pack and pulled out the bank draft. She pressed it into the herdsman's hand. "Get that to them no matter what. They need it to pay back taxes—and Konzin . . ." She looked into his eyes. "Tell them I love them, and that I'll be fine. Don't you let them know I was scared."

"Aye, madine." Konzin nodded, and before she could say anything else, slipped through the crowd and out into the night. Behind her, Amourgin asked, "Who was that?"

"Our chief herdsman, Konzin. He's worked our ranch since before I was born. He can do magic with horses."

"Horses . . ." Amourgin repeated. "Karah, what did you say your full name was?"

"Maybe I didn't," she said. "It's Grenlaarin."

"Of *the* Grenlaarins?" Suddenly he looked impressed. "The *horse-master* Grenlaarins?"

Karah grinned briefly. "*The* Grenlaarins. Champion Grenlsteeds for twenty-six generations." She nibbled at the tip of her braid and looked off to one side. "Or will be if I survive this."

"I know what you mean. I'm no soldier. And I've no wish to die on infidel soil, either."

The line moved forward again. Karah realized there were only three people ahead of her, one of them the ugly whore with the teeth. Godsall. Karah decided she would give anything for a way out of this mess.

"I know a Jawain Grenlaarin," Amourgin added. "Got my main saddle horse from him."

"True? You know Uncle Jawain?" She shook her head. Funny how people got around. "We cross stock with him sometimes. You might have a horse from our lines. What's the get of your horse?" she asked.

"The get?" He looked bewildered.

"Your horse's dam and sire. You're a city boy, aren't you?"

Amourgin gave a dry little chuckle. "Through and through. Wide-open spaces give me hives." He sighed, and said, "Jawain told me. Didn't mean anything to me, but I'm sure it will to you. Ah, Broucher's dam was, um . . . Mountain Fancy, I think—"

"Wait." Karah cut him off. She couldn't believe the words that had come out of Amourgin's mouth. She stared at the citified law-speaker in his dandy clothes and his silly little spectacles, and very slowly, she said, "I think I must have misheard you. Uncle Jawain sold *you* Broucher? Big, solid gelding, six years old, seventeen hands, five gaits, mountain-trail trained?"

"Your uncle sold me a big brown horse named Broucher. Unless Jawain had several by the same name, it's probably the same horse." Amourgin's words were a little clipped—Karah supposed the tone of her question must have insulted him.

The line moved again, and she walked with it, feeling dazed. Her uncle's prize show horse, the savvy, talented gelding who ran like quicksilver and took fences like a bird, sold to a man who knew nothing more about him than that he was a big, brown horse. "Why?" she finally asked, not caring that she was being rude.

"Why what?"

"Why in the names of the Three would he sell Broucher to *you*?"

"Because I paid him a lot of money. And what exactly is wrong with me?"

Karah snorted. "Broucher was never for sale. Oh, I could see Uncle perhaps selling him to someone who knew horses, who was capable of appreciating what a masterpiece he was getting—but to you—" Karah shook her head and turned away. The line moved again, and it was her turn.

"Oh," he muttered behind her. "So those of us who just want a nice horse to ride from place to place don't deserve a good one."

"Broucher isn't just good. Some day," Karah snapped back, "I'll show you what your 'nice horsey' can do."

She turned away from Amourgin, fuming.

The sergeant asked her name, her county, her next of kin, and where they could be found. She answered, only part of her mind on what she was saying. The rest was puzzling out what insanity might have possessed Great-Uncle Jawain to sell his favorite trail horse to a nose-in-a-book city boy.

"Occupation?"

"Horse breeder and trainer."

The man stopped, looked over his notes, and glanced up at Karah. "You of *the* Grenlaarins? With the famous horses?"

"Yes," Karah said. *Good*, she thought. *Now that they know who I am, they won't keep me.*

"That's good," he said. "We got some rough horses need work. And some dancey-assed riders to put on 'em. They'll be more'n enough for you t'do. Y'got yer own mounts, I 'spect."

That was far from the response she'd hoped for. "Two," Karah said stiffly. "Both stabled here."

"Good. Got yer gear?"

"Bedroll, sword, bow, quiver, knife, cookset, tarp, two sets of clothes, tack and travel kit."

The sergeant grinned. "I'll be. Full complement. Yer the best catch we've had so far t'night. Lucky fer us."

"Not for me."

"Nope," he said agreeably. "Never is. All right, then, Grenlaarin." He waved to the priest who clamped a bracelet around her arm. Karah felt a sharp magical sting—then the band constricted until it found her measure. For an instant, the metal glowed, then fell dormant. The sergeant nodded. "Over with the other recruits and wait to go in t'get yer horses." He studied her and sighed. "And, favor t' me—don't do anything stupid—like tryin' to sneak off, maybe. With the bracelet there's no place you can go that we can't find you. An' you're more use t' everyone alive than dead, huh? Includin' yerself."

Amourgin faced the questioner. The man wore a field sergeant's badge on his arm, and a field sergeant's no-nonsense expression.

"Name?" he asked.

"Amourgin Thurdhad."

The sergeant's metal-tipped pen stopped scritching across the page. "Turvahad?"

"Thurdhad. T-H-U-R-D-H-A-D."

"Ah. Right." The pen resumed its scritching. "County?"

"Briar." The one that held Olmya, capital of the New Empire.

"Aw, shit. Another city boy." The sergeant gave Amourgin a narrow-eyed once-over, noting the glasses, the book held in one hand, and the fashionable clothing, and returned his gaze to the log in front of him with a deep sigh.

"Next of kin?" Mostly under his breath, he added, "Reckon we'll need it."

"None."

"Makes it simple, anyway. Got yer own mounts? Any idea how to ride 'em, city boy?"

"Yes. Two, in the stables—I've just taken up riding—"

The sergeant stared up at him with an expression of clear disgust on his face. "Aw-w-w-w, fer godssakes—just *taken it up*? Like it was embroidering or somesuch? How'd y'ever get from place to place?"

"That's what carriages are for," Amourgin said.

"Shit. What's yer occupation—librarian?"

"Law-speaker."

"Wonderful. We'll take you out and shoot you now—save ourselves a load of grief."

Amourgin leaned forward and rested one hand on the field desk. "I know I'm not much. I'm afraid I'll be of no benefit to a unit—I never had the skill for weapons, nor the courage to deal with large animals. If you could see your way clear to send me on my way . . . I could make it worth your while."

The pen froze in mid scritch. The sergeant kept his head down, and sat perfectly still. "Worth my while?" he asked in a low voice. "How so?"

"I have sealed vouchers of credit in my possession. I could sign a goodly number of them over to you—say . . . ten crowns?"

The sergeant's pen began to move again.

"Twenty?"

The pen slowed, then resumed its pace.

"Thirty?"

The pen stopped dead and the sergeant stared up. "Thirty crowns? That's the best offer I've had tonight. Actually, that's the best offer I've had in many a night."

Good, Amourgin thought. "I could make them out to you now," he said softly.

"In fact, that's such a big offer, I can't ignore it. I usually ignore those offers," he added. "But thirty crowns—"

Amourgin reached for his pouch to pull out a voucher.

"Leave 'em where they are," the sergeant said. "Mercele!" he bawled. "Front and center."

A man larger than many houses presented himself in front of the master sergeant. "Sir?"

"This *gentleman* appears to be entirely unsuitable for military service. You are to help him through this rabble to get his horses, and then you are to provide him with a personal escort. Where did you wish to go?" the sergeant asked the law-speaker.

"Any reasonable hostel would be fine," Amourgin said. He couldn't believe his luck. He'd been ready to go to fifty crowns—and could, if forced, have covered a draft of as much as sixty.

"You hear that, Mercele? Any reasonable hostel."

"Yes, sir." Mercele stood impassively in the darkness, watching his sergeant.

"Any reasonable hostel," the sergeant repeated, and chuckled. "He thinks he can *buy* his way out of service to Emperor Shemro an' the Three. Offered me thirty crowns to let him run. So take him to get his horses, and then you take him to the fort, and stick him in the stockade, and if he gives you any trouble, you beat him 'til he can't move." The sergeant grinned at Amourgin. "And if he tries to bribe you, take the money, and *then* beat him 'til he can't move."

The corners of Mercele's mouth twitched in the smallest of smiles. "Yes, SIR!" he said with considerable enthusiasm.

Amourgin stared at the sergeant, feeling he'd been hit between the eyes by an ax. "But—but . . ." he sputtered. "You yourself said I wasn't suitable to be a soldier."

"Oh," the sergeant said, and flashed Amourgin one final genial smile. "We'll fix *that*. Or kill you trying."

"Move," Mercele the mountain whispered.

Amourgin moved.

First Captain Sir Bren Morkaarin looked over Sergeant Ddrad's roster at the unlikely additions the XIXth Imperial

Foot had just acquired, and thought if he weren't standing in the courtyard with the best of the XIXth watching him right then, he would weep.

Lord Colonel Gonstad looked down his nose at the First Captain and said, "These are your charges, then, Morkaarin. Get them back to the fort. I've other things to do." The Lord Colonel flicked his leopard skin back over his shoulder and snapped his fingers. His personal guard leapt to attention, brought his horse to him, and followed him out.

Leaving Bren with the mess. Nothing new there.

So what did he have? A pimp; five whores; a two-hand complement of water-spined merchants and overweight traders; from the earlier part of the night's work, not one, but *two* chicken farmers; four bank clerks; a handful of assorted potscrubbers and street cleaners, beggars, shopkeepers, and thieves. One sheep of a law-speaker, and a horse wrangler. He noted the horse wrangler's name and pursed his lips. A true horsemaster would be a valuable commodity. Of gentle birth, so technically she shouldn't be a common soldier—but time pressed, and technicalities could wait. The rest of the recruits looked dismal.

He rubbed his temples and sighed before he replaced his helmet. *Time to round them up and move them out,* he thought.

"Ignore him," he heard a feminine voice say from somewhere in the midst of the mob of recruits.

"I'll rif his t'roat out!" another voice snarled.

A man laughed. "Y'whore. H'I'll make as much money off yer ass here as h'ever I did before. H'I can still sell you, y'stupid bitch, even h'if we are in t'army. H'and there'll be plenty of takers."

Bren heard a low, terrible growl, and a shriek. Sounds of a scuffle broke out, and suddenly several voices were yelling at once, "Don't kill him! Don't kill him, Eowlie!"

Bren ran into the midst of the recruits.

"Clear!" he bellowed. "Get clear! Back off! Make way!"

The recruits scurried out of his path, until only two were left. The fat pimp, and one of his former whores with her teeth sunk into his neck and murder in her eyes.

"Don't bite down!" one of the young piebald whores screamed. She tugged at the gauzy back of the fanged whore's see-through tunic, trying to pull her off the pimp. "Oh, mercy, don't kill him or they'll hang you!"

The pimp's eyes had rolled back in his head. Bren wasn't sure whether the man was dead or saved his life when he fainted. The man himself would be no great loss if he *were* dead, Bren thought. The woman who'd downed him was another matter, however.

She looked up at him out of cold yellow eyes, her teeth still in the pimp's throat.

"Let him go," Bren said. Their gazes locked. He kept his voice low—and kept his hands away from his sword. He didn't want to panic her into killing the bastard if he wasn't dead already. She looked like she might have some potential as a soldier. It would be a shame to have to hang her over such a sorry specimen as the pimp.

She let up and backed off very slowly. And then she grinned at him, the sort of wolfish grin from which nightmares were made. "Mayve the war kill him for me, hey?"

Bren did not allow himself to respond to her comment. He knelt next to the downed man and felt for a pulse and breathing. The pimp was still alive. Good. He gave her a cold look and said, "You'll spend the next two days in the stockade, recruit. This ever happens again, it'll be lashes."

She nodded slowly. "It von't haffen again."

"It won't happen again, *sir*."

She grinned. "It von't haffen again, SIR."

He stood, brushed off the knees of his breeches. The rest of the recruits were watching him. He beckoned over one of the musketeers. "Take her to the stockade."

The musketeer looked from the pimp to the weird fanged woman, and then back at the ranks of musketeers who stood along the wall. Bren saw him swallow hard. "Me, sir? I mean—you will want several of us to take her together, won't you? Sir?"

"You can handle it." Bren kept his face impassive as he looked from the musketeer to the woman. "I believe I could trust her to go to the stockade by herself. After all, she volunteered. But I need somebody along with her to give my orders to the watchman to put her inside. You're going to ride along peacefully, isn't that right, recruit?"

Those yellow-gold eyes fixed on him, and the smile became something other than wolfish. "Yes, sir. Thank you, sir."

Bren nodded. "Right, then. She has a horse. Get it, and let her ride it."

This should make an interesting object lesson for the troops, Bren thought, as the musketeer and the woman walked toward the stables. *Don't push her, because you might end up alone with her.* The musketeer taking her to the stockade was a good man—not one given to abusing women, not one likely to do anything to set her off. Not, he thought, a man like the several men behind him who were muttering, thinking themselves unnoticed.

"Wish he'd a sent me. I'd a shown her a thing or two 'tween here and the camp."

"Don't you know it. Girl wouldna' of sat down t'whole time in the stockade."

They chuckled. Bren sighed. *That isn't what would have happened,* he thought. *I'd have ended up burying one soldier and hanging another.*

At his feet, the pimp opened his eyes. "H'I want to press charges," he said. "H'I want that bitch court-martialled."

Bren glanced down at the man and permitted himself a slow, gentle smile. "You're lucky I don't stick you in the stockade with her, recruit, and then forget to check on you. You don't own her—or any of them—anymore. And if you try to act like you do again, I'll have *you* up on charges. The XIXth hangs panderers, too, you know."

The recruits who had horses took them out of the stables under heavy guard and saddled up.

Bren watched them. The majority of the horses were candidates for the renderer. The riders mostly sat like bags full of tubers, round-backed and sprawled all along their cantles. There were exceptions. He saw a few good mounts—and two he would have given his own eyeteeth and his lord colonel's right arm for.

Grenlaarin horses, he thought, watching the Grenlaarin girl vault into her saddle as if gravity had no meaning. The Grenlaarin horses were a good two hands taller than the largest of the other horses, deep-chested, heavy-boned and well-muscled, with the characteristic arched necks and shortish backs of the breed. Top Grenlaarins were the ultimate utility horses—good jumpers, good trail mounts, smart enough for advanced schooling, sturdy enough to work as light draft beasts. And unflappable.

And she had *two* of them, matched black-point dapples.

He gritted his teeth, envious. He wondered, briefly, how much she'd want for one, and decided as quickly that he wasn't likely to have that kind of money any time soon—and she wouldn't trade for what *he* had.

"Line up the foot recruits," he yelled. "Halberds to either side! Riders behind, recruits to center, musketeers lead off."

The milling mob shifted, re-formed, took on shape and order. Bren's aide brought him his horse, and he swung into his own saddle, feeling the eyes of the Grenlaarin girl on him as he did. He wished for some of her grace right then—wished for a nobler horse with which to impress her. He hated to know there were people better than him at the things he thought important. Worse, he hated having those people watch him, he told himself. That was the only reason he wanted to impress her. Certainly it was nothing more.

He shifted in the saddle, cued his mount to move to one side with the pressure of a knee and the faintest twitch of reins. He waved a hand. "Move out."

❂ CHAPTER III

"Morkaarin," the man said. "Bren Morkaarin . . ." He snapped his fingers. "The bastard!"

"You know him personally?" Willek said.

"No, no, my liege. *Literally* a bastard. His mother was careless, although she insisted under geas-oath that his father was noble."

Willek raised an eyebrow. A noblewoman had access to the best contraceptive spells available, and even the common-or-garden variety issued to the troops was virtually foolproof. Bastardy was not much of a disgrace, but it was a severe social handicap, since the child had only one set of parents and kinfolk for backing.

"Find him," she said. "Find him and kill him."

"Shouldn't be difficult," her cousin said.

Willek looked him over critically. He had the family looks, tall and slender and quick; his black boots, fitted trousers and shirt, and short-sleeved jacket showed off his build to advantage. He had less of the family wealth, though a stranger couldn't have guessed that by the gold at his belt and swordhilt and on the clasp of his peacock-plumed hat. He tended to vanity, and pomaded his hair with too much lavender, but he was competent. She'd taken him on as liegeman and guard captain because he was a relation, needed the job, and seemed both able and unencumbered with an excess of scruple.

47

"Don't try it alone, Valwer," she said. At his frown: "That's an order. No fuss, no formal challenges, just dead. Take as many as you need."

There was no need to mention the magical complications. Cousin Valwer had the psychic sensitivity of a turnip. If he ran into difficulties, well, that would give her valuable information too.

The aide peeked his nose around Willek's door. "Lieutenant Cöado to see you."

Willek made a flicking gesture with one hand. "Go." Her cousin bowed with an ironic flourish of hat and cloak, and left. She took a deep breath and settled into her high-backed chair, and rested her baton of office across her knees. "Send him in."

The aide showed a whippet-lean man in the elegant grey tunic of the special troops into her headquarters. The man bowed slightly. Willek inclined her head fractionally. Both waited, unspeaking.

The aide stood in the door, waiting.

"I'll call you when I need you again, Ketos."

The aide pursed his lips and backed woodenly out of the room.

"Ketos doesn't like me," the lieutenant said. "Neither does that blond beanpole . . . what's his name?"

"Valwer Tornsaarin," Willek said. "I don't like you either," she added flatly. "But you're . . . useful. So, Chevays, how are you finding life in the special division?"

"Very bloody." The man smiled his thin-lipped smile and leaned casually against Willek's desk. "I like being an official interrogator. It suits me."

"I'm sure." She crossed her legs and tapped her baton against her knee. "Please remember you are now official, and show the appropriate respect."

"Being the Tornsaarin family assassin doesn't confer special privileges, hey?" He smiled his thin, humorless smile and stood in front of her desk, his at-rest position just across the line of insolence.

Willek raised an eyebrow. She waved him into the chair across from her. "I want you to do me a favor."

He grinned. "No one ever asks to see me because they enjoy my company."

"That's because no one enjoys your company." She opened a drawer, and pulled out a small box. She checked the latch—it was firmly in place. She tossed the box to Chevays, and smiled tightly when he gave her a questioning look. "Open it."

He fiddled with the latch, opened the box—then nearly dropped it as ghostly forms sprang out at him. He slammed the lid shut and glared at her.

"Very funny."

She almost laughed. He wasn't completely without nerves, then. "Open it back up. They can't hurt you."

He did what she asked, and the forms flew out again, and gathered coherence and opacity. The lieutenant studied them and frowned, his expression puzzled.

Three ghostly people shimmered in the dim light of the office. One was a bland-looking blond man of medium height—he wore a first captain's sash. The second was a stocky, ruddy girl; almost as dark as a Derkinoi, but with Tykissian lodge-marks on her face. The third was a tall, lean woman whose lower face stretched into a deadly-looking muzzle—she was no breed of human or near-human Willek had ever seen. Her slanted yellow eyes seemed to look through Willek with vicious intensity. The Grand Admiral was pleased with the quality of the images she'd managed to capture from the blood-demon.

"Dull, except for the beast-girl," Chevays offered at last.

Willek leaned back and slapped the palm of her hand with her baton. She imagined Chevays the sort who'd find the wolf-muzzled woman appealing, but then, she suspected him of all sorts of nasty perversions. "I want you to find them all. The man is Bren Morkaarin; he's First Captain in the XIXth Foot. I don't know what their connection to each other is—but they have some strange link to me. The other two I don't know at all. Find them. Once you do, let me know who and where they are. One or more of them is likely to be God-Touched."

Chevays raised an eyebrow. "Could be dangerous. Luck takes bizarre twists around the gods' playthings." He didn't ask how she knew. Willek suspected he was aware that she dabbled in unpriestly, forbidden magic. He knew better than to ask for further details.

She leaned back in her chair and templed her fingers in front of her face. "I'll tell you what to do next after you've located them."

"If you think you're going to want me to kill them, let me know now. I'll have to make special preparations."

Willek closed her eyes and saw, once again, her head falling to the executioner's sword. She saw the expression on her face—horror and disbelief and pain in that instant when the blade sliced through her neck but when life had not yet left her. She squeezed her eyes tightly closed and said:

"I'll most likely want you to kill them. But it may not be that simple. If Fate's taking a hand the timing may be critical. In any case, find them, find out their connection to each other. *Then* we'll think about killing them."

Konzin patted his bedroll and heard the reassuring crinkle of the bank draft. It was secure—but he had a hard time feeling comfortable while carrying that much money. Something he'd have to get used to, he decided.

He shifted in the saddle. He and the rest of the ranch hands had started out for the Grenlaarin ranch long before first light. They were already well into the scraggy open fells and broken bluffs that ran from the sea to Olmya, following the river's eastern bank. The open lowlands on the west were barely visible, a checkerboard of small fields and orchards protected by levees along the waterfront.

By late morning, the air was already sweltering and humid. Konzin mopped the sweat off his brow with the back of his sleeve and took a swig from his water jug.

Lion Abt, the taciturn Olmyan, rode first. The Taghylfa

brothers followed, occasionally heckling the sailors who went below in their little river boats. Brunnai Grenlaarin, on loan from a city branch of the family so she could "learn the business," rode next to Pot Foute, who was apparently not in a mood to be spoken to.

Brunnai, the youngest of the ranch hands, loved to talk, and hated to be ignored. She reined back and waited for Konzin to catch up. "You're sure we canna' get Cousin Karah back?" the lanky brown-haired girl asked.

"She was pressed. T' army isn't goin' t' give her back to us just 'cause her ma and pa will be unhappy."

"I know the army would have traded good, battle-ready horses for her. The army always wants good horses."

"Horses ain't mine t' trade," Konzin snapped. "If t' madine wanted to trade her way out, she should have told me. Should have give me a note or somethin'. But she didn't."

Brunnai nodded. "You know, it's funny, the press gang going to an inn like that. You'd think they'd have come through and pressed all us first. More likely to get good cavalry out of a bunch of working ranch hands than a mess of fat merchants."

Konzin said nothing.

"Sure unlucky for Karah," Brunnai continued, oblivious to Konzin's silence. "You know, Uncle Iano was just over to Feugtuld's ranch dickering dowry with the Feugtuld boy. There'd have been banns before the end of summer. Feugtuld's offered two gold pirate plates and two matched hackneys and two brood mares . . ." The girl shook her head, and a wistful smile crossed her face. "Couple years, I'll be gettin' dowry offers. I'd ha' loved that one."

"Two old families like that . . ." Els started to say.

Konzin cut him off. "I don't want to talk about it," he snarled. Brunnai looked surprised.

From ahead, Lion snorted. "Guess not. Her pa wouldn't talk about dowry with Konzin. Hey, Konzin? Ain't that so? Wanted a young boy of family for his one and only child—not a grown man from the back hills."

Konzin felt familiar rage twist in his belly. "There won't be banns now," he muttered, too low for any of the others to hear. He snapped, "Turn here."

The others looked at him in surprise. The low-level road along the river was an Imperial highway, cut into the cliffs above the cool tannin-stained, deep brown water of the Olmya; it was twenty-five feet broad and surfaced with pounded crushed stone. The laneway he turned his mount's head toward was a local track, rutted dirt, and much steeper if a little more direct.

"Easier on the hooves," he said, which was true enough. The others slowed to a walk as they passed him and climbed. Scrub pinyoce overhung the dusty road, providing scant shade. The heat was oppressive. Brunnai kept talking, but Konzin quit listening, and soon enough, the girl rode ahead and chattered at someone else.

There had been a breeze off the river; on this back lane away from running water, there was none. The air hung still and damp and heavy. Konzin pulled off his tunic; some of the other ranch hands did the same. The quiet, dull thud of horses' hooves on dirt lulled Konzin. He let the reins go slack in his fingers. His head bobbed forward and his eyes drooped. The white glare of the sun shone through his heavy eyelids; the horses kicked up little puffs of chalky dust as they walked. Horse sweat plopped into the dust, making little dark craters. The smell rose heavy around Konzin, as familiar as breath.

Then one of the horses whinnied, and from somewhere up ahead, another horse replied.

They'd passed a few traders earlier—and, Konzin thought, there would be plenty more on the road later in the day, but right then the sun beat down oppressively. Few traveled the road in the worst of the heat.

"Come from the spring up ahead," Pot guessed. "Folks pulled off at the well and waiting 'til dusk."

"Be good to stop and water t' horses," Brunnai added. Her face brightened at the idea of stopping and resting.

The horses perked up, too. Instead of their leisurely walk, they moved into a brisk trot of their own accord; those on lead lines shouldered and pushed, trying to get past the saddled mounts.

Konzin was suddenly and completely awake. He dropped back further, and rested his hand on the hilt of his sword. He said nothing, and the first of the ranch hands trotted around the bluff.

He heard a man call out, "Hail, travelers. What is the news from Derkintown?"

Lion answered, "War and more war. The army is pressing in the taverns—I'd not go to Derkin again without good reason."

"Thanks for the warning, then," the man's voice said. "Care to join me for some bread and cheese while I wait out the heat?"

"Oh, sure," Brunnai's voice chirped.

Konzin stopped completely, waiting.

"Where's Konzin?" Pot asked.

"Scouting the area, I reckon. You know Konzin."

Konzin heard the creak of saddle leather, the thud of boots into dust, travelers milling around a well and being social beneath the shade of the well tree. A windlass creaked, drawing water. He drew his sword, and walked his horse quietly to the point behind the bluff, just out of sight of the clearing. He sat still, his heart racing, his palms beginning to sweat.

He heard laughter.

Now, he thought.

He heard movement on the top of the bluff above him, and the sounds of men running. Then he heard cries of fright, and the clash of steel against steel. Horses whinnied. He heard someone land in a saddle, heard the hooves pound, and "Konzin, help!" shouted by one or the other of his men. The voice was so distorted by fear he could not identify it.

Then young Brunnai, bleeding, came tearing around the corner toward Konzin on one of the horses. The girl's eyes were white-rimmed. "Konzin," she shrieked, "it was a trap! Help them!"

Konzin dug heels into his mount's flanks, and man and beast charged forward. Konzin's sword, already in hand, seemed to leap of its own accord. *Die, little bitch*, he thought, and felt the satisfying jolt in his arm as metal split bone. The hated Grenlaarin sat in her saddle a moment after her head left her shoulders. Then her body slithered from the saddle and fell with a thud to the dirt.

Konzin had never killed like that before—a single stroke, at close quarters. He was surprised at the ease of the deed, and surprised at his pleasure in it. He listened to the fighting going on around the well, and looked down at the body of the dead Grenlaarin, and at the horse which stood trembling beside him, waiting to be remounted—and he smiled. He had done this thing. He could do the things that came after.

The screams died down. He heard laughter, and Derkinoi pidgin loudly chattered, and the sounds of bodies being stripped of their valuables. Still smiling, he trotted around the corner.

A dozen tattered men with rag-wrapped faces looked up at him, then went back to stripping bodies. One man, better dressed, his face masked instead of wrapped in rags, walked over to Konzin and looked up at him.

"We got all but the youngker."

"I got her. Body's out on the road. You have my silver, Ugin?"

"You have the draft?"

Konzin nodded. "I have it. You'll take the horses with you, save one I'll claim I managed to capture. Follow a week behind me to show up at Grenlaarin Five Points. Not the Jawain ranch—that's Grenlaarin On The River. And not Grenlaarin Beechgrove. When you get there, I'll hire you all on. I figure a month, two months beyond that and I'll own the place. We'll divvy then."

"And meantimes, we get wages?"

"Wages and board."

Konzin fished the bankdraft out of his bedroll, while Grey River Weasel Ugin pulled two heavy bags of silver from his waist pouch.

"Silver for half the written value of the draft, as we agreed," the man said.

"That was the agreement," Konzin said. "When y' sell the note, make sure it can't be traced back t' me."

"We've no wish t' see our own heads roll. The draft won't be traced."

The men exchanged, spit and slapped palms. Konzin took his choice of second horse—the fine bay mare Brunnai Grenlaarin had ridden. Then he stripped, and exchanged his clothes for dead Pot's which were bloody and rent and filthy. He stood patiently while one of Ugin's men beat him. When he felt the coming bruises, and tasted the blood running down the back of his throat, he said "Enough."

He would look convincing. He would take to the Grenlaarins his tale of woe. And he would win the ranch they did not think him good enough to marry into.

Amourgin woke on a bunk with the uncomfortable feeling he was being watched, and with the itch of a thin, lumpy cornshuck mattress beneath him. He kept his eyes closed and his breathing regular until he could get past the headache and the foggy certainty something unpleasant had happened the night before. He tried to remember where he was, and how he had come to be there. There had been, he thought, soldiers. And a fight.

Was he in lockup for drunkenness, then?

That didn't seem right, but Three knew he had the hangover. Amourgin hated waking spent and sick. Things took so long to make sense.

Lockup? No. This was not a lockup. He'd had no childish brawl with men over a mere difference of opinion—over the horse races or the qualities of a champion verdal player. This had been much worse than that.

Memory returned to him with the force of the foul taste in his mouth, and his eyes flew open.

"Pressed," Amourgin said, and groaned. And then he saw, blearily and through a haze, that he was indeed being watched. The occupant of the bunk above him hung over the edge and stared at him. He rubbed his eyes, hoping that the picture would improve when he could see clearly.

It didn't.

"Ah—" he said, looking into fierce yellow eyes. "You're here, too. In with me?" Amourgin looked around the tiny confines of the cell, and discovered that only he and the whore called Eowlie shared the tiny room. "Oh." *There is no situation so bad,* Amourgin thought, *that it cannot be made worse by a creative bastard with a sick sense of humor.*

"I got thrown in vecause I was going to kill that f'ig of a man, Zeemos," Eowlie said, and grinned at him. "Vut I did't. I let the vastard live."

"That was, ah . . . good of you."

She chuckled a throaty, deep chuckle. "No, it wasn't. I didn't want the caf-tain to hang me. I think the war will kill Zeemos without my help, yes?"

"Probably." Amourgin studied the gleaming teeth and the wicked smile, and wished deeply and passionately that he had not tried to bribe the sergeant the night before. "How long are we going to be in here?" he asked.

"I'm here two nights. I don't know about you. The caf-tain may decide to hang *you*. Vri-very is a crime."

"Thanks," Amourgin said, and rolled over facing the wall. He tried hard to remember which of the Three he had offended, and how. An appropriate sacrifice might not get him out of the army, but at least it could save him from whatever horrors the outraged god had planned next.

Tramping boots echoed in the hall outside the cell, and metal screeched across metal. "Up and out, both of y'. Y'll spend yer nights in the stockade, but First Captain says your butts are gonna work all day."

Amourgin jumped out of the hard bunk before the guard could change his mind. Anything, he thought, would be preferable to spending day and night locked into a tiny cell with the ferocious Eowlie. Even if the First Captain intended him to scrub floors or shell wettelnuts, he would do it gladly.

Beside, he thought, *out of this cell, I might find a way to escape.*

Somewhere away from the camp, Amourgin's mission waited. His contact would come looking for him sooner or later, and when the man came looking, Amourgin needed to be there. Not in the XIXth's camp, and not shipped across the sea to fight an idiot war on foreign soil at the behest of the Imperial government the Reform fought.

Karah couldn't believe that jackass of a First Captain was still testing the new recruits in the midday heat. First it had been running. Then lifting big rocks. Then they'd shown what they could—or in Karah's case, *couldn't*—do with pikes. First Captain Morkaarin hadn't been satisfied with that. Now he had them climbing over and under fences and crawling through the dust on their bellies.

The absolute worst of it was that *he* seemed able to do anything he told the recruits to do, only much better. Right now he was wiping down his torso with a towel while his orderly held his shirt and jacket. He bore a surprising number of scars for a man so young: bullet marks, and the long white lines made by edged weapons. He looked less bulky out of the armor and clothing—heavy shoulders and arms and the enlarged wrists of a swordsman, but he tapered to the waist and his belly was flat.

Damn, Karah thought, crawling harder. *So he's pretty. I still hate him.*

"I'd like to—vite the v'alls off that—stinking First Captain," the yellow-eyed whore next to Karah snarled.

Karah dragged herself along on her elbows while red dust

coated her skin and worked inside her clothes. "I'll hold him down," she muttered, "and you—do the biting."

The whore grinned.

They were at another fence. The whore gathered herself as a dog or a horse would, and sprang over it on all fours.

Karah was envious. She had to climb, got hung once, and dropped to the ground on the other side, panting.

"Keep your heads down!" the First Captain shouted. "Down, *down*, DOWN! Or somebody will shoot them off!"

Just to add some realism, a squad of musketeers were firing over their heads occasionally. The thumb-sized bullets whistled spitefully overhead, just a fraction of a second after the *thump* of discharge and the long sulphur-smelling jet of dirty-white powder smoke. That would have been less nerve-wracking if the musketeers hadn't been novices, too, doing their basic drill. She could hear their corporal bellowing in a rhythmic chant:

"Load. Load in nine times. Present your firelocks. Prepare to—no, no, *no*, you pig-futtering farmer, take the shit-stirring ramrod OUT before—"

Karah and the whore shoved their faces close to the dirt and moved in a fast belly-on-the-ground elbow crawl toward the trench that meant the conclusion of the dirt-gathering test. At that moment, Karah thought she envied the whore her small breasts even more than her jumping skills.

"You can—call me Eowlie," the whore said.

The two women dragged along in the dirt, breathing hard.

"Karah," Karah answered when she had the wind. "*Grenlaarin.*" She gave the last considerable emphasis, but the whore didn't notice. *Or else*, Karah thought, *the name means nothing to her. If that's the case, she must be from way out in the hinterlands.*

"You know," Eowlie continued, "the testicles are—very tasty." Karah looked over to see if she were joking. The whore had a thoughtful expression on her face. "Either cooked—or sometimes, if the—conditions are right, raw. Right now, I think—the conditions would be verrry good for raw—yes?"

"Yes," Karah said. A pebble had just ground itself into her right hipbone, and she thought Eowlie could do the holding, and *she* would do the biting. "I'll bet—your customers loved it when—you whispered *that*—in their ears."

"I keft those thoughts—to myself, and was haffy to—think avout it. I—did not choose to ve a—whore."

They were at the trench. Karah tried to hang on to the dirt edge while she swung herself over, but it crumbled beneath her fingers. She fell into the bottom of the trench, landed hard, and lay there swearing.

Eowlie dropped lightly into the trench, again alighting on all fours.

I could get very tired of her, Karah thought. She tried to brush the dust off. The effort was futile. It was embedded in her skin—she would die coated in this very dust, she decided. The whole camp was alive with it; twenty or so regiments, sprawling out around what had been a fairly modest provincial garrison fort, kicked up a *lot* of dust. The air was humid with the nearness of the sea, too: sweat stuck to the skin, and so did the dirt it picked up, like an oily abrasive.

Eowlie brushed at herself, too, and said, "I am not a whore in my country. I do other things. I am a hunter, and a hunter on sea. Vut that fatherless devil Zeemos caught me when I was sick, so he traffed me with his collar. It made me weak, so that I could not fight." She laughed; a deep, growling laugh at the back of her throat. "I will get Zeemos."

Karah leaned against the wall of the trench, appreciating the tiny line of shade it offered. "I don't blame you," she said. "Tell you what. We'll cut the balls off Zeemos and that pig First Captain, and you can show me your favorite recipes for testicles."

"I like you," Eowlie said. She, too, leaned in the shade. "You are like me—vut with not-so-good teeth."

The First Captain walked over and looked down into their trench. Karah noted that the sound of nearby shooting had stopped. "Either of you use the sword before?" he asked.

Both women looked up at him.

"We don't use the sword in my country," Eowlie said. She grinned at the captain, and her long teeth gleamed.

Karah studied that ferocious smile and thought Eowlie's people wouldn't need swords. She, however, had used them in practice many a time, and in competitions at the county fairs. "I've trained with the sword," she said. She crossed her arms over her chest and glared, daring the First Captain to make something of it.

He ignored her hostility. "Good. You and the law-speaker are going to take practice blades, and lead off in the fight circle."

The practice blades were split bamboo, the tips and grips leather-wrapped, with a heavy cord from one end to the other that marked the edge of the blade. It was the training version of the long straight-bladed, single-edged saber most Imperial horsemen carried. Karah had worked with such practice weapons before. Used properly, they hurt almost as much as the real thing.

She slipped on the padded jacket and hat that would be her only armor, and stepped into the fighting circle. The law-speaker across the ring from her had done the same. His city-folk finery looked less gaudy for his having crawled in the dirt all morning.

Karah felt better.

"I'll call the fights," the First Captain yelled. "Stay in the circle and don't hit anyone but your opponent. Begin."

Karah and Amourgin faced off. Both held their weapons in the two-handed grip for fighting on foot. Karah kept hers directly in front of her, the tip up and steady. Amourgin moved the tip of his weapon in the loops favored by city-schooled swordsmen. Karah had seen a man fight that way before, but hadn't been able to discern a benefit to the technique. She waited and relaxed, circling. Amourgin did not so much move with her as change poses. His fighting style looked artificial and silly, and Karah began to doubt that he would last a minute against an attack.

She saw a straightforward opening, and jumped at it. Immediately, she found the purpose of Amourgin's fancy poses. He slipped out of her way, stepped to one side, and caught her solidly across the ass.

The circle of recruits laughed, and Karah felt heat rushing to her face. *Damn*, she thought. *I should have seen that coming and parried it. That was a sucker move, not something he'd use in a real fight.*

She realized she'd fallen for a school trick because she hadn't learned her bladework in a school. He'd studied her style of fighting, and figured out she wouldn't recognize the setup—and he'd done it to make himself look good. Karah faced off against him, keeping her anger under control. She was willing to bet there were things she knew that he didn't—if she could just figure out what they were.

They resumed their duel. Amourgin cut and cut and thrust, and Karah parried, stepped, parried, turning the blade into the path of his with quick flexes from the wrists. He tried to lure her into his trap again, but she didn't fall for it. She waited, focusing on him so intently the sounds and smells and sensations of the world around her ceased to exist. This time the fight went on and on, while the two of them tested each other, moved in, and quickly retreated. Finally Karah saw the briefest of smiles flicker across her opponent's face. He evidently thought he'd seen something. He stepped toward her, his sword low for a gutting slash. She moved quickly aside, parried the blow, and kicked the back of his knee so that he sat abruptly in the dirt. She completed her circle to finish behind him and lay her practice weapon along his throat. She said softly, "You're dead."

The sounds came back in a rush—the laughter and the mocking calls of the recruits, of "Ho, law-speaker!" and "There's 'un fer the city boy!"

"I would note," Amourgin said stiffly, "that a kick to the back of the knee is hardly one of the Nine Cuts and Four

Thrusts. I would have expected better swordplay of you than what I would have gotten from a common streetfighter."

"One," Karah said, holding up a finger, "we weren't playing, and two," she held up another, "if I'd been a common streetfighter, you'd been dead instead of dustin' your ass in a practice ring."

Amourgin looked to the First Captain, who shrugged. "She cheated, but she won. We aren't comparing styles for points. We're trying to win a war."

The law-speaker stood and brushed himself off. "I see. Very well. I shall try to remember that."

"Nonetheless," the First Captain said, "I'm pleased to see you know which end of a sword to cut with. I'd feared we were going to have to tie you to a stake and use you as bait in the field."

Karah thought it would be impolitic to laugh. She laughed anyway. Amourgin glared at her, and she could see in his eyes a determination to trounce her the next time they fought. She wasn't worried. She knew how to fight him—and he would never get another chance to smack her with a practice sword.

The afternoon wore on. She stood outside the circle and watched the other recruits thrash away at each other. From time to time the First Captain called her in, and she beat one of them. Among her fellow recruits, none matched her with the practice sword. The only one who came close was Amourgin, and she had proved from the beginning she could beat him. She felt, she thought, justifiably smug.

The recruits sat once for a meal. The First Captain continued his tests, taking notes and watching, often having a recruit do something again so he could compare them against the little marks on his note sheet. Late afternoon became early evening, and the air grew cooler and once again bearable.

Karah looked down the hill at the camp. Musketeers led a line of horses out of the stables and up the dirt path toward her.

The First Captain watched, too. "I have you ranked by foot

skills so far. Anybody can use a pike or a musket with a little practice. I've been asked to create a unit of mounted scouts. Those of you with good riding skills will be considered for the scout unit, but that means being able to ride, use a sword, and shoot. Double pay and an allowance for your horses." He looked from Karah to Amourgin, and Karah saw his eyes narrow. "Those of you inclined to view everything as a competition may consider this to be one as well."

Karah looked at Amourgin and smiled sweetly. She'd beat the pants off him at swords. She would *humiliate* him at horses.

Amourgin raised an eyebrow in her direction, then shrugged and watched the horses being led into what had been the fighting ring.

First Captain Morkaarin cleared his throat. "All recruits who do not wish to compete for scout positions are hereby excused to take mess."

Half the recruits wandered down toward the mess tent immediately. Karah was not surprised. Nor, for the most part, was she surprised by those who remained. Eowlie was there, and Amourgin, and the ox-like Tseldene whore. The traders, none of whom had fancied the pike or the crawling through dirt, had all stayed around. Some of the pack peddlers might even make it; they'd be used to horses, and they went into some rough areas. Zeemos, the pimp, was going to try to win a place in the scouts.

Loud-mouthed evil lard-bellied fiend, she thought. Eowlie had been filling her in on the doings of Zeemos. There were a few others, all unlikely-looking.

The First Captain evidently thought so, too. He picked the two least likely, and walked them into the ring. "First round—" he said to them, "you'll go once around the ring—walk, trot and canter. Then once over each of the jumps. Then stop in the center. Don't fall off."

The men and women around the ring chuckled. Those in it did not.

The First Captain walked along the line, then picked out a

horse from those the musketeers presented. He led one of the horses forward, and Karah recognized him. "Hey!" she shouted. "Glorylad is mine!"

The First Captain turned to her wearing a cold expression, and she added: "Sir."

He nodded stiffly. "I'm aware of that, recruit. If you want to ride him, you'll have to win your place. In the meantime, I want horses I can trust not to balk at the jumps."

The other horse he chose was Amourgin's Broucher. Karah recognized the horse as definitely *the* Broucher. She glanced over at Amourgin, who looked as unhappy as she felt. Her second mount, Windrush, was in the line as well.

Karah gritted her teeth and glared at the First Captain.

Eowlie came up beside her and nodded toward the First Captain. "Raw or cooked?" she whispered.

"Raw," Karah snarled. "Definitely raw."

"I thought so."

They stood, watching the first two riders mount. Both of them looked terrible.

"Do you suffose they've ever seen horses vefore?" Eowlie asked in a conversational tone.

"You certainly wouldn't think it to look at them, would you?" Karah answered loudly. "Why, I've seen dogs climb trees as well as they mounted."

Both riders frowned in her direction before starting around the track as the First Captain directed. The man on Broucher didn't look too terrible at the outset. The one up on Glorylad, however, rode as if he thought he were sitting on the back of a plow horse, with one rein gripped firmly in each hand. He sawed away at Glorylad's mouth until Karah couldn't stand it anymore.

She ran forward and grabbed Morkaarin's arm. "By all the gods' sakes, First Captain sir, he'll ruin the horse's mouth doin' that," she wailed. "He's no farm horse. He took the bit 'cause he's a gentleman, but I don't even use one on him."

The First Captain studied her. "You're out of line, Grenlaarin, but I'll let it pass this time. *This* time. I'm starting to think I could have saved time throwing the whole bunch of you in the stockade."

Karah started to argue, then caught herself. She looked after her horse mournfully.

The First Captain watched her an instant longer, then nodded as if satisfied by something. "Very good," he said. He looked to Glorylad's rider. "You—Gowdsooki—that's not how you ride a horse. Get down and head for the mess. You're out."

The ungraceful Gowdsooki scrambled down from Glorylad's back and stomped out of the ring. He paused long enough to mutter to Karah, "I'll remember you."

The captain overheard.

"Best not to," he said softly. "You wouldn't like army justice."

The man scowled and walked away. Morkaarin looked at Karah, a strange half-smile on his face. But he said nothing, and Karah didn't ask what the smile was for.

She stalked back to Eowlie's side and tried not to see the procession of idiots who rode her horses. The captain alternated beasts so they didn't tire. Windrush stood several turns, too, some of them with hopelessly inept riders.

Finally, though, the truly awful were weeded out and the better riders got their chance.

Eowlie did well. She moved like a part of the animal—Karah wondered if it was because she was part animal herself. She would be in. Zeemos rode better than Karah would have guessed. Surprisingly, so did the short, overmuscled Tseldene woman. The Shillraki could stay on and steer the beast, at least.

Karah and Amourgin went last. Karah strode out to the ring beside him, smiling. "Perhaps," she said softly, "we should each ride the other's horse. Then the question becomes one of general skill, and not one of practice with an individual animal."

Amourgin nodded, his face impassive. "They're both horses. Ride whichever one you want."

Karah smiled and vaulted into Broucher's saddle. She was a trifle disconcerted with Amourgin's graceful mount, but reminded herself that he was tall. Tall people always had a slight advantage getting up and down. She tied the reins together and draped them along Broucher's neck. He snorted and looked over his shoulder at her resentfully, then quieted as he felt cues that told him she knew what she was about. Grenlaarin horses despised bad riders.

"Sorry about that, Broucher," she said softly. "It won't happen again."

Then, with her hands in the pockets of her pants, she cued the horse to a walk. She looked over at Amourgin, intending to give him a smug smile, and found he had imitated her, even to the detail of riding without the reins, and was shadowing her without apparent difficulty.

She cued Broucher to a trot. Glorylad and the law-speaker also moved smoothly into a trot. Karah frowned, and urged Broucher into a canter. She thought surely that would dislodge the law-speaker—few people cared to ride a horse at a canter without holding the reins for security. But the law-speaker continued to mimic her every move.

She swore softly. The law-speaker was a fraud—he knew horses, the miserable bastard. He'd feigned ignorance. She should have known her uncle would never let someone who didn't know horses have his beloved Broucher.

Which still didn't mean he was as good a rider as she was. More than ever, she wanted to rub him into the ground. She wanted to humiliate him so badly he would never dare cross her again.

She clenched the muscles in her jaw and frowned with concentration. Still cantering, and still with her hands in her pockets, she took the law-speaker's horse over the first of the jumps. Broucher moved over it like the gem he was. The law-speaker and Glorylad sailed flawlessly in her wake.

She took the round of jumps, and so did Amourgin.

Angrily, Karah brought Broucher to a four-squared

show-stop in the center of the ring. Amourgin, his hands still casually in his pockets, did the same.

He smiled at her cheerfully. "You know, it isn't all that hard if you just see it done once."

Isn't it? Karah thought. She took her left hand out of her pocket, and smiled tightly at him. She refused to let him see that he'd impressed her with his skill. "Perhaps not—but two simple loops around a ring doesn't make a horseman." She untied the reins and balanced them lightly between the fingers of one hand. Beneath her, Broucher tensed for her next cue. She cued him into a standing pace, segued into a standing show rack, and finished with an aerial, where all four of Broucher's feet left the ground at once.

Amourgin raised a single eyebrow and said thoughtfully, "Yes. Yes, I think I see how that was done." He and Glorylad danced through the same steps.

"I know your game, you swine," Karah snarled.

"Tsk, tsk. Such temper is unseemly in one who would lead." He allowed himself a slight smile.

"Try this," she snapped. She walked Broucher over to the perimeter of the ring, and indicated the single line of square-cut logs that lay on the ground around it. She pointed to them. "Once around," she said.

She urged Broucher up onto the rail, and gave him his head. He catwalked along the top of the line of logs, balancing cautiously on the square-cut surface, his steps slow but precise. It was the hardest stunt to train into a horse—and only the finest rider could give even the best horse the confidence to try it. Broucher was a fine horse—and Karah a superb rider.

But a third of the way around the circle, Karah looked back and found Amourgin and Glorylad, again in her wake, pacing out the circle. He was her equal, then—at riding, at least, though perhaps not at training. And far her superior at subterfuge. When she reached the halfway mark, she snarled with exasperation and urged Broucher back to the center of the ring.

She dismounted by two-handed vault and crossed her arms and glared as Amourgin, on his horse, trotted up to her. He matched her, even to the vault, then stood beside Glorylad, smiling.

Outside the ring, the onlooking recruits applauded—and even Bren looked impressed.

"I still like my big brown horsey," the law-speaker said. "But you have a nice horsey, too."

"You only have two ancestors, and your children will have two heads," Karah hissed.

Amourgin chuckled. "At least the boys," he agreed. "By the way—sometime when it's just the two of us, you might want to try a rematch with the practice blades."

"I'd rather use real ones."

"For shame, for shame." Amourgin dropped Glorylad's reins to the ground and shoved his hands into his pockets. "I wouldn't. I'd hate to be hung for killing a fellow recruit." He paced casually away.

So would I, Karah thought. *Though I'd be tempted to make an exception for you.*

✪ CHAPTER IV

Amourgin woke from exhausted sleep, and dreams of swords and horses and execrable first captains, to the crack of thunder and pounding rain. Wind shrieked and water blew between the bars in irregular sprays. *Back in the stockade,* he thought. *Can't seem to get used to the fact that I'm here.*

The stockade was black as coal tar, except when lightning outside the barred window cast dancing shapes on the far wall.

Every muscle in his body ached, and he yearned to return to the oblivion of sleep. But his pulse raced, and his skin tingled, and dread seeped into his mind and overwhelmed him. He stared around the room with the next lightning flash; the illumination showed it empty except for Eowlie, who now slept in the opposite bunk, unbothered by the storm. He could see no reason to fear, and yet he was afraid.

Flee! his nerves screamed. *Run! Hide! Something is coming!* He felt the irrational urge to turn his face to the wall, or to burrow under his thin blanket. He resisted, and waited, while the storm outside grew worse, and the lightning nearer, and the wind harder. A heaviness settled in his chest, and his stomach churned and roiled.

Suddenly he knew the source of his dread—whatever it was—had arrived. Lightning stabbed steadily just outside the barred window; thunder rolled in endless terrible riot; sheets of icy water blew over him and soaked him clear to the skin.

Across the room, Eowlie slept on, oblivious.

Then it stopped—thunder, lightning, and torrential rain. The instant hush after the storm was more terrible than the storm had been; an enveloping lightless void. The unnatural silence went on and horribly on, stretching out to impossible lengths, until Amourgin feared the storm had rendered him both blind and deaf. Then, from outside the camp a deathbird sang, and Amourgin heard footsteps coming toward him. Freezing wind blew in gusts around him, reeking of rotting flesh. Chill bumps rose on his skin; his hair stood on end.

When a spot of light grew on the wall next to the window, and shimmered like a spreading sheet of water turned end-up, he tried to crawl out of the bed to hide underneath it. He discovered he was pinned in place.

Out of the sheet of light, a man walked—his eyes white and glowing; his skin faintly luminous, waxy. He pointed one clawed finger at Amourgin and smiled a ghastly smile.

"Wait," he whispered, and his voice dripped ice down Amourgin's spine. "They come."

Amourgin heard creaking, sibilant whispers, soft moans, squelching footsteps which grew louder, closer, closer, and through the shimmer-ported wall stepped dead men, flesh hanging tattershawled, bones gleaming with their own pale light. Seaweed draped from skulls and arms, wove in and out of bare, gleaming ribs like weavework, and the men reeked of death and the sea, and nothingness stared out of the places where their eyes should have been. They surrounded Amourgin, and reached out their rotted hands, and they whispered, "Come."

Amourgin shrank back, praying wordless agnostic prayers for rescue, and the dead men lifted him up and carried him out through the wall, and Amourgin believed he was surely dead.

They were on the sea, he and the dead men. In weird procession, they walked across the water, while black clouds ate the string of moons, and the storm returned. Thundercrack and fire in the sky whipped the sea to madness. Waves rose up like mountains and crashed over the hapless law-speaker. Saltwater filled his mouth, his nose; it burned in his lungs and he clawed upward, up toward sweet, distant air; up, while bony hands held him back and the dead men marched inexorably.

The waves fell away, and a drowned city rose before his eyes. Its bells dirged, tolled long across the water, chased back the storm. The dead men wailed, and the corpses of women and children rose from the submerged streets and pointed accusing fingers at Amourgin. In their empty eyesockets, pale, soft-bodied things curled, giving them expressions of appalling madness. "You live!" they bubbled.

Amourgin, still choking from his near-drowning, wondered how much longer that would be true.

A ship rose out of the sea in front of the procession of the dead. Its hull was rotted, and slimy water poured out of holes in its sides.

"Come," the dead men whispered again, and the sounds that came from their ruined throats, Amourgin thought, would drive a man mad.

I am mad. He refused to walk over the water on his own—instead, he made the corpses carry him. The ship loomed over him, dead as the animated bones that dragged him to it. He thought, *I am mad, and lost, and the gods truly live—and they have cursed me for my unbelief.*

Now the sea grew glassy still, and the moons hung out of place for the season, and raced across the sky like stones tossed by giant boys. Night never left—Amourgin believed himself in a world at the end of time, when the sun had died and all the hells broke open and freed their damned. The dead men took seats at the rotted oars, and with creak and snap, the ship raced through the windless night.

Amourgin saw only the sea for a wearying time, and then began to believe the sea was coming to an end. He thought he could make out a darker line along the horizon. His heart leapt—he dreamed of escape—he looked with yearning at what surely was land. Then the white-eyed old man appeared before him, and screeched, "No time. No time."

Amourgin felt himself thrown backward, and with a crash and a shriek of pain, he landed on the floor beside his bunk.

Eowlie jumped so high and so fast she hit her head on the bottom of the bunk above her, and turned, growling, on Amourgin.

He lay on the floor half-stunned, bone weary, aching, soaking wet. A few pale rays of sunlight crept into the stockade at the sharp angle of early morning.

Eowlie stared at him, and shook her head. Her eyes expressed bewilderment. "What haffened to you?" she asked.

"Storm caused bad dreams," he muttered, and started to crawl into bed. But as he pushed against the floor to lever himself up, his hand covered a piece of seaweed and something hard. He closed his fingers around the hard thing, and took it into the bed with him, and held it in his palm, and stared.

"Storm," Eowlie repeated. "There was no storm. It was hot and quiet all night."

Amourgin did not answer. He stared in silent horror at the talisman he held. It was a finger bone. The bone of a dead man.

The law-speaker lay back in his bed and wept.

In the early dawn, Lieutenant Chevays Cöado, dressed not in his uniform, but in the disguise of a wealthy outland merchant, rode through the streets of Derkin. He played the part of the rich foreigner with studied ease: stopped to watch the mourners at a Tykissian wake dancing in formal circles around the deceased, who sat in a chair and missed all the fun; leaned back in his saddle to watch workmen sliding a carved monument along a path of scaffolding lined with ice blocks. He avoided the naked street urchins peddling stolen fruit and the vendors selling shoddy sandals and fly-covered meat. He smiled politely at dark-eyed women who called after him with promises of wondrous and secret delights.

He made his way over the cobbled streets, swathed in an aura of foreign elegance and deadliness, and took some pleasure in being one above the thronging masses.

But the pleasures of the moment could not make up for the torment which awaited him.

He rode steadily uphill, and finally passed beneath another gate, under the fierce gazes of red Krevaulti guards in private liveries, onto the main boulevard of the Hill of Ancients. The Seven Hills of Derkin wore the city's wealth upon their shoulders, but the Hill of Ancients wore the city's crown. Polished granite walls fronted the streets, set with ornamental carved marble and very practical glass blades along their tops. The colored mosaic tiles of the sidewalks spelled words of power and wealth. Metal gates set in the walls gleamed with intricate wrought brass and gilded iron, some set with spell-jewels to keep out thieves. Behind the gates, huge, terrible dogs and their keepers waited, watching Chevays silently as he rode by. Even the character of the street changed, as the rounded, worn cobblestones gave way to shaped white limestone. Pariah streetcleaners worked in the long shadows of morning, scrubbing at the white stones with strong-smelling soap and heavy brushes, removing the marks of the previous day's traffic.

Chevays continued upward, from Broad Street to Banker Lane to Seaview Cliff, where the sidewalls had mosaic murals glorifying the owners of the mansions, or their ancestors. He reached at last The Pinnacles, where the road split into three branches blocked by guarded gates, beyond which each spiralled around a peak upward to a huge estate. Chevays chose the second road. The words inlaid in tiles and gems above that gate said "Footsteps of the Sun." The first time he'd read those words, many years earlier, he'd thought them grandiose. He'd discovered they merely described the demesne beyond the gate, and that with less than sufficient poetry.

"Who comes?" The guard was Krevaulti, the dogs the

notorious Krevaulti warhounds, which had in common with their masters that they were fanatically loyal, mad as weyrds, and could rip skin from bone in an instant.

Chevays cleared his throat. "Chevays, come to say the largest fish in the sea have begun to jump."

The Krevaulti looked through Chevays for an instant, his gaze fixed on things beyond the realm of the natural. Then he nodded. "Yes, I was told to expect such news." The guard unbarred the gate, and let him pass. The dogs, twice the size of wolves, watched him, their pale blue eyes seeming too intelligent and too cruel to be found looking out of the faces of beasts.

Chevays passed three checkpoints on his way up the spiralled outer path to the top. The flowering shrubs and vines set in rock terraces were ornamental, but the weapons of the guards were entirely functional. At each, he gave a different message and was permitted to continue upward to the next. He never failed to be aware of the dogs behind him and in front of him, of the arrows trained on him from hidden vantage points, of the character of those who watched him pass. Chevays feared little, but in The Footsteps of the Sun, he was never out of the clutches of dread.

Beyond the final checkpoint, servants led his horse off, while he was taken to a stone room and stripped and searched with some vigor by big Krevaulti women who seemed to enjoy their work. When they finished with him, they studied the packages he carried, and laughed at the little trinkets he brought as gifts. Once separated from all his weapons, he received a short silk wrap and his packages, and one of the women, with *her* dogs at heel, led him into the public room. The floor was white marble set with designs in amber and lapis; the tall windows were shuttered, veiled with rose-colored silk.

She was already waiting, smiling, enjoying his discomfiture and the knowledge of what she'd just had him put through. She sat in her tall chair looking lovely and very young, and very cold. It was always this way with her—she was much older than she looked, old enough to have picked up some very nasty habits. Pain was a habit of hers—but other people's pain. Specifically, sometimes, *his*.

She pulled her knees up to her chin and wrapped her arms around her legs, and she gave him the sweet little-girl smile he'd learned had nothing of the little girl beneath it. "That's fine, Eaney," she said to the grinning Krevaulti behind him. "I'll call you in when I'm ready to have you and the puppies sweep out the pieces." Her laugh was soft and bright and pure, gold notes in the perfumed air. Chevays had no idea whether she was joking or not.

When the guard was gone, she kept watching him, chin propped on knees and that half-smile on her face.

"So," she said finally, "you've come to tell me little sister is finally making her move."

He nodded.

"You have proof, of course."

She never asked him questions. She made statements, and when she was unsure, said nothing and let him flounder for words. This time he rummaged through his packages and pulled out the box Willek had given him. He handed it to her, and she frowned.

"Yes," she murmured. "This has the taint of blood magic about it." She opened the box, and didn't even blink when the characters inside flew out and billowed into glowing quasi-life in front of her. "Hmmmmmm." She studied the images. "How very interesting."

"She wanted me to find them and possibly kill them. She wouldn't say why."

"No. She wouldn't." The woman on her chair released her knees and stretched and yawned. Chevays could see the small, tight muscles ripple under her delicate silk gown. When she finished stretching, she stood and smiled up at him. "You would not have come to me just with this, however."

"No. I found her courier. I . . . extracted . . . the information you wanted from him."

She smiled brightly, no doubt picturing the extraction. "How delightful. You'll have to tell me all the details later. But right now, you must just give me the meat of your news."

"She's in league with Darkist."

It was the first time Chevays had ever seen the woman lose her composure. Her face went white, and the color drained from her lips. She sat down heavily and stared again at the figures from the box. "Darkist," she whispered. Her fingers dug into the padded brocade of the chair, until Chevays almost expected it to rip. Then she shook off the expression of shock— he could see her forcing herself to calm. She tapped her fingers on one knee and stared thoughtfully past him. "Such a pity Shemro's little brother was assassinated. It would have been lovely to pull him out of hiding, as a legitimate heir to the throne. I fear we would have had use for such an heir— soon." She smiled a cold little smile and added, "So blood really will tell. Assuming he got the right story."

Chevays had no idea what to make of that.

"I was *very* thorough in extracting the information," he said.

Her eyes focused on him again, and for the first time he noticed how like the Krevaulti wardogs' eyes they were. Fierce, mad eyes, that held no mercy in them. "Of course you were. You know what I would do to you if you gave me the wrong information."

She said thoughtfully, "You must not kill these people on her command. First, I will have to know why they are important. And if, perhaps, I find them of more use to me alive than dead, I shall want you to keep them alive. If she has allied with Darkist, and they pose a threat to her, then perchance they are my allies." She cocked her head sideways and studied the images again, then clicked her tongue. "One gets such dreadfully shabby allies when one goes adventuring."

Chevays waited, feeling the dread growing in his belly.

Her expression brightened, and she turned to him, and slowly licked her lips. "Well, then. That's enough business for one morning. Certainly we can take time out for pleasure, and then we'll make sure you have enough of whatever you need to carry out my tasks—while acting as my dear sister's trusted assassin the rest of the time. Come with me."

He swallowed, feeling his mouth go dry. He reminded himself that he could get through what was coming. In order to survive, he could take the humiliation, and the pain.

He followed her through the beautiful rooms, the vast and breezy sunlit rooms, and down the stairs at the heart of the house to the dark and terrible place where she found her amusement. He remained aware at all times of the eyes of the guards and their dogs who watched him from out-of-the-way places. He remained aware of the arrows trained on him, and of his danger.

It wasn't the money. He didn't do what she wanted for the money. He would have gone back to being a poor street thug in the time it took for his heart to beat once, and would never have questioned the decision. But he'd discovered his truths too late. Her servants were ubiquitous and fanatical and as lethal as he. She had a death grip on him. He breathed by her command—no matter where he went, he could never move beyond her reach. And she—she was beyond the reach of all but the uncaring gods.

There were things they understood about each other, he and she. They both took pleasure in pain—in other people's pain. It was simply the measure of her power that she used him the way he used his victims. If he didn't let her do what she wanted, and in doing so maintain some measure of control, at least in his own mind, she would have done what she wanted anyway.

He could get through the things she would do to him. He would try to learn something while she was at it.

And the dark-eyed girls in the streets of Derkin who called after him like chattering birds would benefit from whatever he learned.

He tried to keep that thought in mind.

❖   ❖   ❖

Karah stared into the blinding morning sunlight. All around her, the world was bone dry and hot. And she was soaking wet, and her skin itched from sand and sea salt. Seaweed soaked her bedroll, and the pulpy tendrils of some pale, stinking jungle vine wrapped around one of her ankles with an air of disgusting familiarity.

Drums called the recruits out of the bedrolls to face the new day. Karah dragged herself wearily out of her one-man tent and trotted to the line. She ignored the startled stares of her fellows.

Eowlie made a point of standing next to her. "You have seaweed in your hair," she said.

"And seawater and sea sand in my britches," Karah snarled. "I had a bad night."

Eowlie raised her eyebrows, and one corner of her mouth quirked into a smile. "Indeed. And where did you have it?"

"In my own tent."

"It's very strange. You look exactly like the law-sveaker looked when he woke this morning falling out of his bed. And he spent the night in the vrig." Eowlie shook her head, bemused, and leaned forward to look down the line. "Yah. He still looks like a drowned alley rat." She grinned at Karah, and looked up at the clear, bright sky. "Funny weather folks have indoors around here."

Karah wrinkled her nose. The taint of her nightmares would not leave her. She could not find within herself the courage to laugh, not even in daylight. "Not very funny at all," she said.

"The law-sveaker felt the same way."

They stood in the line beside the dusty main road that led out of camp. The air was already getting hot. Such breeze as there was blew the heated air around, but offered little relief. Karah's clothing and hair began to dry and to stick to her. The salt and sand itched fiendishly.

First Captain Morkaarin worked his way down the line, making comments from time to time, discussing things with his aide and the regimental priest. Karah dreaded what he would say when he came to her. She tried to think of something, anything, that would explain her condition.

The First Captain reached her and stopped and studied her from top to bottom and back to top again. One eyebrow rose fractionally, but other than that, his expression didn't change. "Turn, please, Grenlaarin. One full circle."

Karah bit her lip and turned.

"Stop," he commanded when she was halfway round.

She stopped, and felt his hand brush her shoulder, and lift her braid.

"Note the fresh seaweed," Morkaarin commented.

She heard the priest say, "Yes, sir. That I do." He had a strong accent—not Morkaarin's central-provinces noble's tone.

"Salt crystals on the skin, bit of vine around the ankle—you recognize that vine, by the way?"

"No, sir."

"No. Well, neither do I. It certainly isn't local flora. Nevertheless, there it is."

"Yes, sir."

The First Captain said, "Finish the turn, Grenlaarin."

Karah turned again until she once more faced him.

"The practical joker who did this was busy last night. He got both you and Thurdhad—who was in the stockade at the time."

Karah felt a burst of hope. A practical joker! What a perfect lie. No doubt the law-speaker had come up with it. She nodded solemnly. "I knew about the law-speaker."

"You'd heard?" He glanced over at Eowlie, and Karah saw comprehension in his eyes. "Oh, yes. His stockade mate. What I want to know is, did you see or hear anything last night out of the ordinary?"

Karah wished she knew what else the law-speaker had said. She wondered if he'd experienced the things she had. "I—ah. I thought I heard thunder, sir." She shrugged, wishing she had more experience lying. "Nothing else." She gave him an apologetic smile.

"Thunder? Interesting. That's more than the law-speaker got. Apparently he didn't wake until the joker threw a bucket of cold seawater on him."

That was a good story, Karah thought. But of course, it was the story of a man who made his living listening to untruths and passing them on for profit. He had the advantage of her. She wished she hadn't mentioned the thunder. If she ever got another visit from the walking dead, she would be sure to keep all the details to herself and try to look as innocent as Amourgin, down the line, was managing to look.

Assuming, of course, he had been through the same ordeal she had. Perhaps she was assuming too much.

She didn't think so. She'd always considered herself a logical person, sensible and practical. She couldn't see, logically, how she and Amourgin could have been soaked with seawater and covered with seaweed without having both been involved in the same ordeal.

"Go wash off," the First Captain said, interrupting her reverie. "Present yourself back here after. I'm announcing the postings and training schedules for the new recruits."

And that gave her something else to worry over. Animate drowned corpses and ghosts on a jungle island were not enough, but she had to worry, too, about getting ready to go off to war. *But then, Konzin ought to be reaching the ranch any time,* she thought. *So Ma and Pa should arrive to buy me out in a day or two.*

She didn't doubt for an instant that the army would accept good Grenlaarin steeds in exchange for herself, or a hefty fee and a few able ranch hands into the bargain if necessary. If they just got to the camp before her unit shipped out, she'd be fine.

Meanwhile, she could put up with anything. Probably.

The light of the new day stretched across Willek's bed, and glared red through her closed eyelids. She was pretending to be asleep—transfixed by the horrible certainty that something in her room was watching her. Which was impossible, since she'd slept alone. She felt the tingle of magical energy race along her nerves. She listened for breathing, but could hear none besides her own.

Her skin crawled, and the tiny hairs on the back of her neck stood on end. She opened one eye the tiniest bit—

—and looked directly into a staring face.

Her sword was in her hand and the blade through the top of the stranger's skull and out the bottom without slowing before she noticed that the face didn't connect to a body.

"Damnable fiend!" she yelled, and sat up. "Get out of my room!"

The face didn't even flinch. "I greet with thousand pardon, Admiral. I did no wish disturb, but I must have speak with you."

He was speaking Tarinese, but with an accent she'd never heard anyone else use. She suspected uneasily that it was that of a native speaker—and Tarinese had been a dead language since the Tykissians came south over the mountains, when the Old Empire fell and brought down the legal study of magic with it. Since that time, magic had been formally outlawed in the Tykissian lands to all but priests. Willek's folk had a long tradition of breaking that law, however, and one of the persistent rumors among the sorcerous underground was that the god-kings of the Old Empire, and possibly its successor realm in An Tiram, had some means of cheating death. Willek wanted that magic—it was one more valuable secret this alliance might bring . . .

Willek climbed out of her bed, still snarling. "What do you want, Darkist?" No need to worry about the guards charging in to do something about her yell. Darkist was a magician of inhuman subtlety, and didn't make mistakes.

The disembodied face, wrinkled and senile-looking, frowned. "I must to be sure of schedule and places. Your fleet leaving is to attack my fleet—three days away from this day, is not?"

Willek stared at him. "Darkist, we agreed on three weeks from this day. *Weeks*, man. That's *twenty-four* days."

"Will not serve." The Tseldene god-king stuck his tongue out—an expression Willek had come to discover meant he disagreed vehemently. "My ships sail in three days. If the ships of you also do not sail in three days, we not have our very large sea war. We have land war, which very messy and destroy much businesses and properties."

"You bastard," Willek snarled. "We've had this launch date set for almost two *years*. How dare you pretend we'd agreed on three days from this one?"

"We agreed." The ancient Tseldene ruler was implacable. "But if you is unhappy with, there other people want to be new regent of New Empire lands under my throne. Other people who not insult me."

Willek thought his glittering black eyes, embedded in layers of wrinkles, would have looked at home in a snake's scaled face. *He might be senile*, she thought. *And he might just want to make sure my troops are enough off-balance that they have to lose.* She held her head high and said calmly, "I'll *be* regent, old man."

And not, for example, Cousin Valwer. This conspiracy was getting too damned big. Maybe the time had come to trim the number of players to manageable size.

"Then ships must sail three days. You must come by west side Cnit, then sail to point of Meltroon. We engage there."

Willek nodded. "I know where my people are supposed to be, old man. Just make sure yours are there to meet them." She thought of all the lovely, vicious things she'd like to do to that man, but kept her emotions off her face.

"Yes." Darkist chuckled. "And how our lady emperor feel these days?"

Willek permitted herself a tiny smile. "Shemro hasn't been herself. But she's left the country in very capable hands."

"I very sure she has." Darkist's face swelled, and for the briefest of instants, Willek had the impression it was about to explode. But he was simply trying to impress her, she realized. When the image of his head was as large as Willek's body, he said, "Bring Emperor Shemro with you when you sail. We will find convenient time and kill her."

Willek shrugged. "I intended to bring her, old man. I have my own plans for that bitch Shemro. We have other problems."

Darkist frowned, the petulant expression of an ancient man used to having his own way for a long time. "You to take care of problems are."

"We have *god* problems. My visions indicate the Mighty Ones are taking a direct hand in this."

"The One of a Thousand Faces is."

"I *know* that!" Willek throttled back her anger. "My family has worshipped the One in secret for nearly a thousand years. My ties to the Old Empire are by more than blood." She glared at him. "I referred to the *other* gods."

Tseldene and Old Empire theology held that all manifestations of the Divine were avatars of the One—who was also mad and schizophrenic. Darkist and she both knew that theology lied. The first part, at least.

Darkist's face wrinkled into petulance. "I will seek, I will make sacrifice. Great things draw gods like flies to dung."

So he *didn't* suspect. With a smooth, swift motion, she drew a glyph in the air over Darkist's ghostly face. The room filled with pale yellow smoke, and a sizzling sound, and the reek of sulphur and iron. Darkist's image vanished.

"Figured out how you did that, finally," the admiral said to the empty room. "And what to do to get rid of you." She rose, rinsed off in the basin of tepid water in the stand, and tugged on a fresh uniform.

She didn't bother getting something to eat, though normally her schedule was as regular as the sun. Instead she charged out of her quarters, slamming the door behind her. Her guard, reading in the guardhouse with her feet propped on the sill, fell over backwards.

Willek heard the yelp and the crash behind her and didn't even stop to reprimand the woman. There was suddenly no time. No time at all.

She charged across the compound. Her aide was just stepping out the door of his own quarters for the leisurely stroll to hers when he spotted her, and he blanched.

"Quickly," she snapped. "Schedules have moved up. Get the senior officers together in the war room—I want *all* of them in there before the end of second bell. Go!"

She felt again the seductive tug of power as she watched the young officer running at top speed for the call system. She was the second in command in the Tykissian Empire, and it was her pleasure to give orders and watch them carried out. With alacrity. With fear. Second most powerful person in the empire—that meant something. Her word was about to mean more, because she was taking the necessary steps to become first.

Within five minutes of her arrival to the war room, the last of the senior officers was seated. The men and women shifted in their seats, but waited silently. Some looked tired, some distressed, some almost angry. She noted the expressions, and who wore them. *Unimportant*, she thought suddenly. *It no longer matters who serves willingly, and who grudgingly. The importance of all that is past.*

Her people were present, and they would serve. Beyond the present, she would again have to watch her back, check for loyalty—and take care of the disloyal. But for the moment, the war—*her* war—was about to begin, and for a while nothing else mattered.

She stood in front of them all. "Our plans for the attack on Tarin Tseld have changed," she said. "My sources confirmed this morning that the Tseldene naval forces are massed in the bay at An Tiram; their rowers have gone aboard, and they've loaded full water casks."

For a galley force, those were last-minute preparations. Every day the rowers were below decks made wastage higher.

"I have analyzed the threat and believe an attack is imminent. I will meet with each of you separately to discuss specific roles, but know this—we leave on the tide at dawn morning after tomorrow."

Bren studied his recruits. He was astounded that so many human beings could be so utterly unfit for military service. He was even more amazed at *his* commanding officer's decision to exercise the press in an inn. Bren felt sure he could have come up with the necessary number of recruits somewhere else in Derkin—and that he would have gotten some reasonably competent people. The human flotsam he had garnered stood staring back at him, panting hard after drills and exercises. Everything he'd seen had convinced him more that the XIXth would be better off short than with such a collection of jesters.

"Assignments," he said loudly. "If you don't hear your name, you're assigned to foot. To pikes—Stepvet Trrallti, Mare Ugin, Hard Rain Ugin, Piglet Ddrad."

One woman and three men stepped forward, identical uncertain looks on their faces. Bren continued. "To pike unit recruit command—Stlagi Mrado. You've fought with a pike before, haven't you, Mrado?"

The one-time merchant nodded. "Yes, sir. Against the Krevaulti during the Twelfth Rebellion."

Bren nodded, while some of the recruits whistled with astonishment. The Twelfth Rebellion was *legendary*—had been one of the epic "little wars" of the last two centuries. Survivors were rare. *The merchant was not such a bad choice then,* the First Captain thought. *He seemed at home with a pike—wonder why he didn't say anything about the Krevaulti rebellion.* But odd personnel mysteries would wait.

Bren announced, "Then you're promoted to File Closer. To Scout Troop—Eowlie Thirddaughter, Borte Ren Toka Paga, Korgi Ren Toka Paga, Doe Ditech." *The Whore's Patrol,* he thought with some amusement; they'd make up

nearly a third of its numbers. Not only had the very strange
Eowlie ended up a scout, but the piebald Shillraki twins and
that muscle-bound half-Tseldene. *Every one of 'em good with
horses and good with knives. And I'd probably rather not
know why.* They were weak in everything else, but the best
available.

"To command scout recruits—Amourgin Thurdhad, with
Karah Grenlaarin as second. Field command."

The pimp Zeemos lunged out of the line and charged Bren,
red-faced and puffing. "Y' can't leave me h'in t' foot patrol. Y'
just can't!" he yelled. "H'I must be a scout! H'I have a good
horse, and you cannot make me walk across t' length h'and
breadth of t' land. Y' just can't!"

Bren had been expecting an argument. He'd already gone
over some possibilities when he made out the assignments,
and he'd come up with a plan he considered brilliant. Not
awfully ethical, perhaps—but brilliant.

He didn't have that many brilliant moments, he thought.
He'd take the few he had as gifts from the Three.

He crossed his arms over his chest and smiled gently. "I
truly should throw you in the stockade for arguing."

"Aw, First Captain . . . show mercy h'on a poor, old man.
Let me ride m' horse."

"But you ride like a sack of vegetables. You'll slow my scouts
down."

The pimp looked at him with wistful puppy dog eyes. "There
must be some way . . ."

Bren hooked his thumbs over the leather belt of his rapier
carrier, and tilted his head to one side. "I can't let you ride with
the scouts. But I might be able to arrange for you to keep your
horse—let you act as a messenger, say—if you could become
a *patron* of the XIXth."

The pimp's eyes narrowed. "H'I'm a poor man, First Captain. Poor. How can H'I be a patron?"

"Well," Bren said thoughtfully, "if you're a poor man, I suppose you can't. A rich man could make a sizable donation for

armaments—leather armor, swords, even . . . horses. But I suppose a poor man—even a poor, fat, old man, will just have to walk with the young men. Carrying a pike. Doing the usual fatigues."

Zeemos spat over his shoulder and growled. "How much, sir?"

"Feel generous, Zeemos. Remember your fellow soldiers. They need cuirasses and shields, greaves and armguards and helms and even tents and rations."

Bren smiled and patted Zeemos on one plump shoulder. Beside him, he could see the rest of the recruits watching intently, the men and women standing in positions of alert curiosity.

"Remember, in battle, your lives will depend on each other. Just think how much safer you'll be if your fellow recruits are well-armed. And think how grateful they will be to their patron."

Zeemos glowered. "Will a hundred crowns satisfy you?"

"I'm not the person who must be satisfied."

Zeemos stared at the watching crowd of recruits. "A hundred crowns," he said loudly.

"Naaah!" the other recruits yelled back. "Let him walk! Let him walk!"

Zeemos yelled, "Two hundred crowns."

"He has more than that!" Eowlie shouted.

The piebald twins yelled, "Make him pay five hundred! Five hundred crowns! He has at *least* that much!"

The women who had been Zeemos' whores all stood there, laughing and yelling. "Make him pay, the bastard! He has the money!" and "Five hundred! Five hundred!"

"So you're a rich man," Bren said softly. "How lucky for you, that you can afford to arm your colleagues well."

"B-b-b-b-but five . . . hundred . . . crowns . . ."

The recruits of the XIXth began to cheer. "Hail, Zeemos!" they roared. "Hail, hail, Zeemos!"

A tear dripped from Zeemos' eye, and into a crease between

two rolls of flesh. "It's all I have," he whispered, and glared at the one-time whores with murder in his eyes.

Then he reached into the folds of his draped tunic and fumbled around. After a moment, he pulled out a heavy leather pouch on a belt, designed to lay flat against the skin. He opened it, and began pouring out silver into the folds of Bren's cloak, which the First Captain held out for the purpose.

When he stopped at five hundred, he still had a handful of silver left.

"But don't you want armor for yourself?" Bren asked.

Zeemos' head jerked up, and he snarled, "Y' want it all, don't y', y' greedy bugger? H'I'll make you pay me back every duc someday, if h'I 'ave to cut it out of yer arse."

"Watch yer mouth!" Sergeant Ddrad gave Zeemos a solid whack across the shoulders with his vine-root swagger stick. It wasn't the first time, but Zeemos had learned better than to object. He shuddered instead, his face going dark red down to the jowls. "Sir!" he said, and threw the remaining silver into the dust in front of Bren.

"Attached as patron to the XIXth, to serve as my messenger," Bren said. "Dismissed. Amourgin, Karah, Eowlie—you will go to the market with Sergeant Ddrad, and you will acquire such armaments as you can with this money. Take Mercele with you, as well, and a wagon and mule. Be back by nightfall."

He turned to the recruits of the XIXth, and grinned. "Ladies and gentlemen," he said, "let's all thank our generous *patron*, Zeemos the Pimp."

The recruits laughed and cheered and stamped their feet. Bren noticed, however, that mostly they laughed. He felt very pleased with himself. He'd skinned the troublemaking bastard, and gotten his unit armaments and supplies to boot. Very few junior commanders could have pulled off such a neat trick.

He was destined, he thought, for greatness.

❖   ❖   ❖

"What do we need?" Eowlie asked, tugging at her uniform jacket. The mule that would pull the two-wheeled cart was sniffing cautiously at her from a distance, made nervous by her scent. The heat of the day baked the very dust, and the midday sun bleached it white. She sniffed back at the mule; the beast had a mildly appetizing smell.

Her tunic did not *quite* fit—the proportions of her torso were subtly different from those of a flatface. On the other hand, issue clothing often didn't fit the locals, either. That seemed to be a constant of military life, along with appalling food. Even the flatfaces thought it was appalling, and they *liked* their prey long dead before they ate it. At least the military clothes covered her body; at least she'd been able to get the cooks to issue her meat to her unscorched. The military was far kinder to her than Zeemos had been.

Amourgin looked up from his notebook. "We need sabers, knives, light-cavalry corselets—torso armor—personal gear, and carbines or saddle bows. Mostly carbines, since I doubt many of our number have any great skill with the bow. Pistols. Cartridge paper, bullet molds, flints, powder horns. Military belts. Canteens. Knives. Thread, waxed thread for repairing harness, awls, needles. Riding trousers. Boots. All courtesy of Zeemos."

"Courtesy of Doe and the rest of us," Eowlie corrected, taking a deep breath. The law-speaker had a more pleasant scent than most flatfaces; alien, but not repulsive. "What haffened to Zeemos gave me a vetter imf'ression of your Empire."

Amourgin snorted. "Don't be deceived. It was fortunate for you, but that was an accident. The government shouldn't sweep up people like that."

"Like you, ey?" She wrinkled her nose, amused. Eowlie's folk bared their teeth only as a threat gesture, though she'd come to discover the flatfaces meant nothing of the sort when they did it.

"Well, yes. But all of us. It's *supposed* to be a lawful, regulated process—but the Throne has been damned careless about the law for some time now, and it's getting worse. In fact—"

He shut his mouth abruptly, with an almost audible snap.

"Vad men make for evil days, even if the laws are good," Eowlie commented, prodding gently.

"True. Although even our laws have some weaknesses; take the pariahs, for example."

"F'ariahs? Slaves, you mean?"

"Some of them are. The Old Folk, the people who were here before the Tykissians, my people, came south. It's all foolishness, really—how many of us are of pure Old Tykis blood these days, even north of the mountains? Yet we still *pretend* we are, as if this were Beltra the Great's time—" He cut himself off again.

"Go on."

"We'd better get the mule harnessed," Amourgin replied, turning away.

Interesting, Eowlie thought. Flatfaces seemed to have politics, just like people.

⊙ CHAPTER V

Karah walked through Derkin's main marketplace with Amourgin, Eowlie and Sergeant Ddrad, going from new armorers to sellers of used armaments. There was still equipment to be had, for those who were willing to pay premium price for ordinary quality. The alleys and aisles were packed solid with customers, most of them yelling and waving their arms; the sweat stink was solid enough to cut into building blocks and use for a fort. The XIXth's stocking contingent edged past a thrall bent double under an enormous pack frame of iron bars. Karah stopped to stare for a moment; the slave was a jungleman from the far south—thicker-set even than a Tseldene, with an enormous shelf of bone over his eyes sloping back into a bun-shaped head. Thick brown hair, not quite a pelt, covered most of a body naked except for a loincloth.

"*Come* on," Ddrad said impatiently. "You don't want bows?"

Karah shook her head and shifted the bundle of sabers she was carrying to the other shoulder. "Takes years to learn how to shoot one from the saddle," she said. "Y'have to be born at it. Eowlie?"

"Ve don't use bows," she said, showing her teeth. "We use—vat's the vurd—" She mimed putting a tube to her lips and blew sharply.

"Blowguns."

"F'oison," she amplified.

91

"In here!" Amourgin called.

They ducked into a gunsmith's. Amourgin looked smug. A dozen pistols lay on the table before him, which was a minor miracle when you thought how many well-heeled cavalry had been through, buying. Nor was that all. He grinned broadly and held up a carbine. It was a wheel-lock, the powder in the pan ignited by a flint on an arm that pivoted down into contact with a spring-driven revolving steel. Common for pistols, but far too expensive for musketeers.

"The latest thing," he said. The trigger guard had a handle attached to the rear. He swung it forward and a threaded bolt screwed down, leaving a hole in the rear of the barrel. "Make up a ball and charge in a paper roll," he said. "Put it in here. Turn the trigger guard back one full circle." The screw plug came back up, flush with the top of the barrel. "That cuts the rear of the paper roll and seals the breech. Prime the pan, wind up the action with this spanner, and you're all set to fire. It's rifled, too."

"Fancy," Karah said, bringing one of them up to her shoulder. There was a notch at the rear and a pip at the muzzle for aiming. "I'll stick to my horn bow."

"Yes," the gunsmith said mournfully. "That's what they all say. The cavalry prefer their bows, and the infantry use matchlocks—I've only managed to sell a dozen carbines in the last sixmonth. Thirty-five crowns each."

Karah yelped. That was what a top ranch hand made in a year!

Amourgin grinned and produced their money pouch with a flourish. "The joys of spending somebody else's money," he said. "All the pistols and five of those carbines, please, with powder flasks, bullet molds and saddle scabbards."

"_Ufff_," Karah said, heaving the corselets into the wagon. They were double-ply nosehorn hide boiled black in vinegar, latched with bronze and stripped with steel for reinforcement, and _heavy_. She and the others packed those and bundled swords, carbines, and other assorted gear. All of them paused wearily, handing around a water bottle. The liquid inside was stale-tasting and warm, yet still delightful after heavy labor in such heat. Even so, Karah thought longingly of a spelled canteen her uncle had, ever-filled with pure, chilled springwater scented with lemon and full of little bubbles. Of course that was an heirloom, and priceless, far too valuable to be taken on campaign.

"It could have veen much worse," Eowlie said suddenly, breaking a long silence.

The mule flattened its ears as Sergeant Ddrad climbed onto the seat and flicked the reins. They all began trudging beside the two-wheeled cart, blinking into the low sun ahead. Heat radiated up off the slimed cobbles. Amourgin stopped for an instant to buy a watermelon from a vendor; they split it with a dagger and began eating as they walked. Eowlie gobbled hers rapidly; her mouth really wasn't constructed to catch juice, so she held the wedge of melon over her head and snapped at it.

"I thought you didn't eat anything but meat?" Karah asked, spitting seeds.

"Not vread or vegetables," Eowlie said. "Fruit yes, sometimes."

"What could have been worse?" Karah asked, suddenly recalling Eowlie's earlier remark.

Eowlie caught up with her. "I was just thinking—it's not vad to ve in the scouts. Vetter than veing a whore. And we could have ended uf in the musketeers. Or the f'ike."

"Fike?" Karah was puzzled.

Eowlie made thrusting motions with her arms, and Karah caught her meaning.

"Oh. Pike. I suppose so—but it doesn't really matter to me. My parents will be along in a day or so to get me out of this mess. Konzin should be arriving on the ranch about now."

"You think the army will let you go home?"

Karah nodded. "My parents will bring down a couple of

good horses to exchange—war-trained horses. They're worth more than I am to the army. Godsall—the army paid me seven crowns each for the green-broke horses I brought down here. They offered more than thirty for Glorylad without knowing he was war-trained. He'd be worth five times that to any warrior who knew how to ride him."

Ddrad called back over his shoulder, "I don't think much of that—wantin' to get out of the service. Won't make your fellow recruits think well of you, girl."

Karah shrugged. "Maybe not. But I didn't volunteer to this unit. I planned to serve with the Farbluffs County Horse. As an ensign."

"Don't matter now. Service is service—and this is where yer needed. First Captain was glad to get you."

Eowlie interrupted. "Karah, what is a war-trained horse? We do not much use horses where I am from—how is such an animal different from other horses?"

Karah glanced back at Amourgin, who was examining his new corselet dubiously. The stiff leather had been patched; when he opened it, the inside showed a star-shaped hole, just the sort a pike point would have made. She didn't feel like discussing horses around him.

"A war-trained horse will fight alongside you. He kicks your enemies, and bites, and will stand on them and crush them for you. He is trained to walk on narrow cliff trails, to cross bridges . . ."

"The things you and the law-sveaker did yesterday with your horses. The fancy tricks. Those are war training?"

"Yes."

"And you have some of these horses at home, and your parents will bring them to trade for you?"

Karah nodded again.

Eowlie sighed. "That would've so nice. I would like one of those horses, you know? Vut more, I would like my f'arents to come take me home."

"Can't you write a letter, and send a messenger for them?"

Eowlie laughed. "My home is on the other side of the, um . . . you call her the Kadash Ocean."

"In Melcan?" Karah was amazed. She'd never actually known anyone from that far away. Tykissian explorers had only discovered the land a century ago.

"No. Melcan is close. My home is much further than that—other side of Melcan and over another ocean—narrow ocean, how do you say?"

"Straits?"

"Yes, straits. No one would go that far with a letter—and the ocean is very dangerous. Full of monsters."

Amourgin had been listening. "So how did you get here?"

"Vy accident."

Eowlie shoved her hands into the pockets of her dark-green uniform tunic and stared off into space.

"I was fishing with my v'rother. He was in one voat, with the anchored end of the net—and I was sailing out to set the far end to start taking the fish out of that end, and to vring in the net. There was a vad storm coming—vut that is when the fish run high instead of deef."

"Deef?" Karah repeated.

"Deep," Amourgin said.

"Yes." Eowlie nodded at Amourgin and smiled appreciatively—and Karah felt a twinge of jealousy. "So we were trying to outrun the storm, and to fill our voats."

"But you didn't make it."

"No. The storm caught voth of us. We were washed out to sea. I don't know if my v'rother is alive or dead—and I'm sure my family thinks I'm dead, at least."

Karah noticed that Ddrad and Mercele were silently taking in every word, as well. She sighed and bit her lip. She needed better tales to tell, obviously. Men seemed to pay attention to anyone with a story.

"Then what happened?" the law-speaker asked.

He was staring at Eowlie as if her story was the most fascinating thing he'd ever heard.

"I was washed out to sea. The storm was terrivle. My voat was destroyed vy sea monsters, and I managed to hang on to the wreckage—I was in the ocean for days, and the currents carried me to Tovor."

"To Tobor?" Karah was astonished in spite of herself. "Why, even from Melcan to Tobor would take a week, sailing fast. What did you drink? How did you survive?"

"I almost didn't. When I washed uf on the Tovoran shore, I was almost dead. That's when that vastard Zeemos found me, and fut a collar around my neck. He fed me, and vrought me vack to health. For mayve two or three months, I was too sick to move. Vut I got vetter eventually—and then he told me how much money I owed him, and that I would have to whore for him. So I fretended I did not understand what he said. Vut that did not matter to him. Not to his customers, either."

Eowlie frowned, and Karah could suddenly empathize with her. It must have been terrible to survive such an ordeal, only to find yourself a captive. She felt sorry for the odd creature.

"I waited a long time," Eowlie said. "A long, long time. Now I am free. And some day I will kill Zeemos. Or at least I will see him dead."

Amourgin had quit paying attention to Eowlie's story. Karah felt a twinge of satisfaction at that. Amourgin was attractive . . . in a stuffy, difficult way. And he knew a bit about horses, for all that he'd tried to hide the fact. She thought she would like to get to know him better. Perhaps a lot better. But she didn't think she wanted to find herself jealous of the ugly, strange Eowlie in the process.

Amourgin rejoined them. "Here," he said, and smiled awkwardly, and handed a fancy dagger to Eowlie. "For you. Don't ever use it on Zeemos unless he comes after you."

Ddrad said, "Or the First Captain will see you hang. Remember that."

Eowlie grinned her sharp-fanged grin. "What if I'm sure I won't get caught?"

Amourgin laughed. Ddrad did too, but he shook his head.

"Self-defense the army will forgive. A vendetta, never. And don't think you won't get caught. Isn't worth it. They'd bring in a priest and geas-question everyone in the troop."

Karah strode ahead of them, feeling unreasonable and angry. *It doesn't matter that he bought her a knife. He didn't buy it with his own money, but with company money. And it isn't as if a knife is a suitor-gift.* She walked faster. *It doesn't matter. It doesn't.*

She reached the end of a row of stalls, and saw a tavern lying straight ahead. The shopkeepers were closing up for evening.

She looked over her shoulder and called, "I'm for a drink and some shade." Then she hurried on, not even checking to see if she were being followed. "It's on Zeemos."

Bren Morkaarin tugged at the locket chain around his neck. He often did that when he was nervous; it held the image of his father, an eidolon spell frozen into a slice of clear quartz crystal, visible only to Bren and his close blood-kindred. His mother had promised to tell him the name when he turned nineteen and came of age; she probably would have, if she hadn't broken her neck riding after a boar three weeks before the birthday in question. *Futility, Mother,* he thought. *Like so much of your life and mine.*

There was a good deal of that attached to being the last of an ancient line. Who would sacrifice at the Morkaarin family altars when he was gone? Hopefully his father's kindred were doing better, whoever they were. All in all, his personal life held even more futility than his professional, and that was a considerable amount. It seemed especially so since he'd just spent an entire day being passed from hand to hand in the Quartermaster-General's headquarters.

"You think too much," Father Solmin said, taking another swig at his beer.

"Odd thing for a priest to say," Bren replied. "Aren't you supposed to be wise and thoughtful?"

The XIXth had a good priest, which was a comfort—besides presumably keeping them in touch with the gods, it gave a soldier someone to talk to when there wasn't anyone else.

"True, but that's my penance—you don't get paid to brood like I do," Solmin said. His small blue eyes almost disappeared as he smiled. "Your lady mother was just the same. Thought a lot. 'Tis one reason Ddrad and I promised to look after you; a man who thinks too much misses things."

Bren snorted. "I've been thinking about those weird ones," he said. "The recruits."

"The Karah girl? She's no more strange than fresh bread," Solmin said. "A good wholesome Tykissian girl, for all her looks."

"Waking up covered in seaweed and glowing is wholesome?"

The priest frowned. "I checked. No malign magic involved. *Possibly* a hint of god-touch." At Bren's alarmed look, he went on. "Beneficent only. It happens—rare, but it happens. Her and the law-speaker both; they're consecrated to the Three, and other deities know better than to poach. Gods alone know what it signifies, of course."

When a priest said that, it was more than a conventional turn of phrase. Bren shrugged.

"As if I didn't have enough to worry about," he grumbled. "With Gonstad screwing up and—"

Meanwhile there was duty to attend to. He sighed, finished the last of his beer, and swept up helmet, gloves and sword from the table. The tavern had been a brief escape, but the regiment was waiting for him. Then he saw Father Solmin's face change, looking over his shoulder.

"If it isn't the bastard Morkaarin," a voice said behind him. A cultivated central-provinces voice, and full of sadistic relish.

Bren turned, carefully and slowly. Whoever it was wasn't going to stab or shoot him in the back, or they'd have done it already, and he wanted to be calm.

"Takes one to know one," he said cheerfully, with a slight bow of courtesy. "But you have the advantage of me, sir, with my name on your lips. I don't know quite which bastard son of a whore *you* happen to be."

The tall blond man was certainly a Tykissian, and from the cut of his black Olmya-city style clothes looked to be of gentle birth. The five bravos behind him weren't, but their scars and the worn but well-kept weapons indicated a degree of competence. The tavern's courtyard was emptying out rapidly as the patrons scrambled for safety, leaving a scattering of cushions and stools on the tile. They were darkening fragments of color in the moving leaf shade of the grapevines that covered the arbor overhead, going dim as the sun dropped below the buildings round about. He rutched his feet slightly, testing the footing the hobnails gave against the brick pavement.

Steel rasped on leather as Bren drew his sword. His mouth was a little dry, and he wished very much he'd worn his armor today, even if it would have looked ridiculous among the Quartermaster's clerks. Solmin made a gesture of blessing, then drew his tomahawk and took up a stool by one leg.

"Valwer Tornsaarin," the other man said, bowing in his turn and drawing his sword. The elaborate guard was gilded brass set with onyx, but the straight blade was water-pattern steel, a yard long and sharp enough to cut sunlight on both edges. The dappled lines in the surface of the steel were more emphatic towards the point. Blood etching, which meant it had seen plenty of use.

The bravos spread out to either side of him and a little back.

"The name should be sufficient reason for this affair, I think," Valwer went on pleasantly.

"Father Solmin, get out of here," Bren said out of the side of his mouth.

Then he continued, in a calm, friendly tone, to the man in black: "Ah, the Grand Admiral's kept poor-relation bootkisser." *I knew she hated all of my name. I didn't know it was this specific.* "The law, however, forbids duels between serving officers."

"But I'm not a serving officer—and this isn't a duel," Valwer pointed out, and lunged.

Bren threw himself backward in a huge bound. In the same motion he threw his helmet into the face of one of the bravos, and kicked a stool into the path of another.

The helmet clanged against a sword, and the second bravo skipped nimbly over the flying furniture, a gap-toothed grin on her face. Bren drew his dagger left-handed and backed away from the line of six points. Despite anything the old songs or the trashy new printed novels said, nobody won a sword fight with six competent opponents. Not unless he was using a cannon loaded with grapeshot. Not even with a fat, middle-aged priest on his side.

One of the bravos gave a warning lunge at the cleric. The sword stuck in the pine board of the stool, and the swordsman jumped back with a yell as the not-so-ceremonial tomahawk flashed by his eyes.

All right, so it's six to two. Still bad odds, Bren thought.

The killers were professionals. None of them wasted time on further words; they spread out in a semicircle and closed, blades poised for long-line thrusts with the flats parallel to the ground so they wouldn't stick on ribs—his ribs, to be exact. He could block two at most; that left four. One for Father Solmin, that left three to kill both of them.

"Father, Mother and Child receive me," he muttered to himself. "And One swallow these seal-rapers."

"May They hear your prayer, my son," the priest said, sidling around to guard the officer's back.

Valwer lunged again, and Bren parried with a quick beat and skipped back again.

"*Morkaarin!*" he shouted.

Karah stopped, puzzlement breaking through her sullen mood. The tavern ahead was losing its usual late-afternoon crowd in a hurry. Some of them still had napkins or handkerchiefs tucked into the necks of their shirts as they spilled out and scattered in all directions . . . and some of them looked to be the tavern's staff. The wide carved bogrin doors with their copper studs swung back and boomed against the adobe walls of the courtyard, and she could see a flicker of steel in the dimness within.

"Morkaarin!" a deep voice shouted, and there was a clash of steel.

Ddrad didn't waste time on words. "Comin', captain!" he bellowed, leapt from the seat of the cart, and landed running; the mule walked on a few paces and stopped, head drooping and ears twitching through the old straw hat it wore. It wouldn't go anywhere on its own. The others charged after Ddrad.

Karah missed a half-step. *Why am I running into a fight for that bitch's get who pressed me?* she thought, with her sword half out.

Because these are my friends, she answered, completing the motion and pounding after them. She remembered the First Captain grinning at Zeemos. *And, oh . . . shut up, you cow.*

The setting sun was still bright in the street, but the courtyard was doubly darkened by the wall and the thick vines overhead. Karah prudently halted for an instant to let her eyes adjust; Pa had been most particular about that sort of thing. The first thing she saw clearly was Eowlie dropping flat beneath the lunge of a swordsman's point. Her breath caught for a second, before the other woman came up off the ground like something on steel springs and fastened her long teeth in the upper part of the arm holding the sword. The two went over together with a shriek of pain and a muffled howl of rage.

Steel flickered in the gloom. Karah came up to guard position, right foot and blade forward, dagger in her left held back. She could see well enough now, enough to see that the scarred face opposite her was half again her age, that the weapon was a plain rapier with a solid steel bell guard, and that this was someone who would kill her if he could. A feeling like a bad dinner of heavy dumplings settled in under her ribcage. *Freeze and you'll die*. The voice in her head was a mixture of her parents' and Uncle Jawain, but she listened anyway.

The point came at her, long lunge. She parried with hilt low—*pretend it's practice*—and let the steel skirl up and over her left shoulder, cutting backhanded. The other caught that on a dagger and thrust again. Karah shouted with anger at the cold sting in her shoulder, and stop thrust to drive her opponent backward. Everything seemed clear and slow as the razor-edged metal moved in its intricate dance, no time to stop and think what it could do to her body. They advanced and retreated across the brick pavement, kicking cushions and low tables out of their way; now and then a cut grape leaf would fall in their wake, as the swords clipped a dangling section of vine. The clash of steel echoed back from the walls of the courtyard, sixfold. Karah found herself next to another fighting pair—next to Bren Morkaarin.

The hilt jarred in her hand as the edge sliced meat. Her opponent yelled and leapt back, dagger dropping from the limp fingers of her left hand, the point of her rapier still drawing small circles of menace to keep Karah off.

" 'T the One with this shit," the wounded mercenary shouted. "C'mon, we wasn't paid enough ter fight the army."

The bravos broke away from the fight, and the XIXth troopers let them go—two of the mercenaries were dragging a third whose arm and shoulder were a mass of rips and bloody tears, and all of them were limping or clutching wounds. The stout priest took a stance as they fled and threw his tomahawk. It whirred into the doorpost with an emphatic *thunk* sound.

That left the tall man in black facing the captain. He stepped back uncertainly, looking at the circle of soldiers around him. Karah's sword was bloody, and so was Sergeant Ddrad's and Amourgin's, although both had small cuts. Eowlie was licking her lips with a disturbingly long and mobile tongue; she had a bruise and cut over one eye that might have resulted from frantic blows with a sword hilt, but it didn't seem to be bothering her. They all stared at the stranger, then took a step forward as if in unison.

"No." First Captain Bren's voice was sharp. He shook his head. "My thanks, comrades, but this one's mine."

He brought up his sword in formal salute. "As you said, this isn't a duel—but still, let's dance."

Chevays did not escape into the lower city again until the sun was crawling down the sky with lizardlike torpor, and all Derkin baked in its own sweat-stinking heat. Rage gnawed at him, and humiliation, and despair. He could remember only fragments of what had happened to him, and was uncertain of what he was supposed to do. She'd said he would remember what he needed, when he needed.

But he wanted to remember *her*. Already she was foggy in his memory—and he wanted to hold her clearly there. He hated her, and he loved her, and he would do anything for her—and she, who was used to being loved and hated, took his attentions as her just dues, and used him.

"You'll do what I want you to do—you'll know what you need, when you need it. Do what Willek wants—find her people. What *I* want will come to you at the right time."

He could recall that clearly—her words, the sweet sound of her voice as she did . . . did . . . as she did *something* to him. He didn't remember what she had done, but his stomach twisted when he tried to think of it.

Then her name was in his head. *Szoae*.

He held those short syllables tightly to him. Her name was something he was not supposed to know—had never, he was certain, known before. But there it was.

Szoae.

And with the name, he could piece together something of her face, something of the way the light played on her gold hair, a picture of the soft glow of her skin. He could recall, suddenly, the angle of her jaw, and the fullness of her lips, and the swell of her small breasts—and he felt surging triumph.

He remembered, and knew he was not supposed to remember. She was a creature of secrets, and he held some of them in his mind. He had served her most of his life, and would serve her until she tired of him and killed him . . . or until he died in her service. Such was the bond between them—a bond linked by pain and adoration.

She had put him in the service of Willek . . .

More memories! Willek was her half-sister—and Szoae despised the Grand Admiral of the Fleet.

He was taking steps to destroy Willek—for Szoae.

He felt secretly pleased. He was not disturbed that Szoae used him—he used people, and did not find that disturbing, either. He was satisfied to know that he served, and that what he did for her was important.

The other things between them . . . he felt a sort of blanket beginning to envelop his thoughts, and he backed away from probing for those memories.

A handcart passed him, with a Tykissian priest pacing it, rattle in one hand and small bronze bell in the other—a death-cart. That didn't surprise him, but the face of the man in it did. *Valwer Tornsaarin.* The Grand Admiral's cousin in the fourth degree, and one of her many hatchet carriers. There was a look of terrible surprise on the corpse's face, and the front of his black jacket was covered in drying blood, already attracting a swarm of flies. They settled on the blood, and on his open eyes and mouth, and on the long curled hair. The hole in the leather jacket was a neat slit, which Chevays had no trouble recognizing. Sword thrust, and very skillful, straight through the heart. That was a stroke more often spoken of than seen, quite difficult to administer. The nobleman's own sword was laid naked beside him.

Valwer had quite a reputation as a duelist, something Chevays despised, priding himself on an approach to killing at once more practical and more artistic. Still, whoever administered that death stroke knew which end was sharp, no doubt about that.

It was growing dark; a lamplighter went by with a slowmatch on the end of a long pole, touching it to the glass-globed oil lanterns the street associations of merchants put up in Derkin. They cast a pale yellow glow on the narrow crooked street and the ancient patched stonework of the buildings, scarcely brighter than the two moons above. Most of the stores on ground level were closed, but candlelight showed from the windows overhead, families sitting out on their balconies in the warm night, calling back and forth to each other in Derkinoi street argot.

Chevays pursed his lips in thought and turned back along the trail of the death-cart. One had to trust one's hunches.

He wandered into an open-courted tavern with tables that looked to the market across the street. A cart loaded with armor and arms was in front of it, the mule resting and munching oats, its tail flipping and swishing lazily. A mountain-sized sergeant leaned against a tree next to the cart, eating a long loaf of blacktwist and a huge sausage roll and washing them down with ale. The huge man watched Chevays with apparent lack of interest. Chevays was initially furious that the man did not salute a superior—and then recalled he was disguised.

Right, he thought. *I'm still addle-witted. Sun to the brain. Some food and a cold drink, and I'll feel better.*

He noted the tables were full, and that the customers' chattering had an edge to it. *Something has happened.* That would make it easier to keep his cover, if he acted the part of a rich outlander, with more money than manners—a congenial role anyway. He settled himself into a cushioned chair at an unoccupied table. A kitchen wench sauntered out—a round-hipped girl with dark eyes and big tits.

He grinned at her. "Iced wine," he said, "and blacktwist and beer-pickled pork." He winked. "And what price the house special?"

The girl eyed him coldly. "Market Tavern dasn't have a *house special*," she snapped. "Y've mistook us fer t' Merry Lass, on t' next corner. Girls there have *house specials*, dey say."

She stalked off, her skirts swinging. Chevays grinned, undiscouraged. She was the sort of girl he especially liked— one with a temper and some fire. The ones who weren't afraid to fight were a hell of a lot more fun than the ones who just lay there screaming.

She came back, carrying his meal and his drink, and while she was setting it on the table, he pinched her ass through her skirt. The next instant, she had his hand in hers and was forcing the palm flat and twisting the wrist—and the pain was so terrible it almost blinded him. He slid off the chair, eyes watering.

"Well now," she said, "y' shouldna' drink sa much of dat hard stuff." She pulled him to his feet, and in the pretense of helping him to stand and brushing dust off his clothes, managed to give his wrist a final, especially vicious twist. "Ah, but y'll be more careful next time, hey?" she asked, and grinned at him.

He sank back into his seat and rubbed his aching wrist. He had no idea where the little Derkinoi bitch had learned that trick, but he wished he had her in his quarters, where he could show her a few tricks of his own. She'd lose that grin . . . fast.

He became aware of people watching him, and looked defiantly at the table next to him—and his eyes met the yellow eyes of the girl Willek hunted. He looked away instantly, feigning drunkenness, and gulped down a swig of his iced wine, spilling some in the process. The girl turned away, disgusted, and resumed her conversation with the other people around her table. His hunch had led him where he wanted to go. The dark Tykissian girl was as he'd remembered, except that she was stripped to her halter above the waist. A man with spectacles was putting a bandage on her shoulder, working with a surgeon's precision—although he wore the green jacket of an Imperial footsoldier, with corporal's stripes. And Captain Morkaarin, right enough, standing by the table with one boot up on a chair, throwing back his head and laughing.

The three at the table laughed with him, saluting as he turned to go.

Chevays shivered, and caressed the memory of dagger teeth and yellow eyes. His heart raced and his mouth went dry. He did not think there was another girl like that in Derkin. He would follow her back to wherever she lived, and find out everything he could about her. *Willek will be pleased,* he thought. *Once I have information to give her, she'll be pleased.*

For an instant, it seemed to him there was another reason why he sought the fanged girl . . . another person involved somehow. He stared into the reddish depths of his iced wine and tried to figure out where that nagging feeling came from, but the harder he thought about it, the further it slipped from his memory.

Finally he shook his head and sighed. *If it's important, it will come back to me,* he decided. *Sooner or later.*

Zeemos collapsed onto his bedroll and whimpered. It seemed infinitely longer than four days since that *accursed* accident at the inn. Everything had been going so *well,* the take was up, he was thinking of settling down, buying a house and some more wenches and then—

He whimpered again. Every muscle in his body ached, and he'd already had to take his belt in two notches. Fat was a sign of respectability to a Toboran. A fat man was a wealthy man, a man who didn't have to labor in the hot sun, a man of refinement and leisure and intelligence. Back when he'd been young and hungry and slender and fast, he'd dreamed of the day when he could take his ease in the shade while others worked. Now he was back where he'd started—worse, actually. A hired knife didn't have to work like a peasant or a soldier.

A silvery chuckle interrupted his next groan. He rolled upright, looking around and clutching at the dagger on his belt. A woman sat cross-legged at the other side of the little tent—how could he have missed her? He glanced around the tent; none of his gear was missing. The woman chuckled again.

Young, slender, dark—a tenth-crown piece, he estimated, with a professional's reflex.

"Get out," he snarled. "H'I've no lust fer camp followers t'night."

"Oh, no. I'm not one of the camp followers," the woman said, and smiled. "I'm an admirer of yours. And I have friends who would like to be your friends."

She sat cross-legged on the waxed canvas floor of the tent, and rested her dainty chin in delicate cupped hands. "That awful Captain Morkaarin mistreated you," the woman said. "Took advantage of you because he could. That's so unfair."

"H'it's that, all right." Zeemos dropped onto his bedroll and lay back, looking at the woman. He could feel the anger, beaten down by exhaustion, coming back to life. "Took every crown I had . . . every last duc. I'm a poor man again, and not even m' whores left t' me so h'I can get t' money back."

"I know," the woman said gently. "I know. But you're smart, Zeemos. Smarter than the First Captain, smarter than your whores. You can still come out of this ahead."

He sucked on his bottom lip and studied her. He *was* smart—smart enough to know that whatever she was in his tent for, she was up to no good. *Pimps know people*, he thought. *And we know "friends." "Friends" are what you buy when you have lots of money—and I haven't a stinking copper duc.* So the question was, then, what sort of "no good" did she have in mind? And what was in it for him?

"How?" he asked.

She smiled, pressed the palms of her hands together, and lay her fingertips to her chin. "I, and my friends who would like to be your friends, would like you to do a favor for us. We want you to spread a few rumors about First Captain Morkaarin, and perhaps stir up some trouble. Nothing major, you know. Nothing that would make trouble for you if you were caught. But enough that, perhaps, Morkaarin could lose his commission . . ."

Zeemos smiled in spite of himself. "Something h'I'd love t' see."

"My friends and I as well."

"What sort of rumors? Did y' have anything particular, h'or just as h'I can think 'em up?"

The woman laughed lightly. "Oh, we won't make you work so hard as to come up with your own rumors. To begin with, just say that the First Captain is a secret worshiper of the One of a Thousand Faces. And that he bears a grudge against Grand Admiral Willek, and is secretly in the pay of the Yentror of Tarin Tseld, and would betray the whole of the Tykissian Empire to get even with her."

Zeemos nodded. "Any truth to any of that?"

"Only that he hates Willek. He has his reasons—but his reasons for hating her will make the lies seem more possible."

Zeemos was beginning to feel a bit livelier. He propped himself up on one elbow and looked at the tiny woman across from him. "H'and if h'I do this, what will my 'friends' do for me?"

"We will make you rich. Very, very rich, Zeemos. The five hundred crowns Morkaarin stole from you today will be as nothing."

Zeemos laughed. "As nothing, hey? Now h'I've heard everything."

The woman shook her head gently. "It's true. Morkaarin's downfall is important to us. We will see you get back what you most desire—if you can make that happen. And we're willing to prove our good faith, Zeemos. We'll prove we're your friends, before you even start to help us."

Zeemos grinned. "So prove h'it."

The woman shifted position until she knelt on the floor of his tent, fumbling with the clasp of the heavy leather pouch strapped to her girdle. "I've brought you a gift," she said, not looking up. Her slender fingers darted over the clasp, and Zeemos had the impression for an instant that she was weaving patterns in the air with them, and not truly working the lock. But when he rubbed his eyes, his vision cleared, and he could see that, after all, the locking mechanism on the pouch was merely balky. It sprang open as he watched, and she pulled something out.

Her fingers completely covered the object. She held it out for him, her hand closed, her palm down. He had no idea what she might be holding. "Our gift," she said.

Zeemos reached toward her, and she pressed a smooth, cool object into his palm. He held it up—thought at first it was nothing but a black stone mounted and fitted with a sturdy chain. But a bit of wayward light from one of the moons touched the stone and filled it with a gleaming ruby glow.

He gasped, and cautiously lit a candle from his supplies. He held the stone in front of the flame, and marvelled at its brilliance and fire and clarity. "Looks to be of fine gem quality," he said after a moment.

"The finest. It's heartstone ruby, from a mine at the far ends of the earth—one of the biggest perfect stones ever found there."

"If that's so, this stone could be worth every duc I lost today."

"After the war, when there is a market again for gems, it will be worth more than that," she remarked. "In the meantime, it is simply a very nice gift, and a token of our appreciation for your future help."

"Why is he worth so much to you?"

The woman pressed her hands to her thighs, and leaned forward. "You are not the only rich man he has made angry, or that he has hurt. First Captain Morkaarin has *not* been careful."

Zeemos nodded. It didn't surprise him at all that Morkaarin had made other enemies besides himself. He ran the ruby's chain through his fingers and dangled the gem in front of the flame again. Then he put the pendant on and tucked it inside his shirt. "Tell your friends h'I said, 'A man can't have too many friends.' "

The woman smiled and rose. "I'll tell them."

"Will I see you again?" He found her attractive and was

vaguely curious about her price. If he was to be a rich man again, perhaps she would find him attractive. Perhaps . . .

"You may." She shrugged. "It is, after all, a world where amazing things happen."

He felt the weight of the pendant against his skin—the ruby warmed to his touch and almost seemed to pulse as it nestled at the base of his throat. "They do," he agreed. "They do indeed."

Lord Colonel Gonstad was waiting in the tiny field hut when Bren entered. He sat in Bren's only chair, with his boots propped on the table at which Bren ate.

"*First Captain* Morkaarin," the Lord Colonel said, and smiled.

"Sir?" Bren was startled. He'd never known the Lord Colonel to stoop to entering a subordinate's hut.

"Willek met with the *senior* command staff early this morning. Our schedules have changed."

Not for the better, either, or Gonstad wouldn't be smiling, Bren thought. It was uncharitable of him, but the Lord Colonel was the sort of officer who delighted in the problems of others.

"How so, sir?" he asked. He kept his tone polite, and tried to ignore the dig about "senior" command staff. He and Gonstad had gotten out of the academy at the same time— but Gonstad had risen through the ranks like a black-powder rocket, fallen back now and then when his screw-ups became too blatant to ignore, then risen again on the gilded wings of wealth and birth and patronage in high places. Bren wouldn't have minded so much, if it weren't for the fact that the man had no feeling for his regiment.

"Have the XIXth packed by tomorrow midday. It's one of the units standing at full strength, so it will be going out first— the following dawn. You'll be at the harbor and boarding ships by twilight, to sail with the tide. Twilight according to the schedule, so don't count on it."

"To . . . morrow?" Bren whispered. "Sir, the XIXth might be at full strength numerically, but nearly a third of our numbers have been recruited within the last months . . . some of them within the last three days."

"I was there to do the recruiting," Gonstad said. "Willek's orders, Morkaarin." The Lord Colonel grinned through his beard. "Units at full strength go first. Incidentally, I'm placing you in charge of leading the scouts. Personally. As well as the skirmishers. I'll take the command of the foot and the pikes myself."

Which meant their company commanders would do the work, actually. It was a serious demotion; Gonstad probably thought he'd better take real command, with their superiors suddenly watching him. Or perhaps he thought he'd prevent Bren from getting any glory out of the coming campaign—it seemed to be one of Feliz Gonstad's aims in life to ruin Bren Morkaarin's prospects.

Bren Morkaarin got a horrible feeling in the pit of his stomach. His superiors had refused him experienced scouts. He'd been told to take green recruits and train *them*. And now he was being put in charge of his green unit, which had existed for only days, and was being sent into the field—and not incidentally, the front lines—first.

He and Grand Admiral Willek had never met. He'd known of the Tornsaarin-Morkaarin feud all his life, of course. That was common knowledge. He knew what her great-grandfather had done to his great-grandfather, and vice-versa, but somehow he had never believed generations-old animosity would reach from the past to affect his career. He'd obviously been far too naive. Somehow, Grand Admiral Willek had discovered a Morkaarin in her midst and had taken umbrage. Killing him hadn't worked, and too many attempts in the midst of a war would look bad even at her station on the greasy pole.

So she'd devised another method of getting rid of him. An efficient one, from the looks of it.

Well, it explained a lot. He should, now that he thought

about it, have been promoted over Gonstad and not the other way around. He was competent, and Gonstad was, to his way of thinking, a moron. But Gonstad didn't have the Morkaarin bloodlines; he didn't have the Morkaarin's feud with the Grand Admiral's ancestors, either. So he held regimental command, while Bren stayed stuck at First Captain—and now he was back doing field-sergeant's work, at that.

A Morkaarin would go down like an officer. "Tomorrow, is it? I'll have my people ready by then."

Gonstad's smug grin dwindled away to nothing, and he sat there a moment longer, feet still on Morkaarin's table, with the disappointment evident on his face. "Well . . . good," he said at last.

He stood at last, and Bren saluted sharply, and Gonstad left.

When he was well away from the hut—and Bren had listened to the sound of the Lord Colonel's footsteps until the sounds of them were swallowed by daysounds—the First Captain sank into his chair and rested his head in his hands.

There are dooms a man can face, he thought. *The doom of defeat in honest battle, or the doom of death in an heroic act— I could accept those. But to die from an act of treachery brought on by a dispute that started and ended before my mother's grandfather was born—that's too much to bear.*

And what of my people? They're as doomed as I, and even less deserving of the doom. Their only sin was to fall into my command.

He grinned suddenly. *I should have let the new recruits drown Gonstad in the trough. Godsall, but I should have. Would have been a lovely thing.* He sat a moment, enjoying the picture of it.

"Things could be worse," he said to himself. "Not much, but they could be worse." Thanks to the pimp's generous donation, and the hard work of some of his new recruits, the unit had a good supply of arms. Second-hand, most of the stuff—but far, far better than nothing. Which was what they'd have had if he'd waited for the Quartermaster-General to find something from the armories. The mills of the gods ground slow, but even they were usually faster than a bureaucrat's response to a request.

"So we are not without weapons," he muttered. "And we are not without talent."

The Grenlaarin scion, and the law-speaker—he felt confidence in them. The beast-girl seemed exceptional, too. They'd piled in without hesitation at the tavern; that was just a brawl, but a good sign nonetheless. The rest . . . well, he'd have to see.

"This isn't without hope," he told himself. "Kremis says, 'In war, the unexpected is the only sure thing, and True Leader rides the unexpected like a fish rides the sea.' " He stood and paced. "I hope Kremis knows what she's talking about."

So the only thing left to consider was whether or not he ought to tell the troops the night before, or let them find out in the morning.

And then end up chasing the green recruits over hill and valley, when they panicked and broke?

So he'd tell them in the morning.

Let them have a final evening of relative peace. They'd earned it.

Chevays had followed his quarry enough to be sure. The yellow-eyed girl was going toward the XIXth's camp. He slipped off to a public jakes just long enough to change into uniform and wash the pale paint from his face. He caught up with the beast-girl again easily enough. The road was crowded, and she and her party were heavily laden. He entertained himself by watching her, by fantasizing about her. She moved like the cat she brought to his mind. *I want that toy myself*, he thought. Several amusing games presented themselves to his imagination. She would fight, he decided. She'd fight hard. He smiled, imagining.

Shillraki mercenaries paced along the embankment, while

buckskin-clad levies from Old Tykis leaned impassively on their spears at the gate and watched from emotionless, tattooed faces. Most of the subsidiary camps inside were Imperial regular infantry, each regiment of foot in a checkerboard around the hutments of the officers and the unit Shrine of the Three, divided from the next by open space reserved for drill.

The cart turned off at the XIXth Foot's encampment, those with it saluting raggedly as they passed by the standard at the gate. Chevays snapped his fist to his breast and out smartly as *he* went by a few moments later, under the pole with the Imperial daggertooth and the blazoned numbers.

The commander's tent was more like a pavilion: definitely nonstandard, three or four times the authorized load. Half a dozen blooded horses waited on a picket string beneath an awning outside. The guards snapped to attention and passed him through; the interior was brightly lit, and surprisingly busy. Most of the officers were unremarkable, the same weathered professionals a man could find anywhere in the New Empire. A half-dozen or so were personal aides to the commander, unmistakable sprigs on various prominent family trees—and all, men and women alike, young and remarkably handsome, their uniforms as gaudy as the flexible regulations would allow, or rather more so.

Gonstad, the filing mechanism in his mind prompted him. Lord Colonel Feliz Gonstad commanded the XIXth; the usual mixture of connections and pull, because he certainly hadn't earned the promotion. *How delightful!* the spy thought. *Corrupt, devious and stupid Lord Colonel Gonstad.* So corrupt and stupid that he'd ended up in charge of an infantry outfit— not a status assignment for the high born; a man with his breeding and wealth should have been a cavalry general at least.

Chevays had a file on Gonstad thick as a man's fist. It was no accident that Gonstad's aides were all lovely young things in tight uniforms. Blondes, brunettes, redheads; Chevays had to admire the Lord Colonel's taste, even if he didn't think much of the man's hobbies. They were entirely too simple and straightforward. Chevays thought he could show the Lord Colonel a thing or two about amusement.

One lithe redhead showed him into the Lord Colonel's office: snow-leopard furs, a flask of Perdiki sweating coolness in a spelled snowbath, incense and a jewelled Three-set, and on a stand a suit of three-quarter armor that had to be Dilaarin-made.

Chevays didn't bother with introductions, salutes, or other proprieties. "I need to see your register of troops," he said.

Lord Colonel Gonstad studied his grey tunic, the special division insignia, and the lieutenant's pips. The expression on Gonstad's face told Chevays the Lord Colonel didn't like the special division, and he didn't like Chevays. Knowledge of that fact made Chevays very happy. He hoped Lord Colonel Gonstad would be difficult.

"Where's your authorization?" Gonstad held out his hand as if he thought Chevays would hand over the usual paperwork.

Chevays walked back and closed the Lord Colonel's door, then returned and sat on the edge of his desk. "My authorization, sir, is that on the fifth day of last month, during the celebration of the Virgins of the Lady of Derkin, you used seventy-four crowns, eighteen coppers of unit money to buy gifts for three of the virgins, lured them to a rented room, and deflowered all three—the gifts including highly illegal aphrodisiac candy. One of the virgins, or rather," Chevays smiled slyly, "ex-virgins, though you may not know this, is the daughter of the Hereditary Totani, the Guardian of the Flame of Derkin. Just turned thirteen, I believe."

The Lord Colonel was turning the most delightful shade of green. Chevays thought that last item was probably news to him.

"Further, we have a complete, word-by-word transcript of your, ah, assignation with the three virgins, and only the fact that the Hereditary Totani doesn't know who you are has kept him from having you gelded. You know, of course, that he has that right?" Chevays paused, waiting for Gonstad's answer.

Gonstad's mouth hung open. He seemed to be having difficulty coming up with a response.

"Well," Chevays said after the silence had continued long enough, "*he* knows he has that right, and he is looking for you. But since you're going to cooperate with the special division, he probably won't find you. Aren't you glad about that?"

Gonstad still made no response.

"Yes. I thought you would be. Your troop register, please." Now Chevays held out his hand.

Gonstad pulled out a large black book and handed it over to the lieutenant.

Chevays flipped through it. The names and equipment of each member of the XIXth were listed in the book, along with such useful esoterica as race, sex, and profession before entering the military.

Chevays was looking through the "race" column—he thought he'd probably come up with the information he needed fastest if he went that route.

Sure enough, on the last filled page, he noted a question marker in the race column about a third of the way down the page. The name on that line was Eowlie Thirddaughter. The profession, he noted, was "whore."

How wonderful, he thought. Chevays loved whores. They lasted so much longer than other women. And they were always so sure they'd seen everything.

It was always a pleasure to show them how wrong they were.

Her assignment now was scout. He thought he'd join her unit and decide how he wanted to deal with her once he'd spent some time with her.

He turned to Gonstad. "You'll write orders for me to join the scouts of the XIXth," he said. "List me as 'specialist in covert operations'—vague, and delightfully accurate."

Lord Colonel Gonstad started to argue with him. He could

see the protests forming. But then the Lord Colonel did something totally unexpected.

He smiled. He reached into his desk, pulled out a standard appointment form, and signed it at the bottom. "Fill it in yourself," he said. "Give the papers to First Captain Morkaarin. If you fill them out fairly fast, you'll probably still find him in his quarters. Why don't you just give them to him immediately?"

Chevays didn't like the sudden happiness he saw in Gonstad's eyes. He didn't know to what to attribute it. But he was getting what he wanted—and if Morkaarin turned out to be a tyrant, or a raving lunatic, or worse, Chevays knew he could handle that.

He borrowed the Lord Colonel's scritoire and filled out the form.

"You've made the right decision," he told Gonstad.

"I'm sure of it," the Lord Colonel agreed.

Feeling vaguely uneasy, Chevays Cöado carried his new orders out of the office and went in search of First Captain Morkaarin.

○ CHAPTER VI

Amourgin couldn't sleep. It was his first night out of the stockade, and he was finding the freedom less to his liking than he had anticipated. Insects bit him; uneven spots in the hard ground under his bedroll dug into his back and hips; and dust blew into the tent on the hot, dry wind and gritted in his eyes and nose. He began to imagine ways by which he could get himself thrown back into the stockade. At least it would get him out of the disconcertingly sharp gaze of the regimental priest, who seemed to be a good enough type, but if he discovered that there was an unlicensed, unclerical practitioner of magic amongst them . . .

Then Amourgin considered his plight and started to grin. He'd gotten *out* of worse. As he intended to get out of this predicament.

For the first time since the night the army had found him, he had some privacy.

He peeked outside the tent. The string of moons slipped in and out of the scattered clouds, casting little light, and most of the recruits were, from the sounds of things, well and truly asleep. At the distant camp perimeter, he heard the guards tramping, the occasional call of sentries, and the lights still burned at the regimental headquarters—but nearby, nothing moved.

Well and good.

119

He turned his head to face away from the tent opening, and rummaged through his kit. He retrieved his copy of the *Consolidated Analects of Mero Rimsin*, and pressed gently but firmly on the top edge of the back cover. The thin margin of a panel slid out, and he tugged at it to work it the rest of the way free.

The contents of the secret panel might as well have been at the bottom of a deep well.

"It's too dark in here," he muttered. He didn't dare light a slowmatch, nor a flare. The idea of checking his supplies by moons' light worried him immensely, but he could think of no other alternative. He turned around again, held the book under the open sky, and was able, vaguely, to make out the contents. He pushed his spectacles up his nose and squinted at the labels on the dozens of tiny gut, wax-stoppered tubes that lay packed in rows in the secret compartment.

Blueginny, he read, *bone, bophrayne, caylene, cidon . . . by the Three, what is that next tube?*

The writing was tiny, and some idiot had done it in an ornate script that was nearly unreadable in the dim light. He wanted to swear out loud. *Don't they consider when they put these kits together that those of us in the field might have to use them in the dark?*

Cuevil. That's what it says. No, they don't consider the dark. That would imply, not just a minimum of intelligence on their parts, but some familiarity with the trials of fieldwork . . . and expecting that out of the flunkies doing kitpacking—all right, where *is* the dolemard? They can't have forgotten that, can they?

He looked through the tubes, increasingly frantic. He had plenty of what he didn't need, but the one thing he needed . . .

He found his tube of dolemard in the R's. *I would have assumed the packers were at least taught the rudiments of filing,* he thought, then remembered, with a twinge of shame, that he had used the dolemard once. Thus, the misfiling was his own fault.

He gave the kitmaker a mental apology for the dolemard—but *not* for the writing.

He took his tube and turned again to face away from the tent opening. He slipped his Wolf sept ring off his hand, and pressed the wolf's ears in, then pushed on the nose of the wolf's head. The silver totem slid back to reveal a dark, polished dome of stone. Amourgin licked the stone to wet it, then sprinkled a pinch of the dolemard into the saliva.

The law-speaker muttered arcane syllables under his breath, and stared into the pale light. The stone began to glow.

A face formed in the center of the light, its outlines hazy at first. It stared at him for the briefest of instants, then snapped in a faint and tinny voice, "Where in the Great Domain have you been . . . and why are you calling at *this* hour?"

Amourgin refused to be cowed. "I've been pressed into the army," he whispered. "I've spent the last few days tromping around playing soldier, and the nights in the stockade for trying to bribe my way out of this mess."

The glowing face looked disgusted. "Got yourself pressed? *That* was clever."

In theory the Movement disapproved of impressment—it was one of the abuses they were sworn to correct—but that didn't mean Jawain lacked the general prejudice against anyone stupid enough to be caught in a sweep.

"It isn't as if I volunteered, Jawain." Amourgin glared at the ghostly image. "I missed my contact."

"I imagine you did. Your contact was murdered trying to get to you. We've had that story now for a day or so—but no word from you."

Amourgin rubbed at his forehead with one hand. "Killed? Then I could have sat in that inn waiting forever." He closed his eyes and sighed deeply. "This is just lovely. I came down to this hot hell and got pressed into the stinking army for nothing. Why don't you send someone to get me out."

"And waste a perfectly good cover story? Certainly not! We've wanted to get one of our people on the inside of the army for a while, but so far, everyone we've tried to slip in has been . . . identified. They must be skimping on the scrying spells because of the rush." Jawain looked pleased. "If you get shipped to Tarin Tseld—and my indications are good that the army should be moving in that direction very soon—you can meet up with someone we've had planted down there. So, since you're there, you might as well do something useful. Just stay put, be a good soldier, and don't get killed. I'll find a way to let our agent in Tarin Tseld know you're coming once the time is right."

The image flickered and smeared. Amourgin sprinkled a bit more powder on the stone.

"That won't help much," the faint voice said. "The *shodin* trails of the magic users are thick tonight. The world is crackling with energy trying to find a place to strike."

Amourgin thought of his earlier encounter with mad ghosts and the walking dead, and decided what Jawain said was probably true.

Then something else occurred to him.

"By the way, I met your niece. She's a hellion. She hasn't liked me ever since she found out you gave me Broucher."

The shadowy face looked surprised. "You met Karah?" Then Jawain nodded. "Ah, yes. While she was down selling her horses. No, she wouldn't like the fact that you have Broucher. She tried to buy him off me any number of times." He chuckled. "She is headstrong, I agree. So how did you meet her?"

Amourgin chuckled ruefully. "We got pressed together."

Jawain's mouth fell open, and he slapped a hand to his forehead. He was speechless for an instant. Then, "Pressed? Holy sweet Madrine, Karah's been *pressed*?"

"You certainly weren't this concerned about me," Amourgin noted.

Jawain apparently missed the intended humor in the lawspeaker's tone, for he snapped, "*She's* a child. Besides, Karah knows nothing about the Reform—she's completely unprepared to go into war—"

"She'll do fine," Amourgin interrupted. "She's already won a place as second behind me in command of our scout unit."

Jawain's image flickered and weakened again. "I cannot believe this! I sent one of my nephews along to keep her and my daughter Brunnai out of *just* this sort of trouble—or has he been pressed as well? Name's Lion Abt."

"None by that name pressed."

"Damnall! What was the man thinking? I suppose I'll find out soon enough." Jawain frowned, and his image turned to look at something behind him. When he turned back, he said, "Someone will no doubt be along in a few days to retrieve her. In the meantime, I'm holding you responsible for her safety."

Then Jawain's image popped like a soap bubble, and Amourgin was left staring at the afterimages of the glowing face.

"I'm in the army, and he's thrilled," he muttered. "That isn't the response I was hoping for. Meanwhile, my second gets her ass rescued by mamma and pappa."

Unhappily, he stared up at the moons in the cloudless sky. He'd always been proud to know the Reform needed him. He just wished by the Three it needed him somewhere else.

Darkist roamed through the tiled marble halls of the royal palazzi, his guards stalking at his sides. He could not rest, nor could he eat, nor could he find pleasure in watching his concubines dance. The night was thick with magic, with spells and counterspells and the taint of intrigue.

I am too old, he thought, *and too weary—and these ancient bones feel the weight of plots upon them.*

That reek of defiled conjury, of witching and hungering after power, came from Admiral Tornsaarin, of course. The Tykissian bitch planned to double-cross him—just as her ancestors had betrayed the last of the Olmyan emperors, the ones stupid enough to rely on northern mercenaries. Some of those emperors had survived to flee to the southern shore of the Imperial sea.

Darkist cackled with glee, just thinking about it. She'd planned to move her fleet out a few days early—he'd discovered all about her schemes, before she found and executed his spy. If she'd been really clever, he thought, she would have let the spy live—would have fed her false information. It was, after all, what he was doing. But the Admiral, he determined with some smugness, was not his equal in the arts of plotting and planning. He knew her routes, knew her planned departure time—and his new spy, her perfidious Krevaulti aide, had been so long in the service of her family that she would never think to mistrust him.

By magic he would control the coming battle. Willek would renege on their agreement, he knew, and would fight to win— and when she did, the magical items he had planted in her midst were spelled to turn against her. The Storm Ruby was in place; the plan was flawless.

He should have felt lighthearted; he was about to complete a plan centuries in the making—the plan to bring the Northlands back under the power of Tarin Tseld and resurrect the Old Empire.

And yet, he thought he could feel the meddling of the gods. Outside the temples, he had not felt their touch in centuries, nor had he seen signs of their doings in the world of men in as long. It seemed to him the gods were wakening and taking an interest in the affairs of mortals again. Along the back of his neck, like the steel of an executioner's blade, he could feel the unloving kiss of the One of the Thousand Faces.

The gods were fickle, and their indulgence was uncertain. Darkist would rather have fought his war to regain the Territories without any gods than with the favor of the One of the Thousand Faces, for the affections of the Cold One could be bought . . . but none could guarantee they would *stay* bought. Once the Yentrors of his line had *used* the One: once they had been sorcerers strong enough to compel the very gods. That was long ago; when the Old Empire went down in a chaos of civil wars and barbarian invasions, the sacred Theophone was lost. A feathered shaman had stolen it, and concealed it with such cunning that for millennia, Tseldene magicians had sought it in vain.

With the Theophone, he could have compelled the One—could have compelled those thousand treacherous faces to look to him for orders. As it was, he could only wheedle and bribe and beg the Cold One, and curry favor with sacrifices.

And if other gods also reached their twisty fingers into Darkist's stew—

But were the gods truly wakening, truly returning their attention to the intrigues of humankind? Or was this an old man's paranoia on the eve of his greatest triumph?

He needed to know.

Darkist reached a decision. He stopped stock-still in the middle of the corridor. "You," he said, and pointed a wavering finger at one of the guards, "fetch my Blossom to the Quiet Room. And you," he commanded another, "get Shaad Shaabin."

The guards he'd commanded ran off down a side corridor. Darkist watched them go, then hurried toward the Quiet Room himself.

The guards dared not enter into the sacred spaces of the Quiet Room. They kissed the stone doorposts, but did not pass beyond the small and narrow white door.

Darkist left them behind. Inside the Quiet Room, he need fear nothing.

The Quiet Room glowed with the light of its own magic. Darkist thought the light had dimmed over the centuries he'd worshipped in its labyrinthine recesses—or perhaps his eyes had dimmed with age. The light was bright enough, though, as he walked along the echoing corridor—as bright as it seemed to have been in his distantly remembered first youth.

The Yentror of Tarin Tseld nodded slightly to the statues of guises of the One of the Thousand Faces which lined the wall. He no longer bowed to kiss the carved stone feet—in fact, he had long considered himself one of them, the living personification of the Cold One. So he greeted them more as a man greeting relatives than as one meeting his gods.

The old saying ran through his memory: *Old men stand up to their gods because they can no longer bend.*

Perhaps, he thought. *Perhaps that is the real reason I no longer kneel.*

He chuckled softly. Amused by thoughts of the false courage of age, he moved further into the room. It was an ancient place—the most ancient place in all of Tarin Tseld, which was rumored to be the oldest city in the world. The Quiet Room was a grotto. Unknown worshipers at the beginning of time had carved the aspects of the Cold One in living rock, and their feet had worn smooth the grotto trails centuries before Darkist's earliest remembered ancestors were born.

Down one face of one room of the grotto, fresh water dribbled from a spring. Over uncounted eons, the spring had painted a rainbow of colors down the wall. Darkist sat on the broad carved stone shelf that ran the entire circumference of the long, narrow room and studied the patterns it made. He kept hoping that someday, the minerals would form meaningful patterns, some special message from the One. So far, however, the One had shown restraint toward the idea of writing its feelings on stone for posterity.

Darkist's ancestors built the first parts of the palazzi around the grotto perhaps fifteen thousand years earlier. Those parts of the palazzi felt incredibly ancient to him. But the Quiet Room felt older still. It echoed with the memories of whispers of newborn gods—it was a place rich with the magic of ages.

This was the one place where he could always feel the presence of the Cold One—his favorite place.

He leaned against the feet of The Cold One in Anger, and let the hum of the rocks purr through his bones. He closed his eyes, and voices insinuated themselves into his thoughts. He could hear the ghostwails of worshipers long since dust; the rich, deep cadences of massed chants; a single voice singing with the pure ferocity of fire. *Dead and dust, all of them*, he thought. *But I live—and while I live, I rule.*

Shaad Shaabin stepped cautiously into the Quiet Room. Darkist watched as his servant knelt and did proper obeisance to the Cold One in its many forms. The Yentror was pleased.

Few anymore showed appropriate respect for the sacred ways.

Shaad Shaabin finally reached Darkist. He was taller by half than Darkist, and thin—the child of foreigners Darkist had bought in an earlier time. He was inscrutable and ugly, bred for service. "My master, what would you of me?" Shaad whispered, and gave Darkist the same honor he gave the One.

"The gods waken. Perhaps you have felt them?" Darkist ran fingers over the cool, smooth curves of the Anger. When Shaad indicated by a gesture that he had not, the Yentror sighed. "They creep into my dreams at night, and carve their names in burning omens on the faces of my days. I must find their intentions, for only a fool trusts the interventions of the gods."

Shaad pressed the palms of his hands together, and touched his fingers to his forehead. The long, narrow hands nearly disappeared under Shaad's deep cowl. "My master wishes to see the future?"

"Indeed, Shaad. That I wish most of all."

"Very well."

Darkist heard the door open again. His lovely Blossom slipped inside, and he smiled. She was the most beautiful of his concubines—her skin copper, her eyes green, her hair black as Shboran anthracite. She moved down the aisles without a moment's notice of the gods who towered over her—her eyes were on her Yentror, and her smile was for him. The palazzi was full of magic and forgotten chambers, but there was only one Darkist.

"Truly you are the fairest flower of Tarin Tseld," Darkist whispered, and the murmurs in the grotto repeated his words in tones of agreement. "Come to me, light of my life, and embrace me."

Blossom did not kneel as Shaad Shaabin had, nor did she acknowledge Shaad's presence in any way; she was not a servant, but instead was Darkist's favorite pet and as such could be forgiven anything. She kissed the old man and ran her fingers boldly along his body. She was wanton, but delightfully so. Darkist loved her with an old man's passion, and wished again that she had been his when he was a young man. He would, he thought, have used her harder, but he would have enjoyed her more.

She turned her back on Shaad Shaabin. It was an intentional slight, and one which had always amused the Yentror. Blossom, from the moment she'd been chosen head concubine, had considered herself above all save the lords of the kingdom—and even those she greeted with a saucy wink and a flash of white teeth.

Exquisite, Darkist thought sadly, as Shaad Shaabin neatly slit her throat.

Darkist watched the lifeblood spurt from her throat, and watched her sag into Shaad's arms. Her eyes glazed.

"Place her on the shelf, and we'll begin," the Yentror said.

As Shaad placed the dying concubine on the shelf of the Quiet Room, and as her blood mingled with the spring water and fed the living stone, the One of the Thousand Faces began to sing. The grotto filled with the deep chords of the earth's voice, rich music informed by madness and bloodlust. Blossom could not wholly die in the grotto, of course—there was no escape for the soul in that chamber, not until it achieved eternal communion with the One.

"Undress her," Darkist said.

His servant obeyed.

"Now, cut for me. From there," he indicated the notch below Blossom's breastbone, "to there," pointing to the rounded curve of her belly below her navel.

Darkist appreciated Shaad for many of his skills, but most of all, he decided, for that one. The man could slice a woman wide open, and never do even the slightest damage to the entrails beneath the skin. When her viscera lay exposed, Darkist stepped forward and prodded around among the loops and coils. He remained conscious of the Cold One's singing as he studied the grey twists of the bowel and the slick, dark mass of liver. The One's song grew dark and foreboding, lacking in triumph and promise. Darkist frowned as he squeezed the bile bag and found it full of stones—always a vile omen. He ran his fingers along the lumpy soulfish, and discovered portents of loss and disaster. Both kidneys and kidneyriders lay in the angle of the betrayer. And both womaneggs were swollen and misshapen and the color of old meat—not smooth and round and pale.

He checked again. He ran his fingers along each organ, each bit of entrail, his anger growing fiercer with each new portent of despair and failure.

I gave the Cold One the very best I had. The very best. And this is the thanks I get?

"No," he snarled. He held triumph in his hands. The whole of the world was soon to kneel at his feet—yet the omens spoke of doom for him and his line, and foretold the end of the world as he knew it.

He would not believe such a thing. He could easier believe Blossom had betrayed him than that the future would turn its back on him.

He turned to Shaad in annoyance. "This won't do. It won't do at all. I will not accept such nonsense."

He frowned and studied Blossom, whose body was beginning to dissolve as the One of a Thousand Faces devoured her; expression remained in her eyes to the very end. He turned away at last and glared at Shaad Shaabin.

"Bring me another concubine."

Karah pulled the blanket of her bedroll over her head to drown out the steady, puzzling hissing and booming that went on outside her tent. She'd only just fallen asleep when the noise woke her, but once she was awake, it would not let her drift back into oblivion.

There was a nagging familiarity to the sound . . .

And then she placed it. It was the roar of breakers on the beach. But she was miles from beach.

She knew, suddenly, what that sound meant, and wished with all her heart that she did not. The dead were returning

for her. Her eyes flew open. Inside the tent was dark; the
night outside was less so, with the moons casting their faint
and changeable light.

*I will not stand for another all-night ride with drowned and
stinking corpses*, she thought.

As though he'd heard her thought, the blind old man rose
through the floor of her tent until he sat, cross-legged and
grinning, next to her.

Karah could see through him. She could, she thought, actually
see shapes outside the opening of her tent right through the
draped folds of his robe, and through his arms and head. It was
somewhat like looking through fog, but there it was.

Chills spiderwalked over her skin.

"Fateborn will walk four-legged on the water," the ghostly
man said in a high-pitched, sing-song voice. "Fateborn will fly
with a hundred blazing wings. Fateborn will dance with the
dead, and eat at the table of the gods, will lie with a bastard
and bring forth kings."

She realized she didn't like spirits. Nor prophecies. "Get
out of my tent," Karah said. "I don't know anybody named
Fateborn, and I don't want to hear anything you have to
say."

The spectral madman stared through her with his glowing
white eyes and laughed a chittering laugh. "Fateborn must
walk through fire and ice—not burn, not freeze."

Karah swallowed. "Not something I can help you with,"
she said. Her voice sounded brave, but her heart felt as if it
pounded in her throat.

He crooked his finger at her.

"Oh, no," she said and gripped her bedroll. "No, no! I don't
want to go back with the dead men—"

The earth beneath her opened up and swallowed her.

"No!" she yelled. The roar of the ocean filled her ears, and
drowned out her voice so even she could not hear it. She
hung in total darkness. She had the terrible feeling that she
was falling, that nothing supported her and that at any instant,

she would crash into the unseen, uprushing ground and shatter like glass. The pallid man with his cackled omens was nowhere around her. Nothing was. She could have been the only living creature in the universe.

Then even sound receded beyond hearing, and the sense of falling passed. Now she seemed to float in nothingness, blind and deaf, unable to smell or taste. She tried to move her arms, her legs, tried to touch herself—and found even that impossible. She was uncertain that she had a body.

Her time in this state seemed infinitely long—and then abruptly it was over. She hurtled at incredible speed out of the darkness into a place of fire and terrible redness. Beneath her, a blazing sea churned and tossed and rolled slow burning waves onto the black banks that held in the fiery liquid. Where she had been surrounded by silence, now noise enveloped her; stentorian, palpable—the weight of it pounded her ears and her gut and made her sick.

Now she knew she fell, and knew how fast, and knew toward what. She screamed. She shrieked until her lungs felt they would burst and could not tell she made a sound.

The noise grew louder, and the light brighter and redder, and the air hotter. She was falling straight into the burning sea. She made swimming motions, tried to angle herself away from the molten lake—it was hopeless.

She fell endlessly, into the fire and the sulphur stink, and then without warning she was at the surface of the sea and the molten waves swallowed her.

She thought she would die—of fright, or of the fierce searing pain, or at last of suffocation when she could no longer hold her breath, and the viscous burning fluid filled her mouth and nose. The boiling, blazing stuff burned through her eyes and into her mouth and into her gut; seared her arms and legs; filled her ears and flowed into her skull, leaving nothing but pain as dire and blazing as itself.

Karah knew she could not possibly live, and yet she did not die. The fiery currents carried her, and tossed her, and ate into her, and she knew what they did. All the world was pain and blinding blood-red light.

She clawed her way up, swimming through fluid thicker than tar. Pain devoured her, and twice she stopped and let the fluxes drag her around and wished herself dead. But both times she changed her mind. Both times, as the burning sea clutched her and dragged her down, she regained her courage and pulled toward the air.

Her head broke free of the lava, and she found she could see. A wave carried her upward, and she noted the direction of the black and featureless shore. Then it crashed on top of her, and buried her in liquid pain again. She swam in a daze, fighting for the shore while the sea in turn battled to keep her from it.

And then she felt solid ground under her feet, and dragged herself from the burning sea onto the burning shore. The beach was smooth as glass or ice; so hot at the very edge it still glowed red and stuck to her flesh as she crawled, though farther away from the lava waves, it cooled fractionally and felt harder. She stood. She was incredibly weary, but there was no place to lie down, no place to rest. She trudged up the beach, her back turned to the searing heat of the sea. Ahead of her was only darkness. Her eyes strained for any feature, any detail—and finally she spotted movement off to her right.

She plodded toward whatever it was that moved. She was battered by noise and heat and pain, and not really curious. But going toward something seemed better than going toward nothing.

She came over the top of a glass dune, and realized what she had seen before had only been the hands and tops of the heads of those who moved. She stopped as realization dawned on her, and threw her hands over her face and knelt on the ground. She faced the Three; the Father, the Mother, and the Child.

Nothing happened to her, and she dared to look up. The Three watched her. They made no move toward her, gave her no sign—but they watched her. The Father was as she'd always thought he would be—falcon-headed, with the torso of a man and the body of a huge lion. His body was scarred and bloodied, and she realized all four of his great paws were chained to rock. The Mother was taller than Karah would ever have imagined. Her hips and shoulders were as broad as they should have been, but all ten of her breasts were withered and dry, her pale skin was bruised, and her face was etched with pain. The Child, a massive wolf cub, threw back his head and howled—and his anguish was blotted out by the eternal roar of the sea. Karah could see that he'd gnawed his paws bloody where they were held to the glass beach by huge jawed traps.

How can I free them? Karah wondered and crept forward to look at their manacles and their chains.

Before she was within range, the Father struck at her with his beak, and the Mother swiped at her with one clawed hand. Karah looked into the Mother's face and backed away. Her eyes glowed like reflected fire from the sea, and she bared long white fangs.

The Child snapped and lunged.

Karah knelt again, carefully out of their reach, touched cheeks and forehead, and prayed.

The wild-eyed ghost from her tent suddenly appeared, and took her hand, and leapt into the air. Karah was again enveloped in darkness and total silence. The sudden absence of heat and noise and pain left her giddy.

And then they were in her tent again, she and the madman.

Dawn was at hand—the sky outside her tent was pink. The air felt cold to her, though she knew it was not, and smelled fresh. Her head sagged forward, and she told the ghost, "Leave me."

The old man whispered in her ear, "You must save them, Fateborn. You were born to free the gods—but you are not yet worthy. You are flawed—you are flawed and must be tempered before you are of suitable metal to cut away their chains. I will be your forge."

Karah fell forward onto her bedroll and groaned, "You will be my death."

"Only if you prove unworthy in spite of me."

Karah opened one eye and squinted up at the madman. He still sat cross-legged, and stared blindly off into nothingness, or the eternal beyond. She noticed that he became more translucent with every passing second.

She closed her eyes, and murmured. "Please, just kill me now."

First Captain Morkaarin's voice said, "If you aren't out of that tent in five seconds, I just might. You've slept through call."

Karah's whole body jerked, and she opened bleary eyes, and noted two legs in high boots outside her tent opening. "Oh, godsall, no. I can't get up," she groaned. "I'm dying."

The First Captain's face peered into her tent. Karah noted that what had been an expression of annoyance on his face became one of—shock? Fear? Incredulity?

"What happened to you?" he asked.

"I couldn't sleep last night," she said. And then she considered what she had been through, and decided a lie would be safest. "Nightmares," she added.

He cleared his throat. "Nightmares . . ."

She nodded.

He gnawed thoughtfully on one side of his bottom lip, then sighed. "We're packing and moving out today, but you can sleep for the moment. And go to the infirmary when you wake."

He walked away.

When he was gone, Karah rolled on her side, ready to let herself drift into sleep. She noticed, however, an odd glow in her tent. She looked down at her legs, and then at her hands and arms.

Then she rolled onto her belly and pressed her face into the coarse blanket of her bedroll. She started to cry.

Her body glowed with a soft, pale light.

⊙ CHAPTER VII

A warm wind boomed across the rolling hills of Farbluffs County. Reddish-green, the knee-high grass rippled and swayed, hiding the rocky soil. The dirt roadway kicked up under the hooves of Konzin's mount, each plodding step sending arrows of pain through his chest. Off in the middle distance, a horse herd grazed under the watchful eye of mounted ranch hands, moving slowly down towards the cottonwoods that edged a waterhole. The stallion tossed his head and whinnied a challenge.

Konzin's horse answered. Two of the ranch hands turned and cantered toward him; the roadway was on Five Points land. As they came closer, they cried him hail. The shouts of greeting turned to alarm as they pulled up and saw his injuries.

" 'Tis Konzin!" one cried, gaping.

He suppressed an impulse to snap *who did you expect?* at her. Both of them pulled out their bows and crowded closer, looking around.

"Bandits?" one said, standing in the stirrups. "Raise the alarm?"

Konzin shook his head. "Master an' Madine must hear me," he said. "Now!"

The hands spun and galloped toward the main ranch, shouting the alarm.

✧　　✧　　✧

135

Just before he rounded the last turn to the Grenlaarin ranch, Konzin paused to be sure all the little details in his appearance and his story were right. The horse was near death—its flanks quivered and its head hung low. Konzin hated to waste good stock, especially when it was going to be *his* good stock very soon.

But the Grenlaarins can't doubt that I was desperate to reach them. If I rode a horse to death getting to them, they won't doubt.

He looked terrible, too. He'd look even worse when he rode up. He decided to deliver his news, then faint. Ought to be good drama. And no sense riding home anything less than a hero.

He savored what would happen next. Iano Grenlaarin and the hands would ride off in search of vengeance, and Konzin's bandits would kill the hunting party on the road. Misa Grenlaarin would die grieving her husband and only child— with a bit of help from the nightshade tea Konzin would give her.

He sat there for just an instant, relishing the picture. When the elder Grenlaarins were out of the way, he would pay Lord Colonel Gonstad the rest of the bribe, and get Karah back out of the army where he'd safely tucked her away.

The army is a wonderful paid nanny, Konzin thought.

She would marry him, legitimizing his claim to the Grenlaarin ranch—and then . . .

He was uncertain whether she would be his loving and devoted wife, or whether she would suffer an unfortunate accident in the barns. Might be easier to keep all the stories straight if she were trampled by a rogue stallion. Maybe after she dropped an heir. It would be satisfying to see the uppity bitch lie down and spread for him and ride her ragged, but she'd be dangerous if kept around too long.

Poor sweet Karah. He smiled, thinking of her demise. *Time later to see about that.*

When he rode onto the Grenlaarin homestead, he hung

across the horn of his saddle like one near death. His horse, foam-flecked and blowing hard, staggered as it walked—man and horse were crusted with dirt and dried blood, both equally gaunt and wounded.

Iano ran out of the barn as he rode up. Misa limped out of the house at a half-trot, her bad leg dragging. The rest of the ranch hands clustered around him gapemouthed. The cobbled courtyard was full of noise and questions, and people looked out of the windows of the whitewashed adobe buildings that surrounded it. Half a dozen dogs ran around the outside of the crowd, barking.

"Dead," he wheezed. "All . . . dead." Then he toppled out of his saddle.

Strong arms caught him and lowered him gently to the ground. "What did he say?" Misa's voice was right next to his ear.

Konzin kept still and tried to look near death.

No one answered her for a moment. Then one of the hands muttered, "I think he said 'all dead.' "

Hands shook him. "Konzin! Konzin! Wake up!"

"Fetch the mediciner!" Iano snapped. "Koethe, take the horse into the barn and rub him down. No water or food 'til he's cool. See if there's any way to save him. Zele, Jorsha, help me get Konzin inside."

Men lifted him up, hands carried him. He cried out once when they pressed against his ribs—then faked delirium. Well Bull, the Derkinoi bandit he'd told to beat him, had been too vigorous, and Konzin suspected several of his ribs were, at the very least, cracked.

The Grenlaarins and their workers settled him onto a soft bed, and someone began removing his filthy, stinking clothes and mopping away the blood and grime. He enjoyed the feel of the warm, soapy water—and enjoyed hearing the horrified whispers as those who bathed him noted his many bruises and cuts.

One of the house-girls finally whispered, "What d'you

suppose happened?" She sounded young, and he didn't recognize her voice. A new girl, then. When his Derkinoi employees joined him next week, she might make a nice prize for one of them. A nicer prize if she were also pretty. He didn't dare look. Not yet. He was still "unconscious."

Quick, uneven footsteps sounded in the hall, and the whispering stopped. That would be Misa Grenlaarin. The house servants never whispered around her—she didn't approve of gossip. She knew they'd been at it, though, for she snapped, "Quiet, all of you! None of you know what happened, and you've no way of finding out until he comes to."

Someone pinched the back of his hand—hard. He fought not to cry out. He did groan slightly. "Don't kill them," he mumbled, thinking it might be good to start making himself sound like a hero. "Let them go—take me." He groaned again for effect, and lapsed into silence.

"Humph!" Misa's snort was right next to his ear. She must have been the one who pinched him. "He isn't dehydrated," Misa said. "Skin snaps back pretty as anything. Eyeballs aren't sunk in, either. So either he's been managing to get water for himself—though the horse looked like it hadn't had a drop— or this happened recently."

There was a thoughtfulness and a lack of credulity in her voice that Konzin didn't care for at all.

The servant girls sounded like birds who'd just seen a cat. "Just . . . happened?" The girl who asked sounded terrified by the thought. "You mean whoever hurt him might be near?"

Konzin liked her. *She* believed.

"Now that I think about it, no. This happened days ago." Misa's voice was crisp and certain. "Those bruises are not new. You see how the edges are yellow and green?"

"Yes."

"That's a sign they're healing. Takes a couple days for a bruise to start to heal and fade. So why, in a ride of at least that length of time, did he obtain water for himself but none for his horse?" There was a long silence, while the hands kept on washing him.

Suddenly Misa added, "Also, his injuries don't look very bad. So if he's managed to get enough water, and if he isn't very badly hurt, why isn't he awake now?"

The question chilled Konzin. Misa wasn't reacting at all as he'd expected. He'd planned on listening to her wail and tear her hair, hearing her mourn the loss of her only child. He'd expected both himself and his story to be accepted at face value.

She was being far too rational. And she was noticing things he hadn't intended anyone to notice—she was, in fact, noticing things he hadn't realized anyone *could*.

Konzin heard running footsteps, and a door opened, then slammed.

"Halloo! Where are you?"

Konzin recognized the mediciner's voice.

"Came fast as I heard. You have an injury? Trampling? Something like—" The mediciner's voice stopped. "Good gods have mercy, looks like the whole herd ran over him."

He felt another set of hands, these colder and less gentle, begin to poke and prod at him.

"Healer Fenaulda, he rode into the paddock just some bit ago," Misa said, "collapsed off his horse, and hasn't said a word of sense since then. He's muttered a bit, and cried out once or twice, but nothing to mean anything. And I can't find any injuries so big or so bad he shouldn't be awake."

The mediciner's hands began pressing and worrying at his skull. "The bruises are all old," she said. "I can find no lumps on the skull, and no holes or depressions. Cuts are all shallow and healing—" She lifted one eyelid, and for an instant he and she were looking right at each other. Then he rolled his eyes back.

"Hmmm," she said. She lifted one of his arms and wiggled it a bit. He kept it limp. She moved it over his face, still wiggling and twisting.

"No resistance," she said. She seemed to be talking mostly

to herself. She abruptly dropped his hand, but he'd been expecting something like that. He let it flop naturally to his side, thinking angrily that if he hadn't been fast as he was, she would have hit him in the face with it.

"Hmmm," she said again. "Interesting . . ."

There followed a long and excruciating silence, during which Konzin yearned to open his eyes so he could see what was going on. Then the mediciner's hands moved to his chest and pushed along the ribs with painful vigor. "Let me see. Ribs are tight," she jammed the edge of her hand into his belly, "belly's soft," she squeezed his balls so hard he nearly levitated off the bed, "testicles aren't swollen—though you would think somebody beat him up this bad, they would have taken a swing or two at those."

They didn't need to, Konzin thought. *You're going to do it for them.*

The mediciner sighed. "Get me a stack of pillows and a horse-piller."

A horse-piller? he thought, horrified. He'd used the piller plenty of times to medicate sick horses. It was a hollow tube as long as his arm and nearly as big around. *By the gods, what's she going to do with that?* he wondered. *Jam it down my throat and shove medicine through it?*

Apparently he wasn't the only one who wondered. "What do you need the piller for?" Misa asked. "Surely you don't want to give medicine to an unconscious man. He'll choke, won't he?"

I'll choke, Konzin thought. *I'll definitely choke.*

"Not going to stick it down his throat," the mediciner said. "I think I know why he's unconscious. I think he has a terminal knot in his lower bowel. Sometimes people who have been badly beaten develop one. The last sign before death is persistent unconsciousness."

There was a long pause. Then Misa said, "Oooooh. Terminal knot. I think I've heard of that. It's supposed to be a terrible way to die."

"Horrible," the mediciner agreed. "Gruesome."

Konzin began to feel some concern. What if the beating Well Bull had given him had caused this "terminal knot," whatever that was? It would be beyond irony to have bribed the Lord Colonel to hold his press in Karah's inn, to have hired the thugs to kill the hands and beat him up so he could get the ranch—and then to die because the idiot beat him too hard.

And what did the mediciner intend to do with a horse-piller to fix terminal bowel?

Then he realized he wasn't unconscious—so he was probably fine. And whatever Healer Fenaulda intended to do with the piller, he didn't need it done.

"I've got the piller," one of the girls called.

"Good. Help me roll him over in the pillows, with his butt in the air."

He didn't like the sound of that.

Misa asked, "What are you going to do?"

Konzin felt keen interest in hearing the answer to that question.

"I'm going to shove the piller up his arse and see if I can straighten out the knot."

Konzin decided it was probably time for him to wake up. He began to groan loudly.

"Terrible, terrible. Roll him over quick," the mediciner said. "He sounds like he's dying even now."

The house-girls grabbed Konzin and flipped him before he could think of a way to stop them.

He rolled back onto his back. "Where am I?" he murmured.

"Oh, he's waking up!" one of the house-girls cried. "He's getting better."

Good girl. Quick of you to notice. I'm waking up, so I certainly won't need the horse-piller.

"He's delirious!" the mediciner shouted. "That's end stage. If we don't straighten his bowel, he'll be dead in five minutes."

If you do straighten my bowel, I'll kill you, Konzin thought. He opened his eyes and stared around the room with an expression he hoped would make the mediciner understand his confusion was rapidly fading. "I know where I am . . . I'm at the Grenlaarin ranch," he wheezed. "By the Three, how did I get here?"

"I'd like to know the same thing," Misa said. Her dark eyes glittered.

Beside her, the mediciner, a tall, thin woman with blunt-cut blonde hair and a menacing expression, smacked the palm of one hand with the horse-piller. The tube looked twice as big as Konzin had remembered. He blinked and swallowed nervously.

The mediciner said, "I'm still concerned. He's got memory lapses and the gods only know what all else. I'm afraid if we don't go ahead and straighten that bowel, he'll relapse and die first thing when we aren't looking."

The woman's mind was nailed to that bedamned horse-piller, Konzin decided. Absolutely nailed to it. "I'm beginning to remember things," he said.

The mediciner cocked an eyebrow at him and remarked drily, "I'm sure you are. Why don't you tell us what you remember, and we'll see whether your recovery is good enough that you can skip treatment."

So Konzin told them his tale of heroism and woe—of how bandits attacked the ranch hands on their way home from the city, of how they killed Brunnai and the rest, except for him and Karah; of how he had fought valiantly to save them, but to no avail. And of how the bandits had robbed Karah of her hard-earned money. "Twenty-two hundred forty-six crowns," he said. That amount would be on record at Bemmah and Daughters of Derkin. He made sure he told it to them correctly.

Partway through the story, Iano and several of the ranch hands came into the room. The expressions on their faces were identical—and grim.

Konzin finished his story by telling them how the bandits had killed Karah, and left him for dead as well.

Konzin's audience listened quietly. When he was done, Iano Grenlaarin said, "So they robbed the lot of you of every piece of silver you had, and killed my Karah . . . and thought they'd killed you, too."

"Well, none of us had any silver. I had a few coppers, and Karah had the draft—well, perhaps a crown or two of her own money. I suppose the other hands had coppers, but nothing much. But the bandits took the draft, and . . ." He hung his head and let a tear run down his cheek. "And yes, they . . . they killed Karah. I wish it had been me."

"So do I," Iano said. "Especially since you had eleven hundred twenty-three crowns silver hidden in a carved hole in your saddle tree. We found it when we were checking your horse."

Konzin could feel the blood drain from his face. The room started to spin for real, and only the look in the mediciner's eye kept him from fainting.

Iano continued. "We'll have to send a messenger to let Jawain know what has happened—he has friends in Derkin, and no doubt he'll be able to find out about any robberies or murders on the road from there to here. Meanwhile—" he paused and looked from one burly ranch hand to the other. "Meanwhile, put this animal in the branding stocks. If I find out he's responsible for my daughter's death, I'll do worse than brand him."

"Hey, girl! Out, out! Roust yersel' or y'll have t' swim fer the boat."

Karah rubbed sleep from her eyes and stretched. The air was still hot, but was now wet and sticky as well. She crawled out of the tent into chaos. Every living soul in the camp was striking tents, loading wagons, yelling and shouting and swearing.

How did I sleep through this? she wondered.

She ran to the jakes, dodging people and animals on the way, and when she came out, dodged them again while she looked for Bren.

She found him checking off weapons and armaments from a long list with his sergeant.

"First Captain!" she shouted.

He looked up, annoyance plainly showing on his face. Then he recognized who she was. He handed the ticksheet to the sergeant and walked over to her.

"What did the medic say?"

Medic? she wondered. Then she vaguely remembered he'd instructed her to go to the infirmary when she woke. She'd forgotten.

"I haven't been yet. I just woke—but I'm fine. I won't need to go to the infirmary—"

"That was an order," he snapped. "Not a request. I need to know if what you have is contagious. The priest says it isn't malign magic, so maybe it's medical. I can't have all my troops glowing in the dark when we get to Tarin Tseld—that would be a hell of a thing, wouldn't it? Try to get into position around an enemy encampment while we were all lit up looking like the Child's Festival of Lights."

"I guarantee you this isn't contagious. Besides, I'm not glowing now—and I'm not going to Tarin Tseld. I have duties and obligations at home—duties to my *family*. Maybe you don't know about family, First Captain Morkaarin. Maybe family doesn't matter to *Morkaarins*—but it does to Grenlaarins."

His face flushed dull red and he glared at her. "Go . . . to . . . the . . . infirmary . . ." he said. "Right . . . now . . ."

Karah crossed her arms and stuck out her chin. "We're going to settle this."

Bren's voice went soft and sweet. "You're going to end up spending the rest of your natural life in the stockade, sore from a flogging, Grenlaarin or not," he said, and smiled gently. "If I don't decide to court-martial and hang you for insubordination."

Karah stared at him, shocked into silence. The Grenlaarin name had always opened doors for her. She'd never really *tried* to take advantage of who she was. She'd always known she could—and because she was of one of the oldest and most respected of Tykissian families, she had been careful of the feelings of those whose bloodlines were not so old or so good. But she realized suddenly that the majority of her compassion for the less fortunate came from knowing she didn't have to be compassionate if she didn't want to be. She'd always simply assumed if she really wanted something, she'd get it. Because she'd earned it, preferably, but because of who she was, if necessary.

The First Captain's eyes showed no hint of doubt, no uncertainty about who would come out the winner in a confrontation between the two of them. *If my parents were here, with horses and money and the weight of the old families of Tykis behind them . . .* she thought, and stopped herself. This time, she was on her own, and the First Captain had the weight of the Tykissian Imperial Army behind *him.*

She turned without another word and walked toward the infirmary. For the first time she began to believe she might not get out of her predicament—that her parents might not arrive in time to cut her loose from the army's ties. She considered the implications of that as she walked down the hill through the dust and dry grass.

Tarin Tseld. The foreign sounds were interesting. She'd never been on a ship. She'd never gone much of anywhere. If she had to go, it might be interesting to see far-off lands and strange people. War—that was not such a fine idea, but she would be a scout. She would ride her horse, and sneak in and out of places. She wouldn't have to do any real fighting unless she got caught.

She'd just be sure she didn't get caught, then.

And on the day she got an opportunity to beat the hide off First Captain Morkaarin, she would be sure to take advantage of it.

She entered the infirmary. Several men and women lay on the cots in the small front room. Karah thought none of them looked particularly ill. *Shirking,* she thought uncharitably, and then winced. That seemed an opinion she'd be better off keeping to herself.

A plump young woman in mediciner's garb but with sergeant's piping on the seams stepped out of the back room and snarled, "What do you want?"

Not a thing, Karah thought, and was grateful she could blame the visit on her commander. "First Captain Morkaarin sent me here. Said he wanted to be sure I wasn't contagious."

"What are your symptoms?"

"I feel fine," Karah said. She looked down at her arms and legs, and realized her opportunity to get her revenge on First Captain Morkaarin had just arrived. "First Captain said he wanted to make sure glowing in the dark wasn't contagious."

The woman stared at her. "You jest."

"No, sergeant. Told me if I didn't come right down here, he'd throw me in the stockade for insubordination."

The sergeant eyed her narrowly. "Did he?" She snorted. "Turn around."

Karah turned.

"Can't see a thing. C'mon back here. Not dark enough in that front room t' tell."

Karah followed her back, and when the sergeant closed the door to the inner room and pulled the shutters, stood patiently in the darkness.

"You don't glow in the dark."

"No, sergeant. I don't."

"Hmph. First Captain Morkaarin, you say?"

"Yes, ma'am. XIXth Regiment."

The mediciner shoved the shutters open again, and said, "You're fine. Get back to work. And . . ." She grabbed a scrap of paper off her desk and scribbled a note on it. "You read?"

"Yes, ma'am."

"Well, don't. Give this to First Captain Morkaarin before you get back to work."

Karah kept her smile inside, and accepted the folded scrap of paper. "Yes, ma'am."

She left, and carried the note to Morkaarin.

"What the medic say?"

"Said I'm fine and I should get to work."

The First Captain wiped sweat off his forehead with the back of a hand and squinted at the horizon. Small fleecy clouds were blowing in from the south—and the breeze was wet and sticky. Karah guessed he was suspecting a storm in the next few days. That was what she would have worried about.

"Damnall," he muttered. He looked back at her. "Fine. Get to work. Strike your tent, pack your gear, then get with your horses and get ready to move out. We don't get out of the harbor and around it fast, we're likely to end up in the middle of a damn storm."

"Yes, sir," Karah said. She started to turn away, then, as if it were an afterthought instead of the revenge it was, turned back and handed him the medic's note. "Mediciner told me to give this to you."

The First Captain took the paper. "What is it?"

"Don't know, *sir*. She told me not to read it."

He looked at the paper thoughtfully, then said, "Fine. Go on."

Karah walked back to her tent—but watched from the corner of her eye.

The First Captain read the note, and his face turned the same shade of red it had earlier. He ripped the note into shreds, and dropped the shreds, then ground them into the dust with his boot. The whole time, he swore. Then he gave a sharp order to his sergeant, and stomped off toward the infirmary, every line of his body speaking his rage.

Karah watched him with satisfaction. When he vanished into the infirmary, she went about the business of getting ready to ship out.

❖   ❖   ❖

"So Gonstad hates you, too, hey?" Bren Morkaarin asked, studying the orders. "Or did you look sideways at the Grand Admiral?"

"Willek?" Chevays said with feigned innocence.

"The same."

"Not that I know of, sir."

The First Captain chuckled and said, "Well, I guarantee you did something wrong somewhere." For a moment his expression was serious and bleak. "At least this will give us *one* trained soldier in that troop."

Chevays studied him behind an expression of blandly obedient enthusiasm. The First Captain's face was nowhere near as memorable as Eowlie's; he might have been any minor nobleman from the central provinces, with an ox-strong look about him. A fast heavy man, from the way he moved. Very skilled, from what had happened to the unlamented Valwer Tornsaarin. But he was the man in the image box.

Two down, the assassin thought, *and a sign from the gods that I'm on the right track.*

The right track can be disgustingly long, he thought a few hours later.

"Heave."

Chevays heaved. The box thudded down on the wagon bed beside all the others.

"What's *in* there — lead?" he asked.

"That's right, trooper, lead," the sergeant said. "Ingots fer bullets."

Not for the first time, Chevays reflected that while the gods seemed to enjoy inflicting pain, they had no sense of finesse. His cover required him to play common soldier, and play it he would, even though it was like being on the wrong side of the bars in the monkey cage at the Imperial menagerie.

The wagon creaked away. The rest of the Scout troop were rolling their tents and packing their personal kits, rather more than most soldiers would have, since they were mounted.

Soldiers, or imitations thereof, Chevays thought. He'd heard the two team leaders didn't like each other, that the majority of the unit consisted of whores who'd gotten the assignment because they knew how to ride horses—that information given with a snickered aside about the other things they knew how to ride—and that there wasn't a single soldier in the Scouts who'd ever been in the field.

So the question becomes, he thought, *am I here to find these people, or am I here because Willek decided having me find these people would be a good way to get rid of me?*

Paranoia was a part of his business. Killers who failed to be sufficiently paranoid died young.

The easy solution would be to kill his targets and get out of the unit. Give Willek some story to explain his taking them out before notifying her.

No. He couldn't. He didn't know why, but when he thought of murdering them, his entire body locked up, and he almost couldn't breathe. Odd response for him. He was capable of thinking about his response rationally—capable of reminding himself that he liked killing people. But the killing . . . no. No. That he simply couldn't consider.

"Hey, you!" Someone jammed an elbow in his back and shouted, "Don't stand in the way, stufid donkey! We have to ve out of here vefore the tide goes."

He spun, ready to rip apart whoever had hit him—

—and found himself face to face with *her*. Eowlie. She glared at him. He noted her claws sliding in and out of their sheaths. She'd drawn her lips back to bare her fangs, and he noticed the upper ones were nearly as long as his thumb. Fear thrilled down his spine, and with it the sense of challenge she posed. He could conquer her, he thought. And he would. Willek would wait for her news.

He realized he was standing in the path, staring at her, grinning like an idiot.

And he realized, too, that she was studying him, her

expression that of a hunter who has crossed paths with a beast it doesn't recognize, and is trying to decide if the animal is, or is not, prey.

Goose bumps rose on his arms, and his grin spread broader. His heart raced. She scared him and excited him. She would be a hell of a ride. If he survived.

He stepped out of her way and watched her pass.

"Yes," he whispered as she carried her load past. "You're mine."

☉ CHAPTER VIII

The Imperial fleet was huge, large enough that it could only leave the harbors of Derkin in waves; the army embarking was large enough that much of it had to wait outside the walls, to leave the roads free enough for movement. The XIXth had spent most of the night sitting around on a hillside overlooking the twin round basins with their narrow exits to the sea. The scouts and their horses stayed together, off to one side, while the rest of the XIXth spread out over a part of the hill. Everyone was in full kit, and the corselet rubbed Karah in unfamiliar places; while it had certainly been made for a woman, it seemed to have been made for a flat-chested one with slightly narrower shoulders. She shifted again, and Glorylad rested his head on her shoulder and blew into her ear.

"I'm tired of waiting, too," she said.

One of the Shillrakis—Borte—laughed, then went back to playing mumblety-peg with her sister and Doe, the ludicrously misnamed Tseldene. Doe had blossomed surprisingly, considering that she'd been a slave all her life—from what she'd said, all women were slaves over the sea in Tarin Tseld. That made Karah glad the army was moving to crush the last remnant of the Old Empire—An Tiram had been a capital city for ten thousand years—although not so glad she had to take part in it herself. The Tykissians had fought their way south over the North Shield Mountains, and farther south to the Imperial Sea; most of the wars had been victorious, but none of them were easy. As Pa said, you could get killed just as dead winning. . . .

The sun reached rose-red fingers in the west, framed by the three moons. Shadows moved through the streets and squares of Derkin, and lit the edge of the harbor and the forest of masts. Morning mist lay on the water, and for long moments the ships seemed to float disembodied on a sea of cloud. Then sunlight struck fire from the bronze caps on the masts of the galleys from Old Tykis which made up the first division, anchored furthest out.

The lean hulls were painted red and black down to their copper-clad bellies, the tall prows carved in fearsome shapes. Some of the ships bore the Father's savage falcon head, some the Mother with her fangs gleaming, and some the image of the Wolf-Child, snarling. The steel-clad ramming spikes gleamed in the sun, and light bronze cannon peered over the bows. Three banks of oar ports lined the sides of each ship— Tykissians had been pirates before they became conquerors, and they built their fleet for speed and agility . . . and piracy, still. Karah had listened to her mother's tales of her fierce ancestors and their raids up and down the coast from the time she was a babe in arms. She felt a swell of pride, watching those lean, ferocious ships. *The finest ships on the sea,* she thought, *and my people built them.*

Gold and silver flashed as priests on each foredeck made the morning sacrifice; the tubular bells and long horns called across the waters and echoed from walls and hills. Karah lifted her hands palm-up and prayed with them, hearing other voices around her echoing the chant.

Most of the Imperial ships were less awesome, built to an ancient pattern common to the southern sea. They were as round-bellied as pregnant women, and relied entirely on their sails and rudders for maneuvering. They had no banks of oars, no dire godheads on their prows. Instead, they wore fanciful carved knots and vines, or fish and sea serpents—but even the sea serpents, to Karah's eyes, did not look particularly fierce. And the colors! Why, she wondered, would anyone paint a single ship in tiny squares of orange and yellow and purple and green—much less paint a whole fleet that way? True, they had a few cannon on deck, while the Old Tykis ships did not, and each of the Imperial greatships carried a boarding bridge on the foredeck—but to Karah's eyes, the southern ships looked threatening as flower-bedecked children at Festival would, were their parents to hand them play muskets.

"The greatships will be used for transporting land troops and supplies," Amourgin said when she asked. "They have more storage space in the hulls. The Navy uses the Tykissian ships for itself—they're warships. The best. But they don't have big cargo holds. A fleet has to have caravels and carracks as well as galleys and corvettes."

Further out in the harbor were vessels that looked like a compromise between galleys and greatships—sailing ships, but longer and leaner, without the high forecastles and a sterncastle only one deck high. Gunports showed along their sides, sometimes as many as ten a side. Those were the race-built frigates, the newest and deadliest ships in the Fleet. Most bore the daggertooth-skull emblem of the Imperial family, but some carried flags that read ITESC—Imperial Tykissian Eastern Seas Company, the great guild who managed the new colonies in far Melcan and traded even further. Karah looked at them avidly; they sailed for far lands, exotic peoples—well, like Eowlie—wealth beyond dreams, adventure. Although right now they'd be convoying the fleet south to Tarin Tseld.

Glorylad whickered and pranced, and Windrush nudged Karah's leg and whinnied. The horses were impatient to get going, to do something, and Karah, now that she knew she wasn't going to get out of service, was impatient, too. She hated waiting.

The first Tykissian ships were already lifting anchor and gliding to the mouth of the harbor, oars dipping and pulling in rhythm, the spray that flew off them flashing in the sun. They flanked a bevy of the tublike Imperial transports, whose red-and-white-striped mainsails bellied out in the breeze.

Pretty, she thought. *Even for what it is, it's a very pretty scene.*

She glanced around to see what the rest of the troops were doing. The main part of the XIXth sat on the grassy knoll, their pikes and muskets and halberds tented in pyramids. Some of the new recruits nervously sharpened weapons or checked their gear; the veterans pulled their hats down over their heads and slept, or were involved in several card games and a vigorous round of dicing. Nearby, Eowlie had just caught some small animal that had crossed her path and was eating it. Karah looked away the instant she realized the animal was still alive.

Over with the gamblers, that nasty pimp whispered something to one of the pikewomen. The woman stared at First Captain Morkaarin, her expression shocked. Karah wondered what Zeemos could find to say that any woman would be willing to listen to.

Amourgin noticed the direction of her gaze, and after a moment, leaned over and told Karah, "Every time I've seen that bastard today, he's been whispering to someone. I don't trust him."

Karah shrugged. "At least he's not our problem."

"No. He isn't. But we have more than enough other problems." Amourgin had been watching the sailing ships, and frowning. "This scout unit is completely untrained. Yet we're supposed to advance into enemy territory and note positions and strengths." He sighed and leaned forward to rest his arms across his saddle horn. "I suspect we've been had."

"Had?" Karah was worried about the XIXth scouts' readiness, too, but she'd tried hard not to think about it.

He sat up again, and held out a hand, three fingers outspread. "Either we're a decoy," he pushed down one finger, "or a sacrifice," he pushed down another, "or the person in charge is stupid beyond belief." He pushed down the third finger, then shook his head. "But Willek isn't stupid—I know it for fact. So you can discount that last."

Karah twisted her fingers through Glorylad's mane. "I don't want to be anybody's decoy, or anybody's sacrifice."

He grinned at her. "And I do? No. I don't, either. But that doesn't change the facts." He was still watching the movement of the troops loading ships, and being loaded themselves. "Best of the ships have already moved out," he noted. "You see that. Older and smaller ships coming to the docks now. If you've been watching, you can figure out the order in which they'll reach the loading docks. And if you look at the army, you can see the order in which we'll load. You see what I mean?"

Now that he'd pointed it out to her, Karah could see exactly what he meant.

"Looks like we're to be last aboard," she said.

"It does," he agreed. "And you see our ship?"

The last ship in line for the end dock barely deserved to be called a ship. It was built in a style Karah didn't recognize, resembling neither the Tykissian nor the southron ships in the fleet. It was tiny in comparison to the warships, and looked battered and old; there were only two masts. The miserable handful of cannon on its deck were made of iron bars welded together—and even a country girl from the backwoods knew those were obsolete.

"What sort of ship is that?" she asked.

"It's a Shillraki fishing tub, the sort that goes out with a bunch of dories and salts down their catch. Commandeered for war service."

She and Amourgin exchanged glances. "It seems somebody doesn't like us," she muttered.

Amourgin coughed and said in a low voice, "Still, I've had . . . dreams . . . yes, I suppose that's what you would call them . . ." He looked down at the tiny ship and shook his head. "No matter what it looks like, I believe we'll reach An Tiram. I just don't think we'll like what we find when we get there."

"Dreams," Karah said. She tugged absently on her braid

and said, "I'd forgotten—but you got a seawater bath the same night I did."

He stared at her. "Seawater bath?"

She nodded. "Sort of a — a ghostly experience."

The law-speaker went pale. "You met them, too?"

She moved closer to Amourgin and leaned over so she could drop her voice to near inaudibility. "I've seen the living dead," she said, "and some god in a jungle, and an old man with blind white eyes—although sometimes he acts as if he can see perfectly well. . . ." She twisted the braid, and rolled one strip of leather between her thumb and forefinger. She wasn't sure if she dared tell Amourgin—but there wasn't anybody else she could tell.

"And last night," she said at last, "the crazy old man threw me into a lake of fire, and when I swam out, I saw the Three, chained to the rock. I tried to free them, but I couldn't."

Amourgin looked down at the ship, now only one place away from the berth and the dock. "I spent last night in the lake of fire as well," he said softly, "but I couldn't get out."

"MO-O-O-O-OVE on down the hill!" Sergeant Ddrad bellowed. "Outta here, y' lazy bums! Pick those feet up, up, pick 'em up!"

Karah mounted and fell into line, and Amourgin trotted Broucher behind her. They couldn't talk anymore, and she wished they could. He'd felt the lake of fire, and she wondered if he, too, had glowed when he awoke.

I believe we'll reach An Tiram, he'd said. *I just don't think we'll like what we find when we get there.*

Karah, too, believed she would arrive in An Tiram. She thought of the realms of the drowned, unresting dead and wondered if she would still be alive.

Darkist sought out the solitude of the Quiet Room, and sent the sycophants on their way outside the door. His anger burned like poison in his belly. Both concubines—*both* of them—had been full of vile omens. He could no longer deny the future; his plotting and planning had hatched forth a monster that was stalking him.

He pressed his face against the smooth stone of the One in Cleverness and prayed for the mirror of time.

All my plans, he thought. *All my many years, and all my plans—they could come to an end for this.*

He wanted to live forever. That was not such a terrible thing—to want to see the sun come up every day, to want to know that it would never come up without him. Nine hundred years he'd lived, in a succession of bodies—and nine hundred years he'd grown and learned. He was no fool, who took his time for granted. He knew the worth of a minute, and the price of life.

And if he wanted greatness, he thought, what of that? It was the due of a man who had learned to beat death. Or at least the due of a man who had learned to cheat it and postpone it.

He could not be sure, right then, that he would beat it after all. He felt very old, and very weak, and very tired. And his bones hurt; fingers and hips and back, knees and wrists and knuckles. The ends of his bones creaked and ground against each other when he moved, and ached when he didn't, so that, these last few years, he could find no respite from pain and no peace.

In spite of that, he wanted to live forever.

One willing, he would.

"Show me," he whispered to the carved stone. "Show me where my plans have failed."

An icy breeze blew through the grotto from nowhere, then died, and the sound of running water grew louder. Darkist broke off his embrace of the Clever One. The perpetual glow of the Quiet Room dimmed, as if a cloud had enveloped the light, and indeed, the first tendrils of dark, creeping smoke slid along the floor.

As you will, then, voices whispered in his head. *Here is the future . . . for a price.*

And out of the spring water that ran down the stone wall, scenes grew. Darkist saw his own ships battling the Tykissian fleet—the fleet of the Tykissian upstarts who'd usurped the name of Empire. The wind was freshening, setting whitecaps across the wine-purple sea.

He almost laughed with glee as the long iron-shod beak of a Tseldene galley rammed into the side of a northern tub. Gun smoke hid the scene for an instant; when it cleared the boarding ramps were down, and warriors in the fluted helmets and scale armor of An Tiram poured onto the northern ship's deck. All around warships were ramming and boarding, broadsides crashed out, powder smoke drifted like fog. Burning ships littered the waters, wreckage, spars and planks and chests, barrels and men . . . Off in the distance he could see the mountainous outline of the island of Meltroon, its peaks shadowed with storm clouds the color of bruises. One Tykissian ship after another was sunken, taken—

And from where nothing should have been—enemy ships appeared, frigates under full sail. Half of Willek's fleet had circled round, and flanked him. He hissed with frustration. The storm he created to devour her moved off, unaccountably chasing after something he could not make out.

"Not right," he snarled. "This is not as it should be. Have you deserted me, then, for these heretics?" he demanded of the Cold One. "Is it your will that my fleet be trampled, and my power crushed? Shall not their beast-god Three be at last put down? I demand an answer."

He heard—he felt—the god laugh, and he shivered, remembering perhaps a moment too late that wise men did not demand answers from gods.

And yet the Cold One humored him. In the crawling images on the wall, Darkist saw a demon step out of a mist, a nightmare built of wind and rage and smoke, that inhaled the sea as a man would inhale air, that stormed across the water to the place where Willek's fleet lay anchored. Counterspells and dismissals burst and popped in futility from the demon's shield of power. Willek's people were effecting repairs, and Darkist watched with unabashed delight as the fiend destroyed her fleet and her soldiers—and finally her.

"Yes," he whispered. "This is what I long for. This is the thing I wish to make happen. How, Mighty One? How do I acquire this demon and bring Willek's destruction to pass?"

And again the Cold One laughed and showed him its desired sacrifice.

Darkist whimpered. It was the way of the dark gods, he knew, to demand those things which were most loved in exchange for their favors. Yet that which the Cold One now asked, Darkist simply could not give. "Ask of me anything else, Beloved, and anything else, even though it is all I have, I will gladly give. All of my concubines I will offer up or all of my riches from my treasure house—but . . ."

He felt the Cold One's amusement at the dilemma it had presented him. It asked for Darkist's immortality, in the shape of his grandson Colchob. If Darkist gave the god Colchob as it requested, and Darkist's body wore out before he could bring another grandchild to readiness, he would die. Certainly this would not be any matter of grief for the god, but Darkist didn't like the idea very much.

The timing was bad, he thought. He'd given others of his lineage to the Cold One . . . but never, never so near the time when he needed them.

Perhaps He of the Thousand Faces tires of my worship, and wishes another to take my place, he thought. *Perhaps the One plots to destroy me, as my own people plot. Perhaps. But I need not fall into its schemes. I do not have to become its pawn.*

Darkist walked away from the tinkling waters of the spring, and from the lovely promise of the demon that would destroy Willek and her Northland fleet. He returned to the Clever One, and pressed his forehead against its cold stone chest. Softly, he said, "Changeable One, All-Knowing, I will bring you sacrifices suitable for the raising of a demon such as this, sacrifices a thousand times more magnificent than my single, lowly grandson. I will give you lords and concubines. I will give you satraps and viziers, dancing girls and princesses. All of these I will give you to feed your demon, but my grandson I will keep. He is of little significance, unlovely and foolish, and not sufficient when I have better to give."

The god chuckled—a subterranean rumble that shook the grotto. It did not tell the Yentror of Tarin Tseld what it thought of his plan. It answered neither "yea" nor "nay," leaving Darkist to think what he would.

Darkist left the grotto an unhappy man. His sacrifices would be wonderful, and he felt sure he could conjure up a demon like the One of the Thousand Faces had shown him. He wondered how the One would respond to a sacrifice other than the one it had requested? Would it be angered? Would it turn against him? He didn't know, couldn't imagine.

And if the One became angry with him, how would his magic stand up against the blows of a god?

"*Cavalry* get special transports for their horses," Bren said. "Corporal-probationer," he added.

Karah gave him a murderous glare along with her salute. He felt an impulse to say *and it isn't my fault*! That was impossible, of course; an officer didn't apologize to the lowest-ranking noncom in the rawest auxiliary unit in the regiment. Even when he'd been effectively demoted himself.

Karah turned and led the blindfolded horse up the gangplank. It snorted and whickered and laid back its ears, but she kept it under control with a firm, gentle hand on the bridle and a steady murmuring. Judging by the sounds coming from further down the dock where the bigger ships were loading cavalry and guns, the horsed units were not faring nearly so easily—*their* mounts were going on board hog-tied and hoisted by cranes. Doubtless they'd lose a fair number from broken bones, panic and the general cursed inclination of horses to die at the least excuse. Armies in the field left a trail of dead mounts; if a campaign lasted long enough, the cavalry would end up mostly on foot.

Karah Grenlaarin had gotten all of theirs into the pen on the foredeck without incident, so far. They'd even managed to back them down the ramp through the hatchway into the hold. . . .

I like that girl, Bren decided. A bit of a hell-bitch for temper, but one had to make allowances. She'd been irregularly pressed, after all—and her birth was good, too good for her rank. She had guts, too, and knew horses; even the tantrum just now had been for the beasts' sake, not her own. If she lived through the first few months, she'd make a soldier.

Besides that, she was pretty. Not court-smooth, but she had a bright, open-air, healthy look—not fussed over.

The transport's captain came up. Bren put on his helmet and raised a brow. "Is the *Sea Mare* ready?" he said. The name was freshly painted on the bow; that and the tar covering her sides were the only new things about the fisher-turned-transport.

"No," the seaman replied. He was slender and weathered, with a receding hairline, in the blue jacket and knee breeches of an Imperial Navy officer. The captain's trident embroidered on the shoulders looked much newer than the garment, but the cutlass at his side had seen use.

His voice was bitter as he went on: "*Sea Mare?* She's a fucking *sow.* Sir. Whatever the Treasury paid for her, they were cheated. And all I've got is a scratch crew of pressed fishermen and wharf rats—only my master-gunner is Navy, him and my first mate, and the bosun, and *she's* recalled from reserve. We need another two weeks to get this wallowing tub in shape!"

"Will she sink?" Bren asked patiently.

"Maybe and maybe not; it depends on how bad the shipworms have eaten out the hull planking—it's a race between them and dry rot. Nobody's ever wasted copper sheathing on *this.*"

The naval officer walked down the wharf. "*Look* at this," he said, drawing a dagger. He probed several times at the tar-black planking, then pushed lightly. The weapon sank half its length into the spongy timbers. "Wolf Mother's *tits*, I'm a sea-man, not a magician."

"Do your best," Bren said, clapping him on the shoulder.

The loading trickled down to a halt; a final cargo net full of barrels swung by overhead. Bren walked up the gangplank—it had an unpleasant flex to it, and no side rails—and made his way to the quarterdeck, beside the captain and the two sailors standing to the tall wheel. The captain raised a leather mega-phone:

"Prepare to cast off!"

Bren looked down the deck; most of the two-hundred-odd troops were below, in the cramped and stinking 'tween-decks. The waist around the mainmast and forecastle deck were nearly covered by bundles of deck cargo. Sailors in loincloths scrambled over the crowded deck and swarmed into the rig-ging; the bosun's pipe tweeted, to the accompaniment of curs-ing from the deck officers in the pidgin Tykissian-Derkinoi-Tseldene *lingua franca* of the Imperial Sea. Sailors loosed the heavy ropes from the bollards on the wharf and jumped back on board. Forward and to the left—*starboard*, he reminded himself—a rowing tug waited. It was crewed by shelf-browed jungleman thralls; they were valued for such work, being four or five times stronger than a true human, if stupid. They hooted and snarled as the overseer cracked his whip.

The *Sea Mare* jerked and heeled as the towline came taut. The deck surged beneath Bren's feet; he smiled as he saw Karah lurch and grab for a rope, wide-eyed. She submerged her own alarm in hurrying below to comfort the panicked horses. He squinted against the dazzling brightness of sun on water, like light reflecting off hammered copper. The great arch of Derkin's buildings swung into view as they moved out into the open harbor, white and pastel and blue and pink; sun gleamed on marble and tile further uphill, on the gilded wings that marked the Temple of the Three, on the frowning ramparts of the citadel.

"Set main and spinnaker!" the captain shouted.

Sailors rushed into the rigging, agile as monkeys; they looked fast enough to Bren, but the naval officer cursed them under his breath. Brown patched canvas rose, a big square sail on the mainmast, and a long triangular one between foremast and bowsprit. The cloth boomed and thuttered before the mild offshore breeze took hold.

"Cast off forward! Set the jib!" The towing tug turned back towards the dock; more sailors heaved on a line, and another sail rose from the boom that reached back from the sternmast over the wheel. "Come two points to starboard. *Reef* that mainsail, you lobster-eating lubbers!"

The *Sea Mare* would never be fast, but it began to make way toward the harbor mouth, past the cliff-like walls of the seaforts that guarded Derkin. The mouths of the great bombards were clearly visible, with cheering soldiers of the garrison waving as ship after ship passed out. The ship pitched as she butted into the larger waves where harbor met sea; Bren gripped a line and held up his other hand in salute as the fortress high priest poured incense on coals held in a tripod, sacrificing for the fleet. Father Solmin did the same from the quarterdeck, his face solemn and his movements precise—he might be fond of a tavern and a stein and a good joke, but he took his profession seriously.

A galley went by just outside, boiling along with tall gullwing lateen sails set on all three masts and oars threshing like the legs of a centipede, foam tossing up from her ram. Ships stretched as far as the eye could see, sails white and brown and blue and striped. Fresh salt air blew away the harbor stink of bilges and garbage.

"Under way," the captain said quietly. "Three have mercy."

Admiral Willek Tornsaarin stood on the foredeck of the *Father's Falcon*, the flagship of the fleet. Sunset was near, but all three moons were up tonight—the Three, looking down on the fleet of Their chosen people. There was a comforting familiarity to the rise and pitch of the deck, the long surge as the sharp bow bit into the swells, the muted creak and groan as water, wood and cordage held their eternal conversation.

The *Falcon* was less than two years old, new-built of swamp oak, teak and bogrin; her masts were each a single blanchpine from the Imperial reserves in the mountains above Derkin, nearly two hundred feet high. She was square-rigged forward, with a towering lateen sail over her head on the poopdeck. The planking shone with holystoning, the cordage was neatly coiled, the crew moved crisply to the whistles and shouted orders of the officers and bosuns—if you were going to war at sea, there was no better way to do it. And the *Falcon* was not only fast and seaworthy, she also mounted forty guns. Ten twelve-pounder bronze pieces on each side below on her main gundeck, as many short eight-pounder carronades on deck, a pair of long eighteens forward and aft for chasers.

Willek nodded to herself and brought up her telescope. The stern-lanterns of the fleet spread out before her, ships heading south and west for the eastern coast of Meltroon— the wind was from the northeast this time of year in the central Imperial Sea. The island of Meltroon was held by the New Empire since the last war with Tarin Tseld, in her father's time; it would be safe enough to hold station off its main port. She *knew* Darkist was sending his fleet in a straight push for the island.

That was why most of her frigates were heading for Saldana Point, northernmost cape on Meltroon; to come round southerly, get between the Tseldene fleet and its home port, and give the monstrous old bastard a very unpleasant surprise. He could have the old-style ramming-and-boarding battle he expected—expected her to deliberately lose—and even if he won it, his fleet would be battered and far from home, while hers could fall back to the island's ports and fortifications. Galleys couldn't keep station for long at sea; their huge rowing crews ate too much food and drank too much water, and no amount of whip would make a dead man row. Then her frigates would come in with the wind abaft their beams, to pound Darkist's galleys into matchwood if they stayed, and chase them back to An Tiram if they didn't.

She nodded again. It was an excellent plan—as long as nothing serious went wrong. A breakthrough by Darkist's magicians, for example; the priests of the Three were chanting, drumming, praying and spellcasting right now fit to brew storms. Battlemagic *usually* cancelled out, but you never knew . . . undoubtedly there would be heavy losses.

There were a few losses she even looked forward to. This engagement should see the end of the last of the Morkaarins. The old stain on the Tornsaarin name would fade with his demise, and eventually be forgotten. She'd never met the Morkaarin offspring, nor did she feel any inclination to. She would be satisfied to receive notice of his death.

She felt very good. Chevays had managed to get a brief message to her even in the midst of mobilizing early. He thought he'd located two of her targets, and was closing in on them. Willek was certain, too, that Darkist and his plans were foiled—the buzzard could not expect her to launch early after he'd moved up the schedule by three weeks. She would catch him off guard and annihilate him.

And then she had Shemro. Willek smiled, looking at her Emperor, who sat in a high-backed gilt chair on the poopdeck, wrapped in a blanket and staring out to the dark and restless sea. Shemro IV, the mighty and hereditary ruler of all the Tykissian Empire, was so totally enthralled in Willek's power she couldn't eat or sleep or speak without Willek's leave—and without Willek's suggestion, she forgot she wanted to. Magic courtesy of Darkist, originally, but never mind that.

Willek strode to the back of the ship and knelt on the wooden deck before her sovereign. This was playacting, for the benefit of anyone who might be watching. In private, Willek did not kneel. But here, in public, at the moment when Tykis went to war, she had the age-old ritual to fulfill.

"All is as you have commanded, Lady Liege. The last of the ships have now embarked. I remain at your service."

Her eyes locked with Shemro's, and she made the magical link. Shemro, dull-witted and helpless, spoke in soft flat tones, "Very good, Grand Admiral. Carry on." And then, as Willek silently commanded her to do, she stood, and gave Willek her arm. "Take me to my quarters," she commanded.

"As you will, my liege," Willek said. Inside, she smiled. Shemro was frail and weak, and failing before Willek's eyes. She left no heirs—in place of heirs, she'd already made Willek her successor when the time of her death should come. There were none left of the royal lines, no siblings or cousins or relatives by marriage with a better claim than Willek's to the throne. And any advisors and nobles foolish enough to fight her would die, after she had a victorious war against the ancient enemy to her credit. The mighty line of Strekkhylfa was about to come to an unfortunate end. With only a little outside help.

Willek grinned, thinking about it. She would be Emperor in name as well as fact. She would conquer Tarin Tseld, and eventually Shillrakin and Shborin. She would reclaim Tobor and that lunatic breakaway Nyokese province, and put down the mutterings of rebellion in Old Tykis. And the whole of the known world would bow to her.

And when it did, then she would seek out her sister, who hid in her pinnacle tower, playing little games. When Willek held all the world in her hands, Szoae would be under her power as well. She would make Szoae grovel and beg for her life. As pleasant as killing Shemro would be, destroying Szoae would be even better.

With the helpless Shemro safely stored in her quarters, the Grand Admiral returned to the deck. The sea spray blew in her face, the sails caught the wind, the ships leapt forward, and Willek's heart sang. Everything proceeded in the manner she had decreed. She had reason to rejoice.

✧　　✧　　✧

"Keep your bloody station, can't you, you bathtub of a hulk!"

The escort galley's captain had a strong nasal Old Tykis accent. The scorn in it was clear even through the bullhorn she used to hail the *Sea Mare*.

The transport's commander pulled the knit cap off his head and shook his fist at the warship twenty feet away, keeping level with slow effortless movements of its sweeps.

"No, I can't, you seal-fornicating pirate!" he screamed. "This Shillraki bumboat won't point a quarter into the wind and she's got a skirt of weed longer than the list of your sins!"

Chevays Cöado looked around, swallowing uneasily. The low waist of the ship didn't give much of a view, but he could see that the transports were straggling badly. Hundreds of them dotted the sea, from the horizon where the dark blue of the ocean merged into the lighter color of the sky, to a few hundred yards from his own vessel. The wind was just strong enough to give the ex-fishing craft a nasty twisting, dipping sway; scores of soldiers lined the rail, mostly hanging over it, even three days out from Derkin. Sailors moved around them just as they avoided the piles of crates and tarpaulin-covered baggage that crowded the shabby, stained planking of the deck. Many of them were still working on the rigging, splicing sound rope into weak links, sewing sails, coiling and stowing.

The warship was one of dozens darting around the edges of the swarm, like sheepdogs around a flock. More stood off to either side in ordered squadrons.

"Put on more sail," the naval captain called.

"With this rigging? With these bumwad sails begging for a chance to rip?"

"More sail or we'll leave you for the Tseldenes," the escort's commander said, and the galley turned—almost in its own length, one side's oars sinking deep and the other flashing up free of the water.

Everything Chevays touched left a coating of fish slime or a sheen of fish scales on his hands; he was a fastidious man, in his way, and the sheer misery of it was beginning to fray his temper. The horses were vocally unhappy too; the drumming of their hooves occasionally shook the deck from the pens below.

And I chose to be here, he thought. He began to regret the decision. His quarters, which he shared with a dozen other soldiers, were tiny and dark; at that, he was lucky not to be in the main hold, with the bilges sloshing at his feet—a detail of twenty worked the ship's pumps continuously, to keep up with her leaky seams. The men and women of the XIXth who shared the room with him watched him suspiciously and whispered in his presence. They didn't like him, he decided. They didn't trust him, he knew.

It bothered him a great deal that he had not told Willek precisely where he was going to be. He hadn't wanted her to know where the people she sought were—at least not until he'd decided what he wanted to do with them. Willek was entirely too efficient, and far too likely to decide she wanted them killed immediately.

He couldn't disobey orders he didn't have, he'd thought.

Now he was wishing he hadn't been so clever.

First Captain Morkaarin was in conference with his subordinates on the quarterdeck—no doubt attempting to plan a strategy that might let the XIXth survive, or at least the one-third of it crammed onto this ship. Chevays found himself suddenly sympathetic to the First Captain. He couldn't help but realize his survival depended on whatever clever gambits the man might devise. So any thought of killing him would have to wait until they were all safely ashore and well behind the front lines.

Bored, Chevays had searched out Eowlie, thinking he might find some entertainment with her—but she'd been catching rats and eating them when he found her, grumbling about the fact that she had had nothing live to eat in ages, and the ship was stocked only with salted meat, and she couldn't stand that. Chevays, disgusted, had left her to her own devices.

He didn't play cards, he didn't dice—and as for what he *liked* to do . . . well, there would be none of that for a while.

Chevays sulked up onto the deck. The *Sea Mare* was out of sight of land, limping well behind the rest of the ships sailing west and south. The Lieutenant leaned up against the wooden bulwark and watched the water flash past. He stared over the sea to the south, and noted the odd green haze which spread across the darkness like a glowing bruise. He didn't like the look of that.

The sailors glared at him, chased him out of the way, and Chevays wandered aft.

He heard voices and stopped, keeping himself out of sight.

"H'it won't make a bit of diff'rence," someone snapped. "The First Captain h'is in the pay of that southron fiend, Darkist. He's a traitor! He'll be hanged, an' when he is, who's going to bother wi' you for havin' a bit a fun?"

Chevays heard a second voice, crude and cunning. "Well— if you can get me those two little piebalds . . ."

A sly chuckle. "H'I can. And I'll get you a bargain, too. A mere twenty bronzes, and the sweets from your next two meals."

"That's cheap, all right. They ain't diseased, are they?" The voice was suddenly cautious. "They's no mediciner on this tub— and it may be a long time t' shore."

"My girls h'are all clean!" Indignant, the voice was—and slightly angry. Chevays grinned. The man, whoever he was, was a fair liar.

"Then why so cheap?"

A pause. Then—"Because you're goin' t' advertise fer me . . . and yer goin' t' do it wit'out either of us gettin' caught."

"I see."

You don't see anything, you idiot, Chevays thought. *He has no overhead now, so everything he makes is profit.*

"H'I have that all figgered out. H'all y' have t' do is be there wi' my goodies and yer pecker."

Both men laughed. Chevays arched an eyebrow and smiled slowly. Enterprise would thrive in the damnedest places.

He moved away from their hiding place, head down, deep in thought. He settled himself on the edge of a capstan and played the conversation back—the comment about Morkaarin's ties to Darkist was especially fascinating. Chevays went through the First Captain's thin file before joining the XIXth. Morkaarin was appallingly pure and predictable—Chevays had found no vices, no indiscretions, and no evils in the record at all. In fact, the only thing he discovered of even mild interest was that Morkaarin's family record listed no father, or father's ancestors. His mother had dallied with someone unacceptable, the Lieutenant figured, and ended up with a permanent keepsake from the tryst.

While he found rumors about an alliance between Morkaarin and Darkist intriguing, he also thought them improbable to the point of disbelief. Of more real interest to him was the conviction in the panderer's voice, and the whorejohnnie's willingness to believe.

He wondered where the story came from. He wondered why.

He decided he would follow the rumor back to its source and find out. He had the time.

Unfortunately.

"Put me down! Let me—!"

Bren heard scuffling from the aft deck. Then a yelp. Then a piercing scream.

He raced over the pitching deck, charged into the gutting house, and came face to face with Zeemos, three of the *Sea Mare's* crew, and two of his scouts, the piebalds who had once been Zeemos' whores. The ex-pimp held one of the women tight against his chest. She fought like a fiend, but he was easily three times her size. He'd stuffed a rag in her mouth, but not fast enough to keep her from screaming. The other woman lay on the filthy floor, with a sailor holding her arms behind her head; he had a bleeding nose and knelt on her hands with vindictive force. One of the sailors had been pawing off her clothes when Bren burst in.

They all stopped what they were doing and stared at Bren.

"Let her go," the First Captain told Zeemos. His sword drew small circles in the air between them. "And I'll let you off with a hundred lashes."

Zeemos ignored him. "That's First Captain Morkaarin," he said softly to the sailors. "The traitor I told you about. If we threw him over the side now, Darkist wouldn't know every move we made."

Traitor? Bren wondered. *What madness is this?*

The sailors, all big men, eyed him speculatively. One by one, they began to smile. None of them looked Tykissian, or much of anything else; they were products of the Imperial Sea's waterfronts, cosmopolitan in origin and eclectic in loyalty.

"Throwing him over the side would be a service to the fleet, then, wouldn't it?" one of them said.

A chill ran down Bren's spine. The piebald girl Zeemos held had stopped struggling. Bren could see her looking from one man to the next, while her eyes grew huge and frightened. They'd have to kill any witnesses, too.

"Don't worry," he told her. "They won't try it." He didn't sound frightened at all, he thought. The sword moved, ready. Actually they *had* to try it, now that they'd spoken.

"Get him," Zeemos said.

The sailors dragged long knives out from under their bloused tunics and spread out. One of them sidled toward Bren; he stop-thrust and pinked the man in the arm, sending him backward with a yell.

"Don't let him shout for help," Zeemos warned.

"I only wanted t' futter the bitches," one of the sailors complained. "I wasn't fer throwing an officer off'n the ship."

"If you let him go now," Zeemos said, his voice still calm and gentle, "he'll have you court-martialled and hanged."

"You set us up," the sailor Bren had wounded said. "You planned this all along."

"H'I did *not*." Zeemos fondled the girl he held, and made his expression mournful. "H'it isn't my fault t' traitor ran in here on us. T' stupid bitch screamed. But h'I don't want t' be keelhauled for tryin' t' help you lot out."

The sailors looked at each other, then back at Bren. A moment stretched, then things happened very quickly.

A sailor crouched and came in low, feinting with the long curved knife, his bare, gnarled toes gripping the planks like fingers. Bren's hobnailed boots skittered slightly on the smooth wood as he attacked, and the lunge spitted the sailor's shoulder instead of his neck. It also jammed tight in the bone; the wounded man shrieked and spun, jerking the weapon out of Bren's hand. The officer whirled sideways desperately, spinning out of the way of the gutting stroke of another knife, snatching his own dagger from his belt, horribly conscious that he wasn't wearing his armor. And a knife fight against odds, in this cramped space . . .

Thunk. A sailor folded, falling at the feet of Korgi, the Shillraki piebald; she held up her breeches with her other hand, and began pounding the hardwood stool into the man's face. Bren moved in on the other man, blade of his fighting knife out and his left hand stiffened into a chopping weapon as well. The sailor backed, screamed, threw his knife at Bren and fled. Bren pivoted again, moving with a smooth economy of motion. Zeemos had his hands full; Borte was slamming her head into his face and kicking to some purpose.

Just kill him, Bren decided. It would be tempting to have him flogged to death, but wasteful.

A cannon roared outside, loud enough to startle the combatants in the deckhouse. More echoed across the water from other ships. Zeemos dropped Borte, then screamed as she turned and slammed a fist into his groin.

"Battle stations!" Bren roared, picking Korgi up by the scruff of the neck and pitching her towards the door. "*Move!*"

❂ CHAPTER IX

The horse stalls in the *Sea Mare*'s 'tween-decks were cramped and dark, lit only by a single swaying lantern. Each horse was in a narrow slot with no room to turn around. Karah and Eowlie moved down the row, securing each bridle to two chains running to beams on either side and blindfolding the more skittish horses. Several times she was glad of the leather-and-metal armor she wore—nervous horses *bit*—and there would be a huge bruise on one thigh where a hoof caught her.

"That's all," Eowlie said. The neighs and whickers were full of heart-rending, uncomprehending fear. She hitched at the carbine slung over her back and fiddled with the chin strap of her helmet—the regimental armorer had had to make substantial alterations to make it fit her long skull and unorthodox chin. "Time to go fight the battle."

"Godsall," Karah muttered to herself, as she blew out the lantern. No sense in risking burning oil splattering all over the straw. *Battle*. And on the *sea*, too.

She licked sweat off her upper lip. They clattered up the companionway, past the raw smell of new planking; they'd torn up part of the decking forward of the mainmast to get the horses below, and hadn't it been *fun* getting them to back down the steep slippery thing? Light stabbed into their eyes; Karah noticed Eowlie shade hers for a second. *She sees well in the dark*, the Tykissian thought. *But brightness hurts her.*

So far all Karah could see was water with Imperial ships on it. Dawn was just over, still red and sullen on the clouds to the west. It wasn't the season for rain—rain fell in the winter everywhere around the Imperial Sea—but those certainly looked like rainclouds to her.

More cannon boomed, further out to sea, like rumbling thunder over the prairies of home. Sailors shouted in the rigging above, calling down the news as they close-hauled the sails, cutting back to the minimum needed to keep steerage way on the *Sea Mare*. The wind was freshening, off the land to their west; they were close enough to see the forested mountains of Meltroon and the yellow-and-green checkerboard of wheat and sugarcane along the coastal plain. A city that looked like a pile of whitewashed dice sprawled along the coast directly opposite the fleet.

"Vat did they say?" Eowlie asked, uncertain of the *lingua franca*.

She fiddled a little at the catches of her corselet. Karah thought she knew the reason; if you went over the side in this you'd sink like lead shot. She hunched her own shoulders, checked the arrows in the quiver over her back, and plucked the string of her short, thick horn-backed bow.

"Smoke southeast. More of our galleys heading towards it." Karah paused to listen. "Some coming towards us . . . oh, godsall, Three protect Your children, they're *Tseldenes* and they're coming towards *us*." The *Sea Mare* was with the rearmost of the Imperial fleet, only a squadron of six galleys further north. Karah didn't know why the enemy were lunging at the stragglers, but she didn't claim to be an admiral.

The center of the deck was bulwarked with piled crates of hardtack and barreled meat. The rest of the Scout Troop had finally turned up. . . .

"What happened to *you*?" Karah blurted, looking at the bruise on Korgi's face.

"Zeemos," she said; beside her, Doe growled deep in her throat.

"Ve'll attend to him after this," Eowlie said.

"If we can," Amourgin said.

Karah swallowed again, resisting the impulse to go over to the water barrel for a dipper; she'd already used the head. Getting your pants down while you were strapped into a leather-and-metal corselet was too much of a production, and drinking more water made it inevitable.

She wiped her hands on her pant legs again: "Remember, we're supposed to hold back and shoot up anyone who gets aboard," she said. *Damn. I actually sounded confident.*

Up on the quarterdeck, Bren Morkaarin was talking to the ship's captain and some of the officers; below him the bosuns were handing out cutlasses and axes from the arms chest to the sailors. Soldiers crowded up out of the hold, as many as could fit. They pitched the deck cargo down and then squatted, concealed by the bulwarks from any smaller ship.

Bren looked confident, doing lunge stretches as he spoke to get limbered up. That reminded her.

"Stretch, everybody. Come on, you pop a tendon now and you're dogmeat."

When she got up, puffing, she hopped up onto the barricade around the mast and used the little spyglass Amourgin had owned—it was her day for it. A line of black dots had appeared to the southeast, stretching neatly across the horizon. They grew larger, into model boats with their oars rising and falling beside them like the legs of insects. Lower and a little broader than the Tykissian warships, she'd heard that they used a single bank of oars, but four or five rowers on each. Black-painted hulls trimmed with scarlet and silver; big black-purple lateen sails still up, each with a godmask on it, each different and all insane. The One of A Thousand Faces, demon-god of Tarin Tseld and the Old Empire. That was frightening, but not nearly so bad as the beast-mask castings at the muzzles of the cannon protruding from the bows, or water creaming back from the rams, or the light breaking in silvery glints off the edged weapons of the marines on their decks.

"They're striking sail," Karah said hopefully. The long angled booms of the galleys' sails came down to their decks and were lashed fore and aft.

"Rigging for battle," Amourgin said quietly; his eyes were hard to read behind the reflecting surface of his glasses. Something reached up under Karah's breastbone and squeezed. She could hear a pounding of drums, the *hortator* in each war galley slamming out the beat for the rowers, none of them quite in time with the other vessels. *Tump*tump-tump-tump . . . it speeded up as the sails went down.

The Imperial galleys moved past the *Sea Mare*, backing until they were in line and then lunging southeast. Their formation grew ragged as each picked an opponent from the warships of Tarin Tseld and went to ramming speed. The Tseldene line was double-ranked and much wider; two of the southron galleys curved in toward each of the Tykissians.

Screams brought Karah's head up. Men and women all over the deck of the *Sea Mare* were pointing and crying out.

A figure taller than mountains was striding over the southern horizon, black against the pale blue of the sky. It was clad head to toe in armor of black steel plates that flickered with fire along the edges. At first Karah thought the helmet was fronted by a mask, but then she saw that it changed from instant to instant. An angel's face of luminous chalk-pale beauty; a staring thing with lolling tongue and a boar's tusks; the laughing face of a child whose eyes vomited nests of worms; a woman with the teeth of a dog and the faceted eyes of a wasp. . . .

Someone was retching, and the screams turned mindless. One soldier began hacking at her own hands with a dagger. Another plunged fingers into his eyes. A band of steel was pressing around Karah's head, tighter and tighter until she could feel her own eyes pressing out like bursting-ripe grapes. . . .

A taut string went *snap* behind her eyes and she staggered, moaning with relief, shaking and sweating. Magic was common enough, but miracles and theophany. . . .

"Illusion!" Amourgin was shouting, a little shrill. Bren's voice joined him:

"It's just a sending. Ignore it. The Three are with us!"

She had her doubts about that being an illusion; clouds breasted about the chest of the image like water about a man wading through a river, streaming backward. Waterspouts a hundred feet high gouted upward from each step. It pounded Its steel-shod fists on Its chest, and the sound rang like all the anvils in the universe.

"Fey certainly are the Three, and with us," Eowlie said, her accent thicker. She pointed back the way the fleet had come; the clawed finger shook a little. "If those are them." Karah twisted to look over her shoulder.

The figures striding down from the north were as large as the one to the south; a lion-centaur with the head of a falcon, a woman with a wolf's dugs, a wolf-headed child.

The horizon-high thing to the south threw back Its head and screamed, and the world trembled around Karah. Then It faded, turning ghost-transparent, vanishing. She could feel her mind trying to reject what she had seen, like a dream fading with daylight. The Three vanished also, more sharply. The light seemed to change around them, back to normal, although they hadn't noticed it was different.

Amourgin's lips were moving, as if in prayer. "Just a sending," he repeated, as if reassuring himself. "Manufactured illusion. Our war priests dispelled it. Nothing to worry about."

Karah's eyes dropped from the sky. One of the Tykissian galleys was burning from stem to stern, sending pale flame and black smoke up into the bright morning sky. Another had two Tseldene galleys locked to either side. The remaining four Imperial craft were in a circle with their sterns together while half a dozen Tseldene ships prowled around them like wolves around a buffel herd. As she watched, an Imperial vessel fired its cannon, and the cast-iron shot went skipping over the waves. One plowed into the bow of an enemy ship in a shower of spray and splinters, and the Tseldene fell away to starboard with a list. Three other enemy galleys were sinking, rammed or hulled by cannon shot, but that left *dozens* boiling by the Imperial warships toward the sailing transports.

"I'm worrying," she said hoarsely.

"That mad bitch of a squadron commander had to go haring in, like a curltusker in *musth*," the captain of the *Sea Mare* said bitterly. "Now we're for it."

Bren tapped the point of his sword thoughtfully on the deck between his wide-planted feet. "Where are Willek and the frigates?" he said thoughtfully.

"I didn't ask the Grand Admiral about that part of her strategy, last time we took tea together," the ship's captain said dryly.

"What can we do?" Bren continued, his voice flat. *This was not the time for jokes.*

"Try to avoid getting rammed," the seaman said. "This hull will pop in like a maidenhead before a marlinspike."

Bren winced—it was an unpleasant image—and looked at the approaching galleys. "Can we avoid it?"

"We may. Harder to manage a straight-on ramming run than you'd think, if we've steerage way." The captain looked up at the sky, then checked the pennants flying from mastheads and rigging. "Breeze is freshening and coming round from the northwest. Pray Three send us a storm; we can stand it, those Tseldene rowboats can't; they'd have to run before it or put in and beach."

Bren shook one wrist loose, then the other. "So all we have to do is worry about boarding."

"Or they may throw fire into us—naphtha and sticklime."

The XIXth's officer nodded. "Captain Tagog! Sharpshooters to the mastheads, if you please; keep their lookouts busy. Sergeant Ddrad; troops to keep their heads below the bulwarks, on pain of flogging." It wouldn't do to look *too* formidable. If a Tseldene ship got close enough to throw fire into the *Sea Mare*, he wanted it to look easy enough to board instead.

Forget the rest of the fleet; that wasn't his responsibility. He raised his voice.

"All right, Nineteenth," he said. "We were going south to fight them, and they saved us the trouble by coming to meet us. It'd be poor hospitality to give such eager guests a disappointing reception, wouldn't it?"

A crashing bark mingled with shrill howls—the old Tykissian war shout. A little thready from the newcomers. He wished there'd been more time to train, but if wishes were horses, no field would go without manure.

"Brace for it!"

Karah grabbed again at the rope beside her—sailors had some sort of name for it, but right now she was more concerned with the Tseldene war galleys coming up on either side of the *Sea Mare*. They were longer than the Imperial ship, but lower to the water; half a dozen attempts to ram had failed, and now they were coming in. The quick boom-*boom* of their pacing drums echoed across the narrowing gap of water, along with the massed cannonade and musket fire, flame crackle and shout of the fleets engaged to the south.

"Keep down," she reminded the scouts; Amourgin came in on the heels of her order.

They were all using the piled crates as a breastwork. The deck was covered with crouching musketeers; pikemen were massed at the bulwarks along the sides, their long weapons poised. Forecastle and sterncastle held clumps of halberdiers.

One of the Tseldene galleys fell behind and swerved. The high sterncastle of the *Sea Mare* hid it from Karah, but did nothing to quiet the massive *whump* as its two alligator-mouthed cannon cut loose, firing over the ram.

The ship pitched beneath her feet, and there was a deafening crash of rending timbers. Then the screams began, bone-chilling screams from the 'tween-decks: the sounds of wounded humans, and of horses bugling their terror.

"Rudder!" Amourgin shouted. "They shot away our rudder!"

The other galley came in alongside, disappearing beneath the bulwarks. Oars shot up and the rowers pitched them up and snatched them back into the body of the galley; the sailing ship lurched and checked as the hulls came into contact. Long planks tipped with spikes were slung from the Tseldene's rigging; they swung down and slammed into the *Sea Mare's* railings.

"Fire!" the master gunner shouted.

Along the rail the four little welded-iron guns barked, shooting backward on their four-wheeled carriages until the thick breeching ropes caught them. Karah knew what was flying out the muzzle ends: bags of musket balls, a whirring blast into the enemy ranks. Gunners leaped forward in a ballet of trained motion; a wet sponge to swab out the cannon, a dusty-dry paper sack of gunpowder rammed down with the other end of the pole, then a wad of rope, then another bag of caseshot, then another wad. The primer rammed a wire spike through the touch-hole at the breech to open the powder bag and then poured fine-grained powder into the hole.

"Fire!" The slowmatches in the gunners' linstocks came down again.

"Head up," Eowlie said.

She seemed to have more consciousness of things above and below her than normal people. Karah and the other scouts looked up; men were firing from the standing rigging of the Tseldene galley, bullets wasp-whining down onto the crowded decks of the *Sea Mare*. Musketeers in the crow's nests shot back at them. Other Tseldenes were swinging across on ropes braced to the masts, or scrambling into the Imperial ship's rigging.

Can't have that, Karah thought numbly; her feelings were very distant. She felt cold and hollow—felt all the world had slowed down and grown quiet and slipped away from her. The noises of battle sounded very far away.

She drew a shaft to the ear, estimating distance. Compared to firing from a galloping horse, this wasn't too hard.

"Shoot!" she yelled, and loosed. Her bowstring slapped hard at the leather guard on her left forearm, a familiar and homey sound. This time she wasn't aiming at a target, or a buffel or wolf or leopard.

The arrow seemed to fly slowly, swooping up like a swallow under the eaves of the barn back home on a summer's night, flying after a moth. There was the sense of inevitability that always followed a good shot. Up on the mainsail spar was a man, a dark squat Tseldene, naked save for baggy white trousers and head cloth, his feet gripping the timber with a sailor's agility, two long knives in his hands. The broadhead arrow sank in under his short ribs; she knew from the angle it must be cutting up through his lungs, maybe the heart. He pitched off the spar and fell soundless back onto the deck of the galley, nearly a hundred feet.

The fall lasted forever. *I just* killed *a man*, Karah thought.

Eowlie screamed something in her ear, loud enough to shock Karah out of her frozen pause. Whatever she'd said sounded like a cat whose tail had gotten caught under a moving wagon wheel. The fanged girl levelled her carbine and fired. Karah looked around; a wave of spiked steel helmets and broad brown Tseldene faces was pouring up the boarding planks from the galley.

"Gurah! Gurah!" they chanted; the first ranks carried spears with spiked and hooked heads, the rear long curved slashing swords and small shields. Their armor was of blackened steel and brass; the officers wore helms with bestial masks of fretted bronze and silver shaped in the manifold countenances of the One. "Gurah! *Gurah!*"

Pikes darted and thrust. Tseldenes toppled, to die in the narrow grinding space where the hulls of the vessels met. Others clambered up the sides of the taller Imperial ship, to meet the long steel heads of the pikes. Karah drew and loosed, drew and loosed; a crossbow bolt sank into the crate beside her, throwing splinters at her face. She ignored the splinters and loosed another arrow, over the heads of the XIXth's pikes and into the press on the boarding planks. The other scouts were firing their carbines less rapidly; turn the breech screw, jab in a cartridge with the thumb, turn it closed, prime the pan with powder from a spring-flask worn on a cord around the shoulder, crank the steel spring with the winding spanner, aim and fire—four times a minute, *bang* click-crank-click-snap and then *bang* again. Stinking smoke blew back into her face.

"NOW!" Bren Morkaarin's voice, inhumanly calm but pitched to carry.

All the pikemen squatted abruptly. The rank of musketeers behind them rose and fired over their heads, dropped down; the rank behind them rose and fired as well.

Instantly the deck of the *Sea Mare* was hidden in the smoke, dense enough to choke; the strong breeze blew it away in patches, and they could seek the long pikes jabbing out again, knocking Tseldenes off the planks. In the silence that followed the crashing volley, they could even hear for an instant the *scrinnggg* of pikeheads on armor, or the dull wet thudding sounds as they punched into bellies and chests. A cheer rose from the musketeers, even as they fumbled with ramrods and bandoliers and priming flasks, answered defiantly from the galley's deck.

"*Watch* it!" Amourgin screamed.

Karah turned in time to see the boarding planks fall on the other side of the ship; the second enemy galley was alongside there. Men in the Tseldene's rigging were waiting. As the hulls touched they jumped free, swinging on ropes, the sudden check to the momentum of their vessel bringing them out over the *Sea Mare*'s deck like pendulum bobs. Those low enough dropped into the midst of their enemies. The Tseldenes were sailors armed with knives and light tomahawks, down amid musketeers and pike-armed infantry crammed too tightly to draw their own close-quarter weapons. They laid about, spreading disorder far beyond their number.

Karah drew and loosed, catching one in the gut. He kept his grip on the rope long enough to swing back over his own ship before he dropped. Another landed on a barrel that toppled beneath him; agile as a dancer he jumped free and landed ready to fight. Karah dropped her bow and went for her sword, sickeningly conscious that it would not be in time. The Tseldene got a clear patch of deck to stand on and poised not five feet from her, raising his light axe to throw.

A swordpoint came out his breast. His expression froze, then melted as he toppled forward off the steel. Behind him was Amourgin the law-speaker, blade extended in perfect line with his arm and back leg, left hand on hip, knee bent—the long lunge of the sword-schools of Olmya.

"Thanks!" Karah shouted, getting her own blade out and drawing a fighting knife with a bell guard in her left hand. Then: "Oh, *shit!*"

The soldiers along the bulwark behind Amourgin had dropped their pikes and drawn their swords as the Tseldene marines swarmed over the side. There was no chance to repeat the measured volley-fire that had saved the other side of the ship; the musketeers were stepping forward, sticking the muzzles of their weapons between the ranks and firing with the business end nearly touching enemy bodies. Then they clubbed the firearms and waded in, or drew their own swords. Knots of the enemy were breaking through, deadly amid the unarmored musketeers and sailors.

One was behind Amourgin. He didn't know, but he did see Eowlie kneel and take careful aim, apparently directly at him. Karah could see his eyes go wide, but there was nothing wrong with his reflexes—he dropped like a stone and rolled. Eowlie fired, the crack of the shot lost in the continuous crackle of musket fire. On his back, Amourgin could see a small hole suddenly appear in the silvered breastplate of the Tseldene officer who'd been raising a scimitar over his head with both hands. Blood shot out from the gilded filigree of the man's face mask, as the bullet and fragments of breastplate and rib bone sawed through his lungs and flooded his gasping mouth.

"*Come* on!" Karah shouted.

There seemed to be nothing else to do, so she led the rush across the pen; tripping and stumbling and jumping over their own baggage, slipping on decks slick with blood—she suddenly noticed the planks were actually *running* with it. The barricade of boxes at the other side was half-tumbled by the press of bodies against it. She slashed a Tseldene across the back of the neck without even thinking about it, and there was a sudden ugly jarring thump up the blade of her sword and into her wrist and shoulder—a little like cutting a sheep carcass, which she'd done for practice—but not much. Somewhere very deep down she knew that later she'd remember this, but there was no *time*. Now there were only noise and smoke, screaming horses and screaming wild-eyed faces coming at her.

Amourgin was up on his feet again, blade in both hands. He whipped it around in a tight circle, cut through a spear shaft, then through both wrists of the Tseldene on the return stroke. The marine pivoted, howling and blinding the one behind him with the blood spouting from the stumps; the law-speaker spitted him through the throat, withdrew with a twist of the blade. Beside him Eowlie swung the butt of her carbine into a man's face, still yowling her cat-in-agony warcry. Karah scrambled amid boxes and spilled hardtack, caught a barbed spearhead on the guard of her knife, chopped down into the back of the knee of the enemy marine who'd thrust it at her, drawing the cut. He collapsed backward into the melee. Something hit her *hard* on the corselet, winding her, utterly without warning.

"Ufff." She staggered sideways, wheezing and trying to breathe.

The Tseldene jerked his spear back, aiming at her eyes this time, below the brim of her bowl helmet. Her arms were moving through molasses, slow and weak. The steel spike glittered; he grinned at her, shoulders tensing. It would go right in through her nose and out the back of her head. . . .

Doe Ditech stuck her long wheel-lock pistol into the side of the Tseldene's head and fired. He had just enough time to realize what was happening as the flint struck the revolving steel, and then his face ballooned with hydrostatic shock as the heavy lead ball punched through behind his eyes. Karah wished she hadn't been looking; the eyeballs popped out of his head as he spun away.

"Thanks," she wheezed, straightening.

She and Doe and Korgi and Borte stepped up to what was left of the barricade together, swords out. To their left Amourgin was moving with easy grace, blocking and thrusting and using an occasional economical backhand cut. The Tseldenes seemed to be avoiding him, perhaps because of Eowlie. The sound of her screeching rose even over the roar and crash of battle; she had a long knife in one hand, but her fanged muzzle was a mask of blood as she prowled crouching around the perimeter of the circle held by Amourgin's blade, and there seemed to be a glistening red glove on her other hand and its claws.

Oh, shit, Karah thought again. They were directly opposite one of the Tseldene boarding planks, and the Imperial line around it was *not* holding.

"Gurah! Gurah!"

The Tseldene marines poured up the plank, forming a knot on the *Sea Mare*'s planking. Behind them came more enemy troops, these armed with monstrous two-man muskets. If they got onto the deck . . .

"Oh, *shit.*"

"*Back*, you sibsucker," Bren panted.

The scimitar crashed down on the basket hilt of his sword. It *hurt*; the Tseldene was even shorter than Bren, but built like an ox and strong as one. Bren pivoted slightly and rammed the point of his parrying dagger home beneath the edge of the Tseldene's armor, through a leather groin protector; the enemy marine shrieked and dropped. Bren stamped on the back of his neck as he led the rush to the edge of the quarterdeck. There was a queasy, crunching feeling under his boot, unpleasantly familiar.

"Not good," he gasped, looking down on the threshing chaos of the main deck.

The halberdiers on the forecastle and sterncastle were holding out; the extra height gave an advantage. On the starboard the Tseldenes were still struggling for a foothold along the bulwarks. There was plenty of noise, shouting and the scrap-metal sounds of hand-to-hand battle. Few shots; nobody had time to reload, but the musketeers on the starboard side were managing to keep up a slow trickle of point-blank fire, saving it for times when the enemy managed to push onto the *Sea Mare*'s deck, helping the pike-and-sword fighters to knock them back.

It was to port that things looked really bad. Knots of the enemy were on the *Sea Mare*'s deck, pushing in against the crumbling defense. If they pushed the Imperial fighters back into their comrades on the other side of the ship, broke their formation . . .

Bren looked down at the Tseldene galley. It was nearly two hundred feet long, but flush-decked except for a low quarter-deck aft—a smooth deck of planking broken by closed grills. Through them came the wailing of the rowers' fear, and a stink that was stunning enough even among the salt-and-shit odors of close-quarter battle. Tarin Tseld used chained slave rowers; on Tykissian ships the oar-pullers were freemen, armed and part of the crew. The grills were closed down, except . . .

"Captain!" he barked. The seaman looked up from helping to reload one of the swivel guns mounted on the sterncastle's rail. "I'm leaving you half the halberds. Ddrad, you take your orders from him. Mercele, get your surprise. The rest of you, follow me!"

Karah grunted through a gummy dry mouth, catching the axe on her crossed sword and dagger. Metal rang and the shock pushed her back, jarring everything down to the small of her back. Everyone else was too busy to help, and the marine was *strong*. The spike of the axe—the blade was reversed—

pressed closer toward her eyes. If she weakened it would be through her face in an instant; she couldn't move, either, the brace of her legs was all that was keeping her upright. Her arms were buckling. . . .

Something flickered at the edge of her sight. The axe stopped pressing at her; she flicked it backward and slashed with her sword in the same motion, across the bare taut throat before her. Blood hit her jaw and throat, running down into the stickiness under her corselet, the thick salt taste in her mouth. She spat without thinking, then saw First Captain Morkaarin moving past her with a cluster of halberdiers at his back. The chopping blades swung in full-armed cuts, sheering through armor and limbs and topping heads like hard-boiled eggs . . . although eggs didn't come attached to spasming bodies.

"Follow me!" Bren roared; his helmet was off, and his tow-colored hair thick with blood. "Follow me!"

Karah found herself responding without thought. She followed, vaguely conscious of the other scouts with her, surprised they were still alive, or mostly—bodies were lying all around, still or twitching or trying to crawl out of the way, and fighters were tripping over them. The solid wedge of halberdiers cleaved through the press, stabbing and hacking, collecting sailors with cutlasses and soldiers swinging clubbed muskets or stabbing with swords and shortened pikes. Bren moved through at the apex of it, and the solid professional she'd known and loathed was transformed, moving like a thing of steel springs and leopard fire, killing with an easy metronomic regularity and shouting from a face gone white pale and staring.

Karah followed; they all did, and the Tseldenes buckled, wavering backward from success. Suddenly they were at the edge of the deck, and Bren leaped up onto the boarding plank, boots rutching on the heavy rope matting nailed to it. A Tseldene officer barred his way, curved sword in hand; for a long moment they fought, steel blurring in a pattern of strike and counterstrike too fast for the eye to follow, and then Bren was wrenching his point out of the southron's face.

"Wolf and Falcon!" he shouted, and Karah jumped up beside him, howling. "Holy Three, Holy Three!"

She batted a spearhead out of the way with her dagger and thrust past Bren's shoulder; they advanced a step, another, the board slanting down toward the deck of the galley. She cut at spear shafts, at the legs of men fighting the man beside her, at sailors trying to crowd around the edge of the plank holding to the rope-and-pole railing on either side. The press stopped them, but only two or three could meet them at one time. Beyond on the deck two marines were taking aim at Bren— and at her—one holding the barrel of the huge musket on his shoulder, the other aiming from behind. Its barrel was six feet long and only three or four times that away. . . . The muzzle looked big enough to put her fist down, and it was pointing right at *her*.

"*Now, Mercele!*" Bren shouted. "*Now, now!*"

A barrel soared over her head; she nearly died watching it as a Tseldene probed for her life. It went an impossible distance, down and down, hitting the deck next to the musketeers who were about to fire. One of them dropped his weapon and leaped for it, fingers closing—no, just missing it as he crashed to the deck and the iron-hooped barrel rolled and bounced, the hissing fuse stuck through a cork-stopped bung at one end drawing patterns of sparks through the air. It rolled beyond his frantic scrabble; even then there was something amusing in a man *trying* to grab a barrel full of gunpowder. Rolled, slowed, tipped . . . and fell through the open grillwork before the galley's mainmast.

The explosion blasted the grill up in a fountain of sparks and smoke and metal, a mushroom with a red flash at the center. The great mainmast of the galley fell seconds later, the stay ropes breaking with plucking noises like giant harpstrings; it fell right onto the foremast and broke *it* off flush with the deck. Fire followed, taking heat-dried pine decking with appalling speed; the screams of the rowers below were like damned souls in a Toboran hell. She could feel the shudder through the hull of the galley in the plank beneath her feet. Bren was backing up; in the cold aftermath of whatever frenzy had made her follow him, that looked like a *good* idea.

"Drive 'em back!" he shouted, as they skipped up onto the bulwark of the *Sea Mare*.

The Tseldenes gave a huge groaning shout of terror as the galley began to burn. Drums and trumpets sounded from its quarterdeck; the marines gave way with the suddenness of water bursting through a dam. Some fought to hold the boarding planks for their comrades; others threw their weapons away and leaped down to the galley's deck. A few even ran across it and jumped into the water, near-suicide for men in armor. The officers raged along the galley's deck, their steel-tipped whips flailing as they drove men to the pumps. The deck and hold belched steam as seawater struck flame and scorched wood.

"*Come* on," Bren said, in a more normal tone.

Halberdiers were prying at the plank with their heavy weapons. The spikes on its bottom edge came free of the wood with a screech, and Karah's shoulder hit it beside the officer's. It slid away; she could see a growing stretch of clear water below, a triangle of blue between the hulls. The planks forward twisted free, as the torque of the separating ships flung their weight against the spikes. The last Tseldenes dropped into the water between the galley and the Imperial ship; the marines sank like stones, but a few sailors bobbed up and began swimming. Almost as one, the Imperial soldiers on the port side turned. The enemy commander on the other southron galley saw which way the fight was going; before Bren or his followers could reach the rail the Tseldenes had retreated in good order to their deck and cast free. The oars shot out on either side, pushing against the *Sea Mare*'s hull and dipping into the water.

The captain's voice suddenly rang out from the quarterdeck:

"All hands aloft! Set the jib, we need steerage way or she'll ram us!"

Gun smoke was still puffing from the crow's nests, but there seemed to be enough sailors to scramble aloft.

Bren's sword sank in his hand. Humanness returned to his face; he coughed and looked around. Recognition flickered as he saw Karah.

"Well, *you've* been blooded," he said dryly.

Karah wiped at her face, feeling the greasy smear of congealing blood on it; the whole front of her body was covered in the stuff, like stinking salt-honey. Suddenly her gut twisted and she staggered to the rail, heedless of the bodies she stumbled over, heaving a few painful cups of sour bile into the water.

"Here." Bren offered a flask.

She rinsed out her mouth; it was water cut with brandy. A second swallow made her feel a little better; she could look around. Amourgin was helping Eowlie bandage a cut on her thigh; Doe and Korgi knelt weeping over Borte—*oh, shit*—soldiers were staggering about, looking dazed. The noncoms were hustling them into action, pushing and shoving and sometimes slapping faces, getting them to pick up weapons and start separating the living from the wounded, taking those below to the priest-surgeon.

"What now, sir?" Karah asked respectfully. She hadn't expected to live when the Tseldene galleys laid alongside.

Bren Morkaarin started to reply, then looked over her shoulder. His face changed; she twisted painfully to follow his gaze.

The water was littered with ships, burning and sinking, locked together or stalking a victim. As she watched, a tublike transport rolled slowly over, its belly black with soldiers clinging and scrambling to stay ahead of the waters. A Tseldene galley backed off for another ramming run at it, only to be caught in the stern by a Tykissian warship and heel three-quarter over itself. Beyond that a long black finger pointed for a moment at the sky, a southron galley going down by the stern—she could see it jerk and hear the rumble as the cannon at the bow broke loose and fell all down through its rowing compartment and out the rear. Then it slid out of sight below the waves with scarcely even foam to mark its passing.

That wasn't what was making Bren stare. The wind was still rising, cold against her sweat-soaked skin, and purple-black clouds hid the coastline of Meltroon. Lightning stabbed through them as they swept down the mountains, and she could see spray blowing from the tops of waves. A moaning shriek sounded as the outliers of the waves hit the *Sea Mare*'s rigging, and the ship heeled sharply, canvas straining and creaking. Sailors were scrambling again, this time cutting sail loose rather than trying to strike it.

"We're in for a bad blow," Bren said in an almost conversational tone. Then a shout as he strode away: "Get everything secured—wounded below! Move your arses if you want to live, damn you!"

Oh, shit, Karah thought. It wasn't original; she seemed to be saying and thinking that a *lot* today, but it fit.

She tried to open her hands, but the fingers seemed glued to her hilts. On the third try it worked; she walked over to Amourgin and the others, looking for something to wipe the steel.

"We'd better do what the man says," she said wryly. "Godsall, but it would be silly to drown after all this."

✪ CHAPTER X

Bren watched the war dissolve in the face of a common enemy.

All around the *Sea Mare*, the ships that were still able to began making for whatever ports they might find. The battle disintegrated into a hasty retreat on both sides. Sailors on seaworthy ships raced up and down ratlines to reef the sails, and in a flock, the oared warships began to turn tail and run for the island harbors. Waves swelled and crashed around the *Sea Mare*, and the sky grew even darker. The first huge spatters of rain hit the blood-soaked deck.

But the *Sea Mare* didn't follow in the wake of either fleet. It wallowed, instead, like a pig in mud, lurching up and down the swells, taking on water as waves hit broadside and seawater streamed across the decks.

Bren raced past seamen intent on their work; he wanted the ship's captain. He found him at last on the quarterdeck, issuing orders to the seamen and completely ignoring the tall wheel that should have steered the *Sea Mare* toward safe harbor.

"What's happened?" Bren shouted.

The ship's captain turned a weary face toward Bren. "We're screwed," he yelled back. "That's the short tale. The long is, they shot off our rudder, and this mudsucking puddle barge has no oars and no backup and a keel like a fucking meadbarrel. We'll try to set a sea anchor, keep nose to tail with the storm and run before the wind, but mor'n likely, the sea will swallow us. With *luck* we'll run aground and a few of us will live. That's with luck. Without luck, I imagine we're all dead. Get your people out of their armor," he added. "Maybe some of them can swim."

The wind shrieked louder, and for an instant, Bren fancied he could hear voices in it. Then the ship's captain stared over Bren's shoulder at the open sea, pressed his fist to his heart and bellowed, "Dear gods, deliver us!"

Bren turned, and gasped. The sea glowed sickly green, and out of it rose the prows of long-sunken ships, crewed by the legions of the dead. The hulks lifted gently through the stormy sea as if they were sailing up from the bottom before a gentle breeze; and in fact, their tattered rags of sails streamed in front of them, blown by no earthly wind. Their rotted hulls glowed with phosphor-weed, and barnacles clung to the broken planking. Water poured out of the holed hulls as the ships lifted—poured back into the sea, while the ships arched up to the surface like dolphins. . . . *Or*, Bren thought, *perhaps the animate corpses of long-dead dolphins*. While the storm raged around them, and the wind screamed and the waves battered the *Sea Mare* and threatened to drown her, the derelicts sailed without regard to gale winds or killer seas—sailed as if for them the water was smooth as glass and gentle breezes blew steadily from whichever direction they wished.

This was no illusion conjured by the wizard-priests and their acolytes to strike terror in the hearts of fighting soldiers, Bren realized. This was real.

The crew that hung on those rotted riggings and strode along those worm-eaten decks were Kevo-Death's own vanguard. Some who watched from the far ships were skeletons with their bones washed clean by the hungry sea. Some still wore scraps of flesh and hair and tattered rags tangled with seaweed and holed by worms. Worst though, were the men and women who could have been still among the living, were it not for their ghastly pale faces and flat dead eyes—and the wounds they bore that marked them as that day's fresh dead.

Tykissians stood on those decks shoulder to shoulder with Tseldenes, Nyokese, Krevaulti, Shillraki.

"Death knows no loyalties," he whispered.

Bren knotted his hands together and pressed them tight against his gut. He saw none of his own people numbered among the corpse crew, but that was small comfort. He knew if he looked closer or longer, he would find them.

The small fleet of corpse-crewed sailing ships and galleys came around to face in the *Sea Mare*'s direction, running with the wind, and two of them brought themselves even with the *Sea Mare*. They began to close, one on either side, and Bren saw the corpses readying the rotted remains of boarding planks.

This was too much for many of the *Sea Mare*'s crew. Sailors screamed and threw themselves into the raging sea, rather than face the armies of the dead.

The ship's captain, Bren thought, looked ready to join them. "That's it then!" he shouted. The captain braced himself with his back to the wheel, and drew his saber. "Hell of a way to die!" he added.

Bren couldn't help but agree. *If the war doesn't get you,* he thought, *the gods will.* He had no doubt but that the hands of the gods had sealed his fate. But he would not go quietly, gods or no.

The boarding planks dropped onto the *Sea Mare*'s deck.

The remaining seamen dragged the *Sea Mare*'s priest up from nursing the wounded and forced him to begin chanting and praying.

The storm grew worse, but the second the boarding planks hit the deck of the *Sea Mare*, she bobbed over the waves as if she sat becalmed. The wind continued to scream and the waves raised high at the mizzenmast, but the corpse crew boarded the little ship as if they were parading over a walkway on dry land.

Bren gripped his saber in one hand and his long dagger in the other. He crouched on the unmoving deck, side by side with the ship's captain, and watched them coming.

The first of the uncanny crew dropped onto the *Sea Mare*'s deck, and Bren's mind finally registered something it had not seen before. "Look!" he shouted to the captain. "They have no weapons!"

The man's sidelong glance held no hope. "Maybe they don't need them!"

But the dead made no move to attack the living as they boarded the ship. Instead, as if they were the *Sea Mare*'s rightful crew, they shambled to the ratlines, and then climbed laboriously up them.

Then, to Bren's astonishment, they began to mime the raising of the ship's sails, though the sails had been cut away earlier.

One long-dead corpse approached the ship's wheel, stood stiffly in front of the captain, and saluted.

"What do you want to do, Captain?" Bren asked.

"Back away, an' let Kevo's damned sail us where they will!" he shouted. "We can discuss later whether it's better t' live in Hell or die in the sea!"

The corpse took the wheel and spun it slowly, as if it still guided a rudder—and slowly, the *Sea Mare* came around into the wind. Those living seamen who'd stayed with the ship fled back to the quarterdeck, and stood gaping at the ghastly cadaverous crew that worked in utter silence while the world went mad.

"Any idea where they're taking us?" Bren asked.

"None. I've nothing to reckon by." The captain shook his head, bewildered. "But I'll be here, watching."

Bren nodded, then turned away from the horrors onboard, and headed for the forecastle, where the living and the dead among the XIXth awaited him.

And he thought darkly that the XIXth—at least the part of the unit under his command—would have no burials at sea. He would not permit the dead who'd served under him to fall into the waiting embrace of the sea, to be made to dance at Kevo's whim.

The ship stopped rocking. Zeemos crouched in darkness among the barrels of wine and hardtack and held perfectly still, listening. The screams of the storm continued unabated, but the horrible pitching was gone—and so was the sound of the ship trying to tear herself apart. So they'd made harbor.

He was surprised. He hadn't really imagined the ship would last long enough to find a safe port.

Since it had, he found himself suddenly to be a man with options. Zeemos carefully considered his situation. He was a dead man now if the First Captain found him. He had to get off the ship—and with it docked or anchored, he had probably arrived at a good time to effect an escape.

He stretched and stroked the ruby. With it, he was a very rich man. However, he still needed some guarantee of an income. Riches did not last forever, and he wanted to live well.

He thought of Eowlie. The ungrateful whore owed him her life; she would have died on the beach if he hadn't found her. As far as he was concerned, that meant she belonged to him, no matter what Tykissian law might say. He'd seen her potential and he'd made good use of it, and he resented having her taken away from him because of some idiotic legal technicality.

The other whores did not matter, Zeemos thought. They were instantly replaceable at any of five or six good slave markets he could think of. But not Eowlie. She was unique. Irreplaceable. And she'd made him piles of money. There were men everywhere he'd traveled who had found her irresistible.

He had a price on his head already. Stealing back his own property couldn't make it any higher, or his situation any worse. He had nothing to lose, everything to gain, and he'd be damned if he ever crossed the Tykissian borders again anyway.

Of course, getting Eowlie back would be no simple matter. He'd only captured her the first time because she was near death. She could—and would—kill him without a second thought if he didn't take her unawares.

His fingers poked around for anything among the supplies that might make a good weapon. He found axes and swords, but he didn't want to kill the bitch. She was useless to him dead. He arched an eyebrow and considered that; he *might* make a few coppers off her for a day or two after she was dead, he decided at last, but only for a day or two—and the clientele who would pay for that simply didn't appeal to him.

So he didn't want to kill her. He just wanted to capture her. He felt around further, and at last found a nice solid wooden club. It would be just the thing.

Zeemos didn't worry about hurting the whore. In truth, he rather fancied the idea. That would be just payment for all the trouble she'd brought him. As long as he didn't kill her, he could pay a mediciner to bring her back to health. Probably find one who wasn't adverse to docking slaves' tongues, so she couldn't go telling tales—though for that sort of mediciner, he'd have to get to Tarin Tseld.

She cared for the horses, he thought. He could catch her out when she was feeding or watering them. Unfortunately, the other girl, Karah, was always with her—and Karah was good with a sword. Zeemos considered his odds and decided he didn't like them very much.

A rat brushed by his ankle, squeaking, and the pimp jumped and yelped. Then, slowly, he smiled into the darkness.

I don't need to go anywhere, he thought. *Not anywhere a'tall. Sooner or later, she will come here, looking for rats— and then I'll have her, and no one will know.*

He felt around until he found a place by the ladder, but well hidden from any who might come looking for him, and settled himself against the bulkhead.

Then he waited.

Time passed slowly, and Zeemos drifted between sleep and waking, starting each time thunder cracked nearby or rats used him as a walkway. She would come sooner or later, hungry for fresh, live meat, and fastidious about having anyone see her eat. She hated being watched, and only ate in front of people when she had no other choice.

A shaft of pale light and the thud of the hatch door as it fell open brought Zeemos awake yet again, and he realized he'd fallen into a sound sleep. He looked up. The light outlined Eowlie's profile. Zeemos grinned and hefted his rock. She hunted well in the darkness, but he would have a brief moment while her eyes adjusted—and she would not be expecting any attack, so he had, briefly, a solid advantage.

She clambered down into the hold with her back to him. She was no more than inches away from him, yet because of the darkness and the stink from the bilge below and the noise of screaming wind and crashing waves, she did not discover his presence.

He smiled, and thumped her once on the back of the skull with his club—hard.

She grunted and collapsed into a barrel.

It was over as quickly as that. Too simple, really, he thought. She didn't know what had happened to her, and did not know she was defeated. He would have time to enjoy her unhappiness later. For the moment, he needed to be certain she was securely bound and gagged when she awoke.

He hurried into the aft hold with the horses and dug around in the supplies until he found some rope and rags from the tack. He could actually see in the aft compartment, though he couldn't imagine why. He looked around quickly just to see if he could identify the source of light.

When he did, he wished he hadn't. He discovered a hole in the side of the ship where a length of carvel plank had ripped away—he couldn't tell whether from rot or enemy cannonfire. The upright frames were more or less intact, but he could see water rushing by the hole, glowing with a pale green light.

It should have been pouring into the ship. In fact, he could see some water on the deck to indicate that it had. There was nothing to keep it out. He crept over to the hole, horrified by what he saw, and yet not believing. He reached out, and touched the racing, glowing water—

—and nearly lost his hand as the force of the current caught his fingers and slammed them against the frame, and kept pulling on them. The water was icy. He jerked his hand out, and pressed one moist finger to his tongue. He tasted salt—so this strange water that did not pour into holes, that glowed with its own light, was still seawater.

He stared an instant longer at the enigmatic sight, then shook his head. All the more reason to get off the ship. There was no telling when whatever held the water out would give way, and then the ship would sink like a stone. He wanted to be well away when that happened.

He ran back to the fore hold and checked his whore. She still breathed, but showed no signs of waking. He bound her wrists and ankles together behind her back, so her back arched into a bow. He shoved one of the rags he'd found into her mouth, then carefully wrapped the other around her muzzle to hold it shut. He wanted her to be able to breathe, but not to bite. He'd seen firsthand what those teeth could do.

He had to climb the ladder onto the deck midships, which would bring him within plain sight of the crew on deck and anyone who looked out from either the forecastle or the aftcastle. He would have to creep aft to steal the ship's single dinghy, which was kept lashed to the *Sea Mare* just behind midships. The ship held three times as many people as it should have. Even in harbor, every inch of free space above was likely to be filled with wounded soldiers and people tending them, while the deck would be covered with sailors working on the rigging, repairing sails, scrubbing the deck.

He pressed his face against the bulkhead and considered. He could drop the whore into the bilge—she'd drown there before anyone came looking for her. A man alone would not be so conspicuous as one carrying a bound and gagged monster on his back.

No, he thought, angry with the idea. *She belongs to me! I just have to find a way to make her inconspicuous.*

He pondered a moment, then grinned. *I could stuff her in a barrel—or, better yet, a bag.*

A bit of additional mischief occurred to him as well. He sauntered over to the barrels. He unlashed the first water barrel, popped out the bung, and tipped it on its side—it was terribly heavy, but he was not a little man. The water poured across the cambered deck and disappeared down both sides. He smiled as he thought of the ship's drinking water joining the bilge. He tipped the next barrel—then decided to ruin the pickled greefish and salt pork, too. He cut the pork down from overhead, popped the hoops on the barrels of greefish with an axe. He spilled as many of the water barrels as he could on top of those. He slashed the bottoms of the bags of tubers and onions overhead and watched them pour out in a lovely, thudding vegetable river. It was hard work; the ship's stores were stacked high from just back of midships all the way fore. He'd never be able to destroy all the supplies—after a few minutes, he focused exclusively on the water and the wine. He managed to dump all of that.

"H'I said you'd pay fer takin' my silver," he muttered.

The sounds of his labor were hidden by storm sounds: crashing waves, the crack and roar of thunder overhead, the banshee shriek of wind. He dumped a final bag of tubers onto the planking and carried the bag back.

Eowlie was beginning to wake. Her eyes, half open, held a bewildered expression. She struggled feebly against her bonds, but not as if she understood that she was bound. Zeemos found his club, knelt beside her, and thumped her on the back of the head again. He was careful not to hit too hard; things were going quite well, really, and he hated to think he might damage his merchandise unnecessarily. She went limp, and he stuffed her into the bag.

Then, with his whore slung across his shoulder, he climbed

up the companionway and pushed up through the hatch to the deck midships.

He wondered where the *Sea Mare* had docked, then shrugged philosophically. He shifted Eowlie's limp form to rest more comfortably across his shoulder and plodded back toward the place where the work boat was tied. He wished the idiots in charge had left a few of the running lights burning. Probably best for him they hadn't, he decided. The darkness worked into his hands—even if it was a frightening sort of night.

No one challenged him. He wondered first if the crew and the XIXth had abandoned the ship when they reached port, but his eyes picked out the movements of seamen along the decks and rigging. Uneasiness gnawed at his nerves. He did not like the stillness of the air; its closeness and mustiness held an undefinable and frightening reek. He did not like the brief impressions of movement his eyes made out off to starboard. He could not make out shapes, could not determine what it was about that movement that frightened him, but he was sure it was not right. He did not understand why he could hear the wind, but could not feel it.

He thought how glad he would be to get away from the *Sea Mare*.

He dumped Eowlie on the deck, loosed one corner of the oiled canvas tarp that covered the dinghy, and shoved her in.

A tremendous bolt of lightning struck next to the ship, and for one eternal instant, night turned to day. Zeemos found himself staring into the empty eyesockets of a dead woman who was walking toward him, her torn jaw held to the rest of her face by one flap of shredded skin, her bare breasts bloated, her belly eaten away.

He screamed and turned to flee as the lightning died. His eyes burned with the afterimages of the strike, with the clear picture of a wave as big as a hill towering over the *Sea Mare* and breaking on top of her—and of the water running off of clear air and back into the sea as if the ship were covered by a shield of glass. And he could not clear his mind of the face of the dead woman, and behind her a dead crew, skeletons on the crosspieces and a rotted corpse at the wheel.

He crawled along the deck on his hands and knees, back toward the hatch, praying none of the dead would find him. Another lightning strike in the distance gave him an instant of dim blue light. The hatch gaped open.

He couldn't think—almost couldn't breath. His pulse pounded in his ears, drowning out even the roar of the storm. All he could think was "down." Down, into the dark and lonely safety of the hold, away from the terrors above—

The ruby around his neck worked free from the inside of his tunic, where he'd kept it hidden. He noticed only when he realized a glowing red beacon hung round his neck.

Disbelieving, he lifted the stone in front of his face, and stared at the gem, which glittered with its own internal fire. It was impossibly beautiful—and it was witched. He could think of no other explanation for the glow.

He scrabbled at the chain around his neck and tried to pull the necklace over his head. It resisted. He pulled harder. He felt the chain constrict in his fingers. He tried to break the chain and it tightened around his neck until it cut off his wind and locked his thumbs against his throat. Pinpoints of light began to dance in front of his eyes, and he heard a wind rushing inside his ears.

He quit fighting, and the chain loosened, and he sucked in air like a man who'd never tasted it before, and who might never again. At that moment, a man carrying a lamp ran toward him, and an angry voice shouted, "First Captain! There's that bastard pimp!"

Zeemos saw—as if from a great distance—that the man was the law-speaker. Heat rushed across his face, and the air he breathed suddenly felt thick and muddy; he discovered the air was almost impossible to breathe. And then everything went dark for real.

Father Solmin knelt over his brazier, muttering bitterly.

Karah crouched beside him. "What does that mean?" The flames, burning in a handful of ugly colors, held no special significance for her.

He looked over at her, frowning. Then she saw his eyes flick from the dots on her cheeks to the one on her brow, and he shrugged.

"Every wizard's magic is different. Each wizard has a signature—little wizards, great ones, necromancers, anyone who does magic. I can read the signatures in the magic that surrounds us. A few ingredients, a simple spell . . ." He shrugged again and stared at the multicolored flames in the brazier.

"I only used the smallest of spells, so that I would be able to read nothing but the biggest of magics." He sucked in the skin of one cheek, and shook his head. "That, right there," he pointed to a red flame with a black heart, "that's Willek. The layered gold, that's Darkist." He studied her sidelong. "You're the Grenlaarin person, aren't you?"

Karah nodded.

"Right. So your family's activities will be no secret. That one is one of your people—Jawain." The flame he pointed out was almost silver.

Karah blurted. "But that's illegal!"

He snorted. "That law's enforced only when it has to be," he said. "Not that the priesthood says so in public, you understand." He indicated a pale blue flame. "I've seen that one before in Derkin. None of my people—but not one of Darkist's, either, I don't think. A free agent."

He stared back at his brazier and fell silent.

He'd said nothing at all about the three biggest flames— one white as new-fallen snow, one black as midnight, one that flickered through a rainbow of colors.

"What of those?" she asked.

"Black is the mage-flame of Kevo-Death, bitter god of endings without beginnings—of loss in battle, of destruction and despair," the priest said. "He gathers his followers from the fallen among the battlefields. I would expect the presence of Kevo-Death—but his assistance . . ." The priest shook his head slowly. "His assistance, I fear, can only mean that he foresees greater death and destruction in the future if we go forward than if we die now. It is nothing to be wished for."

Karah shivered. She was afraid to ask, but she had to know. "What of the other two, Father Solmin?"

The priest sighed. "I don't know." He looked at her, and in his eyes she could see dread. "I don't know, and I fear to guess."

Amourgin knelt by Zeemos and drew his knife. "He breathes," the law-speaker shouted to Morkaarin over the continuing roar of the storm. "But not for much longer."

He raised the knife to bury in the pimp's heart.

First Captain Morkaarin, kneeling beside him, put a restraining hand on the law-speaker's wrist.

"First we question him!" the First Captain shouted. "Then I'm going to hang him!"

The pimp opened his eyes and stared up at the law-speaker. Then he smiled. "I have that piece of ass you fancied," he shouted. "She'll die if I don't live."

Amourgin looked over at the First Captain.

"Who?" Morkaarin raised his eyebrows and mouthed the question.

Amourgin frowned. "Have you seen Eowlie recently?" he yelled to the First Captain.

Morkaarin shook his head "no."

Amourgin gripped the knife tighter and said, "You'll tell me what you've done with her, or I'll run you through!"

"Look out!" Morkaarin shouted.

The law-speaker looked up and jumped to one side—one of the animate corpses crewing the ship collapsed nearly on top of him, and did not rise. Others of the dead moved to its side, and without ceremony pitched the body into the sea.

Something about that scene unnerved the law-speaker. What could kill the dead? he wondered. But he pushed the worry away. He was more interested at the moment in killing the living. One of the living, in any case. And the dead, now illuminated by the hurricane lanterns he and the First Captain had carried up, didn't bear close scrutiny. Amourgin didn't consider himself squeamish, but a man had limits.

He nodded toward the back of the ship. "Aft?" he shouted.

Morkaarin nodded, and both men grabbed Zeemos to drag him back to the aftcastle.

The instant he touched Zeemos, pain worse than fire, worse than hot iron, blazed through Amourgin's hands, up his arms, into his shoulders. His flesh glowed red; his body arced backward; he felt his lips peel back in rictus while his vision blurred in a crimson haze. His throat locked shut, and he could not scream, nor even breathe.

He toppled backward and in falling broke contact with Zeemos. He was dimly aware that beside him, the First Captain had suffered the same fate. He could do nothing about it. His muscles were locked, he could not breathe—he was dying.

He willed his heart to beat, willed his blood to course through his veins. The world receded from his sight, the lanterns dimming as he starved for air, hungered for air. He felt his heart fluttering like a trapped bird in his chest, a dying bird that beat its wings against the cage of his ribs. Flights of fancy, the unsteady rush of his blood in his ears . . . so much he wanted to do . . . so much. . . .

And as much as he hungered for air, he hungered for something else as well. *Eowlie*, he thought. *I never touched her—godsall, how I wish I had. . . .*

Something released inside, and like water gushing from a burst dam, air poured into his lungs. He gasped, sucked greedily at the flesh-stinking air, pulled it in and savored it as if it were the sweet, cold mountain air he knew in childhood.

The pain receded, but slowly, so slowly. After what seemed eons, his muscles unlocked. His vision returned, fuzzily at first, so that initially he could make out nothing but a faint light spot in a sea of darkness. These resolved into two, which became lanterns. A shadow grew up between the points of light, and blotted one of them out, and the shadow resolved into the form of Zeemos.

Zeemos with a knife in his hand.

Bending over the First Captain.

Amourgin scrambled to his feet and lunged, hit Zeemos with his shoulder, and again felt that sudden horrible agony. But he bounced off before it could down him. Zeemos spun—*fast for a big man,* the law-speaker thought muzzily. And then he charged at Amourgin, knife held low.

Morkaarin grabbed the pimp's foot and jerked. Amourgin saw a fiery glow surround the foot and the officer's hands, saw the pimp stagger toward him, hands out. Amourgin jumped out of the way, started to draw his sword—and stopped, as the fat man staggered to the rail and fell heavily against it.

Bren charged across the deck, sword out. Zeemos saw the blade coming, and his nerve failed him. He screamed and started to throw himself backward over the rail, scrabbling for purchase on the slick deck. The First Captain's sword slid into the fat man's belly so hard Amourgin could see the First Captain's arm jerk as the point hit the wood of the ship rail on the other side. The pimp and the sword glowed red—but not before the First Captain had let go of his weapon and backed off.

Zeemos stared at Morkaarin, and down at the blade run through him. He opened his mouth, and Amourgin thought for an instant that he was going to say something. But blood ran from the corner of his mouth, down the side of his face. Zeemos glowed red, lit up from the inside as if he were suddenly made of glass. The glow spread around him as he hung, transfixed on the rail. Then the ship pitched—hard. It threw Amourgin and Bren up against the rail, while Zeemos' body toppled over into the sea. The First Captain and Amourgin stared down into the darkness. They saw nothing but the glowing blob that was Zeemos floating in the water, and that only for an instant before the sea swallowed him.

Good riddance, Amourgin thought, gripping the rail—then abruptly the sea lit up. The waves flashed crimson, illuminated from within by a magical fire. The glowing red stain spread until all the sea seemed to burn; false dawn, with no hope in it. In the suddenly glowing water, Amourgin could see the silhouettes of huge fish hunting schools of shadows that darted and fled before them. He found himself looking over the edge of the ship to the sea floor, full of large rocks, frighteningly near. Then a glowing waterspout grew out of the sea—out of the center of light that marked the point where Zeemos' body floated beneath the waves—toward the still-black sky; rose until it lit the bellies of the nearest clouds so they looked stained by gods' blood, while the glowing waves around the spout grew taller and wilder, while the rain slashed down just outside the invisible barrier in sheets and thunder roared and lightning cracked.

As the fiery glow touched the ships of the dead which had paced the *Sea Mare*, those wrecks sank back into the water, and tumbled beneath the waves to lie on the murky sea floor.

The *Sea Mare* once again rode the waves, and did not ride them well. The wind tore at her, the rain pounded her, and the angry sea threw her nearer and nearer the towering pillar of glowing water. Then the tip of the waterspout blossomed high above the little ship and began to pour down like a rain of fire.

Both men fought their way across the pitching deck toward the shelter of the forecastle.

It was then Amourgin realized the situation was worse even than he could have imagined. The dead who had crewed the ship now lay along the deck, unmoving. No living sailors had yet taken their places. The ship rode the sea with no more guidance than a piece of driftwood.

✪ CHAPTER XI

"Don't you have t' feed the flames?" Karah asked Solmin. "How do they burn without wood or oil?"

The priest crouched over the brazier, drawing imaginary lines above the flames with a finger. "The magic feeds them. Each flame draws a bit of energy from the magician who sends it."

The two of them crouched by the brazier a few moments longer, and the priest shook his head. "I fear these many flames. We are the focus for evil intent, and I cannot understand the meaning of the crossing of these magic trails. Darkist aims evil at us—but if I read the flames aright, Willek too has cursed this ship. Jawain weaves some protections around us, as does the stranger from Derkin. And the three greater flames indicate conflict on a grand scale, with this ship as the prize."

Karah wrapped her arms tightly around herself, shivering. Magic frightened her. She stared at those colored lights, burning steadily; tiny fires that indicated the wills and workings of people over whom she had no control—and most of whom seemed intent on working ill against her.

Without warning, the flames flattened out and streamed sideways as if a strong breeze blew them—though Karah felt no wind in the forecastle, and the hatch which led to the deck remained closed.

"Oh!" the priest whispered.

Karah didn't like the way he said that.

The ship began to sway and rock, but it steadied after a moment and sailed smoothly again. Karah felt as if she were trapped in one of her nightmares—as if the walking dead on the deck above, and the howling storm, and the creaking, battered ship were all elements of a horrid dream that would vanish at sunrise. She wished wholeheartedly that were so.

The air above the brazier crackled and snapped, and abruptly all the magical fires save one went out. That one grew, grew from a tiny flame to a conflagration that threw off golden light without heat.

"Darkist," the priest whispered, and threw a handful of powder into the flame, and muttered a fervent prayer.

The flame flickered out—and in the same instant, the waves caught up the *Sea Mare* in their furious grasp and threw her forward, sideways, backward in a sudden, violent game of catch. Karah fell, skidded into wounded comrades, then flew in a tangle of bodies against the bulkhead next to the hatch. The ship bucked again, and she found herself hurtling into the starboard hull. She lay in a heap on the decking, ribs aching. She could feel blood running down the back of her throat, and she was pretty sure she'd broken her nose. Someone's knee jammed into her belly, someone else's elbow into her jaw. One of her eyes was swollen shut, and her left leg twisted agonizingly underneath her.

The ship groaned, and the hull shuddered. And then it was still.

First Captain Morkaarin staggered into the forecastle and shouted above the roar of the storm, "We've run aground!"

The ship's captain burst in behind him. "Ship's startin' t' break apart. Get into the dinghies before she goes down!"

The horses, Karah thought. She got up and ran with the press of the uninjured, but where they ran for the single dinghy, she ran to the hatch in the center of the ship that led down into the hold.

The *Sea Mare* was caught fast on rocks, battered on all sides by waves—she groaned and creaked, and even as Karah went down into the darkness of the hold, the mainmast over her head snapped with a gunshot crack and fell into the sea, trailing rigging and rope. The horses were panicked. She realized why fast enough. She stepped into water that swirled around her thighs, warm and dark. Something cold and slick washed up against her—she recognized the feel of a human body, and her skin crawled. She slogged toward the bulkhead that divided the storage compartment from the makeshift stable, her gorge rising in her throat. She felt along the hull—she'd been into the hold for supplies, and thought she remembered where a couple of sledgehammers were.

"Karah? Are you down here?"

She recognized the voice as the First Captain's. Her fingers located the sledgehammer, not too far from where she remembered it. "I'm here!" she yelled. "I'm goin' after the horses!"

"I'll help. We can't winch 'em out, though. Masts are all gone."

"Thought I'd knock a hole in the side, if the sea hasn't done it for me."

She reached the bulkhead door and opened it. The panicked whinnies of the horses grew louder.

With a terrific groan and the sound of splintering wood, the ship canted to port. Karah fell heavily against one of the horses; the beast kicked out at her and connected solidly on her gut. She yelped in a strangled voice and climbed uphill to the central corridor between the stalls, forcing her diaphragm to work.

The ship shuddered again, and she fell to one knee and got a mouthful of seawater. A warm, strong arm slipped around her waist and pulled her upright. "Careful," the First Captain yelled. "Head to the uphill side. More likely it will be out of the water."

She went clear aft, and on the starboard side of the ship, began beating against the hull with the sledgehammer.

Morkaarin joined her, working on one of the framing timbers with an axe. The wood splintered easily—Karah broke out a horse-high section of the hull between one set of timbers and started on the planks between the next section.

"Damned ship was held together by wishful thinking," the First Captain shouted. His words echoed her own thoughts. The hull was rotten—it was nothing short of a miracle that they weren't all dead already.

She thought of the walking dead and the priest's flames in the brazier while she swung the sledgehammer and decided she'd had a miracle, all right.

Waves slammed into her through the hole she and the First Captain made and added to the flood in the hold. The ship creaked again, the horses plunged and reared, screaming all the while, and above their heads on the main deck, something else crashed.

When Karah began pounding on the next section of wood, the First Captain yelled, "That's going to have to be good enough! Afraid we're going to go down with her if we don't get out."

Karah slogged along the canted deck to the first of the makeshift stalls, fought her way past the panicked animal, and untied the rope that bound it to the ship. In the dark, she couldn't see the horse, and she was so shaken she couldn't remember which beast it was. She thought she knew where Glorylad and Broucher were, but she couldn't be sure. She backed the horse out, dodging hooves and teeth, and handed the lead rope off to Morkaarin. While he shooed the horse through the hole in the hull into the sea, she went back for the next.

It all blurred together on her—the dark cold wetness; the kicks and bites; the terrified, almost human screams. But it got harder, as the water rose to her waist and as she wearied. The bit of sleep she'd gotten on the hard floor in the forecastle hadn't been enough; she found herself fighting uphill with no clear idea of what she was doing or why.

The ship heaved again, and the creaking changed in

character and became a steady roar—the sound of wood ripping loose from wood.

"Out! Now!" Morkaarin yelled, and when she shouted back at him, something incoherent about not leaving the rest of the horses, he lashed a length of rope around her waist, then around his—he dragged her to the hole they'd made and leapt through, taking her with him.

The sea swallowed them, smashed them up against the side of the ship, then threw them back into its depths. The sea pounded Karah, tangled her against a limp, heavy body—left her half-dazed, but not so dazed that she gave up and inhaled the water. She clawed her way up to the heaving swells on the surface, gasped and spit and coughed until her lungs were clear, and found a piece of wreckage to cling to.

And then she remembered the rope around her waist and pulled on it experimentally. It resisted—and she pulled harder, suddenly remembering what was on the other end. She hauled with all her strength, and the First Captain's body came toward her, face down in the water, unmoving. In the faintest of light, light that promised true dawn at last, she could make out his pale form.

No! she thought. She reeled him in, using one hand and her teeth, while her other arm clutched the remains of the *Sea Mare's* framing timbers.

The waves dunked her under the water, but she held fast to the timber and the rope, and came up quickly with the First Captain's body right beside her. *Drowning,* she thought, and recalled the farmhand her parents had pulled out of the watering pond, and the children who fell into the river from time to time. Sometimes they could be saved, she recalled. She pulled Morkaarin's head up and held his body so his back was to her chest. The two of them rode the swells, and Karah prayed. She pushed on his stomach with her free hand—knotted the hand into a fist, punched up beneath his ribs. The first time, nothing happened. The second time she was equally unsuccessful. On the third punch, the First Captain vomited up seawater and bile and coughed and gasped. She kept his head leaning forward, and heard him draw in a shaky breath. Then another, and a third. He still hung limply in her arms, but now he breathed on his own.

The storm was dying down. Morning had come at last, grey and bleak—but even that dull light filled Karah with hope. She saw the dark line of land ahead—the waves were washing her toward it.

She was alive, and she was not alone. For the moment, that was enough.

The ship was going down. Amourgin dodged a falling mast and looked frantically through the darkness for some sign of Eowlie. The pimp as likely as not had thrown her overboard. She was probably already drowned, or lying with her throat cut in the hold. But what if she weren't?

The men and women of the XIXth streamed toward the one dinghy, as the ship settled further onto the rocks. They crawled over the tangles of downed rigging, the buckling planking—clambered into the little work boat, and started pushing.

There wasn't going to be enough room for even part of them, Amourgin noted. He wasn't about to get into the middle of that mess.

He ran for the corner of the aftcastle where he'd had his hammock, and dug around in the debris until he found his rucksack. It held his book, his magic supplies, a spelled knife, and a flask with water in it, among other things. He'd need whatever he could get.

Supplied as best he could manage, he went back on deck—in time to see several men pitch a bag of something out of the dinghy and swing the boat over the side. A whole herd of pan-icked men and women climbed in and let the boat down by pulley—Amourgin noted that Sergeant Ddrad had taken command, and Mercele was enforcing it, and between the two of them, they'd restored order.

He made his way to the bag, which in the faint light of

coming dawn seemed to be moving. He tried not to let himself hope—it was as likely to be extra supplies as the bundle he hoped to find.

The ship heaved, the bag kicked, and he heard a muffled groan. He pulled his beltknife out of its sheath and slit the bag open, careful not to cut the contents. Eowlie came up at him, eyes wild. He jumped back; the action was mere reflex, but he decided his reflexes were good. She was angry enough to kill.

The pimp hadn't been taking chances with Eowlie, Amourgin realized. He'd bound her wrists and ankles and then tied them together, gagged her, wrapped her muzzle shut—*then* stuck her in a bag. Amourgin looked forward to telling Eowlie the pimp was dead. Later.

He cut the ropes that bound her and untied the cloth gags. He was cautious—he admitted to himself that for all the odd attraction he felt for the woman, he was more than a little afraid of Eowlie, too.

She studied him, her expression unreadable.

"Can you swim?" he yelled.

She gave an affirmative nod but said nothing.

"Good. We're going to have to. Ship's going down!"

She held out her hand, her yellow eyes staring at him all the while, and he pulled her to her feet. She was far lighter than he would have thought. She placed one hand on his chest, slid her claw-tipped fingers up to the hollow of his throat, and then wrapped both arms around him. He pulled her tight against his body, ran his hands along her hard-muscled back down to the tight, hard curves of her buttocks.

She licked along his neck and the back of his ear—her tongue nearly dry, warm, the slightest bit rough. He groaned and pulled back. *There is something about a shipwreck makes a man horny as a stag in rut*, he thought. *Must be the wish to die happy*. But, his body's urges to the contrary, he preferred to live—and get laid on dry land. He pointed to the low side of the ship.

He pointed out a good-sized piece of debris, she nodded, and both of them jumped over the side of the ship together.

✧   ✧   ✧

Willek lay in her cabin, enjoying the gentle rocking of her warship. The day had dawned bright and fair, with no hint of the storm that had raged through the night. The tiny globe of wizardlight that indicated the continuing existence of the *Sea Mare* had just flickered and died. Her fleet was the victor in the battle with Darkist—at least before the storm struck—and though she would have to see to repairs and refitting here in Cnit before she took her fleet south and finished the bastard off, she had the funds and the manpower to see that the job was done well.

The refits would take—oh, not more than several weeks. Her spies told her Darkist's fleets had scattered like jackals before a lion, limping back to Tarin Tseld. What was left of them, in any case. The bloodstone showed her scenes of the Tseldenes rioting in the streets, massing to overthrow Darkist, burning the nobles in their homes as news of Darkist's defeat spread. The scenes were as fine as anything she could have wished for—and better than she would ever have dared hope to receive. She would finish off whatever resistance she found when she reached Darkist's domain. The rest of the realm of Tarin Tseld was preparing to welcome her as its rightful ruler.

Shemro's Strekkhylfa dynasty was at an end, and Darkist's as well. Willek decided she would style herself Majestic Deity of the Two Empires.

The only niggling worry besetting her was that she had not been able to identify all the extra players in her little military exercise. Darkist's spells had been plain enough a magicless moron could have marked them. She'd noted the craft-signatures of one of the Tykissian underground people as well—but that was to be expected. Her sister's work was right in the thick of things—and Willek had to admit Szoae's interference surprised her. Szoae, like the spiders she reminded Willek of, did not usually go out after prey. She preferred to spin wide webs and let it come to her. But Willek could not deny the presence of Szoae's spellworking in the battle. She was unsure of her sister's intent or of what she'd accomplished, but the motherless fiend had been there. That left three major players Willek had never so much as come across before, any one of whom had twice the power of Darkist. She couldn't guess their purposes, she couldn't divine what they'd done, and now that they were gone, she couldn't even discern any difference their magic had made on the course of the battle.

That much power combined with that sort of subtlety left a bad taste in Willek's mouth.

Just a minor bad taste. She wasn't about to forget she'd won.

She thought it might be pleasant to create a little victory-sending to dispatch to Darkist. Something small and unobtrusive—perhaps a spell to age him further. He looked like he was dancing at Death's table already—a little thing like that could push him the rest of the way over. Certainly it wouldn't hurt.

That can be a bit of entertainment for this evening, she decided, and got up to prepare to review her troops.

The grandcabin of the *Falcon* was in the usual place at the stern, one level down from the poopdeck, with big fantail windows over the ship's rudder. Two long eighteen-pounder bronze guns occupied some of the space; they were lashed home now, but the smell of powder smoke still lingered amid the gilded woodcarvings and hangings. A long table split the cabin from fore to aft, with the Admiral's bunk on one side of it and a desk with cubbyholes, bookshelves and map boards on the other. At that moment the table was crowded with men and women in the uniform of high rank or in priests' garb, many of them wounded and bandaged, all of them looking tired enough to collapse.

The Grand Admiral shuffled through the last of the papers. "About four thousand lost, then," she said. "Troops, that is; maybe two thousand sailors, mostly pressed civilians on the transports."

"My lady," the general replied, with a stiff bow of his head. There were red semicircles of exhaustion and strain under his eyes.

"The Tseldenes undoubtedly lost more than that," Willek said thoughtfully.

Several of the squadron commanders seated about him nodded vigorously. "If we didn't sink a third of their tonnage, I'm a pariah," one hawk-faced man with the tattoos of Old Tykis said. There was grey in his braids. "These frigates . . . I take back everything I've said, they're a terror to galleys."

"And we rode the storm better than the southrons, too," another naval officer said.

Willek leaned back in the tall padded leather chair. The storm might have been natural or a byproduct—there were so many spells flying back and forth that women would be dropping wolfcubs and flowers starting to sing for years on every island about. The ferocity of it had still been to her advantage; most of the Tykissian ships were built to take the outer oceans, while the Tseldene fleets were designed for the gentler waters of the Imperial Sea.

"We'll call it a victory, then," Willek decided.

She turned her head to look out the windows, blinking at the fierce sunlight. The coastline of Meltroon lay a thousand meters off; between the flagship and the shore were scores of other vessels, and more drawn up on the shelving beach for emergency repairs. The sound of hammers and saws mixed with shouting, cursing, and the splash of oars as longboats shuttled about with coils of rope, barrels of pitch, tools, and workmen. Beyond the beach and the military road that lay along the coastline, hospital tents had gone up to tend the wounded, and foraging parties were cutting ripe grain and sugarcane as fodder for the animals aboard the transports.

"Two more days, and everything that can float heads south," she said decisively. "That'll be all then, gentlefolk. To your commands—Shoddo, Lord Pelkar, Brigadier Multin, your Reverence, please stay."

She waited until the others had left, then rose and pulled a short black archwood rod from beneath the pillow of her bunk. It was plain except for brass buttons on the ends; there was a muted *pop* sound as she touched it to the four corners of the room.

"Safe now," she said.

"Are you a traitor or not?" the man in the embroidered buckskins and ear-to-ear tonsure of a War Priest of the Three said, fingering the archaic tomahawk at his waist.

Willek snorted mentally behind the impassive mask of her face. Fanatical dedication was all very well, and it took a true fanatic to successfully infiltrate the Church of the Three. The thought of what they'd do to a secret follower of the One of a Thousand Faces discovered penetrating the mysteries made even Willek wince a bit. But the priest took it entirely too seriously; also he'd picked up the odd ideas the southrons had about women, and answering to her made him deeply unhappy.

Well, he won't have to bear it much longer, she thought. Aloud: "I am in continuous contact with our lord Darkist," she said soothingly. "All changes in plan are made with him fully in mind." It was best not to lie directly to a magician, even if you were shielded. "The battle served both our purposes, disposing of the inconvenient. And Darkist's land forces have not been weakened at all. Merely destroying warships would leave an invasion of the coastlands of the New Empire very difficult. If the army is lost under the walls of An Tiram, everything up to the North Shield Wall will fall in a year. Darkist will rule, and we as satraps under him."

The priest nodded grudgingly. Willek went on: "And you know the peril our foreseeings found. The battle seems to have disposed of it."

"The *Sea Mare* is gone," the priest said. Willek smiled slightly, and the man's face contorted. "Not *destroyed*, you—*gone*. I cannot *find* it. It is not even in the power of Kevo, which a sunken ship would be. Simply *gone* from all sight and scrying."

Willek blinked, feeling her smirk turn gelid. *I cannot turn my plans aside from fear alone*, she thought. That might itself be the thing that brought disaster on her.

"Well, *find* them, then," she snarled. "Go!"

"I hope there aren't *too* many more like him," Brigadier Multin said, stroking his beard.

Willek spread her hands. "I don't think so. It's difficult to keep hereditary enthusiasm all that warm through centuries of danger without reward. Are your troops ready?"

"As ever," the brigadier said cheerfully. "My Shillraki mercenaries and Krevaulti levies really *don't* much care whose backside warms the throne. Neither do the Tykissian regiments I've had under me on the western border—Shemro's ah, *loss of touch* over the past decade has eaten away a good deal of her popularity. Late pay, bad rations, that sort of thing. We'll start the acclamation, and the rest of the army will join in before they know what's happening. Win big, hand out the donatives and plunder, and you'll be the most popular emperor since the founding."

They exchanged a thin smile. *I'll definitely have to do something about him*, Willek thought. He wouldn't stay bought.

Shoddo nodded judiciously. "I'm sure the civil service will welcome a new regime." Pelkar nodded in his turn; they both had the sleek air of Olmyan city nobility.

"It's in the hands of the gods, then," Pelkar said.

That, Willek thought later as she sat alone in the admiral's cabin, *is what I'm afraid of.*

Darkist luxuriated in the deep silky folds of his couch-robe and opened his mouth so one of his nubile young dancers could feed him another tiny strip of sugar-cured *keri*. When she leaned over, he tugged on her nipple-bells and listened to her squeal and laughed quietly as she darted just out of his reach.

To the victor go the spoils, he thought happily. The Tykissian navy, its power broken, lay at anchor in the harbor in Cnit. The wall in the Quiet Room showed him the twisting, dark streets of cities throughout the dead Tykissian empire, where news of his victory spread, and people danced around bonfires in the village squares, rejoicing at the downfall of the hated Shemro. His own navy at that moment sailed toward home, triumphant—he would greet his ships personally as they cruised between the giant legs of the statue of himself that acted as gate and guard to Tarin Tseld's greatest harbor.

The One of a Thousand Faces had found his sacrifices good and granted him the triumph he deserved. "I bought this battle with the coin of blood," he told the concubine who knelt at his feet, awaiting his merest whim. "It is the only coin gods respect."

She kept her eyes down, as was proper, but Darkist noted her shudder and smiled. She did well to fear him. A hundred of her sisters had gone beneath the knife, along with the senior lord of every household Darkist suspected of havening treason; the sacrifices had ceased only when Darkist read the footprints of magic in the entrails of a prince of the realm and saw the omens of Tarin Tseld's defeat change before his eyes to a crushing defeat for his enemy, Willek.

And the instant after that, the bothersome tampering of several hidden wizards had ceased as well. The dread certainty of pending disaster which had gnawed at his guts for days was gone.

His troops would require perhaps two weeks, and possibly a few days beyond that, to make necessary repairs and resupply; then they would sail to the Tykissian empire and claim their prize.

He considered his grandson, out in the garden chasing and futtering concubines like the young ram he was, and Darkist's smile grew broader. First the prize of empire—and then the greater prize.

"Enough," he told the slaves. He could not sport with his

women all day; he had much to do. The greatest burden of work fell on the winner of a war.

He rose slowly and slapped the dancer on her bare buttocks in passing. The greater prize . . .

He would send an energy creature to devour Willek, he decided. Something that would feed on fear and grow huge on its way to her so that when it reached her it would be unstoppable.

He headed for the Quiet Room.

Karah slogged through scum-specked knee-deep water toward the neck of high ground. Overhead, sharp-beaks and fearegulls wheeled; Karah suspected each of the little clumps of birds on the ground of harboring one of the *Sea Mare*'s dead. The low mournful wails of the big black sharp-beaks; the shrill cries of the gulls; the steady slosh of waves around her legs as the tide went out—all of those were sounds of a land unwanted by humans. *A place far from help*, Karah thought.

She had never seen such a desolate place; endless pebble-strewn flats and tidal pools that, perhaps, parted company with the sea somewhere off in the blue haze in the distance. The sun beat down on Karah's head and the glare reflected off the water into her eyes. Scrubby bushes struggled for existence on the little rocky islands of higher ground. Barrels and bits of planking and timber floated in the pools or were strewn across the sand and rock. Wet gravel shifted underfoot.

She staggered out of the water to the next high spot with Bren leaning on her for support. He was feverish and coughed constantly.

"You're beautiful," he whispered. "I love you with all my heart and soul."

"You're sick," she said calmly. "So I won't hold any of this against you." The sicker the First Captain had gotten, the more he'd adored her. The last hour or so, while they were still clinging to their wreckage and before they'd floated within reach of land, he'd asked for her hand in marriage, tried to undress himself, tried to undress her, and recited a surprising amount of passionate poetry in between coughs.

He was so terribly sincere, and his body felt so marvelous pressed against hers—she found herself wishing it was him instead of his fever talking.

They walked to the highest point of the piece of land they were on. It was sparsely covered with scrub-brush—the whole place was overwhelmingly flat, but this little rise was high enough and had enough live plants on it that Karah felt sure it would be above the water during a normal high tide. The shrubs would give Bren some shade. She was afraid if he walked much farther in the heat, he would die. Karah found the heat and glare and the biting of uncounted tiny insects nearly unbearable.

"Wait for me," she said. "Right here. I'm going to see if I can find anyone to help us." She also hoped to find at least two of the horses, and supplies washed ashore from the ship—and she had less pleasant things to attend to, as well. She had to find water and perhaps a febrifuge. Those she was most likely to find still attached to the bodies of the crew.

Bren wrapped his arms around her and pulled her into a fervent embrace. "Make love with me," he said.

She struggled out of his grip. Even sick, he was extraordinarily strong. His fever-bright eyes looked at her with longing, his cracked lips parted, waiting her kiss.

She still thought he was pretty—and she would have bet he looked better out of clothes than in them. "Godsall, I wish I knew how much of this you were going to remember later," she muttered. But she pulled away. If he were still inclined to randiness when he was in his right mind, she thought she'd take him up on any offer he might make. But this—

"Stay." Karah climbed off the rock. "I'll be back as soon as I find us some water."

"Water all over," he said, pointing to the salt sea.

"No! Don't drink *that*! You've had more'n enough already. Godsall! Wish I had someone t' stay with you—keep you out of trouble."

"I'll stay if you give me a kiss before you go." He looked forlorn.

"I just know you'll remember I did this," she said mournfully, and leaned over to kiss him. When he rolled onto his side to receive her kiss, a medallion slipped out of the open neck of his shirt. It glinted with gold and a complex design that blurred when she tried to study it—after a moment, the design hurt her eyes so much that she looked away. She brushed her lips against his—and he wrapped an arm around her and pulled her against his chest. His kiss was no mere peck, but a passionate embrace. When she finally managed to break away, she said, "Remember. Stay. You promised." She made him give her his overshirt, tied it to the highest of the trees so she would have a landmark, then hurried off before he could think of other demands.

"He's goin' to remember," she muttered as she headed toward the first cluster of birds. "I'll be charged with fraternizing with an officer, or takin' advantage of a man not in his right mind, or Three know what else. Kissing an officer will probably get me hanged."

She shouted and waved her arms at the birds as she neared, and they flew up, screaming rage. Two bodies lay in the tidal pool. She recognized an assistant priest and Doe, the Tseldene whore, and one of the horses, a scrawny brown one. She didn't know if the horse was one of those she'd managed to rescue or one that drowned aboard the ship and washed out after.

She searched both bodies, averting her eyes from the bird-ravaged faces and hands. She searched in vain—neither of the two had carried anything she needed.

Karah stood, scrubbed her hands in the water, and looked for the next place where the birds fed. She was as afraid as she'd been when the ship foundered. But standing there, she had more time to think about her fear—and more time to imagine surviving the wreck to die of thirst. Or hunger.

Or madness. The bleakness, the emptiness—they were enough to drive someone mad, she thought.

She wished she knew which horses she'd managed to save.

She wished she could find someone else alive.

She wished most of all that she could be sure Bren was going to be all right. If he lived, she wouldn't be alone. She wasn't certain when he'd quit being First Captain Morkaarin and started being Bren, but she decided she preferred the change.

Karah walked—stumbled—continued because she had to. She was exhausted, parched, sunburnt, bruised, and frightened. *"Grenlaarin" means nothing here,* she thought. *I could die unnoted, could be lost forever. My family can't help me here.* She'd always thought herself tough and capable; she never considered herself a snob.

She suddenly realized that she didn't care much for the person she'd been. She hoped she'd live long enough to find out what sort of person she could be.

Karah reached the next body. He had been one of the XIXth's pikemen. Both of his legs were gone, bitten off cleanly by something huge. *I was in that water,* she thought, and shuddered.

She rolled him face up, and was grateful the birds hadn't been at his face yet. He was a hideous shade of blue-grey and starting to bloat. She realized she wasn't going to have very long to search bodies—the task would soon become unbearable.

He had a flask strapped to his waist, and a dagger. She managed, with some struggle, to remove both. The flask was full, and whatever it had in it would be better for Bren than seawater. She didn't taste to find out what it contained; she was so thirsty she feared she would drink the whole thing. She moved on.

At the next cluster of birds, she found a sealed barrel and a broken one in the tidal pool with a dead woman—another member of the pike unit—and two dead horses.

One of them was Glorylad.

Karah choked on the sudden lump in her throat, and her eyes filled with tears. She waded into the water and stood beside the dead beast. Seaweed tangled his mane, and water covered his hooves. His head was thrown back.

"Oh, Laddie," she whispered. She'd raised him from a colt, trained him, spent every spare minute with him. She'd told him all her secrets—about the fights she had with her cousins when she was younger, about the boys she bedded as she grew up. Lately about the odious Kreugfeldt boy her father wanted to marry her off to. She didn't care that Glorylad didn't understand. He'd always listened, ears pricked forward, happy just to hear the sound of her voice.

She knelt in the water next to him, and stroked his jaw, and hugged his neck once. Still crying, she stood and brushed the tears from her cheeks. She pressed her lips into a thin line and took a few deep breaths. There was no time to stand and mourn. She had to move on.

She checked the woman's body, but found nothing of use. She aimed herself for the next black clump of scavengers, fighting tears, forcing herself not to look back.

"Hey!" someone shouted. She looked up—realized she'd been walking without looking around her. The voice came from a shrubby spot of high ground to her right. She turned and headed toward the voice and caught sight of movement beneath the low trees. Someone was sitting propped against one of the scrawny trunks. The person stood as she approached. It was a man, one she only vaguely recognized.

"You're the first I've seen alive," the man said.

Karah recognized him—he'd joined the unit the day before it shipped out. Karah didn't know his name, but she didn't like him very much. He was always watching, every time she saw him; watching Eowlie, watching Bren . . . watching her. But he was alive—maybe he'd managed to save something from the ship. "I'm Chevays," he added. "I've seen you before a few times."

I noticed, she thought. "Karah." She introduced herself. She almost added the "Grenlaarin" and decided against it. It didn't matter much here—wherever "here" was.

"The captain's alive, too. You find anything useful?"

He shrugged and didn't answer her question. "Did you?" he asked instead.

He made her nervous—she didn't tell him what she'd found and where she'd been looking, though she realized he'd been able to see what she was doing quite clearly while she was hugging her dead horse and searching the drowned pikewoman. She didn't answer.

He smiled—thin-lipped, a half-smile. Raised one eyebrow. She didn't care for his expression; it was condescending, amused at her, superior. She wanted to get away from him.

He said, "We'll have to go inland eventually, I suppose, but I was hoping to find more people first—and maybe some more water. I got the flask from the woman you were searching—but it won't last long, I don't imagine."

Karah said, "No. Probably not."

"So the First Captain's alive, is he?" Chevays studied her, his dark eyes thoughtful. "What about the girl with all the teeth?"

Karah became more sure that she did not like Chevays—not the way he looked at her or the way he talked to her; she didn't like his rat-thin face or his shifty eyes or his pointed questions. "I don't know," she said stiffly. "I'm still looking."

"Well," he said. "Well, well." He crossed his arms over his chest, tilted his head to one side, and stared down at her. He was very tall—and for all his leanness, muscular as well. His gaze wandered from her face to her breasts and downward, then back up again. He clicked his tongue. "You're going to need some help, aren't you? Why don't I come with you?"

"I don't think so," Karah said blandly. "We'll cover twice as much area if we split up and meet back here."

He rested his hand on the hilt of his knife. "I think separating would be a very poor idea."

Karah's hands slipped to her own knives. "I don't." She glowered at him.

"Wouldn't it be a shame for one of the ship's only two survivors to die so soon after the wreck?" He smiled again, and she thought he looked terribly like a sand viper.

"I told you—the captain's still alive."

"So you say. But if it were true, he'd be with you."

"Bad guess." She sized Chevays up, backing a step. He had the advantage over her in both reach and weight—and the way he looked at her, she thought he would kill her and enjoy it. She would not beat him in a straight fight.

Tall and lean as he was, she would bet she couldn't outrun him either. She couldn't scream for help—there wasn't anyone to hear.

"I outrank you," he said, and his smile became sly. "If you fight me, I'll still win—but when I'm through with you, I'll make sure you're hung for attempting to kill a superior officer. If you do what I tell you to do right now, you'll probably live."

"What a brave man you are," she snarled. She sheathed her left-hand knife, stuck two fingers in her mouth, and whistled shrilly—a low tone, rising.

"Calling for help? That was stupid, dear girl. Now I *have* to kill you."

He came in fast, knife low. Karah had no experience with knife fighting—she pretended her right-hand knife was a short sword. She deflected his cut, he grabbed her left wrist to stop her off-hand stab and she dropped that knife—but she slammed her forehead into his face and stepped as hard as she could on the arch of his near foot, then brought her knee up into his groin.

He yelped and lost his grip, and she scrambled out of his reach. Whistled again, the same shrill rising tone—slim chance it would do any good, but she judged her odds of survival slim. She'd take any chance at all.

He charged her again, limping.

She fled, hoping she'd hurt him enough to slow him down.

When she heard his harsh breathing right behind her, and felt the impact of his footsteps on the rocky ground, she realized she hadn't. She ran around a tidal pool, he tripped her, and she slammed headfirst into the stones. Her other knife skittered out of her hand across the stones. She rolled onto her back, pulled both knees into her chest, and kicked out at his face—managed to smash his mouth with one boot.

Blood spattered—blood and teeth. Chevays howled.

But he kept coming, and the white blade of his knife reflected the sun into Karah's eyes.

He landed on top of her, one knee in her stomach. She lost her wind and saw stars. Bile burned in the back of her throat. She grabbed the wrist of his knife hand with both her hands, and he punched her in the face with his free hand. Her nose, already broken when the *Sea Mare* wrecked, crunched beneath his fist.

Karah screamed. It was all she could do to keep from throwing up. But she didn't let go of his knife hand.

She heard a whinny and hoofbeats clattering over the rocks toward her at a canter. "Windrush!" she yelled. She couldn't see her horse coming—she hoped he got to her in time.

"You called your *horse?*" Chevays laughed.

Karah wedged her feet on the ground and bucked her hips up, hanging onto Chevays' knife hand with all her strength. She threw him off-balance, pulled his knife hand across her chest so that he fell onto it, then rolled. She bit him on the side of the forearm, clenching her jaws and trying to bite clear to bone.

He screamed.

Black hooves and black forelegs flashed over her head, and Chevays' skull gouted blood—teeth sank into one of the man's shoulders and pulled him up and threw him.

Karah rolled on her stomach and scrambled out of the way of the horse's hooves. "Trample!" she yelled, and Windrush dropped Chevays onto the stony beach . . . reared . . . smashed down with his forelegs on the man's chest and head. Reared and plunged . . . reared and plunged . . .

It seemed to happen so slowly—she watched Chevays fall forever, watched her horse pound him into the stones, endlessly—watched Windrush pound his skull into a pulp on the ground, until he didn't have a face anymore, only smears of blood and grey tissue and skin.

She'd spent years war-training horses. She'd never seen the results of that training before.

"Stop!" she said at last, when there could be no doubt that Chevays was dead and beyond any hope of miracles. Then Karah crouched on hands and knees, vomiting. The combination of nerves and fear and the sight of the man's shattered body proved more than she could bear.

Bent over and retching, she almost missed what happened next. Almost—but Windrush backed and whinnied, and swirling movement above the body caught her eye.

She looked up and stared in horror. Smoke rose from his body, pale and wispy, curled and looped and coiled above him until it coalesced into the face of a beautiful woman. The wraith-woman looked from the man to the horse, then over at Karah. Her expression held annoyance and infinite disdain. "The idiot," she said in a soft, cultured voice. "He got precisely what he deserved." Her mouth twitched into a smile. "I would have preferred to take care of him myself—but I must say, you did an adequate job, considering what you had to work with." She shook her head. "I'm coming with you. You won't know I'm around—I'm not planning to advertise my presence. But I feel the need to keep an eye on my sister." Her face uncoiled, back into hazy tendrils, and with an unexpected burst of speed, the tendrils came at Karah and started to wrap around her—

They stopped.

"How terribly, terribly strange," a muffled voice from within the haze said. "I cannot so much as touch you." The smoke coils hung there for an instant, and the voice said, "Nearly out of time. I'll take what I can get." And Karah saw the layers of smoke wrap around Windrush's face. The horse reared, and his eyes rolled back until Karah could see the whites around the edges.

Then the smoke vanished up Windrush's nostrils, and the horse stood, shivering.

Karah didn't know what to do. She got up and walked to her horse. "You, woman," she said. "Spirit. Ghost. Whatever you are. Can you hear me? Can you answer?"

The horse gave no sign of being anything but a horse. "You won't know I'm around," the woman had said. Perhaps, Karah thought, she could not control the horse. Karah wasn't certain what the smoke-woman might *gain* from going into the horse— but if she wasn't going to bother Windrush, Karah needed him.

Awful as it was, Karah searched Chevays' mangled body. The flask was intact, and she found another knife, and around his waist, a pouch. She took everything. If he'd kept it, it had to have some value. She gathered up all the knives.

"Rot in a cold hell," Karah told his body.

She staggered. She was exhausted, her body hurt everywhere and her face felt like it was about to explode. Her nose was swelled so much she had trouble looking around it, and both her eyes were swelling shut.

"Down," she told Windrush.

He knelt.

She climbed wearily onto the big grey's back, and his muscles tensed and trembled beneath her thighs. The animal had never used his battle training before. Karah, her own recent battle experience still horribly fresh in her mind, could sympathize. She patted him on the neck and crooned to him, "Good lad. Brave lad. You did a fine job, boy."

Windrush calmed as she stroked him and praised him. He was frightened by the corpse; she needed to get the horse away. She needed to get back to Bren, too—to give him something to drink, to see if he looked any better for having rested.

"Up," she said.

Windrush lurched to his feet, his front legs straightening fast so that she nearly slipped off his rump, his hind legs shoving. *So tired I can't even ride,* she thought, amazed that she could be that tired.

Karah clucked her tongue and headed back the way she'd come, guiding the horse with knees and words.

I wish I was home.

❂ CHAPTER XII

Amourgin was the first to spot the red shirt blowing from a tree—but Eowlie was the one who found Bren, unconscious and breathing shallowly beneath the meager shade of a few scrubby bushes.

"He's nearly dead," she said.

Amourgin knelt by his commander and checked the unconscious man's pulse. The pulse felt fast and thready; Bren's skin was hot and dry, and his color was very bad.

Amourgin said softly, "I wonder if things would go better for me if he died."

He looked up, and saw Eowlie staring at him. She shook her head. "No. If you can save his life, you should. He was fair to me. He set me free from Zeemos."

The law-speaker sighed. "Yes. Of course." He stared down at the First Captain, and sighed again, more deeply. "Eowlie—" he said. "I believe I can save his life. And I agree with you that I should—he is a good man, and fair, and he deserves to live." Amourgin lay his hands on Eowlie's shoulders and looked into her odd gold eyes. "But I could be hanged anywhere in the Tykissian Empire, at any time, if you were to tell anyone how I saved him."

The girl's eyes widened, and she asked, "How can that ve?"

"I do magic. I am a wizard, though not a great one—but anywhere in Tykis, the sentence for wizardry is death."

Eowlie looked bewildered. "Vut the f'riests do magic."

"Yes. But I am not a priest."

She frowned. "Stufid, stufid rules." The girl sighed. "Then no one will know how you saved him."

Amourgin laughed quietly, and pulled the *Analects* out of his pack. "I imagine I worry for no reason," he said, more to himself than to Eowlie. "It isn't likely we'll live through this little adventure."

Eowlie said, "We'll live."

She said that with incredible confidence. He wondered if she knew something he didn't.

He squatted in the sand next to Morkaarin, and slid the secret panel out of the back of the book. "Watch my back for me," he said. "If you see anyone coming, I'll have to hide the evidence of what I've done."

She nodded, silent, and turned away to stare over the flat, bleak land for signs of life.

Amourgin removed several of the tiny tubes from their hiding place, and mixed their contents in the palm of his hand, all the while muttering. He added a febrifuge, an expectorant, two varieties of spirit balm, and as an afterthought, one of the new powders still being tested for effectiveness—a variety of leaf mold, he'd been told, and surprisingly good against some forms of lung sickness.

It would be interesting, he thought, to see how well the powder actually worked. He poured a bit of alcohol from his flask into the concoction, stirred it around with a finger while muttering an incantation against illness, and smeared the resultant gooey mess against the captain's lips. Then he called upon the Three to witness his work.

That finished, he rocked back on his heels to wait for results.

The changes were not long in appearing. First, the high color faded from the captain's cheeks. Then his breathing slowed. After a few moments, the rasping and gurgling that came with each breath the First Captain took disappeared.

Eowlie looked over her shoulder at the law-speaker and said, "I see someone. Looks to ve coming this way."

The First Captain wasn't better yet, but he looked less likely to die, Amourgin thought. The law-speaker looked up at the girl. "How many, and how far away?"

"One f'erson on a horse, riding slowly. You have a few minutes."

The law-speaker waited and watched, still squatting, shifting his weight from side to side to keep his feet from falling asleep. The First Captain groaned, and moved his arms and legs—swimming motions. "Karah," he mumbled, and then something else the law-speaker couldn't understand.

"He's waking," Amourgin said. He poured a few drops of the liquid in his flask onto his sleeve, and wiped the captain's mouth with the damp cloth.

"Is he well again?"

"Better." The law-speaker shrugged. "He's better. Let's hope that will be good enough."

The First Captain rolled onto his side and groaned.

Amourgin heard the thud of horse's hooves approaching. He shoved his little tubes back into the book cover and slipped the book into his pack.

"Can you see who it is?"

Eowlie was still watching, crouched in the middle of the stand of shrubs. For a long time, she gave no answer.

Then, "Karah," she said.

"Karah?" Amourgin smiled. "Then in all probability, she's the person who tied the captain's shirt to a tree."

Eowlie growled—the sound made the hair on Amourgin's arms stand up.

The law-speaker asked, "What is it?"

"She's hurt."

Amourgin swore. "I'm running out of supplies," he muttered. "Already."

Eowlie stepped out of her hiding place and waved her arms. "Karah!" she shouted. "Over here!"

The Grenlaarin girl was close enough for Amourgin to make her out easily. He saw her wave, then sway and clutch her mount's mane with both hands. He cringed. The girl was either exhausted or severely hurt—he could think of nothing else that would make her ride so poorly.

"Ah—more vad news," Eowlie said softly.

The law-speaker felt the muscles in his jaw tense. "What?"

"Tide is coming in. Very fast."

He stood then—turned away from the captain, whose breathing had improved enough Amourgin was sure he was out of danger—and walked to Eowlie's side. She pointed.

Lines of blue slipped between the hillocks and dunes and tidepools of the lowland. Little runs of breakers rolled toward him, coming closer with every wave. Even as he watched, the sea encircled another tiny island not far away.

He looked up. Two of the three moons rode high in the sky—Mother and Son. For the tide to be rising so quickly, the Father must be on his way. He looked at the ground under his feet—low ground. But there was no higher ground in sight.

"Is it going to cover this island?" Eowlie wanted to know.

Amourgin wished he'd been thinking of the tides. Or—he shook his head angrily—that he'd been thinking at all. "Can't say," he said. The water was rising fast. The edge of the oncoming water licked around Karah's horse's hooves. "We'll have to hope it doesn't. We've no time to get to higher ground."

Bren came out of the haze he'd been in for so long. He'd been someplace hot and dangerous—he vaguely remembered that. The air around him was finally cool and smelled sweet— he took a deep breath, hoping to identify the scent, but it was foreign to him. He looked down at his feet and noticed they were floating above the ground. This seemed wrong and annoying to him, but he realized it was a minor point. He couldn't be bothered with trivia. Something important was about to happen in front of him.

Fog rolled back like curtains, and on the lake in front of

him—*Oh, I didn't realize I was standing on the shore of a lake*, he thought—something moved. A boat, he decided first. Or perhaps a large bird, flying low.

He realized what he saw was a horse, galloping across the surface of the water, with Karah on his back. She charged toward him across the lake. He kept expecting her to fall in, but she didn't. Something gold gleamed in her upraised hand—gleamed with its own light. Karah shouted, "A gift from the gods, your majesty!" and threw the golden thing.

It spun through the air, end over end, growing brighter and more radiant as it flew towards him.

He held out his hands.

The glorious golden thing tumbled closer, slowing as it approached.

He grabbed for it.

It slipped between his fingers and fell into the surface of the lake with a terrible hiss—

—Bren shouted and sat up. The world around him was dark, illuminated only by the merry flickering of a campfire.

Karah, Amourgin, and Eowlie all turned to stare at him. Light from the fire gave them all a ruddy glow and threw long shadows across their faces. The shadows emphasized the length of Eowlie's jaw and threw her gleaming fangs into sharp relief. Beside the wolfish woman, Karah and Amourgin held long sticks over the fire and roasted small animals speared on the tips.

"The sleeper wakes at last," the law-speaker said, and chuckled.

"I was beginning to think you would never wake at all," Karah added. Her smile was bright, but Bren could see real concern in her eyes. He realized that some of the darkness on her face wasn't shadow. Her nose was swollen, and both her eyes bore dark bruises that spread from the bridge over the outer edges of her cheekbones.

Bren frowned. "Karah—your nose—"

She waved a hand and laughed. "Fell while wandering all over the flats looking for other people."

Something about her laugh didn't ring true to the First Captain—something about the laugh, and about the narrowing of her eyes when she spoke. He let it pass. In private, later, he could find out where she'd gotten her bruises. For the moment, he'd act as if he believed her explanation.

Eowlie smiled at him, too. Bren could see nothing but friendliness in her broad, toothy grin and glittering yellow eyes, but he still shivered. Those teeth seemed sharper every time he saw them. "I caught some little animals that came onto the island to escape the tide, sir," she said. "I already ate mine. Vut I caught extra, so we have some left for you."

Bren stood. He was surprised that he felt so good. He thought he remembered being sick—but perhaps that was part of the dream. "I'm starved," he said. Then he started upright.

"My troops—"

He stopped at the look the others gave him and sank back. The law-speaker handed him a sharpened stick and pointed to a lumpy pile of something built on several large leaves. The First Captain discovered the pile consisted of many more of the little animals the others were eating, already skinned and gutted.

He skewered one on his stick and went to sit beside Karah. He remembered closeness between them—shared kisses and perhaps even her saving his life. He hoped that wasn't part of the dream.

As he sat beside her, she gave him a shy smile.

Good, he thought. *Not part of the dream at all.* He thought about it for a moment—thought about the implications of being in love with one of his scouts. Then he considered everything that had gone before; the army's refusal to promote him, Willek's attempt to kill him off, his situation—shipwrecked and lost and likely to die at any time—and he leaned over and kissed her low on her cheek, well away from the bruises.

She scooted closer to him and kissed him back—but hers

was no chaste peck on the cheek. She kissed him on the lips, firmly and with considerable passion.

He got caught up in the kiss—pulled her against his chest with one arm and held her there, relishing her warmth and the firmness of her body pressed against his. Amourgin and Eowlie made comments to each other, but he ignored the joking remarks.

He heard hissing and pulled away from the embrace to see what was causing the sound. His dinner had caught fire. *Appropriate*, he thought. Amourgin and Eowlie laughed, and when he pulled his intended meal out of the flames, the law-speaker tossed water on it from a little flask.

"Gods, don't waste the water!" Bren said.

"Seawater," the law-speaker answered. "We had a nice bit of *woala* in it, but that's gone now. Besides putting the fire out," at that, Amourgin laughed again, "the seawater adds some flavor to the meat—it's rather gamey." He put the flask down and picked up his own cooked beast, and tore strips off with his teeth.

"Better than starving by far," Karah said.

"I won't starve unless nothing lives within the distance I can walk," Eowlie said. Her smile was smug. "I hunt vetter than anyone—and I don't use guns or vows and arrows or nothing like that. I just catch the animals with my hands." She grinned again and flexed her fingers so the claws extended. They were sharp and gleaming white, with none of the paint on them Bren remembered from the first time he saw her.

"We're lucky to have you with us," he told the odd woman, and he meant it.

He tried his own meal and found, aside from the charcoal taste of the burned places, that it was not bad at all.

Amourgin said, "The Mother and Son are up, but setting, and the tide is just below washing over the top of this island. I sat down and figured out the rising time on the Father. It conflicts with the Mother and the Son right now, keeping the tide from going as high as it could. Next time the Family comes around, all three are going to rise together, and this island will be under water. We need to get out of here as soon as the tide starts going out. Run straight for the mainland without stopping for anything. Otherwise, we'll be trapped here—or worse, on some sorry stretch of ground even lower than this between here and the mainland."

Karah finished swallowing the last mouthful of her beast and grabbed another one to roast. "Are we even sure there is a mainland? What if we've wrecked on a cluster of low islands out in the middle of the sea, and this is all there is?"

Amourgin shrugged. "Then next moonrise, we're all going to drown. Let's hope there's a mainland and that we can find it."

Bren said, "I don't suppose there's a chance one of you managed to salvage an astrolabe from the ship."

Amourgin laughed. "None at all."

The First Captain nodded. "Ah, well. It was a hope. And this is all who survived the wreck?"

"Can't say. This is all we've found. I can't believe no one else made it—but we've seen no signs. We've been watching for fires, too—hoping some of our people landed on different islands and just stayed put."

Karah started to say something, then stopped. She stared thoughtfully into the fire, and Bren wondered what she was thinking. Finally she said, "I found the bodies of a number of the crew." She touched her nose gently and kept staring into the flames. "None alive. Found Glorylad drowned."

"I thought *that* was Glorylad," Eowlie said, pointing to the horse tethered behind them, who was asleep on his feet.

"That's Windrush." Karah got out the words, but swallowed hard when she said them. Bren saw the glitter of tears slipping down her cheeks.

He slid an arm around her shoulders. Odds were that he would never see his own friends and comrades again—Ddrad and Mercele and the other men and women who'd served under him for the past several years. He feared them all dead.

He could sympathize with Karah's grief, too. A horse didn't seem so important to him—but horses had always been her life. He wondered if she'd ever had time for human friends.

"What direction will we have to go?" he asked Amourgin.

"Tide came in from the north. Our hope of escaping it will be to run south."

Bren nodded. "So if we've reached mainland, we could be near Tarin Tseld—even near An Tiram."

Amourgin said slowly, "It could mean that. Although this doesn't look like the Tarin Delta; from what I've heard, that's mostly mud. Could mean we're on the Spectre Islands, too. Considering the crew that was manning the ship—" He broke off the sentence, and Bren saw him shiver.

The First Captain nodded, not liking that idea at all. "We could be just about anywhere within the Imperial Sea, I suppose." He gnawed on one of the tiny bones, cracked it, and sucked on the marrow while he thought. "Considering who—or what—sailed our ship, I suppose we can't even say for sure that we're still within the confines of the Imperial Sea. We could be anywhere."

"The gods know," Karah said.

Both Amourgin and Karah touched the dots on their cheeks and forehead, and quickly ducked their heads. Bren, from a far less conservative branch of the religion, merely pressed three fingers to his forehead.

"The gods may know, but men must act in any case," he said, and the others nodded. "I'm setting watches over the tide. I'll take the first, since I've had some sleep. Eowlie, you have the second, Amourgin the third, and Karah the last."

Karah protested. "I slept the sleep of the dead when I got back here. I feel fine now. Besides, I wasn't sick—"

So he had been sick. He thought as much. No matter. He felt fine right then, and he intended to keep the watches short.

"That was an order, scout," he said. He smiled when he said it, but left no room for argument.

Karah proved she truly had learned to follow orders. She nodded and didn't say a thing.

Bren was impressed.

Willek had no need to summon a blood demon this time. The working she chose had nothing to do with demons; she would simply build an energy circle, which drew power from a single chosen target, and send it on its way. What she planned was the tiniest of spells—unobtrusive, silent, completely lacking in flash and drama.

If her guesses about Darkist's age and general health were anywhere near correct, it ought to kill his current body within the week. Then he'd be forced to jump to the new body—a young, healthy, magically inept body.

She chuckled. One of her spies in his court, at her behest, had sent her a little packet with a few tiny clippings of his nails and hair, a bit of his spittle dried on a piece of paper, and a single drop of his blood. Willek wondered how her spy had collected that last. But Shaad Shaabin was a wonder.

She smiled. It certainly paid to hire clever help.

She laughed. "Darkist, now you find out what youth and cleverness can do to doddering, feeble old age."

The ship rocked from side to side, and waves slapped against the hull. Soothing—so soothing, the pulse of the world. In her cabin in the forecastle, Shemro lay in a spelled coma, eyes open but seeing nothing. The last of the Morkaarins was dead; Tarin Tseld hung on the edge of internal collapse; Darkist was doomed.

Willek held the whole of the civilized world in her hand, and she was ready to tighten her fingers around it.

She wove up the energy spell—a tiny swirling ring born of Willek's magic, but of Darkist's body. At first it was so energy starved it flickered with its own light, but she slowed it down, made it invisible—and then sent it streaking over the sea on a path to the wretched old man.

"By the smallest of magics, the mightiest fall," she whispered.

Then she rose, and left her cabin to walk among the crew. It was her job to encourage them, to spur them to greater efforts while they repaired the fleet—and it was her desire to win their admiration and their loyalty. When Shemro suffered her sad demise—soon, wonderfully soon—Willek wanted none to question her authority.

Darkist cackled over the vast, black circle of a huge bloodstone. A tiny circle was carved out of one side of it, along the thick edge—the missing circle might have been a bit of decorative work . . . but it wasn't.

"Like calls to like," Darkist whispered, stroking his fingers over the smooth, cold surface. "Like calls to like," he said again, and touched the place where the circle had been carved out. The stone glowed, and the circle glowed brighter. Out of the stone, a dark red mist oozed, and coalesced on the stone's surface into the fat, shapeless mass of the blood demon.

"Has she fed you well, then?" Darkist asked the spawn of hell.

"Yes, master. I am rich with her blood."

"Give me a drop of it."

The demon shrank back from Darkist's reaching hand. *Silly, stupid creature*, he thought, *to begrudge me a single drop of blood.* Fire crackled from his fingers, and the demon's blood-engorged tentacles hissed and blackened. "One drop," he said again. He could not take from the demon, but he could make it want to give.

"Yes, master," it finally whimpered. It excreted a single drop of blood onto the flat surface of the stone and backed away as fast as it could, its tentacles flopping and squishing as it moved.

Darkist despised the blood demon. It was weak and cowardly—but in some circumstances, it was very useful. He scraped the blood off of the stone into a tiny crystal vial, and told the demon, "Go back now. Go back and wait on her every wish. But whatever you tell her, be sure to come afterwards and tell me."

The blood demon oozed back into the surface of the stone, until no sign was left that he'd ever been there.

Then Darkist held up the sparkling vial to the rays of two moons. "The time has come to send you a final gift, my dear girl," he told the tiny container. "I send havoc to you and your people, and even the ground you stand on, since you skulked away from battle with your tail between your legs.

"Like calls to like," he whispered to the blood, and hurried out of the bloodstone room and down one hall, and then another, and then a third, until he reached the salt baths. The tide was high, and the baths were full to the next highest level. When the moons pulled the tides out, other baths, carved in lower levels of stone, remained full.

Darkist stripped, then lowered himself into the seawater. He sat on the carved stone step, feeling the power of the sea swelling around him. He touched the surface of the water, and said softly, "Live, O terror from the deeps, O avatar of the face of the Thousand Faces; creature that is the soul of the madness of watery graves; monster with the strength of the sea. Come forth and serve me."

The surface of the water swirled and darkened, and then began to swell and bulge in front of him. A watery monster rose up, and howled with a drowned and bubbling howl, and then sank back into the pools until only its liquid head broke the smooth surface.

"Yes, master?" it gurgled.

Darkist dripped the blood into the water, on the monster's head. The thing he'd made absorbed the blood and shivered with delight.

"Thank you," it said, and Darkist laughed.

"She's yours when you find her. But you must find her. Like calls to like," the old man commanded. "Her blood is now your blood, and the scent of her will take you to her, no matter how far she may flee."

"Yes," the creature agreed.

Darkist smiled slowly. A pleasant idea occurred to him.

"Once you have left An Tiram, you need not hurry to her. Feed and grow great. Devour all who cross your path. Spread terror and destruction, so that when you find her, you will be huge and mighty and fearsome. Let her know real dread before she dies."

Again the creature said, "Yes, master."

Darkist waved his hands over the pool in which he sat, and felt currents swirl around him as the creature began to move. He shooed the monster on its way. "Begin," he whispered. "Go now. Find her. Make an end of her."

Konzin stood in hastily erected stocks out in front of the ranchhouse. He'd been there for several days, with the sun burning down on him during the day, and the cold night air chilling him once darkness fell. They'd given him a sip of water from time to time—and one of the house girls had shoved bread in his mouth, though she'd been rude about it, and told him she hoped the missus ripped his eyes out with her bare hands before they killed him.

He'd had a bad time of it. He'd soiled himself early on, and the ranch hands, walking past carrying tack and crops, never failed to take an extra step out of their way to kick him.

He was afraid. He knew he was going to die, but he didn't know when, or how. Thoughts of that "when" and "how" occupied his every waking moment.

He was positioned so that everyone who came up the road could see him, standing there in his shame. The only advantage of his position was that he could see people coming up the road before anyone in the house knew they were on the way.

Karah's parents had come out of the house to greet Jawain Grenlaarin when he came riding in on one of his fine cobs. The three of them talked in low tones near Konzin; at intervals, they glanced in his direction, and when they did, their expressions grew cold and hard.

By being very still and concentrating, Konzin could make out most of what they said.

"—and she was alive a couple days back," Jawain was saying. "I had a man in place in Derkin—doing something else for me, but that didn't work out. It's of no matter now. He was pressed in the same bunch as Karah—from the inn. Told him to keep an eye on her, and even when they shipped out, he was right there. Course, she did all right on her own."

"They shipped out!" Karah's mother's voice rose.

"On their way to Tarin Tseld to war on Darkist. I followed them until the storm at sea, keeping two, three spellcasters going all the day and night. But after the battle, we lost them. Something stopped our spell." He shuddered, and Konzin got the impression that the something had been too terrible for words.

The trio's voices dropped again, then rose as Jawain Grenlaarin looked in the herdsman's direction and said, "He's the bastard killed my Brunnai?"

"Can't be sure it was by his hand she died," Iano said softly. "If not, it doesn't matter. It was by his plan."

Jawain's expression made Konzin wish he'd never thought to steal the ranch. "Right enough. Then he'll pay," the man said, and turned away. The ice in his voice sent shivers along the herdsman's spine.

Iano looked at his wife and said, " 'Course, there's the matter of the note."

Jawain said, "They find it yet?"

Misa's voice could have sawed through stone wall. "Aye, they found it. In the hands of a couple of kid beggars who said they'd stolen it. Like as not they were paid t' say that, but then, you can't catch the little vermin and beat the truth out of 'em in Derkin—'s against the law."

Jawain muttered something that Konzin couldn't catch, no matter how hard he tried. Then, "—should hang him now."

Misa's back was to Konzin. He couldn't hear what she said at all—he only caught the anger in her soft reply.

Iano said, "We have to find out if Karah's still alive—though the traitor can't tell us a bit about that. But maybe he can tell us who he gave the note to, and why?"

Jawain's expression as he looked over Konzin became calculating. That look frightened Konzin even more than the angry one. Iano glanced over at him too, and his eyes bore the same cold, terrible craftiness.

"Torture?" Iano asked in conversational tones.

Jawain's mouth slowly—horribly—stretched into a smile. "Oh, for certain."

Not torture, Konzin thought. He was a rugged man—but he had no illusions about his ability to withstand the things the Grenlaarins would do to him. He rolled his swollen tongue over his cracked lips and croaked "I'll talk."

Three faces turned to stare at him, wearing matching expressions of disbelief.

"Sure you will," Jawain said. "After we've hurt you."

"No!" Konzin shook his head wildly. "No! I'll talk now. I'll tell you anything you want t' know." He babbled, "I didna mean for things t' turn out the way they did. I didna mean for anyone t' die." He felt the heat of a tear roll down his cheek.

The Grenlaarins looked uncertain.

Konzin pressed his slight advantage. "I meant to steal the money—by the Three, I know I was evil t' do so, but I've wanted for so long to have horses of my own. I thought with the money, I could buy my own spread and . . ." He hung his head. ". . . and buy a stud and one or two Grenlaarin brood mares from you for cheap—when you . . . when you couldn't make taxes.

"So I hired a few men t' 'rob' us when we left the city. Their pay was t' be half the note. But then nothing went right. Madine Karah got pressed, and gave me t' money t' bring t' you, so if I'd have been of a mind, I could have stolen it all. But I didn't want t' leave t' Madine trapped in t' army. I tried to find the men I'd hired, to tell them the deal was off, but they were gone. We all rode back here, fast as we could—I was hoping we would miss them. But they waylaid us—followed us. When I told them to stop, they started killing people. They left me alive and gave me my half of the money . . . but . . . but that was only so they could blackmail me. They told me I had to hire them for my ranch, or they'd come to you and tell you lies about me."

Misa and Iano stared at each other, eyebrows raised.

For a moment there was silence.

"I think we should still torture him," Jawain said.

"Ye-es," Iano said, but he didn't sound certain.

"I can tell you where to find the killers," Konzin said. "And how many there are."

He studied the three Grenlaarins. Iano and Misa seemed swayed by his story; they hovered with doubtful expressions upon the precipice of uncertainty. Jawain, however, was still plainly unconvinced. He stood with his arms crossed over his broad chest, glaring down at Konzin.

"So tell us," Jawain said at last.

Konzin said, "There are nearly twenty of them, if the band has stayed together. All of them are seasoned ranch hands, most from up around Olmya. Most are Tykissian, though a few are Krevaulti. The leader's name is—Rale Gonstad."

He dropped that little bombshell as casually as he could. The Gonstads and the Grenlaarins had an ongoing feud over the quality of the horses each house bred. The Grenlaarins were well ahead in public opinion—so the idea that a Gonstad was behind the treachery was certainly something they could fathom. There had been killings between the extended families before.

Indeed, Jawain sucked in air through the gap in his front teeth, and beside him, Iano's fingers clenched and unclenched. Both men stared at each other, and Jawain said, "Gonstads—"

Misa said, "It all adds up. Damnall—we should have known . . ." She looked down at Konzin. "Why didn't you tell us this? Why did you make up a story?"

He hung his head. "Because I didn't think you'd believe me. And I was so ashamed that I couldn't save Brunnai, or the hands."

Iano was the next to speak, and he spoke, not to Konzin, but to Jawain. "Meet me by morning on the north road, with every hand you can muster. We'll wage war on the damned Gonstads and have our revenge for Brunnai."

"The County Justicar—" Jawain began.

"May the *One* take the Justicar!"

"I meant that we'll have to be careful, breaking the Imperial peace."

Misa nodded. "I wish I could ride with you—but the house girls and I will mind the stock until you get back. Bring us their heads on pikes," she added.

The three Grenlaarins turned to leave—and then Iano turned back. "Don't leave him in the stocks," he told his wife. "Give him the run of the outer buildings while we're gone."

Misa nodded. "Shall I permit him to stay in his old rooms?"

Iano said, "Until we get back, yes. He'll have to make us a restitution, but I've no stomach to kill a man who was double-crossed by *Gonstads*." Then Iano turned to Konzin. "If you run away, man, you'll never know another minute's peace in the rest of what will be a short and terrible life."

Konzin nodded his understanding. "I'll be here when you get back," he said, and his voice rang with conviction.

Why wouldn't I be? he thought, as Misa ran off to get the keys and Iano and Jawain ran for the stables. *By the time you fools get back—if you survive the wrath of the Gonstads—my men will be here and the ranch will belong to me.*

Karah woke to someone shaking her shoulder and shouting, "Tide's receded enough we can make a run for it." It was the law-speaker who woke her. Bren and Eowlie were moving over by the embers of a dying fire. The sky was grey and overcast, the clouds scudding near the ground, and tatters of fog still hanging on the water and into the shrubs.

She remembered where she was and how she came to be the regretted waking.

Karah sat up, and immediately her nose and cheekbones began to throb. Sleep had been a wonderful reprieve from pain—but the other three were already slinging their meager belongings into two packs. Karah realized they intended to use Windrush as a pack horse.

There was something she needed to remember about Windrush. She closed her eyes to think about this, and the pain in her head grew worse, until she gave up trying to think at all. She rose unsteadily to her feet and struggled to Bren's side.

"I'm ready," she said. She didn't add that she felt ready to die, though she thought it. She was a country girl, and not about to be shown up by a citified law-speaker.

Bren looked at her and wasn't fooled. "You'll ride," he said. "You won't be able to keep up otherwise."

She started to argue, but Bren had waved to Eowlie, who brought Windrush over. Bren gave Karah a knee up, and she sat astride the horse, swaying slightly. The others put their makeshift packs in front of her, balanced over the horse's withers.

"Fine," Amourgin said. "Let's go now. We have no idea how far we'll have to travel, and the Father has nearly caught the Mother and the Child. The next tide will be severe."

They took off across the pebbled beaches at a trot.

From off to their left, someone shouted, "There they are!" The shout was nearly lost under the cries of the shorebirds and the distant roar of the surf—but the cheer that followed wasn't.

Karah looked left when she heard that ragged cheer, and saw a thin line of people running towards her from a tiny, scrub-covered island.

"Survivors!" Bren shouted, and his face lit with a radiant smile.

The four of them came to a halt and waited. Karah couldn't help counting the runners. There were thirty of them—and as they came toward her, she realized they were running in formation, many of them with muskets or halberds over their shoulders.

"Ddrad!" Bren bellowed as he recognized one of the runners; he sprinted across the flats and tidepools to meet them. "Father Solmin!"

"I thought you dead, sor," Ddrad shouted. "I'm right glad to see you." The men embraced as men often did, slapping each other's backs and laughing.

"Mercele?" Bren asked. Ddrad shook his head. Karah saw tears welling in Bren's eyes as he and Ddrad and the rest of the survivors ran back to join up with the smaller group, then vanishing as his face set. He smiled when he looked at her, though; she felt a glow of satisfaction at that.

"We got the boat back thataway," the sergeant added. "It won't hold this lot."

"Leave it," Bren said. "It's too big to carry, and we have to hurry. Next tide will be the start of the three-moon tides. We *have* to make higher ground."

Karah studied the survivors from the doomed *Sea Mare* and shivered. None of the men and women who lived to get on that boat had been from her unit. Of the scouts, only she and Eowlie were still alive.

Eowlie had evidently been thinking the same thing, for she looked from the soldiers to Karah, and her yellow eyes were narrowed. "We will liff, you and I," she said fiercely.

Karah nodded. *Or we'll take Darkist's bastards to hell with us,* she thought.

They formed up, and they were no longer four survivors pitted against the unknown. They were a company again, Karah discovered, a company with purpose.

They sang while they marched—the men's low voices and the women's higher ones blending beautifully, so that if she hadn't known the words they were singing, Karah would have thought the songs lovely. But they sang about how they hated to march, and about spending life belly-down in the mud, and about the old battles—Kunheero, and Poke Mountain, and

An Tiram. Karah led them off on the one about Sergeant Sara, whose amulet failed so that she got the crud, got pregnant, and finally got away.

Then they sang of home and how they wished they were there—and Karah stopped singing along partway through the song and closed her eyes and let Windrush have his head. She wished she were home, with Glorylad still safe, and her working side by side with her parents.

Of course, if she'd stayed home, she would have ended up married to the Kreugfeldt boy.

She didn't like to think of the advantages of going to war, *but,* she thought, *there you have it. Give up every other man I've ever known for the likes of him. It seemed reasonable before, but it doesn't now.*

When I get home, that's the first thing I'll tell Ma and Pa. No Kreugfeldts. For that matter, the Kreugfeldt heir didn't like *her.*

She grinned. She didn't for a moment believe that was what she'd really tell them first, but it amused her to think it.

God, but she missed home.

The company came to a channel, and ran along it for a while, hoping it would lead to higher ground.

Bren dropped back to her side and waved a hand for her to stop. She reined in Windrush, and he vaulted up behind her. "We're going to ride in a bit," he said. "See if the ground gets better or worse. I don't want us marching into swamp with the high tide coming."

Karah nodded. It didn't seem to her they'd gone uphill much at all. Of course, if she'd run the whole way like everyone else, she probably would have felt differently. She was sure the ground hadn't raised enough to put them out of the reach of a three-moon tide, and they were running out of time. The day wasn't gone yet, but it was wearing thin, and there was no true high ground in sight.

The two of them cantered away from the rest of the company. They got their answer sooner than they would have liked.

Tall, waving reeds and brackish water spread off in the direction they'd hoped to follow as far as they could see, broken only by rare, twisted shrubs and the skeletal, upreaching fingers of larger trees that had once lived there.

"Ugh!" Karah said.

"No hope there," Bren agreed. "We'll have to get back and try across the channel. There *has* to be higher ground somewhere."

"Not really."

He said nothing. Karah looked back over her shoulder at him and saw his rueful smile.

"Thanks," he said. "You're such a comfort."

"I'm only trying to share some of the happiness being here has brought to me," she told him.

He laughed.

They rode back, met the company, and passed on the bad news.

"Then you want us t' swim the channel, sor?" Ddrad asked.

"Didn't look deep enough to swim when we left," Bren answered, and looked at the water.

Karah looked, too. It hadn't been all that deep before—maybe to her neck, and she was short. It was far deeper now.

"Tide's changed," Bren said, and his face went dark and bleak. "Straight ahead, double-time march—and pray for hills."

Karah was stronger. Strong enough, she thought, to do a double-time march, while Bren rode Windrush ahead to hunt for hills.

She shouted that suggestion as she trotted beside him. He shook his head. "No," he yelled. "I need to stay with my people. You ride ahead, Karah. See what you can find for us. Within running distance."

She nodded and took off.

She managed a canter some of the time; but where there was grass, it grew in hillocks, and where there was level ground, the ground was usually covered with stones. She paid attention to Windrush's gait, in case he went off a foot or stumbled. All the while, she hoped to see high ground.

For a while, she could hear the company behind her, feet thudding in a fast rhythm. Some of the old troopers still sang, though the young voices of the recruits had washed out long ago. Then, when she wasn't really thinking about it, the voices were gone, and she realized she was alone.

The land around her remained bleak. Seabirds screamed and brief squalls soaked her and beat the grass down, then stopped as soon as they'd started. The greyness of the day made time almost impossible to tell. The channel beside her was definitely filling.

Time, she thought. *By the Three, we need more time.* She made that into a prayer, touched the marks on her face, and gritted her teeth.

She came to a miserable thicket—tightwoven thorny branches with canes that braided from the ground to high over her head in an impenetrable wall; those were laden with evil-smelling berries of a noxious off-purple hue. Karah thought she'd never seen anything more poisonous-looking than those berries. She skirted the thicket, riding away from the channel.

She rode, but the thicket didn't seem to end, and she couldn't seem to get back to the channel again.

She stopped. "I could get lost out here," she said to Windrush—but more so she could hear a voice than anything. Windrush snorted and his ears flicked back and forth. The bleakness and the lonely sound of the wind as it rattled through the thicket and the birds screaming overhead had all blended to make her afraid. It was a hellish place, this place where they'd come to ground.

"Well enough," she said softly. "I'll not make any turns—I'll just keep going straight round this thicket and sooner or later I'll have to come back to the channel."

She didn't, however. She worked her way along the thicket, keeping Windrush at a steady trot, until she realized another thicket grew down to meet the first, with only a narrow passage between the two thorny barricades, and that on spongy ground. She frowned and rode forward, not liking at all the way the darkness seemed to press in on her, though there was still daylight left. The thorns gleamed, rattles and creaks and cracks echoed from either side of her, as well as clickings and whistles and little soft coughs, so that she knew she was not alone—and wished she were.

The barriers grew closer, and she realized the space had become too narrow for her to turn Windrush around. She pressed her lips together firmly. "Higher ground," she said out loud; but her voice, which she had hoped would sound fierce and so give her courage, trembled instead.

Windrush flicked his ears from side to side and pranced. The two of them were slowed to a walk, with no hope of proceeding faster. The horse was clearly unhappy with the situation in which he found himself. Karah could think only that he was a sensible animal to be frightened. Godsall knew, she was.

Please let there be higher ground on the other side of this, she prayed.

The narrow path between the thickets turned to the left in a steady, sweeping curve. Suddenly, she was riding up a tiny hill. She whooped and clicked to Windrush. The path widened slightly, still in that left-sweeping curve—and the hill grew steeper.

"Yes," she whispered. "Yes!"

The hill grew steeper, the curve tighter. She looked up, caught a glimpse of something ahead over the tops of the thorns, and then lost sight of it. She kept up the hill, for the path was still too narrow to permit her to turn. This was it, she thought. This was her high ground.

She was spiraling around the base of a hill, she realized—going steadily upward. She considered the likelihood of wild thorns growing in a spiral path around a hill all of their own accord and decided there was no chance of that. Someone had made the path she rode. She hoped that someone was friendly. She drew her sword—just in case—and a moment later, broke out of the confines of the path, and onto the top of a hill.

A stone structure, graceful white carved pillars and smooth white stone cupola, sat at the top of the hill.

She studied the building for an instant. It was worn. Dust and debris littered the entryway, and birds' nests hung along the cornices and capitals. Some of the stonework was crumbling and showed no sign of having been disturbed in ages.

"Temple, then—or shrine," she said. "Abandoned."

It would do. She turned Windrush around and charged down the hill as fast as she dared, to go find the others.

Amourgin had found that last bit of the trek too close to disaster for his liking. He was soaked to the knees from the water that had swirled around his boots. *Still rising*, he'd kept thinking. The fact that the regimental priest walked beside him most of the way, talking genially of books and scholarship, was nerve-wracking.

Karah had urged them all on— "high ground," she'd said, "with shelter at the top." The three-moon tide, which had dried the lowlands at low tide, was racing them to the high ground as the darkness came on and two of the three moons crested the horizon and almost immediately disappeared behind the thick blanket of clouds. Then, shortly after, the third came up—the merest blink of white, before it too was gone—and the rise of the tide began to outstrip the company's forward progress. They were fighting not only distance but the pull of the surging water as well, and Amourgin thought they would be victims of the ultimate irony—to survive a shipwreck only to drown on land.

They made the questionable safety of the thickets, and though water still tugged at them, still pulled at their feet and knees and dragged at them, they gained hope, and they marched faster, and fought harder. They made the spiraling path, and their feet rejoiced in those weary upward steps; they left the sea, at last, behind. Amourgin stepped foot into the open air at the top of the hill in time to see the last rays of the sun glimmer on the horizon, in the slit between the clouds and distant hills. Then true darkness fell.

It was an odd place Karah had found, he thought. He knew of no religion that guarded its temples with mazes of thickets and bogs and tides. Plenty built on hills, but all in his knowledge built where people lived—for the religions were dependent on their worshipers . . . and on their worshipers' tithes.

The building was nothing but a darker hulk against the black sky until several of the company found wood and tinder and one of the men brought out his salvaged slow-light and set them a merry blaze going. Then, as they sat around the fire and cheered their survival and their success, Amourgin sat back and watched the blaze dye the white stone to gold and send shadows flickering along the fluted columns.

It was an astonishingly pretty temple . . . or shrine . . . or . . . Amourgin wasn't sure what to make of it. It had the feel of great age and of long abandonment. Someone had once cared a great deal about it—had carved stone in fanciful shapes and worked pictures into the walls. Had made it a place of beauty— and then had stuck it out of the reach of nearly every living thing. He wished he had a better idea of where in the world he was. If he knew that, he might have been able to make an educated guess about the builders.

"Pretty, isn't it?" Bren asked.

"Catches the imagination," Amourgin agreed. "I'd love the chance to look through it, maybe study the inscriptions. If I saw them, I might even be able to figure out where we were."

Father Solmin heaved himself up and took a torch to look at the eaves. "Very old," he said. "I think I recognized one or two of those glyphs—similar to something I saw in an Old Empire text once. A very *old* Old Empire text, from its early days; even the protective spells barely held it together."

"What was the text about?" Amourgin asked, impressed. He'd taken Solmin for a simple hedge-priest.

The priest shrugged and smiled. "A survey of ancient

history," he said. "Ancient to them, that is—and it was three thousand years old. Impossible to tell what in it was legendary. I *hope* most of it was legendary."

"Maybe we *should* take a look inside," Amourgin said.

"Tomorrow," Bren said. "No telling what serpents have made the place home. If you decide to stir them up, at least do it when you can see them as soon as they see you." He chuckled. "You'll have a more even chance that way."

Amourgin said, "And that, sir, shall be my life's philosophy. Never seek fights with hidden snakes."

All three laughed.

The company was merry, in spite of the hardships of being shelterless, nearly without food or drink, and lost in unknown and possibly hostile countryside. Amourgin thought, *Our needs are much simpler than we would think them. Air and solid ground, something to eat as opportunity presents, and a place to lay our heads at night.* Like the rest of them, he made his bed on the ground and fell quickly to sleep.

Amourgin woke again to find tendrils of mist curling around him, faint and luminous green in the starless dark. Their damp tips felt oddly solid and almost fleshy until they broke and drifted around him. He sat, shivering at their cold, damp touch.

The wild white-eyed man sat at his side, crosslegged— perched *through* the middle of a sleeping soldier. The effect was awful, and Amourgin gave a strangled cry of shock.

"Quiet," the spirit said, and pointed that gnarled, claw-tipped finger at him again. "Come with me. We will walk."

"No," Amourgin said, but his body got up as if it had a will of its own and followed.

"In there." The madman pointed into the dark maw of the temple, which somehow didn't look as lovely and inviting as Amourgin had remembered. The delicate cornices and graceful pillars seemed twisted and malign to him, though they were unchanged in form. The carved forms in the friezes had come to life and watched him with glittering, malefic eyes.

Magic in the temple! he thought. *Idiot, idiot, you should have done a spell to bind the temple.*

Man and spirit walked under the arching doorway, into the first of a series of vaulted rooms. Amourgin could see their outlines running back, much further back, in fact, than he would have thought possible. The temple hadn't looked that large from outside.

"What is this place?" he asked, so taken again by curiosity that he was willing to seek information even from the wild-eyed spirit who led him.

"This is the House of the Gods."

Amourgin looked around the first room, at several little wooden idols sitting on plain pillars. "Obviously. But *which* gods?"

The spirit cackled. "These are the Youngest Gods. Mefitose is there—" he pointed to a statue of a crouching cat with an evil man's face, "—and there is Mother Hunger," and he pointed to a skeletal woman whose flat breasts sagged and whose needlelike teeth ripped to shreds the carved bodies of tiny, open-mouthed people. "Finally, that little toad is Patience."

"I don't recognize *any* of those," Amourgin said, puzzled.

"You'll meet them some day, I suspect. Though I don't suppose you'll like it when you do." The spirit cackled again and beckoned. "The young gods tend to be rabble. Come, come. We've far to go, and little time."

Amourgin followed the radiant form. The two of them wandered deeper into the temple, and in every room, Amourgin noted, the trimmings became more lavish and the idols and images were of finer materials set in more elaborate shrines. The Youngest Gods in the front had gotten short shrift, he decided.

"These are the Strong Gods," the old man said, answering his question before he asked it.

Amourgin suddenly realized he recognized two of them. "That's Hoth-Hoth, the Shillraki god of prosperity," he said, startled. "Right across from her are the Zesillan Furies." He stopped and frowned. "But—they aren't gods of the same religion. What sort of place *is* this?"

The old man shook his head slowly. "This is the House of the Gods. I already told you that." His voice became shrill. "There is something you must see. Hurry."

More rooms followed, one after another after another, deeper and deeper. Still there was no end of rooms in sight. "The Great Gods," the spirit muttered, and the two of them hurried past The Three, carved of gold and set in shrines of gold and silk and gemstones, and that Tarinese nightmare, It of the Thousand Faces, as richly formed and honored.

"Blasphemy," Amourgin muttered. He made to dash the idol of the Thousand-Faced Monstrosity to the ground, but the clawed hand of his ghostly guide clutched his back with surprising strength.

"Touch nothing," the old man said.

"Why are the true gods in the same room with that abortion?" the law-speaker demanded.

"They are contemporaries." The old man shrugged and hurried onward. After a moment, he added, "Relatively speaking," and tittered, finding something about that tremendously funny.

"Why *me*?" Amourgin said plaintively. "We've got a priest along."

"He would be too narrowly partisan," the old man said. "Shut up."

Still deeper they went, now almost running.

Each room back became progressively darker and dustier, and the gaudy trappings that had been so sumptuous in the room of The Three, were moldering and tattered. The idols were dust-coated, the metals tarnished. The smell of rot and mildew, which had been faint initially, became overpowering.

The spirit slowed, and began peering into the face of each idol they passed. "The Forgotten Gods," he said as he walked.

Amourgin thought he could have figured that out by himself. Gods gone to seed, he thought. Beggars and bums. He was awed by the sheer numbers of them. The temple still went back as far as his eye could see. There was no end of forgotten gods.

"Ahah!" the madman shrieked, and Amourgin jumped. "Here, here, here!" he yelled again. He jumped and pointed at one dusty old idol, and when Amourgin didn't comment, turned to see why.

Amourgin stared at the god the spirit had found, but he could find nothing about the idol that would logically explain his guide's excitement. The idol was formed of some dull grey metal; the subject was a priapic, round-cheeked statue with a leering grin and vacant eyes that crouched over a mound of cogs and wires. This idol was no more attractive or appealing than any of the rest of the sorry lot of forgotten gods, and perhaps less so.

"What about him?" the law-speaker asked.

"He's Heinous."

"Yes, he is—but what does that have to do with me?"

"He's the *god* Heinous, you idiot."

Amourgin put on an air of righteous indignation. "Since he's a forgotten god, I could hardly be expected to know that, could I? Wonderful name for a god, anyway."

The old man wasn't mollified. "In his time, he was the greatest of all the gods, and heinous once meant the same thing as majestic. The language has changed since then. Back in his time, he was the Overgod, as well as being God of Lust and Invention."

Amourgin grinned at the idol. "Lust and invention, eh? Certainly an obvious pairing in *my* mind."

"Don't mock. Heinous gifted his worshipers with wondrous devices; machines that flew across the sky and sailed under the sea, that created wondrous food out of the air and turned the basest of ingredients into rare gems and noble metals."

"Probably gifted his worshipers with lots of little worshipers, too," Amourgin muttered.

The spirit heard him and gave him a hard look. "They didn't complain."

"I'm sure they didn't. Old man—if that is what you are— why have you dragged me in here in the dark of night to stare at a dusty old idol of a forgotten god?"

"Because one of his devices still exists, and you are going to have to wake him from his long slumber to ask him for the key."

Amourgin looked from the dusty idol to the spirit of the mad old man and back. "Wake him? Now, wait. What is this device? Why do I want it? Why do I want the key—" He stopped and crossed his arms over his chest. "No. There are a lot of things you're going to have to explain before I go waking up sleeping gods, old man."

The spirit turned to Amourgin, eyes blazing. His voice, which had quavered with the frailty of great age, was suddenly huge and hollow and booming as he roared, "You will not ask questions, nor will you make demands, little mortal. The gods have brought you to this place, and you are alive only because they have something for you to do. Otherwise, you would be at the bottom of the sea feeding fishes with the rest of your comrades. You *will* wake Heinous, and you will win his favor."

Amourgin looked at the spirit, who had stretched during that tirade to three times his size, and who filled the room, blazing with angry red light—and he decided cooperating would probably be a good idea.

"Right. I'll wake him." He sighed. "*How* do I wake him?"

"You worship him."

Amourgin arched an eyebrow and studied the leering grin and outthrust member of the forgotten god, and said, "Just what sort of worship does old Heinous prefer?"

"Candles, hymns, dancing girls, sacrifices . . . the usual sort of thing."

"No doubt. And here I am, not a candle or a dancing girl to my name—"

"*SING . . . TO . . . HIM!*"

"*O Heinous, O Heinous,*" sang Amourgin, improvising fast,

"How heinous is your name,

And far will spread your fame,
And this song sure is lame.
Glory, glory, gloria-a-a-a-a-a . . ."

He stopped singing and sort of hummed while he squinted at the idol. Old Heinous was looking brighter. His trappings weren't quite as shabby as they had been, either.

"SING," the old man snarled.

"Glory, glory, glori-i-i-i-a-a-a-a-a-a."

Amourgin faked another couple of verses, fitting in everything he could think of about inventions and women, and hitting the Heinous motif as hard as he dared without raising the suspicions of the crotchety old ghost.

There was no doubt the attention was paying off. Heinous positively gleamed, and Amourgin thought he recognized the metal in the statue as platinum. *Worth a lot of money, platinum,* he thought. *Wonder if Heinous would like to come home with his worshiper—*

"WHO CALLETH MY NAME?" a voice bellowed out of the ether.

Amourgin jumped.

"Say something, you idiot," the old man hissed.

"Ah!" To the best of his knowledge, Amourgin had never spoken directly to a god. "I do, your—your, ah, Heinousness."

"WHAT IS THY NAME, O MAN WHO IS BORN TO DIE?"

Ever cheerful, those gods. I certainly hope he doesn't mean right now. Amourgin cleared his throat. "Amourgin Thurdhad, law-speaker of Olmya."

"WHERE ARE MY OTHER WORSHIPERS, AMOURGIN THRUGHEAD?"

Thrughead? Amourgin frowned. *Heinous was one of* those gods. "I'm it," he said, and realized when he did it that some of the snappishness he felt had come out in his intonation. He hoped Heinous didn't notice.

Heinous didn't. Instead, he yelped, "ONE! I HAVE *ONE* WORSHIPER?! THIS IS PREPOSTEROUS!"

Until a few minutes ago, you didn't have any, Amourgin thought.

"IS THAT SO?" the god's voice rumbled. "THOU SEEMS TO THINK, PUNY MORTAL, THAT I SHOULD BE GRATEFUL TO HAVE ONE ACOLYTE—I, WHO ONCE HELD THE WHOLE OF THE WORLD AT MY FEET AND BALANCED THE SUN AND THE MOONS ON MY SHOULDERS, AND SWALLOWED THE CONTINENTS FOR MY BREAKFAST AND DRANK THE OCEANS TO WASH THEM DOWN."

Amourgin thought it patently unfair that the god could read his mind—but he tried not to think it too loudly. "I didn't mean anything by that, glorious Heinous."

The god's volume dropped, finally, to a tolerable level. "No, probably not," he agreed. "And I suppose I should be grateful, since thy worship and praise have rescued me from complete obscurity." The god sighed windily. "Once, long ago, I blessed my faithful with wondrous blessings. Would thou like a blessing, Amigrin Thudded?"

"You would like a blessing," the ghost prompted.

"Yes," Amourgin said. "Thank you."

"What blessing would thou ask? I could make thy member as long as thy arm, so that all women would adore thee."

"They adore me already," Amourgin snapped. He stood there, considering Heinous's offer. He couldn't help wondering if the men of Eowlie's land were better-endowed than he was. He hated the idea that they might be.

"NO!" yelled the spirit. "You want the key to the Theophone."

"I do?" Amourgin asked. "I liked his idea rather a lot, actually."

"Whose idea?" Heinous asked.

"The key, imbecile. Trust me here."

"Right." Amourgin gave up, for the time being, the idea of being as well-hung as a Grenlaarin stallion. "I'd rather have the key to the Theophone, if that wouldn't be too much trouble," he told Heinous.

The god didn't speak for a moment. When he did, he sounded petulant. "I could make thy lust as great as mountains, puny human. I could make thee a legend among women. And thy request is for a key—"

"If you don't mind." Amourgin was having a hard time giving up the idea of becoming a legend among women. He didn't do too badly, he thought, but a bit of help never hurt, either.

The god sighed again. "How will I get more worshipers if thou hast not the lust of a thousand men?" he moaned. A moment later, he said, "Ah, very well. The key to the Theophone. Call me sometimes."

A metal rod half the length of Amourgin's hand appeared in the air in front of him. He took it and studied it. One half of it was covered with jewels—the other half was plain, with notches running down one side.

"Don't waste time!" the spirit snarled. "Put it in your pouch and let's go."

The spirit turned and fled, and Amourgin, made nervous by the unseemly haste, dropped the key into his pouch and raced after him.

The way back was not as long as the way in. Amourgin considered that for a moment, then realized Heinous, no longer being one of the Forgotten Gods, must have instantly moved into the ranks of the Extremely Obscure Gods—which were nearer the front door.

The crotchety spirit accompanied him as far as the door of the temple, then vanished.

Amourgin, suddenly weary beyond measure, stretched out under the temple's eaves, and fell into deep sleep.

Karah woke to the warmth of sunlight on her face, the sound of waves gently lapping nearby . . . and a strange soft rustling. She sat up and rubbed her eyes. Then she looked up at the sky and rubbed them again.

In the air above the temple hill, a mass of contrivances she could not recognize flew—she squinted, trying to make sense of what her eyes saw. The first few dipped nearer, and made as if to land in front of the ancient temple. She saw what they were, then, and shuddered. They were carts—ancient, decrepit carts, drawn by skeletal horses, driven by skeletal men. Never built to fly, they nonetheless soared and dipped in the air above the temple, and when the troops scattered to make room for them, they landed.

The minions of Kevo-Death had returned.

Karah found herself next to Bren. "What are we going to do?" she whispered.

Her captain frowned and swallowed hard. Karah could see his adam's apple bob up and down. He looked around the temple hill, cut off on all sides by the lapping sea, then out at the distant, tiny islands that would become islands again and again while the Three rode the heavens together. He said, "We could be here for days—we could drown trying to get to another bit of high ground—and from the looks of things, the gods don't like our chances. So we're going to load orderly, ride quiet, and get off where the . . . drivers . . ." He stumbled over that last word, and looked at the carts with a haunted expression. "Where the drivers put us off."

"I don't like it," Karah said.

"You don't have to like it. You just have to do it."

The dead beckoned with their bony fingers and grinned their fleshless grins. The survivors of the XIXth, loyal every one, stepped forward when ordered and climbed into the carts, and each cart, as it was full, leapt back into the air and flew toward the high ground.

Karah did not let herself flinch when the dead harnessed Windrush, or when she climbed into the next-to-last of the carts. She thought, *We are beloved of Kevo-Death. Even now we go to do his work, else we would remain on the temple hill.*

Beloved of Kevo-Death. That, Karah decided, was an ugly thought.

✧   ✧   ✧

Willek stood on the foredeck of her great flagship, the morning sun warm and welcoming on her face. She smiled. Beside her in a deck chair, Shemro sat passively, her once lovely eyes deep-sunken and hollow, her hands—now nothing more than skin-covered bones—resting limply on her lap.

Willek smiled broadly to the assembled troops. Her image, carried by the priests' magic to all the ships of the fleet, would inspire confidence and courage in this next step in the Grand Admiral's plan.

"Today we sail to Tarin Tseld as its conquerors. We have destroyed loathsome Darkist's fleet, and his ground troops quake in fear at the very thought of us. For the glory of our beloved Shemro, now ruler of the two greatest nations in the world, let us go forth. Let us win for her the greatest prize there is!"

A roar rose up from the anchored ships. Men and women, weapons raised in a triumphant salute, cheered Shemro.

The priests brought their focus to Shemro's face, excluding Willek entirely from the image they sent to the ships. Willek fought down rage, and commanded the nearly-dead Shemro. *Smile, you bitch! Give them something to fight for.*

Shemro smiled faintly, and Willek used a tiny thread of her magic to stretch the smile broader.

The volume of the cheering doubled and redoubled, echoing across the water in the harbor as a solid wall of noise.

Then one by one the ships raised their sails, and the report of a cannon boomed. The oars of the galleys dipped in unison, flashing in the sun. Willek's flagship led them out; the rest of the fleet fell in behind. They were only two days from Tarin Tseld—the winds were favorable—the prize was within reach.

Two days, Willek thought. *In two days, I'll own all of the world worth owning—and then I'll take the step I must to make it all official.*

She smiled down at Shemro, who stared straight ahead, beyond caring.

❖   ❖   ❖

Darkist walked the parapets of the ancient Scholar's Wing of his palazzi, Shaad Shaabin at his side. The air was hot and dusty, and in the narrow twisting streets far below, the men and women of the great city of An Tiram moved slowly, and kept to the shade where such existed.

"Master, you must come from the sun," Shaad Shaabin said. "This heat will boil your blood and addle your mind."

"I am cold," Darkist snapped. "My bones rattle and my flesh crawls. The weight of my years sits heavy upon my back today."

"I'm sure it will pass," Shaad Shaabin said, and his voice was soothing.

"I'm not." Darkist glared down at the people below. "I need to make more sacrifices. More children, I think. Young children—infants, perhaps. Their youth for my sake. Don't you agree?"

Darkist looked over at Shaad. His eyes were hooded, and glittered like the scales of a wet viper. His beaked nose stuck out beyond the folds of his green hood. Green robe, green boots, green gloves—Darkist tried to remember if he had ever seen Shaad in anything but unlucky green, and decided he had not.

"I think, master, that perhaps you near the time you have discussed."

Servants who speak their minds are vile creatures. Shaad is vilest of all, he thought. But Shaad was probably right. He had forgotten how old his body was, but he'd worn it far beyond its physical limits. The old man cleared his throat. "Do not say those words to me again. We've beaten the Tykissians, but I must see them driven into the ground, so that they have no hope of rising again, before I can take that step."

The two men paced further along the parapet. "How much longer," Darkist asked, "until the fleet is ready to sail? Have they sped repairs?"

"The masts from the forests of Kalim have been delayed by typhoons," Shaad said, "and provisions for the galleys are in short supply. By the time the masts arrive, One willing, we will have sufficient food as well."

Darkist hissed and swore. "When, then, do the captains say they will be ready?"

Shaabin backed away. Darkist felt the man's fear as a tangible thing, a sweetdaache to be plucked from the tree and devoured. "They say—seven days from the arrival of the replacement masts."

"Then how many of my ships are ready to sail now?"

"Only a third, master."

Darkist swayed as the heat of the day suddenly enveloped him. By the One, he felt old beyond measure, so weary every breath required conscious effort. A week? Could he wait a week, and the several days of sailing his fleet would take to reach the Tykissian shores—and then, however long his people needed to grind the Tykissian countryside to dust?

Every heartbeat shook him. Every breath burned. His blood crawled at a slug's pace through his veins, and his mind was turning to rot. Several more weeks like this—

"No," he whispered. "I already destroyed Shemro, and my vengeance stalks Willek. Youth awaits me, and I weary of this decrepit bag of bones." His power would be enough, even after what had to come, to conquer Tykis. His head snapped up and he glared at Shaad Shaabin. "Take Colchob to the Quiet Room, and ready him for me."

Shaad turned away and stalked toward the passage that would lead, eventually, to Colchob's suites.

"Run," the old man shouted.

And then he delighted in the picture of Shaad Shaabin, the most dangerous man he permitted to live, fleeing like a frightened kitten at the sound of his voice.

Darkist's muddled thoughts circled—he could not recall why he put off this change for so long. "How much more will you fear me," Darkist whispered at Shaad's retreating back, "when I have regained youth and strength?"

☉ CHAPTER XIII

The Grenlaarins were arming themselves for battle, Jawain's people joined with Iano and Misa's—six-score fighters in all, both relatives and hirelings. Most had served in the Imperial forces; those who hadn't had done their stints locally. There wasn't much in the way of law in Farbluffs County, or the other Counties of the Plateau—locally, law was the sort of thing folks took care of themselves.

That was what Konzin counted on.

"Mount horses," Iano shouted, and over a hundred riders settled into saddles and reined in. The horses pranced and snorted, excited—good Grenlaarin horses all. Konzin hated to see so much breeding stock ride out, especially when he had no way to get it back. But the yearlings, the two-year-olds, the green-broke mounts, and the older brood mares and pastured studs were safely tucked away in the near pastures. There was enough good horseflesh left on the ranch for Konzin to start out with.

Misa Grenlaarin stood on the porch of the house next to Konzin and the fool Gowdgeki, a flintlock cradled in the crook of her arm. She and the house staff were staying behind to guard the ranch—less than twenty of them all-told, with the least fighting experience and the oldest and most unreliable weapons. Konzin struggled to keep the grin from his face—just thinking about it made his heart beat faster with excitement.

Jawain gave the signal. With loud whoops, the mounted fighters spurred their horses once around the yard at a slow canter, then charged out of the gate and up the road—heading north. The whole troop broke into a gallop, and Konzin frowned. They wouldn't be able to keep *that* up for long. Still, it made his life easier, for the riders vanished out of sight behind the nearest hill just that much faster.

When the last was gone, Konzin turned to Misa, and with a respectful bow, said, "Madine, should I go up to the roof to keep watch?"

She studied him with a look he would have expected had she just discovered pissbugs in the flour. "No," she said thoughtfully. "I think you'd better spend the day mucking out the stables. And Gowdgeki—" she turned to the hulking young idiot beside them, "—you go with him. If he tries to leave, hit him with your shovel. Understand?"

The simpleton's round face beamed; he was always happy when someone set him a task within his capabilities. "Take 'im to the stable. Make 'im shovel shit. Hit 'im if 'e leaves. Yus, madine."

Konzin felt the bottom of his stomach drop. Gowdgeki could put a fencepost into hard ground with two blows of a maul. They'd found him hammering a plow-point into the shaft with his naked fist once. Worse, he adored Misa Grenlaarin with a devotion Konzin reserved for money.

So I'll be shoveling shit when help arrives.

Konzin nodded politely to Misa and walked across the yard with Gowdgeki right on his heels.

It's just something else they'll pay for.

The first moments of the transfer were hell—Darkist's ancient body burned with racking pain, and as he linked with his grandson, he felt the magic burn through both bodies— pain twice, fed back through a circuit unbroken and inescapable. His grandson's mind resisted; his body, tied to the One in Change, struggled against the bonds.

Youth and youth's attachment to its flesh created a formidable obstacle, but Darkist's mind, toughened by centuries of cunning and the uses of power, battered down the boy, who'd done nothing in his young life but play and futter and eat.

The boy's soul slipped away from his flesh, slid into the decrepit hulk Darkist had occupied—and Darkist shivered, slithered, coalesced into the firm, hungry, powerful flesh he'd bred to become his new home. Then Darkist—Colchob XXIVth, now—straightened and looked at his hands. *No liver spots. No swollen knuckles. No pain.* He'd become so used to the pain that he didn't feel it. Not until it was gone.

He closed his eyes and forced himself to remember the pathways of magic—the tenuous, once-again fragile links that ran between him and the power that moved the world. It was the most dangerous moment, that single pause while the old man struggled in his new flesh like a butterfly just emerged from its cocoon, wings still damp and crumpled. If the boy knew any magic at all, he would have, in the old man's body, sudden access to the well-worn channels through which power flowed like a river. He could kill Darkist in the magically weak body easily.

But Darkist kept his young bodies fed and entertained and busy for just such a reason. Ignorance served the purpose of his power—the boy knew nothing.

Darkist found the first of what would someday be many magical channels, and called the magic to him, and with it burned away the bonds that held him. He lifted Colchob's massive arms and gave a single shout of exultation.

The walls of the Quiet Room drank the sound. Colchob-Darkist shook back his shoulders and gave a final smile to the shrivelling husk that had held his spirit for so long; his grandson's soul looked back at him with melancholy horror before the hungry stone and the devouring presence within sucked him down. Then Darkist composed his features and strode out through the doors.

"Where is the Yentror?" the guard captain barked.

Behind him the war-slaves growled and rattled their swords. The crowd of nobles paused, hushed and still.

"The tyrant Darkist is dead!" Colchob-Darkist roared. What lungs! he thought. Not a cough, not a wheeze. "With my hands and my magic I slew him, who slew my father."

A long sigh went through the crowd. As one, the jewelled headdresses sank in obeisance. Noble and bureaucrat and servitor alike went to their knees, then forward on their faces. The gilded iron of the guard captain's facemask clanked against the pavement as he threw himself forward in the first of the three ritual prostrations. Uncertain, the war-slaves snuffled at his scent with their broad nostrils. Colchob-Darkist met their eyes and they bowed, acknowledging the spirit that had ruled their bloodlines for a millennia.

"The Yentror is dead—may the Yentror rule forever!" the crowd began to chant. "Hail to the Lord of Ten Thousand Years!"

Colchob-Darkist swept through them, hearing their cheers, hearing the sound spread outside through all the labyrinthine corridors of the palace and then the twisting streets of An Tiram. This too was ritual. It was mildly unusual for the new claimant to have killed his grandfather rather than his father, that was all.

If only you knew, he thought, looking down from the balcony on the backs of his subjects as they grovelled before him. *If only you knew how* familiar *all this is!*

A new shout arose: "Lead us! Command us! Lead us to victory!"

But I already have *led you to victory,* he thought.

One of the generals coughed at his elbow. "The latest reports, my Yentror. The barbarian fleet has been sighted off the eastern Delta, or at least part of it."

Colchob-Darkist clutched at his throat. The hand was strong and young, but the magic within his flesh was weak, weak as a newborn's. Memories of technique drifted sharp-edged through his consciousness, without the slight blurring of a failing brain, but also without the power channels a lifetime of sorcery cleared. He could remember them, but he could no more perform most of them than he'd been able to run and leap and climb in that ancient withered husk.

The storm scattered the towhair ships! There can be no more than a few!

"What . . . what troops have we in the area?"

"There's the garrison of Melduk-on-Marsh, mighty one. An infantry brigade and a regiment of light cavalry, with some guns—sakers and falconets, light pieces."

The new/old emperor of Tarin Tseld took a deep breath. "Send them. Let them meet the towhairs on the beach and throw them back before they can repair their damaged ships."

He grew conscious of the general's curious stare. *Towhair* was the old, old term of abuse for Tykissians, not in common usage for centuries.

"Go!"

"Dawn, Grand Admiral," the priest said. "They . . . see nothing."

Willek frowned slightly. The magician-priest was sweating more than the hot southland night would justify, the lanky muscles of her tattooed body trembling with exertion. For this endeavor she was stripped to the ancient shaman's dress of Old Tykis, beads and feathers and deerskin loincloth.

"Prepare," she said quietly to the officers around her.

Tense waiting, with the sounds of the ship and the fleet about her. Pale light to the east, then flickers of crimson on low clouds. Mist lay on the water even then, turning the standing rigging above her to traceries in the gloom, cutting off the deck past the foremast. It smelled hot and damp, alien, with a longshore stink of rotting seaweed and fish under it, and a hint of city smells. No more than a hint; they were a good ten miles east of the city of An Tiram, off the dunes and reclaimed marsh-lands that fringed the Tiram delta. A thousand years of for-tress building guarded the channel into the Tseldene capital, and she wasn't about to do the enemy the favor of sailing in there. But there were more ways of killing a cat than choking it to death with cream.

"Now," she said.

The shaman slumped to the deck of the *Falcon*, boneless; another priest leaped into the air beside the brazier, screaming in pain as he whirled in a circle that ended with him toppling to the deck rigid as a board. The mist shredded, drifting towards shore in tendrils and pockets. In less than a minute the low ground was visible, or would have been if it hadn't been crowded with Tseldenes drawn up in ranks.

Willek suppressed an impulse to giggle. Even at three hundred yards, they looked so *surprised* at seeing a whole fleet, rather than the single storm-battered squadron they'd expected. Time seemed to hang suspended as the fog revealed the line of Tykissian frigates lying at anchor just off the beach. A long rolling thunder of wheels on oak planking sounded and their gunports flew open, the bronze muzzles of the deck cannon nosing through.

She chopped her hand downward, the armored gauntlet glittering in the sun.

BAMMMMMM. The world disappeared in noise and foul-smelling smoke. The ship heeled under the recoil, surging back erect as the cannon slammed against their breeching ropes. A deep cheer rose from the crowded decks of the Imperial vessels. What mostly rose from the beach was screams, as a hundred twelve-pounder cannon spewed canvas bags full of musket balls and chain links into the crowded regiments. They had a few light field pieces with them. Willek saw one standing amid the tumbled bodies of its crew; where the shot struck, the enemy *splashed* backward in wedges of red against the fawn-colored sands. Another fired, the little stone ball skipping out over the mirror-calm water. It passed a longboat crowded with soldiers waiting to make their run in, leaving a yell of alarm in its wake.

Down below her along the deck the gun captains were at

work, their crews moving with the smooth economy of dancers. This time cast-iron roundshot followed the flannel powder bags down the muzzles of the guns. The *Falcon* fired first, then the other gunships in a ragged volley timed by the speed of their crews and the judgment of their master gunners. The Tseldenes were moving back fairly rapidly, but there were no dunes to hide behind, and they were too disciplined to just run. That cost them heavily as the cannonballs knocked down whole rows, or trundled along the ground smashing legs off at the knee, or hit rocks half-buried in the sandy soil and bounced up at unpredictable angles. . . .

"Pour it on!" the captain of the *Falcon* shouted, pounding his hand on the quarterdeck railing. "Pour it on!"

A new fogbank of smoke was drifting shorewards. Willek narrowed her eyes into it; the enemy were nearly out of range. She let the fleet deliver another three broadsides before she spoke.

"Cease fire. Send in the landing parties." *Darkist must be hearing the firing in An Tiram,* she thought gleefully.

Flags broke free from the *Falcon*'s masthead, and the longboats darted out from among the warships and transports. Hundreds of them—some of the cargo vessels had carried them stacked on their decks, and every ship had a few. They grounded on the coarse sand of the beach, keels grating, and the soldiers leaped out—musketeers holding their weapons and bandoliers high over their heads, halberdiers and pikemen moving forward to establish a perimeter. Some of the smaller transports followed, to ground themselves in the shallows and let their cargoes down over the side. Order grew on shore as the Grand Admiral watched; skirmishers with daggers making sure of the enemy wounded, the first regiments forming up and stepping off inland. . . .

"How long to low tide?" she asked.

"Four hours, Lord Grand Admiral. It's making now." The sailing master of the fleet pushed back his cap to mop at his red, bald scalp. "Anything that stays will be grounded, but it's a gentle shelf, good sand—no rocks. Firm and hard for six hours before the sea comes in again."

Willek nodded. They could get the horses and artillery off while the troopships were grounded, and then refloat them—the warships could take station offshore and pace the fleet towards An Tiram. And . . .

"Colonel Gontuld," she said. "I'll be moving my headquarters ashore now; see to it. Captain, the frigates are to stand to sea for maneuvering room. Use the galleys to keep contact and send two . . . no, three squadrons forward to scout."

Gulls were circling overhead in clouds, and giant claw-wings—even ravens. Idly, she wondered how they knew when a battle was due, and how long they'd wait to stoop down on the feast she'd spread.

"By the Three, that felt good," Bren said, dropping the wooden bucket back on the stone coping of the well.

The cold water was welcome. The way the peasants who lived in the little adobe shacks around it cringed wasn't; Bren expected a certain amount of fear from the natives with armed foreigners about, but this had a slimy, servile edge to it that turned his stomach.

He noted a small open shrine with a four-faced, eight-armed brass idol of surpassing ugliness, laneways of pounded dirt, and an abundance of naked snot-nosed brown children, dogs and chickens. The smell would have reminded him of a thousand farm hamlets he'd seen back in the New Empire, were it not for the overpowering reek of alien spices.

The squat, wrinkled little headman gabbled again. Bren spoke fair Derkinoi, but this peasant dialect of Tseldene was another matter, so archaic it was almost Tiranese. He could catch perhaps one word in ten.

He turned to Amourgin. "What's he saying, corporal?"

At least the law-speaker didn't turn around to find out who the corporal was any more. He pursed his lips and spoke, slowly and clearly. The gabbling slowed, and a weak smile revealed the village elder's lack of teeth.

"I *think* he's saying they don't know a thing and just do what they're told," Amourgin said at last. "It's not much like High Tiranese."

"Well, tell him we need food," Bren said. He held out a small silver coin; money would get you more than steel, in most places.

The villager fell on his face and gabbled louder while the soldier stared at him.

"He says," Amourgin said dryly, "that he's a law-abiding peasant and *never* touches money, and will the great lord from hell—I think that's their term for anywhere foreign—will the great devil lord from hell please take what he wants and not kill too many of them."

"Nice country," Bren muttered.

Father Solmin spat, glaring at the shrine of the One. "We ought to cast down the abomination," he grumbled.

"Not right now, Father—we're scarcely a victorious army yet." Louder: "Sergeant Ddrad, foraging party. Nothing rough, just get what we need for the next couple of days."

"Sor." Ddrad began his you-have-volunteered bellow, then cut it short. "It's the scout corporal."

Karah was riding up on Windrush. Nothing surprising about that, she'd been doing most of their scouting. The string of horses behind her *was* surprising; small-headed, long-legged beauties, with expensive high-cantled Tseldene saddles on their backs, studded with silver.

"Trust a Grenlaarin to find horses," somebody muttered. "Or steal 'em," another added.

Karah grinned; she didn't look so bad, since the swelling and discoloration around her broken nose went down a bit. Bren grinned back at her.

"The delta starts just over the next ridge of hills," she said, pointing westward. "Thick sown country, villages and towns everywhere, with the grain harvest in. Everything's shut up tight, except the fort on the main road—that's abandoned."

"Where did you get those horses?"

"Beauties, aren't they, sir?" Karah said, grinning. "A couple of Tseldenes were riding along, but they got right down when I pointed this at 'em." She patted the pistol stuck through her belt. "One of them had a nice little saddle bow, too." That weapon was now cased at her knee.

Bren nodded. "Well done, Grenlaarin." Karah glowed. "That sounds like they're calling in all their troops, and the gentry are heading for the cities," he went on. "Which means the army must have landed somewhere west of here, between us and An Tiram. We'll push through and link up."

"Beggin' yer pardon, sor," Ddrad said. "There's only thirty of us. Won't their levies swamp us?"

Bren shook his head. "Tseldenes don't have levies. All their soldiers are full time—born to it. The countryfolk aren't armed at all."

The Tykissians all looked faintly revolted; so did Eowlie.

"Amourgin, Eowlie, take two of those horses. Ddrad, you too." He looked up at the sun. "We can make four or five miles before full dark."

Konzin heard the clatter in the yard—shod hooves, and lots of them. He put down his shovel, but Gowdgeki raised his.

"Peace," Konzin said.

Gowdgeki looked unimpressed, and his shovel stayed in the air.

"Listen, man—they're back already. They must have had a quick win."

Gowdgeki heard the horses outside, and the men's voices, and his silly face grew puzzled. "Back?" he said, and turned to look.

It was all the opening Konzin needed. His own shovel came down on the simpleton's head, edge on—Gowdgeki might have been strong as an ox, but his skull split as nicely as any other man's. He didn't even cry out; he just fell forward. Konzin left the shovel wedged into Gowdgeki's brain and ran out to direct his men.

Weasel Ugin stood at the front door of his house, hat in hand, speaking with Misa Grenlaarin. The madine wasn't going to be trusting, Konzin realized. She had her flintlock aimed at his chest, and every other weapon in the place was aimed out windows, too. Aimed at his men. From up on the roof, someone shot off a flare that arced high into the air blazing brilliant red, and hung there one long instant before guttering out and falling back to earth.

Your folk are too far away to help you now, Misa, Konzin thought.

And most of his men weren't even in the courtyard. They were hiding, waiting for Weasel Ugin and the rest of the advance troops to put suspicion to rest. The men in the courtyard carried no visible weapons, rode broken-down nags—looked, Konzin could see even from his hiding place just inside the barn door, just exactly like the migrant herdsmen they were supposed to pretend to be.

Why was Misa so damnably suspicious?

And now his men were turning, their heads hanging, their every step eloquent of dejection—for all the world like weary herdsmen sent away.

She *must* see how they need work, he thought. She's running short-handed, and she believes Iano and Jawain and the rest won't be back for a week at least—she'll call my men back, Konzin thought. Misa, though, kept her gun trained on Ugin, and the muzzles of the other guns followed the movement of the rest of the "migrant workers."

Konzin frowned at the scene. I'm going to have to think of another plan. I'm going to have to—

Screams inside the house! And gunshots! The ranch's defenders pulled their guns out of the front windows; Konzin's men in the courtyard, drawing pistols they'd hidden inside their shirts, charged into the house; a body fell out an upper window—one of the old men who cleaned indoors.

The rest of my men snuck in through the back!

He hadn't thought them bright enough to come up with a backup plan on their own, but they had. Konzin was elated— he raced out of the barn and around the back, keeping out of sight of the house, then along the hedgerow. The hedgerow was sparse and low and made poor cover, but the folk in the house didn't seem to be watching anymore.

He pulled a knife from the sheath tucked inside his breeches; and at that moment Misa backed one of his men out the front door and blasted him as soon as he moved to the edge of the porch. She moved out of the open doorway and kept her back to the wall; good tactics, except that Konzin was in her blind spot, because she was turned toward the door, poised to shoot whomever came out.

He charged behind her, knife still drawn—

And heard impossible sounds.

He thought he heard whoops, and the thundering of hundreds of hooves charging at the ranchhouse from all sides. A few feet from Misa, he looked into the yard and saw he'd heard aright. The Grenlaarins hadn't ridden of after the Gonstads. They had ridden no further than behind the nearest hill, and there they'd waited.

Misa had her eyes on the approaching fighters—she still didn't know he was behind her.

It's all lost, he thought.

But I'll still have mine.

He raced out of the last of his cover—heard Iano's men shouting at Misa—saw the Grenlaarin bitch turn toward him even as he made the leap up onto the porch—and her flintlock swung up to point at his chest, the tip of the muzzle moving slow, slower, slowest as he neared his objective. He dropped and rolled, and two blasts sounded, both over his head, though he got the burn of powder and the lancing pain of splintered wood that buried in his skin from the porch.

He kept rolling, came up with his knife out and ready, made it inside her guard before the flintlock had time to fire again. Time moved slow, so slow and sweet as he shoved the blade into her belly with all the force he could muster and saw her eyes go round. He heard another blast, but he couldn't let it bother him—the knife moved up through her round belly as if it were cutting through butter, and wedged into her breastbone, and he shoved up, harder, up and in. Her scream was sweet in his ears.

Konzin realized he was falling forward, into her, though— tried to move his leg in front of him to catch himself, but the leg wouldn't respond; was ablaze with pain. He looked down and saw a bloody ragged hole where his knee had been. He fell, screaming, as the agony reached his brain, and landed on the bloody mess of body and entrails that had been Misa Grenlaarin.

Iano Grenlaarin touched brow and cheeks with fingers wet with his wife's blood and stood. The fight was over. A body arched from a second-story window, one of the bandits; it landed with a *crump* not far from him, still moving.

Jawain and his foreman each held one of Konzin's arms— they'd dragged him from the porch and through the dirt of the yard to stand him in front of Iano. Behind stood the bandit chief, swordpoints resting over his kidneys; Grey River Weasel Ugin held himself erect. His expression made it clear he still couldn't believe what had happened.

Iano said, in an even, almost conversational tone, "You're going to die now, Konzin. I only wish we'd decided to kill you the day you rode in, instead of waiting to catch the rest of your band first." Iano wished that whole-heartedly—his clever plan to gather all the killers together had cost him Gowdgeki, Kari, and old Evetstur—and Misa. He pressed his lips together, and clenched his fists. Nothing would pay for what Konzin had done to Misa—but Iano was going to get whatever satisfaction he could.

Konzin began weeping, big slow-moving tears. Iano raised his head and pointed to the balcony above. "Rope over there."

Jawain nodded and took his own lariat from his saddlebow, tossing the noose over the railing above and snubbing the end to the pommel.

"Oh, Three, y'can't hang me, master, it wouldn't be right, *please*—"

Iano grabbed the man by the jaw as the foreman held him, drawing his knife with the other hand. Relentless fingers pried the teeth open, and he sliced once. Konzin's screams turned to gurgles as blood from his slit tongue welled between his lips.

"I'm not going to hang you, dirt," Iano said.

The ranch hands snubbed the noose around Konzin's ankles. Jawain's horse backed away at a touch on his neck, dragging the ex-foreman of Grenlaarin Five Points along the dirt and then into the air to swing head-down with his hair only a few feet from the packed earth. Two of the watchers began throwing scraps of kindling and firewood underneath the dangling form, and Konzin began to scream.

"Not too much," Iano said, speaking sharply for the first time since his wife's death. "It needs to burn slow."

He turned his eyes to Weasel Ugin. "Kill me, then," the bandit said, spitting at his feet.

Iano smiled. "I don't think so," he said. "We'll give you to the house-girls instead."

The bandit started off at a run.

He made it a dozen paces across the yard before house-girls and farmhands pulled him down. Kisi elbowed the others aside.

"First cut," she said.

Iano turned away as the bandit's scream went high. Kisi hadn't cut his throat, then.

Jawain put his arm around his brother-in-law's shoulders. "You did all you could," he said.

"It wasn't enough. If only—"

"There's no use in that. Karah's still alive, and she needs you—think of that instead."

"Damn, but that's like something out of a bad historical novel," one of Willek's aides said.

They were all looking into the same crystal, a flat oval twenty inches across and thirty high, set in an oak frame on an iron tripod. The operating priest stood swaying and chanting under his breath, eyes tightly closed and rivulets of sweat pouring down his tattooed face. Occasionally the image would flicker, and the priest give a yelp of pain or stress. Acolytes stood by to take over when the strain of cutting through the Tseldene shielding grew too great, but that would degrade performance—few had the natural talent or the years of training it took to produce a good staff wizard.

In the crystal the armies of the southland poured out of the tall gates of An Tiram—the Desert Gate, facing eastwards. In the lead were war mammoths, fifteen feet high at the shoulder, covered in sparse reddish hair beneath the gorgeously inlaid chain and plate armor. Swivel guns were mounted on the steel-box howdahs, and tall bamboo poles carried gaudy flags.

"Ceremonial," Willek said. "The Tseldenes hate to give anything up. The real stuff will follow."

More mammoths followed, but these were hauling massive bronze guns. "Sixty-pounders, battering pieces," an artillery specialist noted. "Good guns, but our new rifled tubes have the range on them."

Cavalry came next, mounted on tall slender-legged horses that paced with knees high and tails like banners. The soldiers were armed with lance, bow, and curved sword, their armor lighter than the Tykissian equivalents. More guns, lighter ones drawn by horses. Rank upon rank of infantry, blocks of spearmen, swordsmen, men with short thick-barreled arquebuses. The sun was blinding-bright on polished brass and steel, on gold and silver and the silken tassels that flew from spiked helmets, on nodding peacock-feather plumes.

The watching officers took notes, or used little prespelled eidolons to record the images as the Tseldene forces tramped through the suburbs of An Tiram and out into the fields.

"I make that . . . fifty thousand, thirty thousand foot, twenty thousand mounted, one hundred light guns, fifty heavy," Brigadier Multin said. "They outnumber us by about a quarter, but we've got the edge in artillery."

Willek nodded decisively. "We'll await them here," she said, looking up.

The Tykissian host was deployed in a north-south line just behind the crest of a ridge; the land was nearly flat, with only scattered trees and rocky limestone soil sparsely covered in lion-colored grass. A few thousand yards to the west, with almost shocking suddenness, the rich flat soil of the Tiram delta opened out. Trees edged the irrigation canals there, and there were orchards and groves and thick-scattered villages; besides which, the ground was fluffy-soft alluvium, a deadly trap for the heavier northern horses. The highway ran from the high ground down onto the delta and continued on a built-up causeway, surfaced with granite blocks.

"We'll meet them here," she said again. "Best ground for it, and the fleet can secure our right flank."

More nods. Willek fought back a grin. *Perfect.* Everything was going *perfectly.* And the troublesome Bren Morkaarin was very dead, along with his odd companions. Dead and at the bottom of the sea in Kevo's cold embrace. Not even their spirits could return to haunt her; the blood-mirror's prophecy had been averted.

The wizard-priest gave a wailing cry and collapsed, blood running from nose and mouth and in red tears down his cheeks. A second later the acolyte toppled forward and landed in an impossible arc with only heels and head touching the ground. Healer-priests rushed forward; one cried out in the ancient tongue and struck the surface of the crystal with a ceremonial whip. The image in the clear hard substance rippled like water and vanished, leaving only a pool of brownish red with eyes opening and closing. The priest struck again and again, until that faded and left inert blankness.

"Counterspell," she said then, wiping the sweat from her face. "Very powerful, very evil—the wizard who cast it drew on the strength of the One."

"Surprised we got that much," a general said.

"The Tseldenes are strong in technique, but they don't have many gifted born among them," the priest said absently. "Too many generations of intrigue, killing off their best before they could breed."

The Tykissians all nodded; that was one reason the Old Empire had fallen. Its rulers had all been wizards, and so prime targets in its internal wars. Their own ancestors had been wiser; all those with the talent were devoted to the service of the Three, and priests of the Three had to have children by holy law, although they were raised by others.

"To your units," Willek said, mounting the horse an aide held for her.

She was a competent if undistinguished rider, and the mount superbly trained. It barely shied at the lumbering six-hitch coach where the stiff, immobile figure of Shemro sat. It *did* start a little when a war-priest came loping up, a wand held loosely in one hand. Willek recognized him instantly: one of her Inner Circle, the loyal traitor. From his expression, he'd realized she didn't mean to throw the battle to Darkist after all.

Her hand darted to her neck and she pulled a talisman free, a common phallic fertility symbol in appearance. She crushed it, twisting it savagely in one steel-gloved hand. Willek had gotten to know the priest well over the years; on one occasion, far better than she'd really wanted to. The result was worthwhile, though: *like calls to like*. The priest stopped, his face opening in a soundless scream of agony. Both hands clutched his groin, but they couldn't stop the spouting flow of blood. He dropped, kicked, and died, in less time than it took for Willek to toss the talisman aside into the dust and confusion of the ground.

"Quickly, someone take that up," she said. "Enemy war magic struck him."

Now, to move those cavalry forward. It never hurt to anticipate a move. . . .

"We'll be before the gates of An Tiram before week's end," she said. The soldiers around her cheered as she spurred forward.

"What's that?" Karah asked.

It was a peculiar sound, like a very large door being slammed shut with a *thud*, somewhere in the distance. The whole party were marching down a road heading north by northeast, and the date groves on either side made it hard to judge where the sound was coming from. The shade was welcome; the day was hot enough to make her think nostalgically about Derkin's weather. No breath of wind disturbed the water in the irrigation canals at the foot of the tall palms. Sunlight glittered fiercely on it, where beams came down through the long serrated leaves; otherwise there was blue-tinted gloom at ground level. Dust and gravel crunched under the horses' hooves, and under the hobnailed boots of the column behind her.

Glad I'm not wearing that armor, she thought, slapping at a mosquito: they'd only recovered a few sets from the wreckage, and none of them fit her. Sweat soaked her jacket and rasped at her skin with salt crystals. Some of the others, the ones from the northern provinces, were turning boiled-lobster red even with their hats on. For once, she blessed the natural olive of her complexion.

Bren pulled his horse in beside her—it snorted and rolled its eyes at the strength of his pull. She'd noticed that the Tseldene mounts were trained to very light aids, as light as a Grenlaarin horse.

"Lighter on the rein there, captain," she said automatically.

"These southron horses don't like being shouted at." Again: "What *is* that?" The sound was repeated, more and more *thuds*, with a muffled popping beneath it this time.

"Guns," Bren said, standing in the stirrups and shading his eyes. "That's artillery. Quite a bit of it, and not too far away."

They cantered out of the date grove and into fields of cotton, just opening their bolls. Pickers' baskets lay abandoned between the rows, full of the white fluffy fiber, startling against the dusty black of the alluvial soil. The road ran arrow-straight before them, crossing canals on round-arched brick bridges. Beyond the cottonfields were squares of maize and durra and wheat, and beyond those more trees; oranges, she thought. And beyond those, dirty-white smoke was rising in straight columns into the aching blue of the southern sky.

"And muskets," Bren added. He turned in the saddle: "Sergeant Ddrad! Troops to drink and fill their waterbottles, then advance at the quickstep!" Under his breath: "Let's see how our great and good Grand Admiral is screwing up."

The sun was like a club on her head in the open field, but suddenly Karah remembered her armor with a good deal more affection.

"A skirmish?" she asked.

"Battle," Bren said shortly, deep in thought. "From the smoke and the noise, a fairly big one, too." He looked at her, opened his mouth, paused as if reluctant, then glanced past her to Amourgin: "Take the scouts forward, corporal." Unwillingly, he added to the three of them, "Be careful."

He watched them go for a moment, then shook his head. *Part of the job, sending comrades into danger,* he thought. Although Karah was perhaps a little more than a comrade. . . . He shook his head again.

Father Solmin came up with a sack full of the cotton bolls. "Packing for bandages," he said. "We'll need it before the day's done," he went on, cocking an experienced ear at the sound of firing. "You might detail the law-speaker to help me with the wounded, captain, when he gets back."

"Amourgin?" Bren said in surprise.

"He's had a little training," Solmin said, adding delphically, "Perhaps more than he should."

"What *is* that?" Karah asked.

I'm getting sick of saying that, she thought. Whatever-it-was was huge, and had four legs, and two tails—one in front, one in back—and it bled as it lay on the trampled field. Windrush kept trying to back away from it. Eowlie sighed and licked her lips.

"Mammoth," Amourgin said, calming his nervous horse. It was not as well trained as Windrush, but being Tseldene it was more used to the scent.

Dead humans sprawled around the beast. Tykissian musketeers and pikemen, and Tseldenes thrown from the steel box on top when the giant animal toppled.

"I thought mammoths were white and furry and lived up around the Ice Sea," Karah said. The old songs were full of mammoth hunts.

"Those are ice mammoths. This is the southern savannah breed, bigger than the northern variety, less fur, different coloring," Amourgin replied.

"Bet you read that in a book."

"True nevertheless. And there are two in the Imperial menagerie in Olmya. We'd better check around."

Karah took her horse out into the fields at a slow trot, back east along the trail of crushed crops and torn-up trees the mammoth had left. There was nobody directly in view, nobody alive, but the noise of battle was loud a little to the north. She found bodies lying amid the corn; the stalks were up to her waist in the saddle, where they still stood. Most of the dead seemed to be Tseldene spearmen and arquebusiers, with narrow stab wounds from pikes, or the massive ragged holes the thumb-sized Imperial musket bullets made. There were a scattering of dead Tykissians too, Imperial regular infantry.

The dead lay in clumps and windrows where the lines had

stood or broken, gaping at the sky, already beginning to swell and smell in the fierce muggy heat. Insects swarmed around them, busy at wounds and lips and eyes. A few weren't quite dead yet, lying with blackened tongues, moaning faintly. She recognized the Tseldene words for *mother* and *water*.

They don't mention this in the songs, Karah thought, swallowing.

She and Amourgin and Eowlie cantered back to the road to meet Bren and the little column of the XIXth's survivors. Amourgin reported.

Bren listened with burning-eyed intensity, looking over the ground. "The Tseldenes are moving back sharpish," he said. "The fight started east of here—out on the savannah. I'd say a couple of hours ago, not long after dawn."

"We're winning?" Karah asked eagerly.

"Not necessarily. We're pushing them back, and that's not exactly the same thing, something I hope Willek understands. Ddrad, get what you need from the dead out there and then fall in in extended order." All the survivors were carrying muskets, but many lacked bandoliers or other equipment. "Hurry."

"Y'*heard* the man, *move!*" the sergeant bellowed.

Karah stayed beside Bren; he stared north, biting at his lower lip thoughtfully until the infantry drew up behind them. "Let's go."

She felt her heart beat less quickly as they advanced, holding the horses to a walk. Strength seemed to radiate from the man beside her, soothing the thought of what lead and steel could do to her. Sergeant Ddrad handed her up a helmet.

"Think this'll fit, miss," he said.

It did, although the sponge lining was damp with something she didn't want to know about. She put it on anyway, fastening the chin strap with a tug. Bren drew his sword; she pulled out the Tseldene saddle bow she'd captured and nocked an arrow, letting the knotted reins fall on Windrush's neck. He pricked up his ears at that, knowing it meant fancy work. Karah blinked thankfully in the shade of the brim, straining her eyes against the brightness to see over the tall crops around them.

The bodies lay more thickly as they advanced, more of them wounded. A lone figure came down the road, staggering. Closer and they saw it was an Imperial in pikesoldier's armor, clutching at an arm that dripped blood. Her head was bare except for a blond thatch, and her face beet-red and wandering-eyed with shock or heatstroke or both.

"What unit, soldier?" Bren asked. "What's ahead?"

"XXVIIth Foot," the trooper mumbled in a yokel drawl. "Sor," she added vaguely, because the questioner was mounted and carried a gold-hilted sword.

"What's ahead?"

"One-lovin' southrons," the wounded soldier said. Her legs buckled, and she sat in the white dust of the roadway in a clatter of steel. "Swordsmen, spearmen, gunmen—t'ousands of 'em. One-lover *cut* me. You got ary water?"

Bren signed with one hand. Ddrad and two of the musketeers pulled the wounded soldier off the road and into the shade of some bushes. She mumbled and struggled feebly as they stripped off the armor and Father Solmin bound her arm in her neckerchief; anyone who wore a breastplate had one of those, to keep the steel from chafing. Ddrad held a canteen to her lips, the other ham-sized hand regulating the gulping until she was conscious enough not to breath the water. The priest busied himself with an anti-infection spell, backup to the amulet. Open wounds in contact with the soil were vulnerable to the gangrene demons and needed special care.

"Easy, comrade," he said. "Easy." His touch drew the pain, and her eyes fluttered closed.

Ddrad added to Bren: "Not a good day fer fightin', sor. Too damn hot fer lobsterbacks." He kicked at the breastplate and thigh guards of blackened steel they'd taken off the soldier.

"You fight when you have to," Bren said.

"She didn't seem to know much," Karah added as they advanced.

"You never do, not if you're in the fighting line," Bren said. "And—"

They passed through a line of big blue-gum trees. A field gun lay on its side in the pasture beyond, one wheel still spinning, the six horses that had drawn it mostly dead except for one that pawed the air and screamed. Fighting swirled around it, cavalry chopping at each other. Some of them were Imperial lancers in three-quarter armor, but more were Tseldenes in light chain-mail shirts and spiked helmets, whirling about shooting with powerful recurved bows or dashing in to slash at mount and rider with their scimitars. Usually they got free again on their light, nimble horses, but she saw one hooked right out of the saddle by the curved spike on the reverse of a Tykissian war hammer. The Imperial trooper jerked it loose and brought the serrated hammerhead down on the man's spine before he landed.

And several score of the Tseldenes were peeling off from the melee and turning to look at the little party of the XIXth less than a thousand yards away.

"Deploy!" Bren snapped. Under his breath, so quietly that only Karah could hear, he added: "All thirty of you, Three help us."

The musketeers trotted past their officer and the mounted scouts, spreading out in a line two deep across the roadway and into the fields on either side. It was knee-deep alfalfa, not much hindrance.

"Fire will be by ranks, reload without countermarch," Bren said, in a voice that carried without shouting. "On the word. Range three hundred. Don't forget to adjust for the second shot, and aim low."

Ddrad went down the line to make sure all the musketeers had clicked forward the grooved ramp under their rear sights; it was a new procedure, introduced a few years ago with rifling and hollowbase bullets. Before then infantry had just pointed their weapons in the general direction of the targets and hoped, and never from beyond about a hundred yards.

"Check your firelocks!" Ddrad bellowed.

The rank of musketeers brought their weapons to their lips and blew on the slowmatches smoldering in the serpentines.

"Level!"

The two staggered rows planted the points of their musket rests in the dirt and let the long barrels fall into the U-shaped rests on top.

"Present your firelocks!"

The butts were snuggled against shoulders. Karah spat to moisten her lips and glanced to either side. Amourgin was winding his carbine. Eowlie was snarling—quite an alarming sight—and holding hers ready. Bren sat motionless and calm as a waiting cat, sword down and the blade tapping at his stirrup iron.

"Wait for it," he said in that iron-calm voice. "The Three are with us."

The Tseldenes seemed to think their One was with *them*. They came on at a hard gallop, a hundred or more of them, riding with short stirrups, crouched almost like jockeys in their high-peaked saddles. The ground shook under their horses' hooves, the round red nostrils of the mounts gaping.

"*Gurah! Gurah!*" the enemy shouted. The spiked helmets bowed toward her, the curved swords raised.

Closer and closer, almost in arrow-shot. Karah locked thumb and forefinger around the shaft on her string. A few of the enemy cavalry were loosing already, black- and scarlet-fletched arrows landing in the soil in front of the musketeers, quivering in the sunlight.

"Front rank—" Ddrad's voice echoed Bren's.

"*Fire.*"

BAMMM. White-grey smoke rose up in front of her, and the horse sidestepped a pace. When it cleared, she saw that half a dozen of the enemy were down, horses kicking on the ground or dashing riderless. And the rest had *stopped*. Not quite pulling up; more as if the horses were spooked, plunging and sinking onto their hindquarters and squealing and pig-jumping.

"Front rank, reload in nine times. Second rank, *fire*."

BAMMM. More smoke; through it she could see the first fifteen musketeers frantically unscrewing the tops of cartridge flasks, dumping the powder down the long barrels, dropping in bullets—a lot of them were holding two or three in their teeth—ramming, priming. The iron ramrods clattered frantically, and then came the dry clicking sounds of the springs that drove the serpentines being cocked.

BAMMM. BAMMM. BAMMM. The enemy were coming on again now, but they'd stayed bunched up while three volleys drove into them. Karah drew the bow to her ear, shot, again and again. The light carbines of her fellow scouts banged next to her ears; then Bren was firing a pistol left-handed over his horse's head. A musketeer fell with an arrow through his throat, heels drumming at the ground.

The oncoming line of Tseldenes seemed to gather themselves, and then something gleamed behind them. Whatever it was *struck*, and the enemy cavalry scattered before it like droplets of mercury on ice. The XIXth's soldiers had been clubbing their muskets, or sticking the hilts of their daggers down the muzzles to make them into improvised spears; they stopped in midaction, incredulous, then cheered wildly and began to reload once more.

The Imperial lancers were in the midst of the Tseldenes. A few of them had kept their fifteen-foot lances, long slender weapons with a ball guard before the hand. They stabbed them into the backs of the fleeing enemy. Others were lashing about them with war hammers and heavy single-edged broadswords. Crammed between the musketeers and the lancers, the light-armed Tseldenes went down, or fled if they could without stopping to look back. The musketeers took slow aimed shots after them, jeering and whooping when a horseman went down.

Karah lowered her bow and forced her jaw closed. "That . . . that was a miracle, wasn't it?" she husked.

Bren handed her his canteen, wiping his own lips on the

back of his hand. "That it was," he said quietly. "Without any pikes to stop them, they'd have cut us into dog fodder if they hadn't stopped and milled around. A miracle."

They looked at each other. There had been far too much of that since they left Derkin . . . but under the circumstances, it would be unwise to complain.

"Thank you." That was the lancer commander, riding up and flipping back the three-bar visor of his plumed helmet. "You got those donkeysuckers all bunched up for us. Oh—Captain Sir Juwis Keldewll, IInd Olmya Lancers. Your servant, sir."

"First Captain Sir Bren Morkaarin, XIXth Foot," Bren replied. "What the bloody *hell* is going on here, Sir Juwis? We just got in—delayed at sea."

Sweat dripped from the point of the lancer officer's brown beard, and blood splashed his inlaid armor and the war hammer in his hand; any other time he might have resented the tone from a mere infantry officer, but not now.

"Eat me for an orca if I know," he said, pointing north with the weapon and flicking brains off it at the same time.

"We were in the middle of a murthering great battle, and winning it, until an hour ago. That *should* be our left wing, and I was covering it—until we got orders to pursue, and then messed up in this *tutti-putti*." That was army slang for rough ground; there were villages and groves all about. "The Tseldenes were moving back faster and faster, and then they weren't, if you know what I mean."

He rose in the stirrups to look past Bren. "Where are the rest of your troops? We could certainly use some infantry right about now."

"You're looking at them," Bren said. "We had a shipwreck. Now, collect your people and fall in to my left—we'll go straight north. From the looks of things, we'll pick up stragglers enough as we go."

Something in Bren's face stilled the question the lancer might have asked. He saluted, clanking a gauntlet against breastplate. "Our horses are blown," he warned. "This damned heat."

They looked it, standing with their noses down and foam dribbling from their mouths and streaking their necks.

"Water them," Bren said. "Five minutes, no more."

"Shall we scout?" Karah asked.

Bren shook his head. "Not now. I want you with me. We'll find out what's ahead soon enough."

Karah fought back a smile, even then. She cocked an eye at the sixty or so lancers, noting with approval that they seemed ready to lead their horses, and that many were emptying their own canteens into their helmets for the beasts to drink.

"I wouldn't count on those for much in the way of galloping," she said, pitying the horses. They were warm-blooded—crosses between draught breeds and light saddle types—and lacked the endurance of true blood mounts.

"We'll all do what we have to today," Bren said. *"Forward."*

What a monumental cock-up, Bren thought, as the fugitives halted wheezing in front of his line. He'd rallied hundreds already, running or just scattered and lost.

He recognized this lot; they were from his own regiment. "Ensign Fulin?"

The bloodied bandage around her head didn't seem to have affected her sight. "Three, am I glad to see *you*, sir! When the *Sea Mare* vanished in that storm, we thought you were all dead."

"So did I, for a while. Where's the regiment?"

"The colors are with Lord Colonel Gonstad, and the Father, Mother and Child together don't know where *he* is," the junior officer said. "He had us going forward at the quickstep, we lost dozens from heatstroke, more than our battle casualties—'til our right was hanging in air and we couldn't see a damned thing. Then the Tseldenes hit us, horse and foot and guns, we were split up by some houses, and I haven't seen him since. Sir."

"All right," Bren said grimly. "Fall your people in, over there on the right."

He nodded eastward. There were about three hundred with him now, a block of pikes in the center and musketeers on the flanks, with the lancers and a few odd dragoons covering his left, the westward extremity. He even had a light gun, a six-pounder. It was all very ragged, dribs and drabs, but he thought they'd fight. He *knew* the six score of the XIXth in front of him would; they raised a tired cheer as they poured by to deploy. From the sounds right ahead, they'd have to fight, and soon.

The firing rose to a crescendo as the band he'd rallied came around a curve in the road and up to the small manor. It was a lacy openwork building, all arches and slender columns and windows, white stone and tile in the Tseldene style; some nobleman's country seat, surrounded by gardens and greenswards. Furniture and farm wagons barricaded most of the entrances, and from the thick scatter of Tseldenes lying in front of them, the Tykissians inside had been giving a good account of themselves. Their prospects didn't look good, though: the huge hairy shapes of two mammoths loomed over the pomegranate trees and pergolas, and they were dragging big bronze guns on wheels higher than a man—battering pieces, fit to knock down castle walls. All around were the better parts of two regiments of the enemy, say three thousand men; mostly polearms, with some arquebuses, and cavalry. Not well ordered, but they looked full of fight and hungry for blood.

A party of enemy riders was waiting halfway between the Tseldene positions and the barricaded manor, high officers from the brilliance of their armor. A white cloth drooped from the lance one held. Another party was advancing down the chipped and battered rose-marble steps of the building, carrying a furled flag. Bren recognized the figure in three-quarter armor beside the standard bearer.

"Scouts, Father Solmin, with me!" he snapped. "Ddrad, Sir Juwis, bring the troops forward at the quickstep, in line."

He clapped his heels to the mount, suddenly conscious that he was advancing with only three riders at his back—and none of them had been a soldier a month before. *Well, it's a parley*, he thought. Besides, there weren't all that many he'd rather have with him than those three, come to think of it.

"Lord Colonel Gonstad," he said, drawing rein in front of the two XIXth officers and the standard bearer, forcing them to stop. Twenty yards still separated the Tykissians from the Tseldene officers. Gonstad didn't have any of his fancy aides with him, only another of the XIXth's captains. "And Captain Tagog."

"Morkaarin!" Gonstad blurted. "You're *dead!*" His face turned pale under the peaked helmet.

"Not quite, sir," Bren said. "Why are you taking the regiment's banner to a parley, my lord?"

Gonstad shook his head violently, seemed to gather himself. "Ah—ah, as you can see, this position is hopeless."

Bren looked around. From the smoke, the main action was only a few thousand yards north—and they were going at it hammer-and-tongs. The XIXth seemed to be covering the main army's flank.

"You're going to *surrender?*" he asked incredulously. "To *Tseldenes?*"

Tagog's face grew bleaker; she was a scarred professional of forty years, discipline bred in her bones. Suddenly Bren knew the truth. Again he saw the faint red mist across his eyes, but this time he didn't hold it back. It swelled through him, stronger than brandy, hotter than the southron sun.

"With a safe-conduct for yourself, while the troops go to the altar!" he said to the colonel, his voice gone flat and deadly. "You faithless *pig*."

Gonstad gestured with his commander's baton. "I *order* you to silence, Morkaarin," he said. "And consider yourself under arrest."

"Consider yourself halfway to being wormshit," Bren said, and pulled the wheel-lock pistol from his boot. Gonstad was still gaping when it went off, the muzzle not a foot from his face.

"Three!" blurted Tagog, wiping at the blood spattered across her face. "I've wanted to do that for *years*."

Bren stooped in the saddle, across the kicking body of the ex-colonel. He seized the staff of the regiment's banner; even then, he kissed the fringe reverently before he planted the end of the staff on one boot toe and shook the heavy silk free.

"Nineteenth!" he roared, spurring out in front of the manor and raising his sword. The flag fluttered behind him from the staff in his other hand.

Soldiers moved in there, hundreds of them, moved and stirred and called his name. He heard more and more taking it up.

"To me!" he shouted again.

No sense in sticking in there and waiting for those siege guns to kill you. The Tseldenes had barely started to move as the troops he'd rallied on the way came around the bend in the road and deployed at the run.

"To me, Nineteenth! For your blood. For the flag and your honor, for the Emperor—for Tykis! *Charge!*"

Howling like wolves, they poured out.

"No," Willek whispered.

"Yes!" Brigadier Multin said exultantly.

The crystal before them was cloudy; flickers and bubbles ran through the image, as the priest-acolytes sweated and chanted and threw pinches of powder into the air to fight through the interference of the enemy war-wizards. But it remained, and it was unmistakable.

The main Tykissian host held its formation, a half-dozen squares, but weakened by the groves and irrigation canals that hindered its interlocking fire. Around the squares the southrons raged in numbers double the most pessimistic estimate; the smoke of battle drifted over the defenders like fog banks, heaviest where the great bronze guns of the enemy mowed hideous paths through the tight-packed ranks of the Imperial infantry. Their lighter fieldpieces replied; arquebus answered musket, and charge after Tseldene charge halted dying before the iron order of the northern pikes. Far to the west, a blue shimmering field of magic marked where the Tseldene Yentror rode his war mammoth and watched the invaders brought to bay and destroyed before his eyes.

What the crystal showed was the left flank of the Tykissian army. The flank Willek had thought broken beyond recall, when it pursued into the jaws of the Tseldene trap.

It had rallied; she saw regimental banners in the crystal, serried ranks, Tseldene cavalry turning to meet them and held at pikepoint while measured volleys tore them to shreds. And at the front, the banner of the XIXth Foot. Beneath it, a stocky tow-haired officer riding with a face like iron, and the soldiers cheering him.

She had seen him before. Seen that *image* before. In a blood-mirror, above her quarters in Derkin, not a month ago. *And Morkaarin was supposed to be dead!*

"Grand Admiral," the brigadier said, pulling at her vambrace. "Grand Admiral, we have to attack *now*. There's only a few thousand who've rallied, we have to attack now while the enemy are thrown off-balance!"

"Yes," she said numbly. Remembering the rest of that vision; the executioner's sword rising . . .

"Attack. Forward in square of brigades, and the lancers stand by to charge."

"That's a real retreat this time, by the Three," Bren said.

Ahead of him the Tseldenes were ravelling away from his advance, caught in the angle of an L between the troops he'd rallied and the massive blocks of the main Tykissian force. Those blocks were moving now, ponderous and sure, crushing the southrons caught between their walls. As he watched, one rank of infantry swung open like a great door and a column of lancers trotted out. They paused to dress their lines and then advanced, walk-trot-canter-gallop and the points came down like a cresting wave, glittering in the harsh sun. Never as steady as northern troops, the enemy infantry gave way before them, crumbling like sugar-sand before the tide. The disciplined Tykissian foot came on to an inhuman hammer of drums, marching over the bodies of the dead, splitting like a stream about the huge abandoned enemy cannon and forming again beyond.

One last assault headed towards Bren. *Trying to split us off from the main force,* he decided. A Tseldene general gestured with his feathered wand from a hilltop, and a reserve force came to their feet and loped forward.

"Advance!" Bren called.

Drummers and bugle boys passed it down the line; not far away he saw a pikesoldier spit on his palms and lower the long polearm. The pikes flowed forward, a six-deep line of two-foot steel blades on sixteen-foot shafts. Ahead came the Tseldenes, a sea of shouting brown faces and gaudy enamelled armor and broad-bladed spears. Cannon thumped out grapeshot into their ranks, and the measured crash of volleys. There was a scraping metal-on-stone sound as they struck the line of pikes; a brief grunting scrimmage, a wild thrashing where the musketeers fought on the edges of the pike phalanx with sword and clubbed musket.

It was like a wave smashing on rock, but it was the rock that advanced, howling and stabbing.

"Press 'em," Bren said. "Press 'em hard!"

The long line of his force swung north and then east, trapping thousands of the enemy against the squares. Packed too tightly to use their weapons; he could see riders in the mass of footmen lashing out with their swords against their own men as they tried to force their way out of the closing trap. Mammoths surged above the crowd, their trunks curled up and trumpeting shrilly. One panicked and bolted. Even then, he found a half-instant to pity those in its path. More and more Tseldenes were streaming out of the narrowing opening and running west, west toward An Tiram. Tykissian cavalry pursued them, cavalry and buckskin-clad figures armed with javelin and tomahawk—tall, swift warriors who yelped and howled as they ran, the levies of Old Tykis.

"Now we've won?" Karah asked beside him.

Bren came to himself with a start, as if from a trance. The godlike clarity left him, and he was only a man on a horse, on a field that smelled of gunpowder and blood and shit. He looked around; the front line was trotting away northwestward, leaving only the dead and the groaning, writhing wounded in their wake.

He looked over at the girl. Her mouth was a grim line as she looked around; he liked her the better for that.

"The only thing worse than a battle won is a battle lost," he said. She smiled at him. Out of the corner of his eye he saw Amourgin's eyebrow raise; well, he hadn't *claimed* to have invented it.

A squadron of dragoons pulled up beside him and the XIXth's banner. The light cavalry's green uniforms were stained and torn, and there was blood on their sabers.

"You're Sir Morkaarin?" their officer asked, swinging the blade up to salute.

Bren returned the gesture. "I am."

"The Grand Admiral's—the Grand Constable's—compliments, and please to attend her. At once."

Bren clamped down on a snarl; he nodded with a jerk. "Ddrad, Ensign Fulin—color party, please."

"Godsall," Karah blurted, as they rode east through a thinning mist of powder smoke.

Bodies lay two-deep in places amid the trampled crops and through grove and orchard, thick scatterings elsewhere; the cries of the wounded and the injured horses were a throbbing backdrop to the fading sounds of battle. Claw-wings and vultures circled lower and lower. The ground where the Tykissian squares had stood at bay was still marked by squares . . . of the fallen, and less regular mounds of bright-clothed southrons fringed every one.

She gagged a little. "I didn't think there could be this many dead people all in one spot."

"There shouldn't be," Bren said grimly. "We must have suffered ten, twenty percent losses. Three alone know what the enemy lost."

"A soldiers' battle," the dragoon commander said tactfully.

"That's a euphemism for *the generals fucked up*," Bren answered shortly.

News of what had happened must have crossed the battlefield swiftly. As they passed the reserves and the units too badly battered to join in the pursuit, more cheers went up as well as helmets on the ends of pikes and muskets and swords. There was an edge of hysteria to the acclaim, as if they knew how close the whole army had come to disaster.

"Bren! Bren!"

He raised a hand.

"Bren! Bren! Bren!"

It only died down as he approached Willek. Officers smiled at him, including many who'd barely have acknowledged his existence a month ago. Bren hid a cold pleasure; now Willek would have to offer honors and promotion to a man she'd hated enough to have set upon by hired bravos. And the Emperor herself was there, in an open carriage, looking tired and strained.

Well, I did a soldier's work today, Bren thought. *No more than my deserts, and I'll see that the rest of the XIXth gets what it deserves, too.*

"Grand Admiral," he said, dismounting and bowing. He went briefly to one knee in the Emperor's direction. "Reporting for duty."

Willek looked *strange*. White around the mouth and eyes, with two burning spots on her cheeks, left hand clenched hard enough on her sword hilt for the nails to turn red. She began to speak, then swallowed and cleared her throat before trying again.

"Arrest him."

Silence fell around the command group and its clustered flags. Willek turned to find a hundred pairs of eyes staring at her incredulously. Bren realized his mouth was open in astonishment, and closed it with an effort of will. He drew himself up and crossed his arms on his chest to keep his hand away from his sword.

Her lips worked, and she shouted:

"Arrest him!"

The captain of her personal guard half-drew his sword. There was a stir from the Life Guards around the Emperor's coach; Bren remembered that that unit had been cut heavily on Willek's orders. Their faces and stance remained still as marble, but there was the slightest tremor in the rigid line of their halberds. In the background the troops were still chanting his name.

"Lord Grand Admiral," Bren said, pitching his voice to carry without seeming to shout. "If you would arrest me, I demand to know the charge."

"Desertion. Treason. Captain, you have your orders."

Whatever had been harrowing Willek seemed to have relaxed its grip; she looked determined now, no more. He met her eyes; whatever her other faults, nobody could say the Grand Admiral was a coward.

The guard captain did draw his sword. He turned to the row of bodyguards and opened his mouth to bark an order. At the same instant, the Life Guards around the carriage moved— as one, they thumped the butts of their halberds against the roadbed, a sound full of menace.

Bren smiled. "I claim," he called, in the same ringing tones, "as a free Tykissian gentleman and nobleman of the Empire, the right of appeal to my sovereign."

The beginnings of an uproar quieted. Voices shouted approval. Willek ground her teeth.

"The Emperor is unwell," she said shortly.

"She's well enough to go on campaign," Bren pointed out.

"And if she's well enough to do that, my lord Grand Admiral, she's well enough to hear a case."

And you're not the Regent, not yet, he added to himself. From the way she looked around her, Willek was thinking that too. Back home, where she could control access to the Throne, her authority was nearly absolute. Not here.

He turned and marched toward the carriage at the regulation pace, head up and helmet tucked under one arm. The Life Guards opened smartly to let him pass.

"My Emperor," he said, dropping to one knee. "I appeal to your justice."

Shemro IV looked less ancient close up. *Not much older than my mother would be, if she'd lived,* Bren realized, with surprise. The grey-blue eyes blinked at him, looking slightly misted, then focused with an effort of will.

"Who—" she said.

"*Silence as the Emperor speaks!*" the officer of the Life Guards bellowed, satisfaction in her voice. "Hear the Voice of the Crown!"

"Who are you, young man?"

"First Captain Sir Bren Morkaarin, Majesty," he said firmly.

"You look . . . very like someone I once knew. Who was your father?"

Bren felt himself flush. "I . . . I don't know, Majesty. My mother said he was a nobleman and that she'd tell me when I came of age, but she died before then."

Shemro nodded. "Is that an eidolon of him?" she asked, indicating the small crystal on his chest. "Let me see it; my eyes aren't as sharp as they once were."

Bren rose and pulled the silken ribbon over his head. It wasn't until he had handed it to the Emperor that he remembered. *Only my blood kin in the first degree can see that image!* The spell was keyed to the tiny coils-of-kinship in his cells, by blood-magic.

Shemro gasped, looking down into the crystal. "It's Eartin!" she said. "My—"

She gasped again, this time in pain, and sank back on the cushions of the coach; Bren caught the eidolon as it slipped from her fingers toward the ground. Shouts of alarm rang out as the Emperor twisted helplessly on the embroidered seat. Bren stood, stunned and helpless. *Eartin. The Emperor's younger brother. Dead these thirty years.* His eyes widened. Exactly his own age. *Impossible . . .*

Willek was beside him, staring, one hand clasped in a tight fist.

"Arrest him, he's attacked the Emperor! Conspiracy, treason, arrest him! *Brigadier Multin, do your duty!*"

She turned and grabbed for him herself. He struck, once, and she folded over and staggered away, wheezing, through the line of Life Guards; none of them looked quite ready to lay hands on the Grand Constable of the realm. A man with brigadier's flashes was moving forward, a squadron of Shillraki mercenary dragoons at his heels. Half a dozen of the Life Guards had leaped into the carriage, holding the Emperor and forcing a leather strap between her teeth. The rest crossed their halberds protectively around the coach and team. Beyond it was chaos, as officers and officials shouted, argued, pushed—a few had even drawn swords, deeply illegal in the Imperial presence.

"Guard the Emperor," Bren said shortly to the Life Guards officer. "And remember."

"I heard," she said, nodding. "But this isn't the time or place, not with a battle going on."

"More than one," Bren said.

The color party of the XIXth were forcing their way through the throng towards him, none too gently. Karah guided her horse toward him, prompting its bared teeth and menacing hooves with her legs, and swung the Tseldene mount she'd captured to his side. He vaulted into the saddle.

"Gentlefolk!" he shouted, drawing his sword at last.

A little of the clamor died down. One of Multin's mercenary dragoons raised a carbine, only to find half a dozen Tykissian swordpoints pressed to his torso.

"Gentlefolk of Tykis," Bren shouted. "You've seen me falsely accused. I won't shed the blood of Falcon and Wolf myself, not while we're at war with the hereditary foe. You know who carried the field this day—think on it. Until then, guard the Emperor from *her*."

He pointed the sword at Willek, then brought it around to slap the haunches of his horse.

"*I'll be back.*"

Willek paced inside her tent. Her own guard had allowed the Morkaarin bastard to retreat in safety, the Life Guard had prevented her any chance to attack—and Eartin. The bastard was *Eartin's* son? An heir, when she'd been sure there were no heirs.

She needed answers. She'd not touched the bloodstone in a long time, but she needed it now. She needed to know what happened in the many places where she could not be, and she needed to know what to do to counter Morkaarin.

She told the guards outside her tent she was in no means to be disturbed, and she made her preparations, and she called for the demon. A weak one came, weak and snivelling, satisfied with her littlest sacrifice and easily intimidated. For once she would have preferred a stronger monster, but hell sent forth its minions on its own schedule.

"Show me," she hissed. "Show me the Morkaarin scion— Eartin's son. What does he do now?"

When the pictures flashed before her, they were confusing. Morkaarin and the XIXth trekked through a jungle, and gods and demons threw their bolts, sometimes at the XIXth, and sometimes at each other; Darkist and a huge force, taking cannon and lighter weapons, went up the same jungle river in boats; and then she saw it. An island in the middle of a rose-colored sea, and a temple in the center, and in the temple *something*—something that even the gods bowed down to. And Morkaarin was first to that rose-red sea.

"No," Willek snarled. "No. He won't be first."

She called her officers, delegated authority as necessary, and issued her orders. She would leave most of her army behind to fight in Tarin Tseld, would let her generals run things. A few of her best people would go with her—go into the jungle, dragging the Emperor and such weapons as they could manage. They were going in light and fast, though. Time was everything. Willek didn't know what the prize in the temple was, but she knew she was going to get it. The gods had their fingers in this—Tarin Tseld and the whole of an empire had become, suddenly, the lesser prize.

The three moons touched at the sky's zenith at midnight, and their light shimmered down on Tarin Tseld. It insinuated itself into the camp where Willek lay, and danced along the parapets of Darkist's palazzi, and crept across the bare ground where Amourgin slept curled next to Eowlie, and where Bren and Karah lay.

It cast eerie shadows and brought forth illusions and spectres and left indelible tracks in among the dreams of the sleepers—dreams of a golden icon far to the south, a plaything of the gods left behind and nearly forgotten; dreams of power beyond imagining, power for the taking; dreams of jungles and mountains, and of a rose-red sea.

The voices of their gods whispered to the sleepers, "Go, make haste."

And when they woke from dreaming, each of the god-touched knew the answer to an age-old puzzle waited . . . and that the first to reach it would command the rest.

As one, they made their plans.

As one, though by different routes and different means, they headed south.

"Sor." Ddrad twisted his hat in his hands and would not meet Bren's eyes. "Sor, I've followed you, man an' boy, these fifteen years. And yer mother before you."

Bren nodded absently, and shifted his grip on the reins; he

was walking and leading his mount with the reins looped over his wrist.

"Then, sor, I don't believe m'eyes when I see you runnin' from a fight!"

Bren turned, grinning. "Don't believe your eyes, then," he said. "I'm not running; I'm going to the armory for a weapon."

The sergeant's eyes were baffled.

"Look, Ddrad, you *have* known me all my life. Did you know me for a liar?"

The older man shook his head.

The moonlit road to the south lay open before them, and on either side the rustling corn was silvered by the light into a wilderness of triple shadows and pale gold. The wind was cooler, but the pavement and the stone and the very earth around them gave back the day's heat. The tall cypresses by the wayside cast a slow flicker of shadow as they advanced. Behind them the steady tramp of hobnails on the hard-packed crushed rock of the road sounded like a drumbeat to the empty land.

"Call the halt."

A bugle note sounded, and the steady tap of the pacer's drum turned to a ruffle.

Bren swung into the saddle and turned the horse to face the troop. "Karah, Amourgin, by me," he said. "Soldiers, stand easy."

They relaxed, leaning on pike and musket. "Comrades," he went on. "I know you, and you know me."

Their answer came in a growl. He nodded. "From the bottom of my heart, I thank you for the trust you've shown me, coming when I called. But you're free children of Falcon and Wolf, and you deserve to know the truth."

He paused, watching their faces. Scarred veterans, fresh-faced plowgirls, all looking at him with more than the moons' light in their eyes.

"I've never known who my father was. My mother died before she could tell me; she left me this eidolon of him—" he held it up. "It's blank to all but those of my close blood kin.

And I thought I didn't *have* any. Until, not two days ago, I was before the Emperor. You know why I was there."

They growled again at the memory of victory. "The Grand Admiral tried to have me arrested. The Emperor, Three favor her, took this eidolon in her hand—and she saw the face of her brother, Eartin."

A mass catch of breath. He held the eidolon up. "My father's name was Eartin Strekkhylfa!"

Sheer silence fell for a moment, then an explosion of cheers that startled sleeping birds out of the roadside trees and the grainfields.

Ddrad stepped forward. "Then strike for the Empire, sir— my lord Prince," he said. "Lead us!"

The soldiers howled and shook their weapons, and the officers knelt to lay their swords at his horse's feet.

"Comrades," he said again. "I thank you again. And I *will* take up my right—not least, to rescue my father's sister, who is in the power of the traitor Willek Tornsaarin. But not here, and not now. The Grand Admiral has followers enough to make a fight of it, and if the Imperial army fights itself here on foreign soil, who'll benefit but the southrons? And—" he paused. "And, the gods themselves have taken a hand in this. Father Solmin."

The priest came to stand by the commander's stirrup. "I swear," he said, signing himself, "by the Three and my oaths to my Order, that the First Captain—the Prince-Heir—speaks the truth. The Emperor acknowledged him; and then she was struck down by evil magic, blood-magic of the foulest kind. And that night, visions were granted the Prince-Heir by the Three themselves."

The troops sighed in awe. The priest went on:

"Long ago—very long ago—in the time of the Old Empire, the wizard-emperors of An Tiram had a mighty talisman. They didn't make it, it was older even than the Old Empire, but it gave them great power. Power to make a channel to the Other World, and call the gods themselves down into this world of men. It made them invincible in battle, for with it they could call on the One of a Thousand Faces to bring madness and death to their enemies.

"A priest of the Three, from Old Tykis, took the talisman and fled south, far south with it. There he hid it and bound it fast around with powers the wizard-kings could not break. Then came the Judgment of the Three, when the Old Empire fell and our ancestors came south over the Shield Mountains to make that land their own. Only here in the south, in Tarin Tseld, did a fragment of the Old Empire survive.

"Ever since then the talisman, the Theophone of the Gods, has lain protected. But those protections wear thin, and soon the Theophone will be loosed among men again, for good or ill."

He drew a long breath: "I believe—the captain says, and I believe him—that he and his companions have been given a vision. If they take this talisman, the Three will be unbound and all will be well with Their people. But if Darkist or the traitor Willek seize it first, then there will be a long night of evil as bad as the Old Empire, or worse."

Silence fell with the moons' light. Bren added: "And they're both after us now. Not with armies, but in parties light enough to travel fast. Are you with me?"

A moment passed, while the stolid faces before him struggled with what they'd been told. Ddrad answered:

"That we are, sor. Against men or devils."

⊙ CHAPTER XIV

Amourgin felt a quick cold shudder down his spine when he stepped beyond the light of the fire to check on the horses. His stomach knotted and doubts whispered into his mind. *You're on a fool's mission,* the little whispers said. *You'll die in the service of a power-hungry, bloodthirsty fool. Escape while you can.*

He looked beyond the field in which they camped to the thin lines of trees that bordered it. Those trees would make good cover—he could keep low, double around beyond the XIXth and head north. No one would catch him. All of them were too intent on their insane trek south . . . and really, it wasn't as if he'd chosen to be on this mission.

Yes, the niggling fears whispered. *North. North is safe, north to An Tiram—you'll be safe in An Tiram.*

An Tiram? He shook his head and stared back at the fire—saw it as a menacing fiend, claws reaching out for his throat. By the gods! He shivered and clutched the amulet at his wrist and murmured a warding spell. In an instant, fog lifted from his mind, and the little voices quieted, and the flame demon became nothing but a cheerful campfire again.

He looked to the north.

It was to be devils, then, and not men that tried them first.

He woke Father Solmin. "Something coming in," he

whispered. "It got past my amulet—subtle but very strong. Almost convinced me to desert."

The priest sat up and stretched his arms out to his sides, fingers splayed. He closed his eyes and inhaled slowly. "Don't feel anything," he said after a long moment.

Amourgin nodded. "I didn't, either. But just beyond the campfire, I started feeling . . . doubts. I'd appreciate it if you'd walk out to the edge with me and see what happens. I've spelled myself . . ." He winced as Father Solmin gave him a hard look. ". . . Ah, sorry, Father. It seemed necessary. And when I did, the doubts and the shivers left me."

The priest stood and brushed himself off. "Very well. Let me take a few tools with me, and I'll see what I can find for you."

The priest walked with him out past the flickering circle cast by the firelight. Amourgin stopped and watched while the priest took a few more steps.

"Oh." Father Solmin fumbled in a pocket and pulled out a small, pale stone. He held it in the palm of his hand.

Amourgin could see the other man beginning to tremble. "You feel it now?"

The priest's voice was soft. "Oh, yes. I certainly do." He said something to the stone, and it began to flicker. "Oh, indeed . . ." He looked up. "Very good, corporal. You've caught something that could have destroyed us in short order. Willek has sent us a . . . a gift. A very clever one, too, I'm afraid. It will take the both of us, and the smiling fortune of the gods, to fend it off."

Amourgin nodded, but said nothing.

"She's bypassed the warding of the amulets very cleverly, by convincing the amulet spirits of her rightful claim as head of the armed forces. Thus, her sendings come at us because we look to the spirits like deserters. I had forgotten that particular implication of backing someone other than Willek." He sighed and stared mournfully at the amulet around his own wrist. "We're going to have to magically establish Bren's rightful position as heir to the throne before we can turn this.

Our only other option is to ward each man and woman individually, and I have neither the power nor the supplies to maintain that kind of a spelling against the forces both Willek and Darkist can bring to bear. I don't know about you."

"I have neither your skill nor experience," Amourgin said quietly. "My magical abilities are small—though they have served to save my own life on occasion, I'd hardly think to try saving the world with what I can do."

Father Solmin nodded, and his lips pressed into a thin line. "I thought as much. I dislike asking this—I know of both your affiliation and your . . . loyalties—but I give you my word I will not pursue any knowledge I gain from you at a later date. Are there any others among the XIXth who use magic, and who could be convinced to help us?"

Amourgin studied the man. He discovered that he actually believed the man—Father Solmin really would not have turned in other magicians to the Inquest Council had Amourgin been able to bring them forward. He clasped his hands behind his back and sighed. "I wish I did."

The priest gave him a shrewd look. "No? Well, I hadn't thought I'd felt any others among us. We'll do what we can with what we have, then."

"Shall I bring the captain?" Amourgin asked.

The priest was squatting in the dirt, spreading out his tools in a circle around himself. "Yes. Quickly, too." He indicated the light that glowed from his sensing stone. It throbbed and pulsed, and Amourgin could see the fire at its heart growing brighter as it did.

He ran quietly through the dark, to the flag at the heart of the camp that marked the place where Bren slept. As he ran, he noted a few men and women beginning to wake, looks of confusion and fear in their eyes. *The spell is getting strong enough to draw them from their sleep. This could become a rout*, he thought. *The XIXth could disappear into the darkness before we can break this spell.*

He ran faster.

Bren was already awake when he got there.

"Something's going on."

Amourgin was blunt. "We're under attack by Willek. Father Solmin needs you at the periphery."

Bren questioned him as they ran, and Amourgin explained what he knew. When they reached the priest, the First Captain understood as much about the danger as Amourgin did.

"Corporal, I need you to draw the captain's blood and spill it into the brazier as soon as I've brought up the amulet spirits. As soon as you see the first flicker of light—you understand?"

Amourgin looked at the First Captain and swallowed hard, but Bren said, "Do what you must, corporal."

Amourgin drew his dagger and crouched next to the brazier. "Wait beside me and give me your hand, then, sir," he said. The two of them waited, while Father Solmin tossed powders and poured liquids from cork-stoppered bottles, and the noises from the camp grew louder. Frightened voices called back and forth in the darkness, and Amourgin felt a sense of impending doom beating down on him, even through the warding spells he'd done.

"Hurry," Bren said.

"Goin' as fast as I can," Solmin said—then, "Say nothing, now, until you must, sir, and if you must answer questions, tell only the truth. Don't guess, don't speculate."

Someone moved past them in the darkness, running. Amourgin, holding onto the First Captain's hand with the dagger point pressed against it, felt the other man tense and felt it, too, when Bren's balance shifted as he started to move after the runner, then checked himself.

Amourgin held his breath and hoped the captain could restrain himself from shouting.

More things went into the brazier. Father Solmin began his incantation. Amourgin, listening to the form and the pattern of it, couldn't help but be impressed by the grace and style of the priest's work. A lot of the effectiveness of magic was tied up in that artistry, he mused. Solmin had the power of the gods, and the soul of a poet. And to think of words of such beauty, to create such moving passages with demons attacking on all sides and the sounds of desertion and despair all around him—such was the mark of a master.

The priest reached over the brazier and sketched out the shape of a dome with his hands. As he drew back, Amourgin saw the first glimmers of light flicker within the shape of that magical dome.

He took the knife and slashed it across his captain's palm, and blood spattered into the brazier.

"Ow, dammit!" Bren yelled.

"Wait for it," Solmin muttered. "It comes now."

The three of them crouched around the brazier, watching as the lights within it flickered and swirled together, faster and faster, and filled and stretched the barrier the priest had shaped with his hands. With an abrupt tinkling sound, the barrier burst, and the spirit of the amulets swarmed free. It billowed upward in the night sky, glowing more fearsomely than the demon that had flickered in the flames of the campfire. It towered to the height of a hundred men, and then it looked down, and from that great height, there could be no doubt that its eyes fixed on the three men around the brazier. It reached one massive claw-tipped hand down and scooped them up in it. "You've called me forth—I, who serve Shemro and those who serve Shemro. Shall I kill you then, little traitors?" it boomed.

They soared up into the sky until the fires below them were lost beneath the swirling mists of clouds, and the air became thin and bitter cold. Amourgin cried out. Beside him, Bren gasped. Only the priest stood fast in the face of this assault. He pointed his finger at the colossal form and said, "You, who are named Intirris, touch the blood we have given you, and see if Tornsaarin or if Morkaarin shall by rights succeed Shemro as heir. See then who serves faithfully."

The spirit guardian snarled and became for just a moment very still. Then it growled, "What treachery is this, that would betray a king?"

Amourgin and his two companions shot back down to the earth again in the spirit's palm, and scrambled gratefully to the earth. The spirit looked down at them. "One would rule by Yentror's choice; one by bloodright were the truth but known. And the Yentror's choice is tainted by foul magic." The guardian stared off into a great distance. "I cannot return to attack those who sent me, for my Yentror is with them. But I will not attack the right heir, or those who serve him." The guardian began to shrink, until it was the size of a man. "Go, with my continued protection," it said.

And then it was gone.

Amourgin's heart thudded in his chest, and his legs shook. *We could all have died,* he thought.

"Went better than I could have hoped," Solmin muttered. He bent and gathered up his things, then trudged back to his space on the ground without another word.

"You cut a bit deep," Bren said drily, studying the slash along the edge of his palm.

"Sorry, sir. I wasn't sure how much blood Father Solmin required—and I didn't want to take a chance on spilling too little."

Bren nodded. "Under the circumstances, the worry seems justified."

Around them, voices called to each other—and dark, shadowy forms crept back out of the lines of trees and back to the makeshift camp.

Amourgin tried to peer through the darkness to get a better look at the faces, but the captain rested his hand on the corporal's shoulder and shook his head. "Don't look," he said softly. "We don't want to know who went—it wasn't their fault. If any remain gone by morning, we'll make note of that. But for now, give them privacy to come back."

He walked away, and Amourgin sighed and went back to check on the horses, as he'd planned to do before.

❖   ❖   ❖

"You should have left me to take care of the siege," Brigadier Multin said. "Gods alone know what those damned loyalists will do while we're gone."

Grand Admiral Willek smiled bitterly. *Left you in charge of the army?* she thought. *Oh, no, this Tornsaarin wasn't born yesterday.* She'd known better than to leave any of her Inner Circle behind; and while she had Shemro along—and back under close control, that had been careless of her—the loyalists didn't matter. If she got her hands on this Theophone, *nothing* would matter. With that, you might as well be a *god*. For the first time, she realized how the wizard-kings of the Old Empire had kept their rule for ten thousand years.

Aloud, she said, "They'll sit in front of the walls of An Tiram and build trenches and fire cannon. That's a sideshow, now. You'll notice that Darkist is making time south, just as we are."

He looked at her strangely—they were all doing that now. "Darkist's dead," he said.

"No, Darkist has just put on a new shell, like a beach-crab," Willek said brutally. "He'll tell us how, before he dies the real death and joins the One. I don't intend to end up like that." She jerked a thumb at Shemro, huddled in her coach and looking older than years.

Multin paled and swallowed, dropping his horse back. *Didn't think through the consequences of your allegiances, did you?* Willek thought sardonically. Multin hadn't been bred to the conspiracy as she had and still had some Three-worshiper scruples buried deep within him. Not that she intended to let *him* have the secret of eternal life. No, Darkist and the ancient wizard-kings had been right about that. One alone should live forever, while the others bred, died, and served, generation after generation. One alone.

Willek Tornsaarin.

Behind her the hooves of the horses were an endless muffled thunder on the arrow-straight road; good highways were a common inheritance from the Old Empire. A regiment of dragoons—Multin's Shillraki mercenaries, who weren't concerned with Tykissian internal politics—and two more of mounted infantry, Imperial Regulars to keep an eye on Multin's hired soldiers, some light galloper-guns, and a minimum of essential baggage on pack mules. Enough to fight through light opposition in the countryside, and as long as she avoided the river, that was all she'd face. Darkist-Colchob would be travelling by water, through the fortress-cities on the Tiram River. Water travel was fast, but you had to follow the river, and it curved widely out of the way. She'd cut across the arc of the curve and then scare up some sort of boat, rafts if need be. A few score sailors were with them, uncomfortably perched on mules, and they'd take care of any boating necessary.

I'll get there first. And whoever gets there first will rule everything, forever.

Darkist-Colchob made a sign with one hand.

The war-slave struck. His huge curved blade hissed as it swung through the air, ending in a meaty *thuck* sound. The nobleman who'd argued with his Yentror barely had time to widen his eyes in alarm before the upper half of his body was toppling to the right.

Darkist's lips moved, murmuring in a language dead seven thousand years. His fingers moved as well, in small precise motions more graceful than a dancer's. The effort brought sweat to his frowning brow despite the cool evening breeze, much more than it should have—this new body was weak, *weak* in magic.

But the spell took hold. The legs and stomach stayed braced erect, despite the flood of blood, and the ropes of intestine that spilled around it like the long limp petals of some tropical flower. It took one tottering step, another—then it went to its knees and bowed. The remainder of the viscera slid forward out of the body cavity with a wet slushing sound.

"A reasonable question," Darkist answered the corpse, raising the bouquet to his nose to cover the hard latrine stink of death. "Reasonable but impudent—quite impudent."

The remainder of the city's nobles were on their bellies, beating their foreheads against the rose-colored marble of the royal docks. Behind them the riverport of Tol Tiram Kulnator raised itself toward the aching blue sky: onion-domed minarets of fretted marble topped with peacock-colored tiles, green copper roofs, gardens where flocks of spellbound glowflies danced in intricate patterns among the fountains and trees and orchids. Beyond lay the tarry workaday sections of the city, blocks of adobe buildings around tangled mud-paved streets, but his business was with the elite.

"We are but worms beneath your feet, Lord of Ten Thousand Years," the city viceroy's vizier said. "Order and we obey, though you command us to bite out our own tongues and eat the flesh of our firstborn sons."

For a moment Darkist-Colchob considered it—beautiful irony—but there was no time for play, despite the way his organ grew erect at the thought. Mind you, Colchob's body did that at *every* opportunity, even when he thought about vinegar and crushed ice. He'd forgotten what a distraction it could be.

"True, the northern barbarians sit outside the walls of An Tiram," he said mildly.

The vizier shuddered slightly as his master's blood slid around him on the slick marble, but he did not dare to move.

"That is no concern of yours," Darkist went on. "My generals will see to that matter. Your Yentror has business in the south. I require of you your battlebarges, powder, shot, provisions, and jungleman rowing slaves. Immediately. Go."

Karah wiped sweat from her face and leaned far back against the cantle of her saddle, bracing the balls of her feet into the stirrups and straightening her knees. Windrush's hooves squelched in a patch of mud. He picked his way carefully down the steep, ruined roadway, stepping over tangled roots thick as thighs that plunged through the shattered paving blocks. Huge trees leaned overhead, almost blocking out the fading sunlight; lianas and vines and festoons of moss dangled from them. Birds flitted between the boughs hundreds of feet above her head, birds such as she had never seen—a flight of thousands yellow as gold and tiny as her thumb, like a shower of airborn coins; others blue and red and orange, wings broader than the stretch of her arm, great curved beaks like swords and crests even longer, gliding with raucous cries. Flowers grew in great tumbling banks down the rough bark of the great trees, carmine and ivory, or hung in single blossoms bigger than her head from the vines. Insects flew and buzzed and hopped between—sometimes the petals of a flower would close over one with a swift vegetable hunger—and slow spirals of glowflies crimson as dawn drifted up like thick smoke through the olive-colored haze of air.

It would have been wonderful, if it wasn't so hot and wet and eerie. Away in the distance, something huge trumpeted and crashed through the vegetation. Monkeys threw things at her and scolded from the branches. The smell was overwhelming, like spoiled beer and yeast and perfume all mixed together. She worked her itching toes in her boots and kept her eyes moving, bow ready. They'd already met one denizen of the forest: a thirty-foot-long snake, a constrictor with a disposition to match and a taste for man flesh . . . or possibly horse. They'd had to hack it to pieces to get it to relax its grip on a pack mule and driver after it dropped down from the branch it'd been dangling on.

It had tasted like yardfowl, although a bit rubbery.

"The country sure changed fast," Karah said.

Dry savannah flanked the irrigated lands of the river valley; then the savannah turned lush, with tall grass and palms and patches of bamboo and unbelievable herds of beasts she'd never even heard of until the cultivated lands gave out and then . . . this.

Behind her, Amourgin and Eowlie were having more trouble with the roadway; their Tseldene horses were not as surefooted and well-trained as Windrush.

"Mountains," Amourgin said, checking the priming on his carbine. "The south shore of the Imperial Sea is dry because it's low-lying. The land's rising here, there are mountains south of us, and we've come four, maybe five hundred miles. And—"

He froze. Karah turned, careful not to raise her bow quickly.

The natives were grinning. At least, she *hoped* those were smiles—the teeth were intimidating, not fangs like Eowlie's, just big and yellow and sugarloaf-shaped. The faces behind them looked to be jungleman by breed, or at least partly so—shelf-browed and lump-nosed, covered in reddish-black hair, on bodies even squatter and browner than Tseldenes. Bodies and faces were painted in startling colors, red and yellow and electric green; it might even be camouflage, in these woods, or decoration like the stridently-colored feathers tucked into their topknots. All of them were men—emphatically so, with their manhood exaggerated by woven penis sheaths, their only clothing—and many of them had steel knives through their belts. Others carried stone-headed clubs, or spears with points of volcanic glass, or six-foot bamboo bows, or long slender tubes.

"Blowguns," Eowlie whispered. "T'ose darts at t'ere belts—poisoned."

The savages hooted in amazement at Eowlie's teeth; more of them were coming out of the jungle, slipping noiselessly through the undergrowth. One of them, probably the chief from the rusty Tseldene scimitar he carried, opened his mouth and pointed at Eowlie to do the same. She barred her fangs at them, bringing more enormous grins and hoots.

"They're closing around us," Amourgin said.

Karah nodded. Besides the body paint, many of them had bones through their noses, or necklaces of bone—human fingerbones, mostly.

She gave a broad, false smile of her own and pointed north.

"Many," she said, opening her hand and closing it again and again. "Tykissians." She indicated herself and her companions.

Let's not try to explain about Eowlie now. "Tykissians, there, many, many."

After a moment, that got through. The savages growled and jabbered to each other when they realized there were more of the visitors; the chief barked orders, and a dozen or so slipped off through the jungle to check. Karah carefully returned her bow to its case at her knee and held up open hands.

"Friends," she said, in the most friendly voice she could muster. "Friends, you brainless no-neck apes, *friends*." At a sudden thought, she unhooked a flask from her saddlebag and took a drink, then handed it to the chief.

From the way he beamed when he sniffed his broad nose at it, he recognized brandy. He swallowed the rest of it down with a blissful flutter of the prominent adam's apple beneath his nonexistent chin. Then he turned and raised both hands to his followers, breaking into a prolonged musical jabbering.

"I think you made a friend," Amourgin said, as the others lowered their weapons to the ground.

"Godsall," Karah said.

The chief belched contentedly and rubbed his stomach. "Fwiend," he said, in a basso lisp.

It was a little cooler by night, away from the bonfire. It burned low now in the square of the ruined city, glowing like the firepits that had prepared the feast. All around were woven-leaf platters of the local delicacies: grubs fried in oil (edible, to Karah's surprise), barrel-thick sections of giant snake, whole roasted forest hogs, baked monkey (she *hoped* it was monkey), plates of giant oranges and bloodfruit and steamed breadplant, salads of palm hearts and peppers, fiery spiced stews of gods-knew-what, bananas, mangos, jungle gooseberries with their sweet red hearts. And palm wine, huge earthen jugs of it, frothy and sweet and cool, with a kick like a skinner's mule.

Godsall, it's good to be full, she thought, hiding a small belch. *And* clean, *best of all*.

For a wonder, the jungle savages *washed*. They even had ancient hot springs still running into huge cracked tubs of granite in the overgrown ruins of what might have been a temple or a governor's palace, and a soapy root that lathered up well enough to wash all the grease out of even hair. The city was enormous, although most of it was barely distinguishable from the jungle itself—giant trees pushing up through roofless squares of tumbled stone, mounds of vines and brush across the lumpy remains of pyramids and avenues and statues. The woven palm and saplings of the tribefolk's longhouses seemed as natural as the undergrowth.

Right above her a broad-nostriled stone face loomed fifty feet high, with lianas and creepers for hair, its heavy features underlit by the flame flicker until they looked very much like the jungleman chief's.

She leaned back on her elbow beside Bren and took another draw at the gourd of palm wine. There was an odd undertaste to it, almost like cinnamon, some spice or other. The Tykissians were taking to it as enthusiastically as the savages were to the barrels of medicinal brandy. Many had joined the local men and women in the capering dance around the central fire . . . even the grim Captain Tagog had thrown off her inhibitions and was leaping with the best of them right alongside the native chief. In fact, she was shedding more than inhibitions; a whoop went up as she tossed her jacket through the air. The chief roared with delight and danced over to her. The dance wasn't suggestive; it was a demonstration. Tagog kicked off her tattered uniform breeches and leaped forward.

Karah grinned, blushed, and looked aside. "Who'd you think built this place?" she asked Bren, for want of anything else to say. "Tseldenes?"

"Maybe," Bren said, shaking off whatever mood had kept him silent. "Maybe the ancestors of our hosts." He indicated the statue above them.

"*Junglemen?*" Karah said incredulously.

"Possibly. Our own ancestors were savage enough, in the

old days, and look what we've done. Although I think they're hybrids around here, not pure jungleman, mixtures—*that's* certainly possible, eh?"

He nodded towards the fire. Karah looked, and blinked. *Godsall.* Tagog was wrapped around the chief like that python that had tried to swallow a mule, her heels kicking at the air. Maybe there *was* something odd in the palm wine; there were more combinations entangled all around the clearing. The natives didn't have contraceptive amulets, either, so a fair number of little half-Tykissians were going to be running through this jungle with bones in their noses in a few years, by the look of things.

The two rose and linked hands, walking a little distance into the ruins. One of the hot springs ran from a rockface, into a pool it had worn for itself. Soft moss grew beside it.

"We nearly died again," Karah said at last. "I don't think we could have pushed on through the jungle much further."

Bren grinned at her, his face ruddy in the light of the distant fires. "We do seem to be making a habit of near-misses, don't we?"

Karah nodded. "I think we're near the end of our journey— and I'm afraid once we get there, and do whatever the gods want of us, they'll throw us away." She shivered and wrapped her arms around herself. She stared into the falling water, watching the almost-pictures made by the dancing flames as they reflected in it.

Bren stared down at his hands, and the grin vanished from his face. "We've been sharing dreams then, you and I."

When he glanced up at her, she stared into his eyes. "Then you feel it, too? That death is just waiting—just biding its time?"

He nodded slowly.

Karah sighed. "I kept telling myself that after this was over, I'd come to you, and tell you how I felt about you. I'd swear my love, and offer you my heartstone if you would have it." She stood and slipped her hands into the pockets of her breeches and paced. "I imagined the two of us courting, and how I would bring you home to the ranch and show you off t' my family. But I suppose I knew that wasn't going to happen. We're going to die here, and there will be no long tomorrows for us."

The silence hung between them, and Karah began to wish she'd said nothing. Then Bren spoke. "I would give you the kingdom as your brideprice if I had it, Karah. I'd give you my heartstone, and my heart with it." His voice broke, and he looked off into the night, into the overhanging gloom of the jungle. "I love you. If we had forever, I would love you forever. But all we have is now." He stood and faced her, breathing hard. "If you'll have me now, I'm yours."

"We aren't safe here." She walked to him, touched her hands to his.

"Love is never safe."

She nodded and kissed him once, lightly. She stared intently into his eyes, trying to discover if she really could see his soul staring back at her from behind his pupils, the way the poets said lovers could. But she saw nothing except her own reflection, and the reflected flicker of flames behind her.

They kissed again, a harder, deeper kiss. Karah pulled away first, but only so she could begin to undress him. He smiled at her, and when he did, his upper lip trembled, and the smile died, to be replaced by a look of raw hunger.

They pulled each other's clothes off as quickly as they could, then, and knelt on the ground, not quite touching, but so close Karah was warmed by the heat from Bren's body.

He lowered his head and put his mouth to her breast. She sighed and ran her fingers through his hair. A part of her mind noticed the way the gold highlights in it gleamed like real treasure, while her fingertips traced the swirling pattern of the hairs themselves—but Bren's hands slid from the small of her back to her buttocks, and Bren's knees pressed her thighs apart and Bren's mouth traced its path from one breast to the other, and slowly up along her throat and the line of her jaw. Karah got lost in the rhythm of their touches, and forgot to notice anything. Then their mouths met, and he lowered her onto the makeshift bed they'd created with their cast-off clothes.

She slipped her legs around his hips and pulled him against her.

"Gods," he muttered, and she whispered, "Yes."

They moved together, desperately. They were a tangle of arms and legs, a restless, shifting, sweat-slicked blur; images stayed in Karah's mind after they themselves moved on—her ankles wrapped around his neck, his chest pressed against her back, her hands pressing his shoulders flat to the ground while she slid down onto him.

When it was over, and they sprawled, spent and panting, next to the fire, Karah clenched her fists tightly and wished she could believe there would be another time and another chance for the two of them.

"We're leaving the *horses*?" Karah asked with incredulous horror, swatting at an insect. The stinging hordes were out in force again, buzzing through the hot mist of morning.

"Be reasonable," Bren said. "We can't take them with us in *these*, can we?"

The native canoes bobbed in the slow current at the end of ruined wharves. Buckled and uneven and overgrown, high with silt on their upstream sides, the wharves still served; even the bollards, stumpy little statues of grinning monkeys, were often useable for a mooring rope. Ropes had worn them half-way through, although the stone was iron-hard basalt, fine-grained and tough. Some of the canoes they'd bartered for with spare bits of iron and cloth were thirty feet long or more, but none of them were much wider than man-broad, even with the outriggers on both sides. They had stubby sails, V-shapes made with two poles pivoting up from a common footing, but no decks—each canoe was hollowed from a single giant log with fire and stone tools. For all the crudeness of their making, they were comely craft, slender and fine-lined, with whimsical carvings at their man-high stemposts and sterns.

"But—" Karah looked into Bren's face. "All right."

She turned and walked away, knuckling at her eyes. Windrush whickered and lipped at her hair, ready to be off about the business of the day. She looked at the natives; one of them was fingering the haunches of a pack mule in a meditative way, while another stropped a knife.

No! she thought, and stripped the bridle and hobble off her horse. She hadn't brought Windrush all the way from Grenlaarin-on-the-River to see him put into a jungleman's stewpot. For a moment she hugged his neck, burying her face in the coarse mane and the earthy, grassy smell of horse. Then she darted back and slapped him smartly across the haunch with the tack.

Windrush bugled and started. "Go!" Karah yelled, waving her arms as the horse circled nervously. "Get out of here. Go! Scat!"

The horse hesitated, then plunged away across the square in a clatter of ironshod hooves. *He'll just be eaten by a snake, or a lion, or a giant lizard or something,* she told herself—a Grenlaarin was supposed to be practical about horses.

To the One with that. Windrush deserved a chance, and *she* wasn't going to connive at cutting him up for giblets.

One of the natives scowled at her, until she threw him the bridle; the metal in that made it a treasure. She stalked back to the docks; the rest of the troops were loading, many of them looking hangdog and a little the worse for wear, but without the brutalized exhaustion of the last days' journey through the jungle. One of Captain Tagog's company smothered a chortle as she winced slightly taking her seat in a canoe, then quickly bent to heave an ammunition crate aboard under her basilisk glare. Karah saw Bren's raised eyebrows, then his smile and nod. Warmth spread through her middle.

"*Dis*mounted Scout Troop, ready for action, First Captain," she said, saluting.

He replied with a courtly bow, and handed her into the canoe. It rocked slightly. "The only throne I can offer you at present," he said lightly. Then in a serious tone: "Although, Holy Three be my witness, there'll be one beside me in Olmya for you, if we live through this."

For a moment she simply smiled back. Then the sense of the words struck her—and the fact that he meant them, down to the bone.

"_Me_?" It came out as a squeak. "I'm just a rancher's daughter!"

"I'm just a bastard of the minor nobility and a first captain of the XIXth Foot," Bren said, and for a moment his square face went very grim. "If the high haughty lords will take the one, they'll have to swallow the other—I'll see to that."

Amourgin was looking at him oddly. "I believe you will, sir," he said quietly. "Well, we've had worse emperors. And odder, come to that."

Bren nodded decisively. "Cast off there," he said. "Dawn's making and we've a long way yet to go."

The little fleet of outrigger canoes loosed the ropes that held them to the ruined docks and slid out onto the broad green surface of the river, through coils of mist that trailed across it and reached up like limp banners to the trees. A wind from the north slid by them, warm even now. The tall narrow sails of the canoes went up, and they turned their carved prows southwards.

"Not _one_? You didn't capture even _one_?" Darkist-Colchob shouted, starting erect from his throne on the battlebarge.

The guard captain knelt again and struck his forehead on the blue-and-green turrwood planks. "Slay me, Lord of Ten Thousand Years, but spare my men. The fault was mine—I underestimated how elusive the forest savages would be."

Darkist-Colchob blinked. "Slay you? A man who actually _accepts responsibility_? Nonsense." He reached down and gripped the young officer by one ear. "Obviously, the towhairs bartered for boats here. A prisoner would merely have confirmed details. You are promoted to Captain of Two Hundred. _And do not fail me again!_"

The officer looked more terrified at his promotion than he had at the prospect of a long death—possibly rightly. The Yentror of Tarin Tseld turned, surveying the ruined city. *Tall were its towers*, he remembered from the last time he had seen it. Tall, and lit with fire, as his armies swarmed over the walls. Now the forest had reclaimed it, and only here and there did stone loom out of the greenery into the hot mists of afternoon. Nothing moved save birds and beasts, no sound came to him save the screams of parrots and somewhere the hunting call of a gurr-tiger. The battlebarges waited, their oars dipping just enough to keep station against the sluggish current of the mile-wide Tiram.

There were a dozen of the craft, each forty feet broad and a hundred long, shallow-draft and carrying light cannon on the deck over the oarsmen. Their sides sparkled with inlay and metal and enamel; his own was a blaze of gold leaf and scarlet and lapis, with the canopy over the quarterdeck cloth of silver. It was still very hot and very damp, and the barge stank like any slave-rowed vessel. Darkist-Colchob waved aside servitors with flasks of iced pomegranate juice and shrugged back the woven-feather cloak that trailed from his shoulders.

He turned to the priests. There were two of them, on either side of a three-foot sphere of crystal held in the jaws of a cast-bronze dragon. Both were naked and had been trimmed of all hair on eyelashes, nose, external ears, and genitalia. One was written all over in scars that traced out the legends of the One in High Tiranese; the other was covered by a network of lines, with a sharp silver pin inserted at each junction. They busied themselves with their work, and the Yentror did not disturb them. At last the pinned man looked up.

"Still south, with the river—we follow their amulets, Yentror of All Men. But look—"

He indicated the globe. An uninstructed man would have seen only empty crystal; Darkist-Colchob made out mist, threaded with points of light. He passed a hand over the surface and felt chill air, the chill of northern snows.

"Shadows grow; the Three Unnamed Ones extend their hand over their votaries. Keep watch."

He looked up. "Southward!"

"Ukk!"

An officer not two paces away from Willek pitched backward into the mud with a blowgun dart quivering in her throat—none of them were wearing their gorgets anymore, not after a month in the jungle. The woman's body arched and quivered, already dead but still reacting to the neurotoxin smeared on the point of the dart. A deafening volley sounded as the musketeers on either side blasted away into the foliage, and then the whole body charged through the screen of bushes and ferns. Willek followed with her sword out and a pistol in her left hand; they'd learned the natives could appear around a tree like ghosts, and always when you least expected them.

Screams and shouts and the clash of metal against stone and wood sounded from ahead. She passed dead junglemen, and dead Tykissians and Shillraki mercenaries, dead sailors, and one man who'd run into a trap and lay impaled and still alive ten feet below in a pit. The natives were good at booby traps, too.

Sweat trickled and chafed as she walked down the path, senses pricked to inhuman alertness; the coat of light chainmail she wore under her jerkin was hot and heavy, but better sore than dead. Soon she passed through the screen of jungle, into banana groves and patchy fields of cassava amid the charred stumps of giant trees, the mark of slash-and-burn cultivation. The barbarian longhouses stood helter-skelter down to the muddy riverbank, full of figures who ran and fought and died. The troops were killing everything that moved, down to the babes in arms.

She came to Brigadier Multin, wild-eyed, stuffing a cassava cake into his mouth with one hand, the other still holding his bloody sword. There were weeping sores on the back of both hands, and another at the corner of his mouth; most of them had them by now. And—

"We surprised them this time," she said.

Only two of the village's canoes had put out into the broad greasy-green waters of the upper Tiram, and both were drifting helpless, emptied by the fire of the musketeers on the bank. Imperial sailors or Shillraki bundled into others and paddled out to tow them in; most of that breed had some experience in boats.

"We've got river transport now," Willek said, sheathing her sword. It took a few tries; she was almost as hungry as the rest of them. "We'll . . . we'll rest here a day or two, feed up, then take to the waters."

Multin choked down the dry cassava and licked the crumbs off his hand, peering at the mud beach. "There aren't enough— we've still got nearly two thousand effectives. Those canoes won't take more than a half of that."

"The rest can make a garrison," Willek said, wiping a hand through the oily sweat that plastered her hair to her face. "Put up a stockade, wait for us to come back."

"And eat what?" Multin said. "Our supplies are about gone, and we've eaten most of the horses and mules. This damned jungle is like a wet desert."

"There's the plantain groves here, and the roots and such; and they can fish and hunt."

Multin looked at her blankly. The jungle was buzzing like a hive of bees behind them after the passage they'd hacked through the sparse native villages, looting to feed themselves and killing to break resistance. Any soldier who so much as stepped around a tree to squat came back in pieces, and the savages were like ghosts, impossible to catch. The river was full of things that ate humans. They were short of ammunition, and the climate made slowmatch and powder sputter so that firing a musket was no better than an even chance.

"And you, my dear Multin, will command the base. You need the rest."

He looked at her with sick horror as she laughed.

❖   ❖   ❖

"*Heave*, damn your arses!" Bren yelled over the thunder of the white water.

The rapids stretched the full width of the river, nearly half a mile. In the middle, spray jumped twenty feet in the air over fangs of eroded black basalt and pale granite; the sound of it toned through teeth and bone like an everlasting earthquake. A hundred early morning rainbows marked the foam. The margins on the eastern shore were calmer, and it was there the Tykissians were trying to tow their vessels past the wild water.

One by one the outriggers were emptied of their cargo on the rocky shore. Stripped to loincloths and boots, dozens of soldiers splashed into the chest-deep water, pushing and hauling at the hulls, the outriggers and the connecting poles. Scores more hauled on ropes from the bank or the shallows, and foot by foot the light craft lurched southward and upstream.

"Sod this for a game of soldiers," Bren called, stripping off his shirt and jumping into the water to a cheer from the troopers. He bent and put a shoulder to the stern of the first canoe. "Let's see you idle lot do a little *work* here."

Whooping, Karah joined him with a splash. The water was cool and silky, caressing her bare skin; she locked her palms on the checkered wood of an outrigger strut and heaved. The soldiers around her were laughing, proud that the commander joined them at their labor; they all took up a cadence chant, with a heave of grunting effort at the chorus, and the canoe began moving at walking pace. Karah could feel the current tugging at her thighs and torso like strong eager hands, and an occasional wave lapped at her face like the tongue of an over-eager dog. She spat out a mouthful of hair and took up the chant.

It almost drowned out the screams of warning from the shore, but not the whipcrack of musket bullets.

Karah looked up. For a moment her eyes refused to accept the scale of what they were seeing; back home on the Nyok plateau, alligators were narrow-snouted little fish-eaters the length of your arm, in the limestone sinkholes that dotted the hill country. In the Olmya River, they grew to a man's length, or a little more, and she'd *heard* of the huge saltwater variety, although those were rare in the Imperial Sea these days.

This one was as long as the canoe, thirty-five feet from the flared nostrils to the end of the massive sculling tail that propelled it forward faster than a horse could run. Its square-tipped jaws were nearly as broad across as her leg was long, and they gaped open like a barn door, edged with four-inch ivory daggers. Breath like an opened tomb washed across her. Then the beast struck the canoe's outrigger like a three-ton battering ram.

"Giant crocodile!" someone screamed.

Tough wood cracked across with explosive force, sending splinters and chunks flying twenty feet into the air. The hull surged back against Karah with the unstoppable force of an avalanche, pushing her down into the water. For a moment she struggled, lost in tumbling green depths with the underside of the hull looming over her and threatening to trap her against the rocks.

Then she braced a boot against a rock and *pushed*, her chest burning with the effort. Two strokes, and she came erect again in waist-deep water, coughing and shaking hair back out of her eyes. The crocodile had shattered the bow of the canoe with one blow of its tail . . . and now it was turning towards *her*. The water clung to her like glue, slowing her, as if she were in a nightmare where she ran and ran, but couldn't move. Only this monster was all too real. She could see musket bullets striking it, but the two-inch scutes absorbed them. Reptiles took a lot of killing, and unless one of the shots found the tiny bone-armored brain, it wasn't going to stop.

"Here, Karah!" A strong arm circled her waist and flung her backward towards the land.

It was Bren, but now the monster was bearing down on *him*, climbing over the wreckage in its eagerness, crushing and breaking wood and bodies beneath it. She floundered six paces to the shore, seized her sword from the pile of clothing, and turned back into the water. All the fear she'd felt while the crocodile bore down on her was gone, lost in the knowledge that Bren was about to die. She raised the blade and shouted, wading out as fast as she could without tripping.

Maybe if I stab it in the eye . . .

Godsall. Maybe it would have a stroke and float away, while she was at it.

There was a body in its jaws, born aloft and shaken like a fish in the beak of a heron—not Bren, Sergeant Ddrad. His open mouth was screaming but he still struck with the blade in his hand, striking sparks from the flinty armor until it shook him apart in a shower of blood. Bren was right there beneath it with a half-pike in his hands, which looked like an eight-foot toothpick against the beast's gape. The great jaws opened again; the beast was half out of the water, its little legs scrabbling at boulders. Even in the hindering stream, Bren's thick-muscled body moved with heartstopping grace. He lunged—upward, into the roof of its mouth. It clamped its jaws down, but in the same movement he'd whipped the butt of the half-pike into its lower jaw.

The whole enormous power of the crocodile's jaws drove the sharp steel of the pikehead into its palate. It screamed, a shrill sound like a thousand steam cookers venting—a sound that stabbed painfully into the ears. Then it twitched its head, and Bren went pinwheeling into the water a dozen paces away. The pikeshaft snapped like a twig, and the crocodile bellowed in a mist of blood. It took one step forward—

"With me," Father Solmin yelled. Karah turned, and saw Amourgin at the priest's side. The two of them began flinging powders into the water and shouting at the top of their lungs.

The water began to hiss—then turned an ugly shade of orange. Smoke rose from it, dark orange and stinking, and curled around the monster. The giant crocodile slowed, though its teeth still snapped and its tail still lashed back and forth.

Amourgin's doing magic in front of the priest, she thought, and noted a few others who gazed at the priest and the corporal with speculative expressions and poorly hidden curiosity. But she had no time to wonder about the law-speaker and his illegal magic.

Even with the mist and the curling smoke, dozens of muskets were able to fire from the shore—not without screamed curses when damp priming powder misfired or slowmatches went out. A rapid stutter of shots built, more and more as musketeers reached their stacked weapons. Water spurted up around the sluggish beast, and blood spattered where the heavy bullets struck home. A file of pikes waded out to it, the long razor-edged pyramidal heads of the weapons punching with the two-armed thrust meant to penetrate cavalry armor. It bellowed and thrashed, knocking the shafts aside or wrenching them out of the wielders' hands, but more took their place. Halberdiers climbed over the wreckage of the canoe and slammed their massive weapons down on its spine and sides.

Blood turned the water pink, the blood of human and reptile. Even in its death throes, the beast was deadly-huge. At last a musketeer came out with her weapon held high overhead and fired with the muzzle not a foot from the yellow slit-pupiled eye. The king crocodile reared out of the water impossibly high, like a great rough-barked tree reaching for the sky, then crashed back in a wave that knocked Karah off her feet again. When she struggled erect, the beast was dead—still twitching, and some of the soldiers were driving their weapons into it with blind fury, moving like wind-up mechanisms.

Bren came to her side, his naked body bruised and grazed, but whole.

"You're all right?" he wheezed.

"Apart from being scared pissless," she said, then hugged him clumsily with one arm, the other fist still clenched on the hilt of her sword. "Godsall, you could have been *killed*!"

He nodded, then turned to the riverbank. "Fall in, there!" he called to the ones still beating on the crocodile's corpse.

"Get those other canoes tethered" —several were drifting downstream— "tend to the wounded, let's have some order here!"

Captain Tagog and the noncoms were adding their voices to his. Bren and Karah slogged their way to shore. "Damn," Bren said softly, looking out to where the dead and injured were being hauled from the water's grip. "*Damn*. Damn you for dying, Ddrad, I'm going to miss you."

"He was a good man," Karah said, sliding her hand under his arm.

"He was a friend. I led him a long way from home to die, him and too many others," Bren said quietly. Karah saw the unshed tears in his eyes, saw the way he bit his lip and looked out over the bodies. "Damn," he whispered. Then he shook himself.

"All right, nobody told you to stop working!" he shouted. The soldiers stacked weapons once more and went back into the river with gingerly caution—all but a much-enlarged overwatch, their muskets primed and pointed out to the waters.

Captain Tagog came up with something that glittered on the point of her sword: a ruddy copper band as broad as a man's hand, covered in raised glyphs. It had been hacked across, but the circular shape was still visible, like a bracelet for a giant. Solmin and Amourgin peered at it with interest, the law-speaker bringing out his spectacles. Then both recoiled with identical grimaces of disgust. The soldier flicked the copper circlet into the mud at their feet.

"That was on the lizard's forearm," she said grimly. "I don't think that writing means 'return pet to owner.' "

"Crocodile, not lizard," Amourgin said absently, in scholar's reflex. "Tseldene script—Old High Tiranese, the wizard's dialect."

Solmin nodded in professional approval. "It's a dedication to the One—in Its aspect as Death-by-Stealth, the Fanged Terror. Crocodile-god cult. And a warding of sight, to prevent a magician sensing the beast's coming, and another of control and domination."

He pointed with a stick. "The wizard's blood would be added to the metal while it was still molten." At Amourgin's raised eyebrows, he went on: "You don't want to know the rest of the rite. Believe me, sir."

"This was a sending?" Bren asked.

Both the magicians nodded. "At you particularly, I'd guess," Amourgin said. "The beast didn't stop to feed, or strike at others in the water. You or Karah."

Bren had been dressing while he spoke. He tightened his belt with unnecessary force, and clashed his sword home in the sheath. "Then you two will see to our protection—together. And that *is* an order."

He turned to Tagog. "We'll build a common pyre and grave," he said. "See to it."

❂ CHAPTER XV

"These fell here: Ensign Towi Fulin, Sergeant Sleffer Ddrad;
Privates Mrado, Dotakbotsl, Trall, Dorax, Galodden. All honor
to them, who faced death unflinching. May the Father shelter
them, the Mother comfort them, the Child be with them,
until the world is made new. By Prince-Heir Bren Morkaarin-
Strekkhylfa, officer commanding, XIXth Imperial Regiment
of Foot. Five hundredth forty-first year of the New Empire,
twentieth day, Month of Falcon Turning."

Grand Admiral Willek felt the blood rushing to her face as
the officer read it, and knew anyone who watched her would
see it; it was a curse of the Tykissian strain. The temptation to
have the little monument blown to fragments was overwhelming, but the troops wouldn't like it, and besides that they were
short of powder. It was only a heap of fieldstone, anyway, with
one naturally smooth slab for the rude chiselwork of the
inscription.

"It's the thirtieth of Falcon Turning now," Willek said. "Ten
days. Now we know they didn't turn up any of the jungle tribu-
taries. We can catch them if we push hard, we're about equal
in numbers."

"The troops are tired," the officer said neutrally. "And we're
a Three-forsaken long way from anywhere."

Willek looked up; the soldiers were standing around their
beached canoes, murmuring among themselves. They looked

338

ragged and hungry, but these were the best, the fiercest, and the ones most deeply committed to her. Everyone was very conscious of the huge rotting bulk of the crocodile, mostly pink bone by now but still swarming with vermin. On the whole, she was satisfied with morale. Except for the group of Life Guards around Shemro, of course.

Their commander came up to Willek and saluted smartly. The Shillraki dragoons around her drew closer; Willek had an excellent reputation among mercenaries—she always saw that they were paid promptly, and in good sound coin, and she'd promised a quadruple bonus to all survivors of this expedition.

"Grand Constable," the Guards officer said. "I must protest. The Emperor is not well—"

The Emperor is under a spell of slow wasting and obedience, Willek thought smugly.

"—and should not be subjected to these hardships. I must insist that she be—"

A cannon sounded further downriver. Around the curve came the prow of a Tseldene battlebarge, its painted oars flashing in the bright tropical sun like the vermilion legs of some monstrous centipede against the blue-green water and deep-green jungle. Four more followed it, their sides bright with metal and paint, their decks equally bright with the weapons of the troops. Another cannon thudded.

"Li' pieces," a Shillraki officer said, in their whistling accent. "Four-p'onders, murtherer guns, swivels. Not'in heavy."

Willek's voice rose with a whip crack of command: "Let's get to work, gentlefolk. Set up the fieldpiece there" —it was a bronze six-pounder, and now worth the living hell it had been getting it through the jungle— "to keep those bumboats at a respectful distance. The rest of you, set the working parties to hauling the canoes. They'll not get those barges up the rapids soon, if at all, provided we give them a warm reception now. *Move!*"

✧   ✧   ✧

"We took their cannon," the officer said. "And pursued their rear guard to the head of the rapids, as you ordered."

He gestured to the pile of sixty or so heads the Tseldene soldiers were piling at Darkist-Colchob's feet. Blond Tykissians, black-haired, hook-nosed Shillraki. Mongrel-looking sailors.

It's interesting how severed heads all have the same foolish expression, the Tseldene emperor thought. Perhaps something to do with the severing process, but there was rarely the fine grimace of agony you otherwise got on a dead face. He couldn't really concentrate, not with the voice of the Cold One forever in his mind, begging, pleading, commanding, promising horrors and delights. There were times when he saw with the One's own eyes, and that was something to shake even a soul as long in the world as his.

"Your orders, Lord of Ten Thousand Years?"

"Go, go—help prepare the barges."

Upstream teams of workers were hammering long steel wedges into cracks in the granite, or spiking block-and-tackle rigs to the larger trees. The musical *tink-tink-tink* of sledge-hammers carried through the background burr of the rapids. On the deck of his barge the first cables were being reeved up through the hawseholes, and rowing slaves were herded onto the deck as long iron bars were thrust through the capstans. Their grunts and howls sounded, gobbling and thick from tongueless mouths as the sweet music of the lash crackled.

"Most efficient, most efficient," Darkist-Colchob murmured, gratified and surprised. When you dealt every day with a civil service eight thousand years old . . .

Ahead, at the turn of the river, something crashed through the thick undergrowth at the water's edge. It was huge—Willek raised her hand and forward progress stopped. She had seen some of the horrors the river held—she had no wish to discover, too closely and too late, that this thing ahead was another of them.

She heard screams, and suddenly a tribe of junglemen boiled

out of the trees and splashed into the river, running heedless.

"You never see them unless they want you to," she muttered to her aide.

The man nodded. Willek's army sat frozen, holding its place along the banks, hidden in the shadows of the overhanging trees, silent.

The last of the junglemen tribe raced into the water—the first were already halfway across, swimming frantically. Willek wondered what would make the natives take to it swimming, instead of in boats. What sort of predator . . . ?

And then the trees parted, and the hunter crashed out, and sloshed into the water. Willek bit on the back of her hand to keep herself from screaming; one of the guards beside her fainted.

It was a creature made of water, entirely magical; in its misshapen body she could see bits of trees and pieces of boats . . . and the limp, bloated forms of those it had consumed. They floated and bobbed inside it, terrible to behold.

It was after the junglemen, reaching out, touching them, sucking them into itself, one after the other. A few made it to the far shore and fled, still screaming. Some of her soldiers raised weapons to fire at the monster, but with the smallest gesture of a hand, she held off their fire. *Silence*, she thought, not even daring to breathe. Nevertheless, the monster paused in midstream, still and waiting, looking around as if it sensed the presence of the Tykissians. *No*, she thought, frantic. She had no idea how to go about fighting off a thing made of water. She thought, but the harder she thought, the more ideas eluded her. The thing rose up and started in a slow walk toward the spot where the first boats hid, and Willek felt doom approaching—but then another of the junglemen struggled onto the far shore and into the greenery with a crash, and the watery horror turned and took off after it.

The sounds of screams and of the monster's lumbering progress grew fainter, and finally disappeared.

Willek sat for a long time after it passed, sucking thoughtfully on her lower lip. Finally she gave the signal, and the boats proceeded upstream again.

That had been no natural denizen of the jungle. She had felt the tingle of magic about it. It had been, for an instant, keenly interested in them—and even though it had been distracted, and had gone chasing off after the junglemen, Willek had felt about the monster a taint she'd hoped never to cross. It was, she suspected, one of Darkist's creatures. And though it was hunting widely and not selectively, she felt from the stink of the magic around it that it hunted for her.

She shivered and thought of the glowing gold icon that lay ahead of her. Time pressed. She needed to find the thing, and lay claim to the world quickly—before the darkwoven magics of those who wished her ill caught up with her.

"I know enough to keep the judges honest and pay the troops on time," a voice murmured softly. "Beyond that, what?"

Karah stirred in her sleep, blinking. She was lying with her head in Bren's lap; his hand stroked her hair idly. She lay still, listening. Amourgin and Eowlie were seated behind them in the big canoe; ahead was the mast and the tall narrow sail. Most of the other crew-passengers were asleep, except for the helmsman and the ones on the simple rigging lines. Moons' light glittered on the still waters of the river, throwing a winding avenue of brightness down their southward path. The other canoes were around them, their wakes phosphorescent streaks. Tall papyrus overhung the river on both sides, dark and ragged against the moons and huge soft stars of the southern skies. It was never quiet, but the hum and buzz and bird calls were muted now, in the third watch not long before dawn.

By night, in a broad channel, with the heat less fierce, the great swamps above the rapids were even fairly pretty. In the daytime, going overside to hack a path through the winding, floating clumps of reed . . . she shuddered inwardly. The leeches were as long as a big man's thumb; what they'd all do when the salt ran out, she didn't like to think.

Amourgin answered, equally quiet. "Make the margraves and the counts pay their share of the taxes, for starters," he said. "Right now, the free-farmers and tenants and small merchants are being ground down slow but sure."

Bren chuckled softly. "Right, you've got the Throne rocking under my fundament right there. I see your point, though. What about the cities? Should I let them go their own way internally, as Shemro has?"

"You shouldn't let the bankers and the Guilds-Merchant turn them into closed corporations, that's for certain," Amourgin said. His voice was passionately earnest. "And try reigning in the Imperial Tykissian Eastern Seas Company and the other chartered combines. They're as bad as the upper nobility, in their way, trying to turn Melcan and the new colonies into their private fiefs."

"Is there any vested interest you *don't* think I should alienate, my friend?"

"You could tighten the laws protecting the thralls, sir," Amourgin said. "And do something about the pariahs."

"Now there's the Tykissian commonfolk and the priesthood you'll set against me, too. Bren the Tyrant, eh? Who'll be *for* me, besides you and your friends?"

Amourgin inclined his head: "Easier to let things drift, I know. But think: why did our ancestors fight the Old Empire in the first place?"

Bren's teeth flashed white in the darkness. "Loot."

"They only became warriors when the Old Empire started raiding them. Oh, yes, they were pirates—but they were a free people, and in the Old Empire everyone but the wizard-kings were slaves. And that *matters*. Look at what we've done, in only five or six centuries—I know we think of the Old Empire as civilization incarnate, but did they ever build ships that could sail the outer oceans? Or make gunpowder or cast cannon, or build watermills?"

"Watermills are civilization?" Bren said dubiously.

"They are if you're a thrall grinding grain by hand every day," Amourgin said grimly. "That's just an example. I could have mentioned printed books, or optical glasses, or even magic—the Old Empire could do marvels, but we're better at common, everyday magic like purifying a city's water supply, or putting the hex on a swarm of locusts."

He adjusted his glasses. "But if we go the way of the Old Empire, what's the point in it all? The Old Empire's wizard-kings ruled for ten thousand years, and that's all they did—rule. No wonder they became sadistic monsters!

"It should be the other way round, but every time we Tykissians have pushed south in last few centuries, we've 1become more like what we conquered. Look at Derkin compared to the central provinces, or the central provinces compared to Old Tykis. In Beltra the Great's time every free commoner could speak to their chief, or carve out a freehold by putting the plow to vacant land. Now a tenant who owes their landlord money can't even move."

Bren was silent, frowning, for a few minutes. "I'll have to think about it," he said slowly. "I don't agree with everything you've said, and I certainly couldn't put it all into practice at once even if I did. Hmmm. It's certainly a bad thing to have too many thralls around; they take away a free man's pride in the work of his hands. At Timlake, we Morkaarins always held a chief is a chief for the folk's sake. . . ."

He glanced back over his shoulder. "You realize you've talked yourself into a job, law-speaker? Not as an infantry corporal, either."

"Job?" The moons' light glinted off Amourgin's glasses, but he looked startled as an owl nonetheless.

"Certainly . . . Imperial Councillor." Bren chuckled again. "I tend to get too focused on the job at hand—need someone to remind me what it's *for*. Although all this is pretty damned academic, right now—my empire is a dozen canoes in the middle of a swamp in a country right off our maps."

Karah yawned and stretched. "I'm glad you're not just pretty," she said, sitting up. "Hate to think I'd have to do all the skull work when I'm Consort."

Bren grinned and kissed her. "I'll have you running the cavalry," he said.

"What's that sound?" Eowlie asked softly.

The river had risen out of the swamps in the last day or so, which was a relief; unfortunately, the wind had also died down, and they were paddling. That was difficult enough, and the canoes were overcrowded, too. The scent of flatface sweat was rank on the air.

"I - don't - hear - anything," Amourgin said, pacing his words to the stroke of the paddle.

"I - do," she replied. "From . . . up ahead.

"*Halt*," Bren called. "Everybody listen."

The words echoed back from the high, rocky hills on either side. The hills were sparsely covered with reddish grass and stunted thorn trees; nothing moved there but a troop of ground apes, baboonlike creatures the size of small humans. They barked alarm and scampered off in a clatter of pebbles and dust. Karah strained her ears to hear something besides the sough of the wind and the low murmur of the river.

"I *do* hear something," she said. "It's loud, but it's a long way away. Maybe some more rapids?"

"We'll find out," Bren said. "Let's get moving."

The Tykissians pressed on, sailing when the wind favored them, rowing more often as the river narrowed and wound deeper into the hills. The rock rose on either side; glimpses ahead showed range upon range climbing towards the southern horizon. Clouds floated above it—either clouds or snowpeaks. The river stayed fairly level, with no more than the occasional stretch of rough water.

Amourgin looked in fascination at the banded stone of the cliff. "That's volcanic rock," he said. "Layer upon layer of it, and the river's worn it away. Must have taken a long time; this basalt is *hard.*"

The river wound through it in sharp S-curves, where the rushing water had found softer veins in the lava. All wind died in the straight confines of the canyon, and sweat ran from the paddlers in steady trickles as they dug their paddles into the swift current. It surged beneath their keels in long smooth swells, like the muscles of a dancer, and they could feel it quivering with life through the wood in their hands. The stone walls rose about them, glossy black streaked with red and umber and green; they plunged into the deep river as vertical as masonry laid with a plumb bob. Tall pinnacles split the water here and there, flat-topped columns soaring overhead and giving welcome shade. The faint noise grew until it echoed back and forth from the half-mile cliffs, grew into an endless roar like continual summer thunder.

"Look!" Bren shouted over the noise, pointing.

A huge space a hundred yards square had been smoothed on the cliff to their right, outlined like a human hand with the flat patch forming the palm. On it, faint with the erosion, was carved in bas-relief the figure of a raven-headed man in a robe, four wings springing from his back. His arms were bare, showing stylized corded muscle, holding up a sword and cup. Across the carven figure were scored deep marks, jagged angular glyphs. They too were worn at the edges, though far less so than the man-god.

"The glyphs are Old Empire," Father Solmin shouted back. "Archaic form. *Here Ruktha-yentror set the boundaries of his realm. From the* . . . I can't make it out."

Amourgin took it up, with a half-smile: "*From the Smoke-that-Thunders to the shores of the Middle Sea* . . ." He hesitated, then went on: "No, that's *in truth, to islands in the vastness of it, all men and* . . . ah, *beast-men and spirits of the earth obey him.*"

Appalled, the priest and the scholar looked at each other, rivalries forgotten.

"Holy Three," Solmin said, signing himself on brows and cheeks. "That's . . . the Old Empire ruled both shores of the sea almost from its founding, for nine thousand years. Ruktha—he's *mythical*. He's the one who drove the ancestors of our people north over the Shield Range into Old Tykis."

"Not mythical any more," Bren said dryly. He shuddered slightly, looking up at the image. It must have been ancient when Ruktha set his masons to overwriting it. *How long was it here before Ruktha-yentror came?* he wondered. The other canoes had stopped and gathered around his.

"Nobody told you to stop working. Bend your backs, soldiers!"

The current grew still swifter, water piling up in a narrow chokepoint only two hundred yards across. The paddles flashed, leaving strings of spray glittering in the bright sunlight like momentary necklaces of diamond. The crew of the lead boat took up a grunting song and then a sea chanty they'd picked up on the old *Sea Mare*; the others took it up, until it crashed through the roar of the waters:

"Rantin' Ranzo, Rantin' Ranzo—
Gave him lashes thirty
Because he was so dirty
Rantin' Ranzo, Rantin' Ranzo—"

For a moment the big canoe hung stationary, shuddering with the force of the water streaming past the hull despite all the paddles could do. Then it slid past the narrows and the sculpted watcher, gliding as if downhill into the broad waters of a lake nearly a mile square, an almost perfect circle in the earth.

"Smoke-that-Thunders," Bren whispered—to none but himself, for if the noise had been loud outside the cleft, here it was an endless bass rumble that thundered through gut and bones, a white roar of sound that filled their skulls and echoed there as it did from the cliffs.

Half a mile away to the south, the whole flood of the Tiram—the Mother-River, three thousand yards across—shot over the edge of the precipice in a single smooth sheet of green. Long it fell, until much of even that flood dissolved in a boiling cloud of mist, and that mist hid the earthquake impact of a million tons of water striking the surface. For long moments Bren and all the others sat and stared, wide-eyed. They could feel that shattering strike through their bones, through the water and the thin wood of the canoe, jarring their very teeth together.

At last Bren waved his hand forward; there was nothing else to do. Only at the sides of the waterfall were the cliffs broken, but the slope was very steep, over huge slab-sided boulders, and overgrown with a dense scrub of thorny trees and vines fed by the eternal mists. A few jungled islands broke the surface of the lake, but none of them were more than a few hundred square feet. The little fleet made a circuit of the lake, seeing nothing but a few monkeys on the cliffs and a promising number of giant catfish in the deep waters. At last they beached on the largest of the islands, the leaders gathering to talk while the troops cut firewood and attended to the endless work of keeping the gear and boats in condition.

"I hate to lose a day," Bren said, leaning back against a tree trunk.

Eowlie looked up thoughtfully and took off her boots—the toes had worn through some time ago and were held with patches of rawhide and thongs. She crouched, spread her fingers, and leaped. The thick trunk took her weight without a tremor, and she scampered up it squirrel-swift. There was a thrashing in the branches, a high squeal of animal terror, and bits of fur started dropping down to the sandy ground.

"We might run into Willek," Captain Tagog nodded, "or worse yet, Darkist—but there's no way up those walls that wouldn't take longer. Back a day, and up into the hills, around these falls, then on foot . . . Sir, you don't know how *much* farther south this is going to be, do you?"

Embarrassed, Bren shook his head. "I think . . . I think not much farther. The stars at night are starting to look like . . . well, like the dreams."

Amourgin and Karah nodded. Father Solmin did too: "Trust the vision," he added.

A soldier came up and handed around palm-leaf platters loaded with grilled catfish and small wild avocados. Karah drew her belt knife and tucked in. The avocados were juicy and messy, but more flavorful than the larger cultivated variety she'd tasted in Derkin. The fish was good, but—she shook the last crumbs of grey salt out of her pouch—a bit bland.

Another squeal came from the branches above, and a satisfied exclamation from Eowlie. *On the other hand*, Karah thought, *it could be worse. Could be eating lizards by the sea again.*

"Godsall, but I miss beef," she said. "And bread. And vegetables. And wine."

"Stop it, you're breaking my heart," Bren grinned. "Some people would complain if they were hung with a golden rope. Here you are, getting to travel, see far-off exotic places . . ."

". . . feed their leeches and mosquitoes," Amourgin put in helpfully.

". . . meet strange people . . ."

". . . and kill them," Karah finished.

Twigs and leaves showered down from above. They all covered their food with their hands or hats and shouted complaints up at Eowlie; the fanged woman dropped down more swiftly than she'd climbed. The smiles died at the expression on her face. She pointed a clawed finger northward.

"They're coming."

"Darkist?" Bren asked sharply, standing and belting on his sword. "Willek?"

"Both."

"This is like the story of the wolf, the cabbage and the sheep," Bren said disgustedly, watching the three miniature fleets maneuver. "Or paper-rock-scissors."

Up in the bows of the canoe, a musketeer completed the contortions needed to reload her weapon in the strait confines of the canoe and knelt. The boat rocked; she waited until it steadied, blowing on the glowing end of slowmatch in the serpentine, and fired. Half a dozen others followed suit.

An armored figure toppled off the battlebarge three hundred yards away—fine shooting at that range, from this platform. Almost immediately one of the light deck-guns replied with a flat *thump* and jet of powdersmoke. The two-pound iron ball came skipping over the flat surface of the lake. Everyone yelled and dropped flat as it went by a few feet overhead, still sizzling with the heat of firing.

The man at the steering oar at the rear of the canoe leaned on the wooden crosspiece. The narrow sail of the outrigger canoe caught, and the light craft went skipping away toward the rest of Bren's vessels.

They were gathered in a clump to the west of the lake's outflow; the three remaining Tseldene battlebarges held the center, keeping in position with long slow strokes of their oars. One more barge drifted half-afloat and still burning, heading slowly back towards its compatriots. The wreckage of several of Willek's canoes littered the water near it; freshwater sharks and crocodiles cruised about among the dead and wounded. Bren watched one Tykissian kicking desperately as he clung to a piece of wreckage; then four-foot jaws clamped over his legs and pulled him under with a last scream and swirl of red-tinted water. Battle smoke was drifting in patches across the northern quarter of the lake, smelling of sulphur and death.

"Gods *damn* Willek," he whispered, suppressing an impulse to shake his fist towards her canoe.

She had the infernal insolence to be flying the Imperial standard, too—and the callous cruelty to have brought the Emperor along on this wild expedition. At least the canoe with Shemro aboard was keeping well back from the action.

"Why like papers and scissors?" Karah finally asked.

Bren pounded his fist on the mast. "The barges can fight but they can't move as fast as we do—if any of them gets separated, either Willek or I could swarm it with boarders. But neither of us can attack the Tseldenes all-out, because then the other would attack their rear. The Tseldenes can't catch either of us and, if they try, the other could attack their rear—or get out of the lake."

"It's a Three-Body Problem, all right," Amourgin said. The others looked at him blankly, save for Father Solmin. "Mathematics . . . Well, something's got to break the stalemate."

Father Solmin gasped. "Something has," he said. The tiny portable brazier before him hissed as he threw pieces of incense on it. "A sending."

He pointed to the largest battlebarge. On its quarterdeck, behind a screen of spearmen and arquebusiers, figures moved. Crystal blazed, a flood of white light that threw shadows stark and blank even in bright afternoon sunlight. A high eerie wailing followed, interspersed with screams of pain that sounded almost like joy.

The world seemed to twist around them, though nothing changed. Then the surface of the water began to vibrate, like coffee in a clay cup dragged over a sanded table. Bren could feel his teeth begin to hurt and clamped them together; there was a pressure in his head, behind his eyes.

"*Help* me," Father Solmin gasped.

Black flames darted over the brazier. Across from him Amourgin knelt, chanting, cursing and fumbling in his belt pouch at the same time. The flames changed color and seemed to flare outward in a film of light.

"Oh, Three," Amourgin stuttered. "Willek's doing a wreaking as well—oh, *Three*, that's foul."

The air above the barges and canoes twisted like heat shimmer in the desert. The firing died down, as warriors waited for what might happen. Bren felt the pressure behind his eyes lessen and sighed with relief; but from above there was a sensation as if the sky were twisting and receding, leaving a blankness like a giant blind spot. Behind that non-space, he somehow knew, were *eyes*.

"Something . . . something . . ." Solmin said. "Is *awake*."

They'd all had enough time for the roar of the falls to become background noise. It still drowned out most distant sounds. The rending, snapping surf of rockfall from downstream was loud even by comparison, and it went on for minutes, as if cliffs were falling. The cry that followed was even louder. It might have been a bird, if the fabled mammoth-hunting *khorg* of the Southern Sea were present hereabouts.

"What *is* that?" Bren asked. His voice sounded tinny in his own ears, stunned by the cry.

The long shriek came again, louder, punctuated by a pounding sound like some giant drum. And around the bend of the river, out into the lake, walked the four-winged, raven-headed image from the cliff.

It had been a bas-relief; now it was fully three-dimensional. It was still black-grey stone, only the stone had turned flexible as living flesh. The Old Empire glyphs carved across its torso *bled*, bled lava that hissed and sputtered and sent up puffs of steam as it fell into the lake. Bren felt his mind stutter in disbelief as he watched it. He'd grown up with magic, it was part of the web and woof of ordinary life—but this was like something out of an ancient song, something from before the fall of the Old Empire.

No, from before the rise *of the Old Empire*, he gibbered mentally. Then: *Why isn't it sinking?*

The thing of living rock wasn't wading through the deep water; even at a hundred and fifty feet tall, it would still have been submerged to the neck. Instead it walked across the surface of the lake. At each slow ponderous stride a huge patch of lake *dimpled*, as if it were some tough elastic fabric compressed under great weight. His eyes hurt when he looked at it, as if not water but the structure of existence itself was being distorted.

"I don't fucking believe this," he said quietly—and he was

not a swearing man, as a general rule. More loudly: "Who raised it?"

"None of us," Amourgin said, sinking back with sweat covering his exposed face and arms in a shining layer. "Even if we knew how, none of us would have the power—the power to transform and move so many tons of rock, maybe not even a *god* would have that much power. Where's it *coming* from?"

The thing raised its wings and opened its beak, screaming again. With the sound came a blast of air, furnace-hot and dry, smelling of rock dust.

"*Put* down that bloody musket," Bren said, turning and making a chopping gesture with his hand. The soldier lowered his weapon, white-faced under his tan and shaking. "*Hold your fire*, everyone."

Somebody on one of the Tseldene barges was less disciplined, or perhaps more hopeful of actually doing something to the thing. They fired a swivel gun, and the half-pound ball knocked a chip loose from one ankle. The creature screamed again as lava leaked out and dribbled down its foot. It turned and strode towards the Tseldene craft, lifting the enormous sword that seemed to be part of its right hand. The strides were slow, but each covered thirty yards of distance. Real matter tolled like a bronze bell under those unnatural feet. The battlebarge spun in barely its own length and began to speed away as fast as the vermilion oars could take it. The rowing slaves could see the . . . thing . . . through the deck grills, and their screams had nothing to do with the overseers' lash.

"I think," Eowlie said, her voice a little shrill, "I think I knowing where is f'ower coming from." Her grasp of Tykissian had slipped a little.

Everyone in Bren's cluster of boats followed her pointing arm. The clouds of mist around the base of the waterfall had lessened. They shrank as the northerners watched, because the water was *falling* more slowly. Bren fixed his eyes on a spot near the top and followed it down. He knew exactly how quickly the torrent should be falling; things always fell at the same speed, and he'd been watching the great waterfall off and on for hours. It pounded down from the heights. Now the weight of water was falling with a dreamlike lack of haste, as if tired, as if . . .

Amourgin's lips were moving, and both hands, in a pattern that Bren recognized. A counting and multiplying mnemonic that merchants and scholars used for dealing with large quantities.

"Oh, there's power enough there," he said.

Bren's mind was working as well. "The hand," he said. "That thing was carved on the palm of an *open hand*. Every folk I know, use this—" he thrust one arm forward, fingers up and palm forward "—use this gesture for *stop*."

The two magicians looked at each other, then priest and scholar went to work. Powders tossed in the air, and words were chanted—words that Bren seemed to hear only at the edge of his ears. Magic was usually like that; he turned and watched the—*guardian*, he decided—instead. The battlebarge was trying to dodge it now, having failed to outrun it. That seemed to be working better. It raised one bare stony foot and stamped. Bren's teeth hurt again, as the fabric of reality shrilled to the impact. The barge escaped the foot; the blow of the sixty-foot stone sword clipped the barge's mast and splinters exploded in its wake.

"A sentinel," Solmin said at last. "A living spirit of anger and vengeance clothed in stone. Set here long ago, oh, so *long* ago to guard the pathways south. The Old Empire glyphs carved across it—"

"—drew on the power of the One With A Thousand Faces," Amourgin completed. His skin looked grey. "They bound it, neutralized the activation spell all these thousands of years. But they wore with the rains. Then Darkist and his priests and Willek—"

"—all called on the One for battlemagic," Solmin took it up. "A god is omnipresent where he's worshipped because devotion thins the walls between the Worlds. Here, away from humans, most of the One's local power was incarnated in This World, in those glyphs made by his followers so long ago. The battlespells drew *all* the power of the One within reach, emptied the theosphere. The glyphs dropped below their effectiveness threshold and their binding failed. That thing, it'll kill all invaders here—and we're *all* invaders. It's got no mind, only reflexes. Whoever designed it is dead ten millennia and more."

The guardian screamed in frustration and *thrust* with its sword. The round tip plunged through the deck of the Tseldene battlebarge, then out through the bottom of its hull without slowing perceptibly. When it ripped free the barge was already settling, water pouring through the huge rent in its planking and boiling out across the low deck. The screams of the tongueless chained slaves belowdecks were even louder than those of the warriors above. Many of the warriors threw themselves overboard without even trying to take off their armor, and they sank instantly. Triangular fins cut toward the disturbance, swimming ant-tiny past the huge stony feet of the guardian. The ones who drowned quickly might well be the lucky ones.

Most of the soldiers in Bren's flotilla were silent and frozen with terror; a few were shouting hysterically, or praying. Faces turned towards him. *What do we do?* they asked mutely.

Karah sprang erect beside him. His arm went around her waist automatically as the canoe rocked slightly, the poles of the outriggers protesting.

She spoke into his ear. "Bren . . . Bren, do all waterfalls hit the rock alike?"

"What?" he said. *What's she on about?*

"Do they all—" she made a gesture "—curl under and hit the rock below their lip?"

Her eyes were alight. "I think so," he said. "Most of the ones I've seen, yes."

"Then I think, I think I know someplace we can go. Back home—there's a fall in Farbluffs County—"

He bent to listen.

Karah raised her torch high. It was only a piece of wood hacked from the canoe and wrapped with rags, but it cast a pool of light into the wet, olive-green gloom. More torches were strung out through the great cavern, ahead and behind, slanting up from east to west. To her left the massive sheet of water hung almost suspended, creeping down in eerie languor. High overhead was the lip of harder rock where the Tiram took its northward plunge. To her right was the excavation made by millennia of in-curling water, that left the chamber behind the falls a jumbled slope of huge blocks like a dice box of the gods. The air was heavy with mist, cold with a shocking chill after the tropical heat outside. The rocks themselves ran with the moisture.

She looked at them, up, then at the water to her left. Bren met her eyes and nodded. *When the water's falling normally, there's no way in or out. There probably isn't any airspace here at all.*

Which meant, of course, that if the battle outside ended or the creature returned to unliving stone, several million tons of high-velocity water would hit them all at once.

Probably worse than that, she thought. The Tiram had to be building up behind the falls, behind the water slowed by sorcery. Something rather like a freshwater tidal wave would come roaring over the falls and into the lake.

"I should watch these bright ideas," she said—aloud, since there was no chance of anyone hearing her.

The long files labored upward. She saw one trooper ahead of her with a musket over one shoulder and a keg of powder over the other, staggering doggedly over the jagged rocks that tore at his skin through his ragged, much-patched trousers. The burden of her sword, bow, and bedroll seemed a lot lighter when she looked at that. Her vision narrowed down to the path before her, climbing, crawling, sometimes rappelling up a rope anchored above with a pikehead for an improvised piton. It was a shock to see natural sunlight again, a gleam through the mist ahead of her. The fog in the air was thicker here, the falls closing in as they threaded the narrow cleft between the water and the outer cliff face.

The torch hissed out. Moments later she was choking, the fog turning to water droplets; then she was out in the open air and holding up a hand against the dazzle of the sun, sinking onto a rock and gasping for breath.

Bren staggered out beside her, coughing. She pounded him on the back; he flicked the water from his face and turned to look out over the lake.

From here the figures below were sand-speck tiny. Canoes and barges still dodged and spun around the feet of a bird-headed mannequin. Only two of the barges were left; they seemed to be trying to get out the exit, and the guardian was dashing to cut them off like the goalkeeper in a village hurly game. It was almost comical, once you were a couple of thousand yards away.

Father Solmin came up, half-dragged between a burly trooper and Amourgin. Karah felt Bren stiffen at the expression on their faces. Priest-magician and scholar-sorcerer both shouted, then gave up trying to compete with the waterfall and pointed.

Karah peered. Then her eyes flew wide. The guardian *was* moving more slowly . . . and the slow-motion waterfall was speeding up. Just a very little, but . . .

Bren sprang to his feet and tried to plunge back into the chamber they'd quitted. Karah wasted no time; she drew her dagger and struck once with the heavy leaden knob on the pommel, aiming at the spot behind the ear as she'd been taught. Bren staggered, eyes rolling upward. Karah grabbed one arm; Captain Tagog took the other, and XIXth troopers grabbed handholds wherever they could. Together they rushed upward and westward, scrambling and lifting and ignoring their commander's feeble struggles. Behind them the noise of the waterfall mounted, and with it, a feeling of tension building to a breaking point—the same feeling that you might get by holding a human hair and stretching it between your hands, slowly, slowly—

Snap.

A roar like the ending of the world. The sunlight vanished and water struck; they threw Bren down and Karah flung herself across him, fingers clawing at fissures in the rock as a wave without ending poured across them. Red-shot blackness swirled before her eyes; the water dragged at her belt and bowcase and the tops of her boots. Grit and stones struck her and whirled away. Then the light returned.

Bren lay unmoving under her. She forced groaning muscles to work and lifted his head, turning it to free his mouth and pinching his nostrils. Karah filled her lungs, blew into his mouth, again and again.

Breathe, Three damn you for a lazy sod, breathe! she thought frantically. She'd done this before—it didn't get any easier or less terrifying. Then he came back to her, coughing and sputtering.

"Give me a hand with the commander!" she called, looking around.

Most of their party seemed to have made it; they were on the very lip of the cliff, with the falls behind them to the east. Rainbows arched overhead, and the ground shook with the pent-up water's release. Huge chunks of the cliff's lip were going tumbling down into the lake below; she could feel the rumble of it through her belly.

Father Solmin limped up; Amourgin with him, leaning on Eowlie, and the officers with him. Bren gave them a baleful glare before he doubled over briefly and coughed up a cupful of bile. They waited patiently, all familiar with the effects of a blow to the head.

"Thanks," he said hoarsely to Karah as she handed him a flask of brandy. "Now, who was the mutinous dog who struck their commander?"

"I did," Karah replied tartly. "You were acting crazy."

"Some of my *troops* were still back in there, corporal," he began coldly, levering himself erect.

"Bullshit." Captain Tagog.

"What?"

"Bullshit. Sir. Majesty, whatever. They were deaders. We lost twenty back there under the water, and I'm sorry for it. But if we lost you, we'd *all* be dead. Unless we want to go back and bow the knee to the Grand Admiral, you're our only hope. Not just the XIXth. You're the hope of *Tykis*, sir; if you die that sorcery-eating demon-worshipping bitch has *won*. Sir."

Bren locked eyes with her for a long moment, then gave a brief nod. "All right." He looked at Karah, and smiled very slightly. "Did you have to hit me so *hard*?"

"I was in a hurry."

☉ CHAPTER XVI

"Beautiful country," Karah said. "It'd make a great ranch."

She switched her sword to the other shoulder; more practical than leaving it on a belt while going on foot. They'd been walking a full month since the disaster at the cataract, and she was just getting used to it. Although she still wished for Windrush.

Above the falls the land sloped upwards, the river broken every few miles by rapids and smaller cataracts. The stifling tropical heat of the flat jungles and flatter swamps had given way to a springlike freshness, just warm enough to be comfortable. Rolling red-soiled volcanic hills flattened out every now and then into broad plains; waist-high greengold grass was starred with flowers and dotted at intervals with odd-looking flat-topped trees. Denser forests of juniper and cedar stood on some of the hills, gallery woods followed the many creeks and streams, but mostly it was grassland. It swarmed with life, beasts familiar and half-familiar and totally strange, herds and clumps in every direction, the air loud with birds overhead.

She shivered slightly. It was all very alien, and too *familiar*. Her mind's eye saw pink waves and silver sand.

Bren shook his head; they exchanged a glance of troubled sharing, both uncomfortable with dreams and visions. "Think you could break one of those to the saddle?" he said, seeking comfort in the familiar.

The animals he pointed at were not quite horses. They were glossy black, but there were white stripes across their necks and forelegs, and their tails were more like a mule's. *Not bad conformation*, Karah thought, with an expert's eye. *About fifteen hands*. The herd stallion threw up his head and snorted at the scent of man, and the senior mares led the rumbling carpet of not-quite-equines away at a slant. *Fast, too*, she decided.

"Depends on their temperament," she said. "And—"

A shrill trumpeting broke the drowsy stillness. The column of Tykissians bristled with weapons, moving into formation with a neatness that belied their ragged, rawhide-patched garments. This time they were only spectators. A small herd of quasi-mammoths broke from the ribbon of trees along a stream; they were about ten feet at the shoulder, grey, hairless, and each had two downward-curving flattened tusks, like ivory shovels. Leaping among them were catlike creatures fifteen feet long, yellow with zigzag stripes of black. Karah watched one jump onto the withers of a shoveltusker, its own hyperdeveloped shoulders bunching and flexing as giant claws sank into the victim's thick skin. The tiger's mouth was open in a ninety-degree gape, exposing the two-foot canines. They stabbed with blurring speed, and the writhing trunk began to spray blood in a great scarlet arc. Others darted in and out, slashing at the flanks and legs of the big herdbeasts. One went flying through the air, caught on the tusks of a big male, but the others closed in, stabbing and ripping.

The Tykissians waited, tense. A lone survivor of the shoveltusker herd fled across the prairie, lesser beasts scattering from its path. The pride of giant sword-tigers settled to their feast, snarling and whacking at each other with paws the size of barrow wheels. A heavy scent of blood drifted to the humans. Others found it more attractive; a pack of several dozen hyenas gathered, each as high as Karah's chest at the shoulder, and thick-jawed wolves, maned lions, a pair of land-alligators rising on their stout hind legs and clapping their long jaws together.

"Let's get out of here before the carnivores' carnival gets properly under way," Bren said. "In column—forward—*march!*"

"I take it back about the ranch," Karah said.

Other beasts were beginning to drift away from the site of the kill. Herbivores, giant baboons, and the two types of upright ground ape they'd seen on the plateau—the big vegetarian ones, and a smaller, more active breed that sometimes carried sticks and crudely-chipped stones.

Amourgin came up with Eowlie beside him. They all looked better fed; anyone who starved here would die of hunger in a butcher's shop. Eowlie looked sleek and glowing with health, tanned brown, lithe as the great cats.

"There might be a good trade to be done here," Amourgin said thoughtfully. "Ivory, hides, maybe dried meat—An Tiram is always short of meat, they don't have much pasture. Some of the new mammoth-drawn railroads around the falls and the rapids, and—"

He shrugged ruefully, aware the two gentryfolk were smiling at his city-man preoccupation with commerce. "I found this, sir."

He handed over the fragment; it was smooth white marble, with the figure of a bird-headed man carved on it. Unpleasantly familiar in form.

"Try scratching it," Amourgin went on. "Looks and feels just like marble, doesn't it?"

Bren raised an eyebrow, but pulled a heavy fighting knife. The point skidded off the surface; he hacked at the broken edge, and swore as it notched the fine Olmyan steel.

"It's smallbit-bespelled," Amourgin said.

"Ah!" That was Father Solmin. He took the stone and weighed it, lips moving soundlessly. Amourgin went on:

"Sir, it's older than anything has a right to be—in a fairly damp climate like this, at least. I checked. The smallbits—the smallest types of matter—they've been frozen by an embedded spellcasting."

At Bren's blank look, he went on. "That's hardly even theoretically possible these days. Not enough ambient power, and no wizard now is capable of *handling* that much power without burning out his brain. There was a human kingdom here once, but perhaps even the gods don't know when. I don't think these people had iron, or needed it. They shaped the stuff of the world with Power alone."

"True, true," the priest said, carefully wrapping the relic away. "The chronicles agree that the Talent and the world's magical potential have both decayed since ancient times, but I hadn't realized how *much*."

"I've done some tests," Amourgin went on. "The theosphere around here is hyperactive but unfocused. Lots of potential, but not used or directed much for a *long* time. It's swarming with non-personified spirits of wind and rain and animals." He nodded to a troop of the ground apes, who grimaced and chattered from a hillock. "Probably that's as close as our distant cousins here get to gods."

Troubled, Bren frowned ahead at the horizon. To left and right—west and east—the mountains receded. Between them lay the waters of the Upper Tiram, and their goal.

"Still nothing?" he said, pointing.

"No," priest and scholar said together.

"Densely shielded."

"I do feel a flavor of Tykissian magic," the priest amplified. "But only a flavor. Very old, by our standards—we're a young people, I realize that now. Primitive texture, but very strong, and linked to the power of the Three."

"Whatever I expected, I didn't expect *this*," Bren said.

Half a mile away, the tumbled ruins of a city sat atop a hill. Not a large city, and the ruins were overgrown with trees, showing mainly as blocks of white stone and an occasional column. Below them in the grassy plain were log longhouses, and the trouble was that they were *entirely* too familiar. In some of the more backward parts of Old Tykis they still built like that, like scores of big log cabins joined at the end. An extended family-clan would live in each. Strips of cultivated land extended out from the village, corn and roots and barley; a small round wooden temple stood by a well, with three carved pillars before it. Smoke blew the scent of cooking and new bread toward them.

Striding over the tall grass were people. Half-naked in the balmy weather, most of them, wearing leather kilts and sandals. They carried spears with long iron heads, tomahawks and knives in their belts, longbows and quivers; some had coffin-shaped shields of thick hide painted in geometric patterns. They trotted in a dense mass that flowed into a crescent moon with the points towards him, several hundred—as many as his own command or more. Moving with smooth precision, if not formal discipline, and coming to a halt all at once. A small party kept moving toward him and the XIXth's banner; they had white heron feathers in collars around the heads of their spears.

Closer, and he could see details of face and figure. All tall, all slender with whipcord muscle showing under their tanned skins. Hair ranging from white-blond to sun-streaked barley color; eyes coldly grey or blue, narrow straight-nosed faces.

They all look like Willek, he thought, only more so. Like a bunch of immigrants right in from Old Tykis, except that even in the far north you'd rarely see so many of such pure blood— too many southron captives had been carried north in pirate raids in the old days. All with whirling tattoos on their faces and bodies as well. *Like a war band out of the folk-wandering when the Old Empire fell*, he decided.

They'd have looked old-fashioned to Beltra the Great, founder of the New Empire.

"Hail," he said, as they halted, staring. They made him uneasily conscious of his own stocky build and the cosmopolitan looks of the Imperial troops behind him. "Ah . . . do you speak Tykissian?"

They leaned on their spears. "Of course," one said, scratching her head. "Better than you." She pronounced it *Beeta twun yöou* with an umlaut on the final word. His skin crawled slightly; it had been a long half-millennium since anyone spoke like that.

A grizzled, middle-aged man spoke. Bren recognized a commander's tone:

"Why do you come to the shores of the Rose Sea?"

Sea? he thought. *At last, an end, one way or another.* "We seek . . ." A sudden feeling of icy certainty filled him. He could not lie. "We seek the Theophone of the gods, lost these six hundred years," he said.

A rustle and murmur as the strangers spoke among themselves. Bren tensed, ready to signal his musketeers to fire. The chief gasped, sweat starting out on his face.

"The Great Shaman took it," he said. "He brought it far to the south." His voice had a singsong edge, like a man repeating a lesson memorized in youth. "Our forefathers guarded him. Without the talisman, the Yentrors could not oppress our people, the Children of Wolf and Falcon. He brought it to the Rose Sea and walked to the Holy Isle, and there he lies with the Theophone on his chest, waiting."

Karah leaned on her sword. "Does this Great Shaman have sort of milky eyes, scrawny old bas—old man, wears a loincloth and sort of orangey tattoos?"

The leader of the native band reversed his spear and thrust the point into the earth, stepping close to peer into Bren's face, then into Karah's.

"It is the prophecy!" he shouted, turning to his folk. "The Broad-Shouldered War Chief and the Chieftainess with the Dark Hair! The Final Battle is at hand!"

He flung himself to his knees before Bren, seized his foot and placed the much-patched boot on his own neck in the ancient gesture of fealty. The strangers threw down their weapons and knelt in a single movement.

"Well," Bren said.

❖   ❖   ❖

Feasted, rested, passed from village to village, the Imperials were still shocked when they crested the final ridge.

Dawn was breaking over the peaks to the east, leaving the western hills in shadow. The mountains shone white and crimson as the sun touched the snowcaps, sharp against the azure sky. Shadow rolled down the slopes, darkness bursting into electric green over copse and ravine and shore; a breath of green reached them, as if the wilderness woke and stretched to meet the day. It was very quiet, though, not much in the way of birds or beasts calling. But they did not need to wait until the sunlight caught the water to see it, for the vast lake before them *glowed* from beneath. Glowed like a sea of rose crystal, glowed like the petals of the flowers that gave its name, a soft crimson. Not like blood; the very sight of it made him think of peace, of rest. It throbbed as he watched, then flamed up to meet the light of the sun until he had to hide his eyes behind his hand.

When he looked again the glow had died down, but the waves still beat salmon-colored on beaches of purest silver sand. He could see islands in it now, small ones where the Tiram left the waters for its long journey northwards, and a larger one perhaps two miles from shore. Part of it was green with trees, but the rest was shining white and gold. The buildings there weren't ruined; they stood, column and tower and dome, metal and polished stone, as if the inhabitants had just walked away for an afternoon.

"There," the chieftain said, in his archaic Tykissian. "There the Great Shaman left the talisman. He set us to guard—our mothers' mothers' mothers' mothers. Have we done well, lord?"

Bren clapped him on his bare shoulder; it was like slapping an old oak. "Very well," he said. "Now, the question is—how do we get out there?"

His eyes turned speculatively on the tall pale-barked trees round about. A raft wouldn't be difficult, even though the . . .

well, not really natives . . . *folk* didn't seem to have boats or canoes.

The chief gaped. "Do you not know, lord? The Rose Sea is death to any but the chosen one. No boat will float upon it."

They went down the hill, on a roadway that was a hint of purpose under ages of erosion and growth. He wasn't particularly surprised that wild rosebushes coated the slopes, the scent heavy in the mild damp air. It felt heavy in his lungs. Towards the shore, his troops had to get their swords out and cut to clear the path. They walked out onto the beach, sand rutching up beneath their feet. Closer to, the water seemed less reddish, more of a blue-green streaked with crimson. It hissed very slightly; he went to one knee and bent, to find the waves full of tiny bubbles rising from the seabed. Intrigued, he bent closer and scooped up a handful, raising it to his lips.

It tasted like water, but fizzy. There were mineral springs back in the Empire that tasted so, and sometimes the water was packed in tight-corked bottles and sold for health's sake. He frowned and yawned. Yawned again and found his thoughts wandering. Then hands dragged him upright.

"I am sorry, lord," the local chieftain said. "Did you not know? Any who stay too long near the surface of the Rose Sea grow sleepy—and if they sleep here, they do not wake."

"Gas," Amourgin said, sniffing. "There's an odorless gas like that in some deep mines. It puts out lights and smothers."

He bent and lifted a section of log, heaving it out into the waters. The wood was light and sun-dried, but it sank like a stone.

The Imperials muttered in awe and touched the markings on cheeks and brow; the locals followed suit. "Magic," someone said.

Father Solmin shook his head. "No."

Amourgin nodded. "Not that I can detect, either." He frowned. "Perhaps the bubbles? But I can see why nobody sails on this sea."

Karah snorted and drove the chape of her scabbarded sword

into the sand. "Well, sod this for a game of soldiers, as our glorious leader says. By the Wolf Mother's tits, how are we supposed to get *out* there?" She pointed to the island. *"Walk?"*

The Imperials looked at each other. Silence fell for a moment, and they all yawned. Then came a sound they recognized, echoing from the hills and down the steep slopes to the water's edge. The dull flat *thump* of distant cannonfire.

"Sakers, falconets," Bren said automatically, his head cocked to one side. "Light pieces—the sort the Tseldenes had on those barges." The thought of hauling those around the falls and over four hundred miles of unroaded country, without draught beasts, made him shudder. *But they did it.*

A lighter crackling underlay the sound of the guns. "Muskets," he went on. Rifled muskets, Imperial issue.

His eyes met Karah's, with the same appalled speculation. Amourgin spoke it aloud:

"That orca bitch Willek's joined up with Darkist," he said. "Long enough to wipe us out, at least."

How many of them could there be? Bren thought. The answer was unpleasant—too many. Perhaps a thousand Tseldenes, if two of the barges had survived. As many again of Willek's troops, Imperial regulars and well-trained. Certainly at least half that of each.

He looked around. There were three hundred of the XIXth left; as fine a body of soldiers as he'd ever seen, but they were critically low on ammunition—no more than ten rounds left for every musket. Perhaps a thousand of the locals, equipped with weaponry out of a museum or a historical pageant, not a helmet or breastplate among them. He had no idea if they'd ever fought anyone, and they certainly hadn't fought modern troops equipped with firearms.

Karah looked back at him, tense but confident. *Confidence in me, Three preserve me,* he realized. So were the others. The XIXth's troopers pounded the butts of their pikes and muskets on the ground and growled a wordless cheer.

"Tell me," he said—to Karah, to the magicians. "If we get

the Theophone, we sweep the table and take home our winnings, right?"

They all three nodded. "With the Theophone, you can call the gods to manifest directly," Father Solmin said. "There's no doubt the Three would—Darkist and Willek are both soulpledged to the One."

"But if we *don't* get it, the world comes to an end, effectively."

Or we go to the Home of the Three, he added. Everyone here was a soldier, and dying was one of the risks of the trade. But what would happen to the people they left behind. . . .

"True," Amourgin said. "With the Theophone in the hands of Willek or Darkist . . . either of them would call on the One. This world would become an antechamber of hell."

Bren swung round in frustration. "We can stand them off for a while," he said. "We can't hold them forever. *How are we supposed to get to that island?*"

Willek and Darkist advanced. Black clouds and whipping winds moved forward with them—the One of a Thousand Faces presented the face of storm and the cover of darkness in the middle of the day.

Bren could see movement below and off to either side. The enemy set up its flanks. "However we're to do it, we won't be doing it now," he said. The bitterness he felt crept into his voice.

A soft voice whispered in Karah's ear, "Fateborn will walk four-legged on the water."

Karah, on her belly in the tall grass, holding a position to the back of the main line with the other archers, felt the lick of ice water along her spine. The voice was familiar—insanely familiar. She turned and saw, overlaying the archer to her left, the ghostly white outlines of the madman—the Shaman.

She turned her back on him.

"It is your time now, Fateborn. The crucible awaits to test you. Perhaps you will be found worthy."

She refused to look at him.

"You cannot deny your fate, child. You can only falter—and in faltering, die."

Karah felt ghostly fingers wrap around her wrist. Her people needed the Theophone—*Bren* needed it—and somehow, her gods had chosen her to go and get it. She thought of her gods, chained in fiery torment, and of the ranch, which she might never see again.

And she thought of Bren. She loved him. It wasn't only the uncertainty of war, the passion that rose after a brush with death. She wanted him.

And he needed the Theophone.

She shook off the Shaman's hand and stood. None of those around her paid the slightest attention to her. The sounds of the battlefield had vanished at the moment the white-eyed ghost spoke to her. Karah realized she existed outside the realm of the real world—for the moment. Her battle was not this battle—it lay elsewhere, where she would fight alone.

"Lead me," she told the ghost. "Tell me what I must do."

They walked down to the water's edge, and the ghost said, "You must go alone, and you must triumph or fail alone. I can tell you only this—that you are not the first Fateborn, nor are you the first hope I have led to the shores of the Rose Sea. But now these gods, the One and the Three, have wakened, and look with interest upon that which you seek. If you fail, you may be the last Fateborn."

He vanished, leaving Karah standing on the pebbled shore, while the wind whipped around her and overhead black clouds blotted out the sun. The wind slashed across the water, churning the smooth surface into a frenzy. The waves tossed and crashed, and lightning crackled over the surface.

"Three help me," Karah whispered. She stepped into the water; the spray lashed her and soaked her to the skin. One step and she was in to her knees—the island was far, far away, and as she waded out, it seemed to float farther away. She was not a bad swimmer, at least not in regular water. This water was witched, though—no one could swim in it. Boats wouldn't even float in it. *Is this where they died?* she wondered. *Has anyone ever gotten beyond the Rose Sea?* She wished she hadn't known about the other Fateborn. She wished she still thought she was the first.

Only a wizard could cross this sea. She took a second step and the water was to her waist. The waves splashed in her face and hit her in the back, and she staggered and nearly lost her footing. *I'll drown in here,* she thought. She could not swim in the water, but she had to cross the sea. Without her, the people she loved would die.

She swallowed tears and got ready to take a third step.

Behind her, she heard a whinny and a snort. She backed carefully, then turned, and stared, and felt her mouth gape open. A grey horse stood on the shore, black-point dappled. He stood at the water's edge, watching her, his eyes dull, his coat lifeless and ugly.

She stepped up, out of the water, and stood beside him on the shore. Waves crashed at his feet, but he seemed not to notice. He simply stood there.

She reached out and touched his nose—it was cold, and the flesh felt stiff beneath her fingers. She looked at him closely. He bore the Grenlaarin brand on his left flank—and the number on his shoulder that identified him as Windrush. He didn't seem to her like Windrush, though. He was gaunt, and marked with scars on belly and flanks and back as if he'd fought off a big cat or a pack of wolves. His hipbones stuck out, and his withers were knife-sharp. She ran a hand along his legs—his joints were hot and swollen. She lifted his hooves, and found the right front cracked, and the tender frog in the center swollen and full of pus. Little remained of the horse he had been.

She took out her knife, and traced the line of the crack along the bottom of the hoof, and began paring away at it. The horse stood patiently, his head hanging, his tail limp. "How did you ever find me?" she asked. "We've gone two thousand miles if we've gone one since we left you. I missed you, too. I

felt sure something would have eaten you by now—I wish
you seemed happier to see me." She carved at the tough horn
until pus and blood spurted from the crack. Then she put the
foot down.

"At least you'll feel better now. I can't do anything else for
you," she told him. She patted his shoulder. "But at least you'll
be able to walk." She turned away from him, back to the stormy
sea, and clenched her fists.

Why was not the Fateborn a magician? A wizard, she
thought, would surely be able to cross the sea. Why her? She
couldn't do magic. She knew nothing but horses.

Beside her, Windrush whickered and knelt. She stared at
him. She'd trained him to do that so she could mount if ever
she were injured. He'd never done the trick of his own accord.
But he seemed to want her to mount.

He looked out over the water, and snorted—had he been
human, she would have thought the snort sounded impatient.

She stared at him and at the raging surface of the sea.

"Fateborn will walk four-legged on the water. . . ."

The Shaman had said that to her once, so long ago, so terribly far away.

"Drowning is no worse on foot than on horseback," she
said, and slipped onto Windrush's back. She clucked her tongue
against the roof of her mouth, and he lifted his forequarters in
a lurch, then his hindquarters. Then, without her urging, he
stepped out onto the sea.

Karah stared at his hooves. They struck the tossing, shifting
surface of the water, and where they touched, rose light glim-
mered. Windrush broke into an uneven trot and headed
toward the island. He picked his way over the shifting surface
of the sea, keeping to the troughs, away from the swells and
breakers. When a breaker rolled unavoidably toward him, he
bunched himself and went over it, scrabbling down the smooth
backside as if he were running on ice.

Every time Windrush reached the top of a wave, Karah
tried to make out the details of the island toward which they

rode. The sun still shone on it, golden and glorious—the clouds which blotted out the rest of the sky circled around it, held back as if by magic. As she rode closer, she could make out the tall spires of buildings, their dun-brown stone washed golden in the light. Small shapes dotted the shoreline, and the light sparkled off of them as if they had been carved of gemstones. The wind screamed around her, and the waves crashed beneath her horse's hooves, and thunder cracked and rumbled—but the island sat, placid, sunlit, and safe.

A seabird shot past her, its shrill cry startlingly loud even against the sounds of the storm. It circled around her, flying low over the waves, and joined another. Those two shrieked and screeched—and then Karah made out, skimming the waves toward her in a thin line, a flock of them. Birds, in her experience, rarely flew in storms—yet these birds wheeled and dove, unhampered by the vicious winds that buffeted her and Windrush. Their circles around her grew tighter.

She tightened her thighs around the horse, and urged him into a canter. The birds slipped and flowed around her, staying close.

Windrush came over the crest of a wave unaware, fell into the trough beneath it, and stumbled hard, going to his knees. He whinnied his fright—and Karah, unprepared, fell from his back and only managed to clutch his mane as she slid into the sea. Windrush panicked and began to spin, while Karah's legs dragged through the water and her grip loosened. "Still!" she shouted, and the horse's eyes rolled and his nostrils flared. He tossed his head, and shifted nervously while the waves rolled beneath his feet.

The waves pulled Karah beneath his belly, though she maintained her grip on the horse's mane. *I can't get back up*, she thought. She dangled, straight-armed. If she told Windrush to kneel, that would only sink her deeper into the sea and give the pounding waves more of a purchase on her. None of his tricks, and none of hers, had been designed for the situation in which she found herself.

The birds circled low. *They're waiting for me to fall,* she thought. *Waiting for me to drown, so they can feed on my body.* Then one of the birds dove at Windrush's eyes, and the horse reared and plunged, and one of Karah's hands came away from his mane. So they didn't intend to wait—but to help her die instead. Her pulse pounded in her fingertips, her wrist ached, and she scrabbled for purchase on his bony withers. Her terror gave her strength, and she lifted herself high enough out of the water that she was finally able to throw a leg over the horse's back and urge him on his way. She regained her seat, but felt unsteady. A trot was the fastest pace she dared. No more cantering—another fall could easily unseat her again and throw her to her death.

The birds resumed their formation and sailed along beside her, watching her with their beady red eyes, waiting. Uneasy, she unslung her bow, felt with her fingertips for her arrows, and nocked one. She didn't have enough arrows to kill all of them—and she thought of the damage they could do her. Their beaks were sharp and hook-tipped, their webbed feet fiercely taloned, and they dove and wheeled in tight formation, disciplined.

Waiting, watching.

She almost loosed an arrow at the first bird in line, but she held back. They seemed unwilling to attack her while she was armed. Perhaps they would leave her alone. She had so few arrows. . . .

So they rode along together—Karah, Windrush, and the birds—while the island grew gradually closer and the storm grew worse. The first spatters of rain blew across her path and struck her, and within an instant the few drops had become a deluge, that whipped in sheets and torrents across her path and nearly blinded her.

Now, she thought, dismayed. *This must be what they were waiting for. I should have shot at them while I had the chance.*

Something huge and grey and toothed rose out of the water in front of her, its maw large enough to engulf her and

Windrush and the birds with room to spare. The carrion stink
of it overwhelmed her; she loosed her arrow down its maw,
aiming as best she could for the tender flesh of the soft pink
uvula, while Windrush turned and cantered up the swell of a
wave to evade the monster.

It roared and sounded, and the splash it made as it crashed
back into the sea threw water up in cliffs around Karah, and
nearly washed her from the back of her horse.

Karah wiped her sodden hair from her eyes, and rubbed
the rain out of them, then nocked another arrow. She looked
down, beneath her horse's hooves. For a moment she could
see nothing but the rosy light that spread each time Windrush
stepped on the surface. But then she made out a dark shape,
rising beneath her. She longed to goad Windrush into a gallop, but she didn't dare. Instead, she urged him into a schooled
sideways leap, and the two of them evaded the nightmare creature—it came up off to one side and slightly behind them, and
Karah twisted around and aimed an arrow at its eye. Her shot
missed, and the creature sounded again and vanished out of
sight.

She readied another arrow. The rain pounded down harder,
so hard that drawing breath became a challenge. Somehow,
she'd lost sight of the island—she had no idea whether she
and Windrush continued in the right direction, or stumbled in
circles while the sea monster that hunted them picked the
place where it could most easily devour them. The water
streamed into her eyes, and she wiped at them futilely. The
toothy sea-thing would be coming—at any moment it would
rise up from beneath her to swallow her and Windrush. She
put the arrow back and drew her sword. She couldn't see to
shoot. She didn't think the blade would be much use against
the giant creature, but holding it gave her some comfort; at
least she didn't feel completely helpless.

Windrush screamed, and the giant toothed maw appeared
directly in front of her. The horse wheeled and bolted, and
when he did, the monster's head brushed against Karah's

left arm. Its coarse sanded-paper skin ripped away her sleeve and abraded pieces of skin, and Karah, in pain, with no time to think, plunged her sword into the monster's eye to the hilt.

The monster dove; its tail smashed against her left leg as it drove itself deep into the sea, and she screamed in agony. She looked down, and found her blood coursing into her boot, washed thin in the pouring rain. The gash in her thigh was as long as her dagger, and deep. She pressed her hand against the wound to stanch the bleeding and swore. She had no sword, she was lost on the surface of the stormy sea, and she was going to bleed to death. The birds circled around her, closing in tighter and tighter, and she pulled an arrow from her quiver. She couldn't shoot the birds, but she could stab one or two of them before they tore out her eyes—or Windrush's.

The birds wheeled, and the first one peeled off from the line and dove straight at her.

Karah shouted, "Damn bird!" Tears ran down her cheeks, so that she tasted salt at the corner of her mouth. She was going to die. She kicked Windrush into an insane gallop straight at it, her arrow gripped like a spear.

The bird whipped up and out of her reach at the last instant, and suddenly a voice from out of the air said, "Very well. You are brave. Continue."

The birds vanished, the rain stopped, and the surface of the sea became, in an instant, still as a reflecting pool. Behind her, the storm still raged, but it no longer touched her in any way.

The island lay off to one side of her, fairly close. She corrected her course, then ripped off her shirt, and with her dagger cut away the remaining sleeve. She tore that into strips and bound them around her thigh, swearing from the pain. She looked Windrush over—his left flank was abraded, but he didn't have any deep cuts. Just as well, she decided. She couldn't have gotten off of him to treat his wounds if he'd needed help.

She pulled her soaked blouse back over her head with

difficulty and, still watching for the sea monster, galloped Windrush over the finally smooth sea.

The shapes that glittered on the island's shore grew clearer as they grew closer—fantastical gem-carved beasts that lined the narrow beach and the cliffs to either side of it, around the periphery of the island as far as her eye could see. She remembered the stone watcher set to guard the river, and eyed them warily. They didn't move—but then, the watcher had not moved either, until it broke free of the Tseldene magic. Had the Tseldenes ever been to the island before her, she thought they would have already owned the Theophone—so there was likely no magic to keep those stone beasts from doing what they wished. And she had no real weapons. She doubted the effectiveness of any arrow against such creatures. She would have felt safer holding the sword, but that was gone.

They surrounded the island—the only break she saw in their line was in front of her, at the point where the waves lapped up onto the narrow, pebbled beach.

I could go around, she thought. *I could see if there's another way on to the island.*

But the thought of riding one instant longer than she had to on the surface of the sea decided her. She took Windrush straight for that narrow tongue of land, riding hard, as fear that the waves would stop holding her up consumed her.

As Windrush's front feet hit the pebbles on the beach, his hind feet splashed into the water. A chill ran down Karah's spine. She turned the horse around with difficulty; he wanted to run away from the water, and walked him back toward the sea. He balked, but then took one step from the beach into the waves. They washed around his hoof, and he drew it back and reared.

Karah slid from his back and stared at the sea. She was trapped—unless she could safely retrieve the Theophone and figure out how to make it work. If she could do that, she would be able to escape. But what if she couldn't?

She turned and studied the carved creatures. They stared

out to sea, unmoving. Some of them were lovely, some hideous—winged serpents and clawed horses and multiheaded birds. Most seemed to have been sculpted of huge single gemstones, though some appeared to have been made of common stone. She saw a sweet-looking giant rabbit, and various frightening reptiles, and a fair selection of creatures that would have been common domestic beasts, if they hadn't had weird horns, or huge fangs, or great furled wings. The only thing any of the carvings had in common was that they were lifeless.

Karah looked around her. The island was dry and treeless, and a narrow path led up the hill in front of her to the high dun-brown walls of a dun-brown city. Windrush, walking on hard, rocky ground instead of the enchanted surface of the sea, began to favor his hurt foot, so Karah started up the path on her own. The Theophone, she decided, would most likely be hidden there.

The horse waited at the foot of the hill, cropping at the sere, withered grass. Karah looked upward, leaning back to get a better view of the edge of the wall, for the path quickly grew very steep. She began to hike. The air around her grew hot. She patted her canteen, and it rattled. Empty! She'd thought sure she'd filled it with water earlier. No time to worry about a canteen, though. She would fill it again when she found some water.

She climbed farther. Odd how the higher she climbed, the more the city at the top of the hill seemed to recede. It was a trick of the light, she decided. An illusion. Dust blew across the cliffs around her and clung to her skin. The sun beat down on her from directly overhead. She realized how very thirsty she was—her mouth was parched, her lips cracked, her tongue dry and swollen, though she had not realized until that moment that they were. *Water,* she thought. She would have gladly given over her bow and arrows for a glass of it.

She thought of the sea, and the water in it, which was fresh and bubbling—but Darkist and Willek fought Bren and her people. She'd been so long already. If she waited longer, it might be too late to save the people she loved and the world she knew.

No turning back, then, she thought. She refused to even look behind her, so afraid was she that the sight of water—even the bubbling rose-colored water, would be more of a temptation than she could withstand.

Her leg hurt terribly; she wished she'd tried to ride Windrush—the horse had been in pain, too, but she'd done much to relieve his when she released the pressure on his hoof. Her own pain grew worse with every step she took. She tried not to think about it—tried instead to think of Bren, and lying with him that one night, making love. That was a better thought. She pushed on up the path.

Gradually she began to realize that her steps were getting smaller—that she was having a harder time moving one leg in front of the other. Her skin felt stiff, tight, almost as if she were stretching out of it. *Dryness and dust,* she thought; but then she looked at her hands, and was horrified to see they were almost skeletal, the flesh drawn across them like paper pasted across bones. Her wrists and elbows bulged around the stick-like lengths of her arms. She felt her face, and her fingers sank into her hollowed eyesockets, and traced the sharp ridges of her cheekbones, and found the thin line where her lips had drawn back from her teeth. Her hair had become wispy and thin—a few strawlike straggles puffed around her face like chick down.

Thirsty—so thirsty. I'll die without water, she thought. She stopped. *I need water. But if I turn back, I'll never be able to make myself do this a second time. Never.*

If she could just get to the top and find the Theophone, she could make everything right.

As soon as she started forward, the heat vanished, replaced by a vicious ice storm and angry winds that nearly blew her off the path. In an instant, snow and hail closed in the world around her until she could not see more than a step in front of her. Her teeth rattled and chills shook her. Her fingertips withered and blackened, and the skin peeled away from them. Pain burned along her hands and feet, up her arms, across her face. Thirst consumed her. She saw the bones of her finger-tips exposed, and watched with mute horror as they fell away. *Magic! This is how the others died,* she thought. The skin of her arms turned to powder, and the slight breeze blew it away in tatters and puffs. The bones of her arms crumbled, and she looked down her legs and realized her feet were gone, and that she stumped along on the ends of her leg bones.

Whoever guarded the Theophone would do anything to keep her from it. "You can't stop me!" she tried to shout, but her tongue crumbled in her mouth, and all that came out was a hoarse whisper.

I'm dead anyway, she thought. *But Bren isn't. Not yet.*

She kept climbing, even when her lower leg bones fell away and she had to crawl upward on the bones of her upper legs and upper arms.

"Stop," a voice whispered out of the air. "She will not be turned from her path. She is faithful. Let her continue."

As quick as that, she was inside the wall of the ancient city, at the top of a giant staircase that led down into the center of a grassy square. The four streets surrounding the square were full of people, lovely and graceful, their skins white as fine linen or black as ebony, their faces proud, their heads held high. They paced along in swirling robes, bowed gently as they passed each other and murmured liquid-syllabled greetings.

Musicians and dancers moved across the green in bright costumes, and the tinkling of music filled the scented air. The breezes were once again gentle and warm; fountains played at the square's four corners, and naked children laughed and chased each other through their sprays.

Karah stood, dumbfounded. Her flesh was once again whole, her body intact, her thirst abated. She looked down into the city wonderingly. She'd expected to find ruins, had expected to dig through rubble to come across the relic that would set her gods free and bring them to her—but instead . . .

Faces looked up, saw her standing atop the stair, and in an instant, a murmur rose from the crowd. More people stopped and stared—they began pointing and shouting. The musicians stopped playing, the dancers stopped leaping and spinning, and the people below quit going where ever they'd been heading, and walked back towards her.

Godsall, she thought, swallowing hard. *What are they going to do to me?* She'd figured her biggest challenge would be in finding the Theophone, not in stealing it out from beneath the watchful eyes of thousands of guardians.

She clenched her hands into fists at her sides and waited to see what would happen next.

"How came you here?" a man shouted from the crowd. His Tykissian was flawless.

The truth? Karah wondered. "I rode my horse across t' sea," she called down, "fought a giant fish, and storm, and hunting birds, came between t' stone beasts that line the shore, then climbed up t' path through parching heat and freezing cold—and came inside I know not how."

The murmur grew louder. "How are you known?" a woman called.

"Karah Grenlaarin!"

"Is that what *he* calls you?"

Little doubt about the "he," she thought. If she and they shared any acquaintances, they would share only one. The ghostly Shaman.

"He calls me Fateborn."

"Fateborn," she heard whispered. "She's the Fateborn! She's come at last!"

The musicians started to play again—but this time the music they played was stirring and dramatic. More and more people joined the crowd already in the streets, and all of them began cheering and chanting. Nearby, and then all across the city, she heard great bells begin to toll, and bright, high bells to ring the counterpoint above them.

"Fateborn!" they chanted, "Fateborn! FATEBORN!"

Long horns sounded, and Karah felt the air around her crackle. She looked down, and found herself suddenly dressed in a green gown of soft, gauzy cloth that draped and folded elegantly.

"FATE-born! FATE-born! FATE-born!"

Karah felt herself blush and stared down at her feet. A man shimmered into existence beside her on the stairs. He was tall and broad-shouldered, with dark eyes and a sensuous smile. Her heart caught in her throat; she had never seen a man so lovely or so fine. He wore a jeweled circlet on his dark hair, and held a jeweled scepter in one hand.

"My lady, my queen," he murmured softly. "You are more beautiful than ever I could have hoped. I will pledge my heart and my kingdom to you forever."

My queen? She cleared her throat, and below her the multitudes called out, "Hush! The Fateborn speaks."

Oh, dear, she thought. "I hadn't planned to say anything everyone needed to hear," she whispered to the . . . prince . . . king? Her whisper carried clearly to the green below her, amplified by some magic, and echoed back to her from the walls of the towers all around. ". . . needed to hear . . . to hear . . . hear . . ." She closed her eyes and swallowed hard. "You don't understand," she told the man. "I've come to get the Theophone and stop a war."

"But of course you have," he said, and smiled gently. "Everybody knows that. You are fated to save the world from an evil magician, and to wield the Theophone to speak to the gods—and to marry me. It has been written on the stone walls of the Temple since near the beginning of time."

"But . . ." Karah said.

He patted her shoulder. "I know. You wish to hurry. As soon as we've wed, I'll bring out the Theophone and show you how to use it, and you can beat the wizard you and your people are fighting."

"Ah . . ." Karah said.

He studied her curiously, one eyebrow raised and his head

tilted a bit to one side. "There's something else? Something you aren't telling me?"

"I love someone already."

"Many people do. What has that to do with anything?"

The crowds in the square below were silent, staring up at Karah and the man who claimed the right to marry her. They seemed to strain forward, as if afraid they would miss a single word. She wished fervently that she and the man were alone. She wanted privacy to say what she had to say—but she wasn't going to get it.

She stared down at the expectant faces, then into the man's beautiful brown eyes. "I don't want to marry you," she said at last.

He chuckled, and below, in the square, some of the watchers laughed with him.

"No, of course not," he said. "Arranged marriages are never popular, are they? And we, who have had our marriage arranged by no less than the gods—" He chuckled again and shook his head. "—To whom do we complain? But come, if we are to win your war, we must marry quickly."

Karah frowned. "What if I don't?"

"If you don't marry me?" His eyebrow rose again. "Then you are not the true Fateborn, and you must die."

That was clear enough, Karah thought. With every moment she pondered, men and women fell in battle. Darkist and Willek would win, and the world would become a place of evil and misery. Compared to that, her happiness was nothing.

"Marry me in the Tykissian ceremony," she said quietly, "then help me win my war."

"The Tykissian ceremony?"

She said, "Yes. It's short. Take my hand." She held up her left, and he clasped it with his right. She drew the dagger which hung from a jeweled girdle around her waist, and slipped the blade carefully between their palms.

"Say you marry me," she told him.

"I marry you."

"And I marry you. Witnessed by the Three—" she spat, and after an instant's hesitation, and with an amused look, so did he.

"Hold the knife with me," she said. He wrapped his other hand around hers. "—and sealed in blood," she intoned. She turned the blade sideways and drew it back quickly, slashing both of their palms.

She gasped at the sudden sharp pain—her blood ran down her wrist, hot and pulsing, and stained the green of her sleeve.

He smiled at her, and she saw that he did not bleed. A soft voice that filled the air around her said, "So she is practical, too. She has been tried by fire and by ice, and her childishness has fallen away from her. She has shown herself worthy. Let her go."

Her groom vanished. The people in the square vanished. The fountains dried up, the grass in the square turned to dust, and the lively city fell silent. Then, the air before her began to sparkle and glimmer, and the wild-haired white-eyed Shaman appeared. He clutched a gold torque, crusted with fire opals and sapphires, and bowed to her. "Lady, Fateborn, daughter of Chance and Destiny—the gods await your voice." He slipped the torque around her neck and said, "Ask of them what you will."

"How do I use this?" she asked.

"Take the key, and press the curved end of it into the hole between the gemstones. Then simply address the gods you would have hear you, and . . ." He stopped. "Why are you looking at me that way?"

"What key?" Karah asked.

"The key! The *key!* I had that idiot law-speaker get it— from a god, no less. I don't suppose he forgot that, do you?"

Karah shook her head. No answer seemed particularly good.

"So *where* is it?"

Karah snapped, "Well, he didn't give it t' me, so you need not shout like that!"

"World coming to an end, and you're upset because I yelled

at you. Hah! Well, we're in for it now. Nothing to do but get back quick as we can, and get the key from that idiot." He turned and walked away from her, down the side of the wall, muttering, "The Three tell me to get you, get him, get the captain and bring you along to pick up the Theophone, and I'm damned if you don't mess the mission up from start to finish."

"Hey!" Karah yelled after him. She stood at the top of the wall, looking down the steep face of it, watching the Shaman disappear down the path toward the sea. "Hey! Wait! How am I supposed t' get down from here, blast you!" The Shaman kept walking. The full skirt of the green dress blew around her ankles. She could just imagine scaling a wall in that. She lifted up the front hem of the skirt and stared at her feet. She was wearing dainty court shoes—little gem-crusted slippers with raised heels and pointed toes. "Pig shit," she muttered. "Nothing is *ever* easy."

She took off the slippers, pried off the tottering little heels with her dagger, and put them back on again. Then she went to work on the skirt, splitting the front of the skirt, and then the back. She hacked off the train and ripped two strips of material from the silk, and used them to wrap the split skirt around her ankles. She was left wearing ludicrous ballooning pantaloons and silly shoes—*but*, she thought, *at least I can ride and run.*

She looked down the steep face of the wall. *And climb . . . I hope.* She nibbled thoughtfully at her lower lip. The stones of the wall were uneven—and the wall leaned inward a bit as it rose. She *might* be able to climb down it. She would have a better chance in bare feet, though, she decided.

She slipped over the edge. Her left leg throbbed. She hadn't thought about that until she moved—but that gash in her thigh was going make the trip more dangerous. Her left shoulder hurt, too, but the abrasions of the skin weren't anywhere near as serious as the lacerated muscle. She climbed, struggled—and hated Amourgin all over again. How like him not to give her the key—she could have summoned the gods and brought the war to an end already, if it hadn't been for him.

Another volley blasted out from Willek's ranks. *Damn, how did they cart that much ammunition this far?* Bren thought, rising on one knee.

The tribesmen caught most of it; they were in full charge, an astonishing loping run that might well have kept up with cavalry at the canter. The heavy bullets ripped through them; Bren thought he would never be able to erase the horror of the sight from his mind. In a volley battle, where lines stood and blasted at each other all day, a quarter of a regiment could die in ten minutes. But these innocents had never seen fire-arms before. Still they kept on, leaping over their own dead and wounded with catlike agility, sweeping past Willek's troops—*Imperial troops, obeying orders*, Bren reminded himself—and then turning just beyond the bristle of pikes to strike at the junction between the Imperials and the Tseldenes.

The tribesfolk struck, a flurry of throwing axes and javelins sparkling in the sun before them; the crash of onset sounded, screams and howling wolf cries and the unmusical clash of metal on metal, the flatter sounds of weapons slamming into leather shields. Bren used his telescope and his lips shaped a silent whistle. *So that was what our ancestors were like in battle*, he thought. They had no discipline, as he understood the term, but they moved in pack-unison like wolves, each aiding their neighbor, stabbing and slashing in a blur of speed. A spray of broken weapons and bodies marked the spot where they hammered a wedge into the enemy line. And—

"Yes, by the Three," Bren said.

The two forces were recoiling, each away from the other; whatever arrangement their leaders had come to, Tykissian and Tseldene were not going to trust each other much. In battle, distrust was worse than acid.

"Now!" he said crisply.

Greatly daring, he'd drawn up his musketeers only three

deep, along the reverse slope of the hillcrest on which he knelt. The first rank stood and set the rests of their muskets.

BAMMM.

They walked six paces backward, downslope, making themselves invisible to the enemy on the other side of the slope, and began to reload. The second line stood and fired in turn, then the third. By then the first was nearly ready again. The enemy formation staggered at the impact, losing a half-step. Men and women dropped, thrashing or twitching or still. The tribesmen were pulling out and falling back to the flank, moving with the same tireless wolf speed. Another series of volleys; here and there one of his musketeers fell to enemy fire, but they could not reload as quickly while they advanced. Closer, and he could see the set faces under helmets and hats, the bristle of points coming down. He looked to either side, at the pikes and halberds crouching below the lip of the ridge.

"Ready," he said, drawing sword and pistol. "Hold fire."

The enemy came on more rapidly, jog-trotting as Bren's musketeers stayed crouched below the ridge. Far behind the front rank, the Imperial house standard fluttered, the Life Guards around it in a clump. *Good thing they're there,* Bren thought. *Otherwise Willek would have had the Emperor . . . my aunt*—the thought was still strange—*in the front.* He didn't know whether he could have ordered the XIXth to fire on the Emperor, or whether they'd have obeyed. *Darkist's well to the rear too,* he noted sardonically. It was tempting to order a volley at *him,* but no. Shooting at an alerted, high-powered magician was a waste of ammunition.

"Wait for it," he called. The enemy were close now, only a hundred meters. Bullets whined about him. "Now!"

All three ranks rose and fired at once. The enemy charge faltered, soldiers going down all along their front, throwing up their arms and dropping or rolling back down the hill. Smoke hid the action for a second.

"Charge!"

His halberdiers and pikes came up off the ground with a howl and ran down the slopes. The musketeers followed, drawing their swords or clubbing muskets. On either flank the tribal warriors swept forward. Bren ran with them, through the smoke. A pikehead came in at him. He knocked it aside with his sword and pistoled the bearer, and her face vanished in a red splash while her helmet rolled away. A halberd chopped at him; he caught the shaft on the braided guard of his sword and clubbed the wielder across his face with the pistol, then turned and thrust a swordsman through the body. Troops of the XIXth closed around him.

Then the tide of battle shifted against Bren and his troops. "They're coming in on the flanks," Captain Tagog shouted in his ear, over the screams and shrieks and clanging. "We'll have to form square—too many of them."

Bren nodded. Outnumbered, flanked, and with superior magic on the side of their enemies . . . *Karah, you're about to be a widow before the marriage.* He wished they'd found a way to go after the Theophone. He'd let down his people, his world, his gods.

The XIXth was going to go down—but it was going to go down fighting. "Form square!" he bellowed aloud.

"Keep low," Amourgin growled. He reloaded his carbine and crouched behind the boulder. Eowlie crouched next to him and reloaded as well.

"We're cut off," she said.

He watched Willek's flank sweep in and pin most of the XIXth down against the side of the hill. His people were losing, and losing badly. He said, "We're out of sight. If you want, we can sit this out—try and escape after it's over. We're back of the action now—the main part of the fighting seems to be moving down toward the beach."

He looked at the dead sprawled across the ground below them.

"This is what you want to do?" Eowlie looked at him, and

her eyes narrowed. Her expression was thoughtful. Amourgin saw her claws flex and retract.

He took a deep breath. "I'll do whatever you want to do. You just ought to know, if we try to join up with them, we're going to die. We might take out one or two of them first, but we're going to die. If we stay put, we have a chance to live through this."

"And what after? What a'vout our friends?"

"Eowlie, I'll fight beside you if that's what you want. I'll die beside you, and die a happy man. But I won't drag you into something you don't want to do." He looked down at those dead bodies again. His hands tightened around the butt of his musket, and he swallowed hard. "I love you, Eowlie."

The yellow eyes stared into his, wide and startled. "I love you, too. I wonder what my f'arents would think." She pressed her cheek against his chest and sighed, then pulled away. She checked the load in her musket, then held it up, sighting down the barrel. "But my f'arents are never going to know." One dark eyebrow arched, and her smile quirked. "Yours, either. I suff'ose you can ve glad avout that."

He imagined his wealthy, snobbish, upper-class parents meeting Eowlie as a prospective daughter-in-law, and grinned back at her. "You'd be good for them," he said. Not that they were ever going to get a chance to see the truth of the statement. Eowlie was already putting the match to her weapon and aiming at one of the enemy officers.

Amourgin nodded and gave his own weapon a last-minute check. It figured—for the first time in his life, he'd found love. And the day he became sure of it was the day he was going to die.

The explosion of Eowlie's weapon blasted in his ear. She dropped beside him and began to reload. Amourgin eased his own carbine over the top of the boulder and picked out a suitable target.

"When we run out of ammunition," she said, ramming the powder tight, "we charge behind them with claws and teeth."

"Knives and swords," Amourgin corrected. He fired, and another of Darkist's Tseldene fanatics fell over dead.

"Claws and teeth." She flashed him a smile as he dropped down to reload and she stood to aim and fire.

He looked up at her, at her lithe body leaning along the boulder, at the sharp angle of her jaw and the way the shadows fell across her eyes. And the only thing he could think was, *I do not want to lose you.*

Karah caught up with the Shaman at the seashore. The ghostly figure stood looking out over the water at the storm that still pounded on the far shore.

"Why didn't you help me down t' wall?" she shouted. "Why did you just leave me there? I had t' climb down with that gash on my hand from marrying that man, and the cut in my leg from t' damned big fish. . . ."

He turned and stared through her with milky eyes. "Why didn't you have the key? If you'd had the key, you would already be back and the war would be over. Now . . ." He waved his hands in circles and turned his back on her in apparent exasperation.

"Pig-futtering fatherless son of a dog." She glared at his back, then turned and whistled for her horse.

Windrush had been out of sight. He trotted toward her. Karah noted that he wasn't favoring a foot anymore, but that his movements in general seemed gangling and stiff. She'd seen the horse born, by the gods—and in all his life, she'd never seen him display a gait that rough.

She frowned, watching him. *Jerky, off-pace, like he was set wrong on his legs.* The Grenlaarins would never have bred such an ugly mover. He reached her and, still frowning, she checked the brand on his flank and the tattooing on the inside of his lip. They were Windrush's. The scars, the markings, the way the hair on his chest grew in the pattern of a horned diamond—all were the same. She lifted his right foot and saw where she'd pared through the horn to let the pus out. He was her horse, and yet he wasn't. She stood and brushed his fore-lock back and sighed.

He looked at her, and the way he looked at her seemed cunning somehow—crafty. At that instant, she realized something was wrong with his eyes. They glowed faintly in the bright sunlight, and instead of the rich dark brown they should have been, they were the deep blue of the autumn sky.

Her nagging certainty that something was wrong with Windrush returned, and she tried to remember why she'd thought that. "Shaman," she yelled, keeping her eye on the horse.

She got no answer. She turned, and discovered the Shaman was missing. *This is all wrong*, she thought. *Why did he leave me?*

"You're trapped here," a soft, feminine voice behind her said.

Karah spun and saw pale wraiths of light and fog curling out of her horse's nostrils. They formed themselves into the head of a woman—and then she remembered the dream from the other beach, where she'd killed a man. She remembered all of it clearly, as if a curtain had hidden the events until that instant, and someone had moved the curtain. "You! I remember you! You made me forget, didn't you?"

"Of course. Give me the Theophone."

"What?"

"I was going to dump you into the sea, but you started to figure things out. I can leave you here just as well. Give me the Theophone."

"When the hells break loose and swallow me."

"If you wish." The woman's lips curled up at the corners in a sweet, childlike smile, and the Theophone at Karah's neck began to tug and pull, trying to get away.

The woman was a wizard, and Karah had no magic. *How am I to keep the Theophone from her?*

She began backing away as the horse, and the cloud-woman in front of it, moved toward her.

"I control the horse," the woman said. "I can have it trample you in an instant if you don't give me what I want. I don't want to damage that trinket you wear—but I'll take the chance if I must." Her eyes narrowed.

Trampled, Karah thought. *Trampled*. . . . She kept backing.

Her horse had trampled that vicious killer, and the woman had come out of the man . . . tried to go into her . . . failed . . .

That's IT!

She drew her dagger and lunged, not even allowing herself to think about what she did. She lashed with the knife across the horse's throat, slashing open his windpipe and cutting through arteries and muscles. Windrush reared and his eyes rolled white. The cut at his throat bubbled blood—he made a horrible, strangling sound. Karah knelt beside him, tears rolling down her cheeks—and the woman shrieked "No! No! Nothing by all the gods, that's MINE."

She rushed Karah, talon-like fingers forming from the mist that made her. But for all her wizardry, when she touched Karah, the vapor sizzled and she vanished with a loud pop and a flash of light.

Karah stroked Windrush's cheek, crying. "I'm so sorry," she told the dead horse. "I'm so sorry."

"Thou had no choice, sweetmeat. Thou didst the one thing that could have won thy battle."

Karah turned, expecting to see the Shaman behind her. Instead, her mouth dropped open. A naked, round-bellied, chubby-cheeked little being with a cock that would have done one of her stallions proud stood watching her. He grinned insanely.

"Nice. Very nice. Thou'rt as smart as thou'rt fair. Yon bitch had a spell bound to the horse—let her work her magic, let her control things. Had thee not killed the horse, had been here a long, long time. Or dead, which I think was her next plan. Good thinking. So, would thou choose to be one of my worshipers? The duties are few and the pleasures many." He arched an eyebrow and smiled a lascivious smile.

"Who *are* you?" Karah whispered.

"Ah, sad, sad is the day when the daughters of women forget the lustiest of the gods. Sad for the daughters, that is. They don't know what they're missing. I'm Heinous. The *god* Heinous. Used to be *the* big god, but business has been slow. And what is thy name, fairest and most delectable of women?"

"Ah . . . Karah. Karah Grenlaarin."

"Akarakara. A fair name for a delicate beauty. A friend of thine has the key to that little whigmaleerie. Thou hast the lock, he has the key . . . so to speak." Heinous waggled his eyebrows and leered. "Locks and keys are, of a nature, specialties of mine." He made a circle of the fingers of one hand, and gestured obscenely with one finger of the other hand.

"I'd guessed as much," Karah said. Her voice gave the god no encouragement for that line of conversation.

"Yes. Well. I noted thou had somewhat in the nature of a difficulty."

Karah looked at him and waited.

"Hast thought how thou wilt cross the sea to thy friends? Thy horse is dead, and thou canst not walk on the water."

"I know. But I had to kill Windrush. I couldn't let that woman get the Theophone."

"Mercy, no. Thou didst only as thou could have, acting quickly, and with great courage. I like those qualities in a woman." He looked away and muttered, "They tend to breed true."

Karah heard the comment and frowned. She knew a lot about breeding—but didn't care much for being looked at as a brood mare.

The god Heinous continued. "Perhaps thou wilt let me help. We can make, ah . . . something in the nature of a deal."

Karah looked at him through narrowed eyes. "What kind of deal?"

"I need worshipers. I have, at the moment . . . um . . ." He glanced in the direction of his feet, but Karah doubted that was what he was actually looking at—considering the size of everything else. He looked back at her, his expression abashed, ". . . one. Only one worshiper. And that one is about to do something tremendously stupid, which I, being an obscure god, no longer have the strength to undo. I need another worshiper, and quickly, before I become once again a forgotten god. Thou needest transportation. And some assistance in finding the key. I can provide both."

"I already worship the Three. I don't think they would look kindly on another god."

"I don't notice the Three standing here offering thee a ride to the other shore. Dost thou?"

He had a point. The Three were chained on the beaches of a fiery hell in the center of the earth. Until she got hold of the Theophone, they weren't likely to answer prayers. She'd been willing to marry a man she didn't even know to save the people she loved. She could risk heresy for them, too. "What would I have to do?" she asked.

"Bear lots of little ones, and teach them to revere the name Heinous. Thou couldst also wear something a bit more revealing. Thou hast the bosoms for such garb. I adore bosoms."

Karah winced and sighed. It could have been worse. "Well enough. I'll worship you. Where's my ride?"

"Oh, joy! Saved from anonymity once more." Heinous pointed to the carvings that lined the island. "Choose a mighty steed that is to thy liking. Leap on his back, and cry the words, 'Ho, away!' I'll take care of all else."

Karah nodded. After a single backward glance at the dead Windrush, she ran to the nearest beast. It was a great emerald tusk-cat, fangs long as her forearm, with giant wings, the feet of a bird of prey, and a tail tipped by a viper's head. "Will this one do?"

"A mighty war beast. He will be loyal to thee, and guard thy life with vigor."

Karah slipped in front of the beast's wings. The gem-flesh beneath her legs grew suddenly warm and soft, though it remained clear and vivid green. "Ho, away!" she shouted, and with a rattling flap of wings, the monster lifted into the air.

"My thanks, mighty Heinous," Karah shouted, remembering her manners at the last minute.

"Make me lots of babies," the god called after her.

That was the sort of duty she thought she wouldn't mind. At least she *hoped* she wouldn't. The idea of bartering with gods didn't appeal to her.

She tried not to think about the flying, about the water far below. But the beast was far faster than any horse. In an instant, she and her monster were soaring over the battlefield. The dead and dying lay everywhere, while the smoke of gunpowder and the stink of blood filled the air. Faces turned up to her, and muskets and arrows began pointing in her direction. The flying tusk-cat screamed as an arrow struck it, and dove straight at the shooter. The huge bird talons ripped the woman's head off before she could move, and the giant wings lifted Karah back into the air again. Arrows rained at her, and she shrieked, "Up, beast, up, or we die!"

Thou art too near the sea, the voice of Heinous whispered in her head. *Thou must go over the first rise, and look for a great upwelling of the earth's bones. Beyond those massive stones, thou wilt find Amigot Thidded, and thy key. But go swiftly, Akarakara, or all may yet be lost.*

Karah located the boulders without difficulty, and noted a cluster of bodies in front of them. She and her monster angled, and as she got nearer, she saw that Eowlie crouched near one of the dead, keening.

Her stomach lurched. She could think of only one person for whom Eowlie would mourn. She brought the monster down a short distance from the beast-woman, and shouted, "Eowlie! What happened?" She told the monster to stay. *He will guard thee,* Heinous whispered in her mind. Karah nodded and ran to Eowlie's side.

"He's dead," the woman whispered. She lifted her chin and howled again.

Karah knelt beside Amourgin, who lay sprawled on his back. He had a massive hole in his chest—his clothes were blood-soaked and his skin was ghost-white. Karah took a deep breath and closed her eyes, and sent up a quick prayer to the Three to watch over his soul.

Then she turned to Eowlie. "I need to look for a key he had," she said.

Eowlie stopped howling, and looked directly at her for the first time. Karah saw tear streaks lining the dirt on her face, and the puffy redness of her eyes. "Do what you must. I won't hurt you."

Karah rested a hand on Eowlie's shoulder for an instant. "I'm sorry," she whispered.

"So am I."

Karah began digging through the dead man's pockets, finding nothing that remotely resembled a key. She heard her tusk-cat scream as she loosened his pouch from his waist and began digging through that. She glanced up long enough to see him attacking several Tseldenes. "Eowlie, you have any ammunition left?"

"No."

"I was afraid of that." She dumped the contents of the pouch onto the ground and rummaged through it.

Jewels sparkled up at her. *The key!* She slipped it into the torque, and turned it, as the tusk-cat finished off the Tseldenes and let out another terrifying scream.

She felt the world hush. The sounds of battle on the other side of the hill fell silent. The wind stilled, the slashing rain became a drizzle and then stopped altogether, and it seemed to Karah the whole of the world waited with indrawn breath. She pressed fingers to the tattoos on her cheeks and forehead—quiet reverence—and whispered, "I call upon the Three, Father, Mother, and Wolf-Child, to attend me in this, my hour of need."

The tension grew greater. Nothing moved. Eowlie, next to her, sat unblinking, wide-eyed, and only the near-imperceptible rise and fall of her chest proved her not frozen.

Then the earth beneath Karah's feet heaved, and an anguished voice filled the very world. "WE—CANNOT—BREAK—OUR—CHAINS."

The sounds of battle began again in a clash and a scream, and Karah gripped fistfuls of the earth on which she knelt and screamed with rage. "For NOTHING?!" she shouted. "All I've done has been for NOTHING?!"

Thou art too hasty, little one, the voice said in her ear. *Thou hast not called upon me—but even so, perhaps I can help thee. I shall go down into their fiery prison and free them as a favor to thee.*

"My thanks, Heinous," Karah whispered. And then she thought of the grinning little god, and thought to wonder about the price he would ask for his favor.

My price? She heard him chuckle, though the sound in her mind grew fainter, as if he were receding into the distance. *We shall decide that between us at some later date, thee and me.*

Whatever his price, she knew, she would have to pay it.

The sounds of battle grew fiercer—and Karah prayed that Heinous would be successful in freeing the Three, no matter what he asked in return. The tusk-cat guarded her and Eowlie, and the two women knelt next to the bodies of Amourgin and the men and women he and Eowlie had killed.

They waited.

"When?" Eowlie asked.

Karah clenched her hands and stared downward. "Soon, I pray."

Willek felt the enemy power build and build—and then she felt the spell go amiss. Elation flooded through her—they had the Theophone, and even with it, they couldn't win! The gods weren't coming. She whooped, and urged her troops onward. That bastard Morkaarin scion and his people were trapped against the sea. Darkist had rallied his Tseldenes.

Shemro was breathing her last, all of this was about to be
over—

She recalled, briefly, the vision of her head falling to
Morkaarin's headsman.

"So much for inescapable visions of the future," she snarled.
It would be nothing more than simple justice, she decided, to
play out that scene, but with his head instead of hers on the
block. She would see to it.

Darkist ran a group of his spears to the front. The upstarts
who'd gotten first to the Theophone were out of ammunition and left with nothing but pikes and swords. Their wizards were holding a good line, but wouldn't for much longer.
The victory that had seemed to elude him was finally within
reach.

Then a delicious tingle of power surged along the back of
his neck—a spell sent out and finally about to home in on its
victim. He closed his eyes momentarily, listening only dimly
to the surge and crash of battle. He was focusing on his weakened magical senses. The spell . . .

He recognized it at last—grown massive and horrible in
the time since he'd sent it off, still aimed for the target he'd
chosen.

He smiled slowly. He would get to watch the lovely Willek
die, devoured by his incomparable water-devil, and would see
the second of his obstacles topple at the same instant as the
first. Death, despair, and destruction—and out of it, the new
god Darkist-Colchob, who would find the Theophone and
graft it to himself, so that none would ever dare question his
power again. He would not rule by divine right, but *as* Divine
Right.

Bren saw his outer line fall, decimated by the enemy's rallied forces. *"If only"—those are the words in a fool's world,* he
thought. But they would not leave him alone. He thought of
Karah, of the future they could have had, of days that stretched

in front of them. If only the Theophone had done what it was supposed to do.

All was lost—hope, his life, the world as he had known it. There was no more time.

He raised his sword forward, and led his troops in their last charge, roaring, "We'll take 'em to hell when we go!" And his soldiers, who loved the man who might have been king, charged willingly toward hell with him.

Karah felt the hot tears start down her face. Help didn't come, and it didn't come—all she'd done had been for nothing, and the battle was lost. She rested her head against Eowlie's shoulder and whispered, "We tried, Eowlie. By the Three, we tried."

"Vetter we die with them than fall on our swords," Eowlie said.

Karah rose. "Then let's go die."

Then a fierce, jubilant shriek erupted from the depths of the earth, and stopped the thunder of guns and the clash of metal. The earth rose as it had before, but this time it ripped apart, and out of the seam rose a giant figure, the figure of the Father, his falcon beak open, his lion paws spread with his claws raking the earth. An instant later fanged Mother leapt from the belly of the earth, and charged after her lover. And last, Wolf-Child chased out of the hells after them, and galloped into the battle, howling.

A ragged cheer rose from the remains of the XIXth and the surviving natives. The Tseldenes screamed and those who could break away from the fighting fled; the Tykissians among Willek's following threw down their weapons and knelt, raising their arms in adoration.

Karah and Eowlie stood where they were, frozen, stunned by the violence of the gods. From the heart of the fight, bodies flew threw the air and crashed to the earth like broken toys thrown by an angry child. The fury of her gods seemed to Karah greater than her plea for help could have caused.

Their fury has nothing to do with thee, littlest, the by-then-familiar voice whispered in her mind. *The One of the Thousand Faces tricked the Three down into that prison it created for them, and compelled them to stay there in silence until a mortal thought to rescue them. The Three have been trapped down there for a very long time. Mortals very rarely set off to rescue their gods, you see.*

Karah saw.

Something inexplicable happened. Those Tseldenes who had been racing wildly away from the sea abruptly reversed direction, and screaming, headed back toward the Three and the combined forces of the XIXth and the Shemro loyalists.

Eowlie growled suddenly. "You smell that?" she asked.

Karah shook her head.

"Strange—smells like jungle water—coming up from the cliffs."

Karah sniffed, but didn't have Eowlie's nose. "I smell nothing but blood and shit and gunpowder."

"Wait, then. Whatever it is, it's coming."

A small company of prisoners marched past them, surrounded by soldiers of the XIXth. The Three stood guard over the captives, who, Karah could see, made no attempt to escape. Then the Wolf-Child turned to face the cliff, and his hackles rose. He bared his teeth and growled so that the earth trembled again.

Over the crest of a distant hill stalked a thing of mud and water, its form uncertain in the long light of late afternoon.

"What is it?" Karah asked.

Eowlie shrugged. "Another god? A demon? I don't know."

Karah looked about for a weapon. Eowlie watched her with apathetic eyes. "Get something to protect yourself with, Eowlie."

"Why? I finally had a life again, and now I don't." Eowlie stood and began to walk toward the water-fiend. "Why should I care whether I live or die?"

"Because *I* care." Karah grabbed her arm and pulled her back down. "There are always reasons for living."

✧   ✧   ✧

The water-demon came across the rolling plains, and Darkist, captured by Morkaarin's troops in the sudden turning of the battle, watched with pleasure as it tread with slow, heavy steps toward Willek. The magic that he'd put into it was greater than anything he could raise in his new body—but it was enough that he could take pleasure in its making, and in the devastation it wrought. His stupid sheep, who had abandoned him to the enemy, were first to be sucked into its ever-expanding maw.

My creature, he thought proudly, and conceived a plan by which his creature could free him. It would devour Willek, of course—he doubted even the gods could stop it from carrying out the reason for its existence. But first, it could come and rescue him.

With what magic he could muster, he called to it. At first he thought his call was too weak, but after a moment he noted a slight but perceptible change in the direction it travelled. That miserable beast-god Father stood in front of it as if to bar its progress, while all the Tykissian fools cheered—and it flowed around both sides of him, not even slowing down. Darkist smiled. The men and women guarding him looked at each other, the priests stared at them and made their futile warding spells, and then all of them looked at Darkist.

"It is *my* creature, come to save me," Darkist-Colchob said, and grinned. He flexed the muscles of his massive arms and legs and added, "Even your gods are powerless to stop it."

The water-demon moved closer, and one of the priests said, "We can do nothing. Fall back!"

The Tykissians melted away, leaving Darkist standing alone on the sand. The soldiers shot their arrows at him, hoping to kill him before he could be rescued, but they wasted their ammunition. Only things of magic could kill a magician, and Darkist, even weak, had no equals. He reached up to embrace his monster, his savior, and it tenderly put down one ill-formed hand to lift him up.

He stepped onto the hand, confident, shouting, "I'll have

you all yet!"—smiling at them with purest joy at this last-minute triumph he'd engineered—

And realized his foot had stepped *through* the hand, not onto it. He was knee-deep in swirling, sucking, deadly water, and his creature was still moving forward.

"Stop!" he shouted, putting his magic into it.

The water-demon was stupid, and its reactions were slow. It rolled forward while thinking about his command, and enveloped him as it did so. He struggled, but the current dragged him in.

NO! he thought. *Not like this!* He held his breath, and struggled to command the requisite magic to break apart the creature's will and to thus kill it, or to float himself away from the circling vortex in its center, but he was too weak, and his old self had built too well.

His chest felt as if it would burst. He felt the cold, limp limbs of the already drowned tangling with his own—an intimacy he would never have permitted in life. He stared out at the light of day's end that filtered through the watery body of his creature.

He swam—but the endless, mindless strength of the ever-circling current that held the demon together was more than his own weakening strength. And at last his arms and legs faltered, and at last his will gave out, and at last he gasped once, with lungs aching for air that filled only with water.

His final thought was, *Anything for one more sunrise.*

Solmin raised his head from his divining sticks, and said to Bren, "It seeks Willek's blood, and cannot be stopped until it has it."

"There is no other way?"

The priest's lips were a thin line. "None. And others will keep dying until it has her."

"Then have the guard bring me Willek. Quickly."

Bren bellowed for a headsman, and one appeared, running.

"This will be quick," he told the man. "We cannot try her, we cannot give her either due process or priest's blessing. When she comes, take off her head, and then run. Don't miss on your first strike."

The headsman nodded. "Who is the woman?"

"The Grand Admiral."

The man paled, but nodded again. "I can do it," he said. "Have the priest shrive me for my sins when the deed is done."

Solmin came running, and the guards with him, dragging a screaming, cat-fighting Willek. Bren saw her up close for only the second time. She was a lovely woman, he thought. Then she saw him, and her glance darted from him to the headsman, and at once she stopped screaming. She straightened herself and walked proudly.

"I knew," she said directly to him. "I already knew."

Bren didn't understand.

She brushed away the hands of the guards, looked the headsman in the eye, and said, her voice cold and authoritative, "Do the job right, you." And then she knelt, and lay her head across the makeshift chopping block.

The headsman seemed for an instant stunned.

"Now," Bren snapped.

The axe flashed—red in the last rays of the setting sun, red as blood.

Willek's head rolled—Bren saw her eyes wide and surprised, her mouth slack, before he turned away.

"Run," he commanded his people.

They fled before the wall of living water that came at them. It swirled around Willek, and kept on coming.

Then, without warning, it roared with the sound of a wave breaking on a cliff, and rolled into the smooth, still waters of the Rose Sea.

Bren watched the sun set beyond the far horizon, over the Rose Sea, and thought, *Tomorrow, the sun rises on a new world.*

Karah and Eowlie were dragging Amourgin's body down to the beach, to be numbered with the rest of the dead, when the Three came to Karah and stopped her.

The Mother raised her hand and said softly, "Daughter, by your will and deeds we are free. We would give you a boon, in gratitude. Name anything within our powers, and it will be done."

Karah knew instantly what she wanted. "Can you make the war to have never happened?"

"We will not, for that is not one thing, but many—and there are things both good and bad that have resulted from the war. To undo it would be to set ourselves back in chains and the foul One back in his seat of power over us."

Karah nodded. "Could you then bring back to life all those from the XIXth who were killed?"

The Mother shook her head slowly. "Again, daughter, you have asked not one thing, but many. It has been our will that those who have died have come to us in due time. We will not reverse ourselves and give up all our souls."

Eowlie gripped Karah's arm. "Does that mean they would give vack one?" she whispered.

Karah looked down at the blasted, torn, fly-covered body they dragged, and said, "Is Bren safe?"

"Bren is safe, and by our word will be king."

I would be most grateful to thee, daughter, if thou wouldst have those gods give back my only other worshiper. I need him much more than do they.

Heinous sounded pitiful and terribly hopeful, and he did not demand the man's life as her gift for freeing the Three— though Karah thought he had earned the right. And Eowlie had life in her eyes for the first time since Karah found her next to the fallen law-speaker.

"Could you give this man back his life?" she asked, and pointed at the body.

"You do not have to take your boon now, child. You can save it for a moment of great need. I would not spend a gift on such a one as that—an ofttimes unbeliever, a man who would defend either side of a point for pay. . . ."

Karah took a deep breath and said, "Can I ask for the return of this man's life?"

The Mother frowned. "You can. It would be a foolish request. There will be many things you desire in the days and years to come, and you will look many times on this moment with regret."

"Perhaps. Nevertheless, Mother, Father, and Child, that is what I ask. Please give this man back his life."

Amourgin screamed—his scream went on and on, while his flesh grew back, and his bones knitted together, while his body reversed rot and decay—his scream went straight into Karah's soul, and burned its place there.

Then he rolled over and crouched on hands and knees, weeping, while Eowlie knelt beside him, whispering to him, stroking his hair with one hand, pressing her face to his side.

Karah felt a lump rise in her throat. *It was the right thing to do,* she thought.

She looked up at her gods. "Thank you," she said quietly, and smiled.

The Mother did not return her smile. "You earned our blessing. Simply remember—kindness is never a sin, but it is often a flaw." The gods vanished together, leaving Amourgin wrapped in Eowlie's arms, and Karah, outside the desperate intimacy of their greetings, to search for Bren.

"She's dead," Bren said. "At the end, Solmin said Willek's magic must have been keeping her alive as much as it kept her in thrall. Willek needed Shemro to live so she could proclaim Willek's right to rule."

"You don't." Karah looked at the wasted body of the woman who had been her emperor, then up at him.

"No. She was family, though—and I never knew her. All my life, I've hungered for family."

Karah held his hand. "Now you'll have it."

Bren turned and pulled Karah into his arms. He kissed her fiercely. "Yes," he whispered, feeling real happiness and a sense of wholeness he'd never known before. "Now I will."

✪ CHAPTER XVII

"You're pardoned," Bren said curtly to Willek's troops—Willek's ex-troops—as they kneeled before him. "It's a soldier's first law, to be faithful to their salt. I won't punish you for following one you thought was your lawful commander."

He turned to the chieftain. "Your people fought bravely," he said. "I don't forget my debts. The Rose Sea will be part of the Empire now, but this land will remain yours, yours and your children's children. Your only tribute will be the duty of guarding it."

Tagog nodded. "Sir—Majesty—if a captain can give advice to an emperor—"

"That's brigadier," Bren said.

"—we'd better start back. Three Alone know what's happening back in the northlands, with the Emperor and the Grand Constable both vanished."

Bren grunted agreement. "I'm not looking forward to that trip—" he began.

Karah groaned and rolled her eyes; Amourgin coughed discreetly into his hand. Bren grinned, and touched the torque about his neck.

Take me— He stopped. Wishing was dangerous, very much so when you got what you wanted. *Take us to the Imperial camp.*

Vast wings seemed to brush across his vision. The cool

freshness of the Rose Sea's shore vanished; the dry heat of An Tiram supplanted it. Cries of terror rose as officers exploded away from the map table in the Grand Constable's tent, over-turning the sand table that held scale models of the city and the besiegers' lines. He watched their faces as they recognized him; his name ran through the camp in an echoing murmur. And from the looks, they were seeing something *else*, not just the band of ragged fugitives behind him. For a moment he felt a tremor of the same luminous awe, reflected back from their eyes. Then the sensation died, and reality returned: with the sewage-horse-and-garlic smell of a war camp, and the distant thud of artillery dueling with the city's defenses.

The Imperial staff officers drew their swords and knelt with the blades across their wrists. "Command us, lord," they said in ragged unison.

Most of them, he thought, probably even meant what they said. The rest he decided he would deal with generously for the time being. Those who did not come around he would have to take care of eventually, of course. But first there was An Tiram—and the Empire of Tarin Tseld, which suddenly owed fealty to him.

"First order of business," he said. "The Emperor—my aunt—is dead, may the Three receive her. We'll hold an assembly of the Army—" an old Tykissian tradition, that the new ruler had to be raised on the shields of the war-riors "—and I'll take the title of Regent until we can hold a coronation in Olmya.

"Second—Count Mustermaster General Feughylfa—arrange for a truce and cease fire. The war is over."

They came, the Tseldenes—sullen and proud, but still they came, in silks and feathers, underneath the blazing midday sun. They attended themselves with musicians, with slaves, with carpets rolled along the ground that their feet might never touch dirt. They stood in the commander's pavilion, eyes cold, heads high, and one of their number read their opening declaration—their requests and demands for terms of surrender.

Bren, newly made Emperor of Tykis, listened, arms crossed over his chest, until they ran out of things to say.

Then, he answered them; his response was shorter, and clearer. "No."

The commander's pavilion fell silent—the Imperial officers on one side, the delegation from An Tiram on the other. Mostly officers there, too, with a clutch of higher nobles. No priests, he noted grimly. Most of the priests on both sides of the war were dead. The air smelled of expensive perfume and fine leather, incense. Bren was dressed with somber elegance in dark blue silks; they felt unnatural on skin used to rags and rawhide.

"We are not here to discuss the surrender of An Tiram and the empire of Tarin Tseld," he went on.

"I am Regent," he went on. "I also have—*this*." He touched Karah's arm, and she turned the key in the Theophone, and whispered something.

The sky above the pavilion went black as moonless night, and all the ceremonial torches guttered out. A falcon's shriek ripped through the darkness—and then glowing, marching over the harbor, the Three came. They walked in the light of their own radiance, glorious, their eyes fixed on Bren. The Father stopped at the great statue of Darkist that stood astride the harbor, and with another avian shriek, slammed it into the water with one paw. The Mother clapped her hands in a sound like thunder, and every ship that had ever died in the harbor came to the surface, and rebuilt itself.

Then the Child howled his long, shuddering, mournful howl, and all three gods leapt into the air and soared into the heavens, to become the familiar beacons of light that were the Father, the Mother, and the Child. They raced across the sky, and not until they were gone did the sun dare to rise.

A rustle of awe went across the chamber. "I will be Yentror. Emperor of *all* the peoples."

He turned to the Tseldenes; they went down on their knees, then on their faces. "My first order—stand up!"

They obeyed, eyes still on the carpets. "There will be no confiscations, no pariahs here in the southlands. You gentlemen will keep your estates, and most of your customs and religion. There will be changes—for starters, no more sacrifices. We'll move on from there."

There were murmurs of gratitude. "Hope you don't expect *that* to last," Karah said in his ear.

"Beat me to it," Amourgin murmured in the other.

Bren nodded. "And there are going to be some changes north of the Imperial Sea, too," he went on. Some of the Imperial courtiers paled. "To begin with, this lady—Karah Grenlaarin—is now Regent's Consort and future Imperial Consort. We'll have the ceremonies later."

A wave of low bows rippled over the assembly. Astonishment showed on some faces at the thought of a consort from the lower nobility. *Get used to it*, Bren thought.

"This gentleman is Amourgin Thurdhad. He is now First Councillor and Chancellor of the Realm."

This time he touched the Theophone lightly to still the murmurs; Amourgin wasn't even of the *lower* nobility.

A man could get too reliant on this, he thought, feeling the god-presence at the back of his mind. He'd have to watch that. Gods, even benevolent ones, strained the human scale of things too much for routine intervention to be tolerable.

Amourgin started slightly at the magnitude of the promotion, and Bren gave him a bleak smile.

Why should I be the only one to suffer? Bren thought.

"There will be other appointments to follow. For the present, we'll see to the reprovisioning of the city and the reestablishment of order. I want the Tseldene commanders to report to me in private, and we'll begin the demobilization. Now—"

Karah could see in her father's eyes that Iano Grenlaarin was stunned by the sight of the Imperial house banner as it came up his road and into his courtyard, and more so when he recognized her riding beneath it, with the ceremonial cloth-of-gold parasols held over her on long poles.

She could see him studying the man beside her. She wished she could hear his thoughts.

The rancher went to one knee as Bren dismounted and bowed his head.

"Majesty," he said.

Strong hands raised him; they were of a height, her two men. "Father-in-law," the Emperor replied.

Karah was off her horse and with an arm under his elbow when she saw him stagger. *"What?"* he croaked. "We'd heard—new Emperor—but—"

"We came faster than the news," the ruler said. "I'd have come incognito, but," he shrugged, "the Yentror's a slave to protocol, I'm finding."

"Pa, I'll tell you all about it later." Karah smiled at him, thinking he would be proud of her—of all she had done, and of all she had become. "But first, where's Ma?"

Her smile slowly faded at the look on his face, and as she noticed the sudden burden of years that stooped his shoulders. Out of the corner of her eye, she saw Bren sign the guards to stand back, as her father turned and wordlessly led them to the family plot in a corner of the ranchhouse yard, beneath a scattering of pepper trees.

Her stomach lurched, and her hands knotted into angry fists.

"Misa Grenlaarin," she read. "Fallen defending hearthstone and family, Five hundredth forty-first year of the New Empire, Month of Wolf Running. May the Father shelter her, the Mother comfort her, the Child be with her, until the world is made new."

She signed herself and turned to Bren. "Just after we sailed from Derkin. Oh, *godsall.*" After a moment she raised her head. "What happened?"

"Konzin betrayed her—you—all of us," her father whispered.

"Konzin? Where——?"

"You can see him," Iano said. "But the ants haven't left much." He took her in his arms. "Weep, girl. I've had my tears."

She held her father tight—and fast on the heels of the anger and the sickness came another thought, a terrible thought. *I could have brought her back. They said I would regret—*

Then she heard a whisper in her mind, the voice, not of her mother, but of the Mother. "You can change your mind. We will allow you that."

The scope of it was more than she could take in for an instant. She pulled away from her father and stood looking at the plot of ground. Her mother was under it. Almost, she asked the Mother for that one gift—but she looked back, to Eowlie standing next to Amourgin, back of the guards. She had given her word. She would have to take one life to get that other . . . and her mother was already with the Three—

She stepped back from the grave, feeling a terrible weight settle in her heart.

Bren stood helplessly, his hand resting on her shoulder. When she looked into his eyes, he whispered, "I know. My own mother . . ."

She had not told him the whole story. No one knew that but her, and Eowlie, and the god Heinous. Not even Amourgin knew he'd died—he hadn't remembered, and at her first opportunity, she'd sworn Eowlie to secrecy. It had been a gift, one she didn't ever want to have to justify to people who could have thought of better things to do with it.

She had never truly believed she would have been one of those people.

She felt tears streaming down her cheeks—her anger and her dismay and her regret—and the only words she could say to her new husband were, "I wanted her to meet you."

Bren held Karah, feeling a sudden distance between them that hadn't been there before. He saw her look at Amourgin, and saw faint anger in her eyes. He wished he knew what that look meant—but then she looked at him, and the anger was gone, and the distance with it. "All things come round in their season," she said softly.

"All things." He pulled her close again, and held her, his eyes closed, as she started to sob.

"I did the right thing," she said, again and again, until at last she stood away from him and blew her nose.

Bren extended his hand to Iano, and they gripped forearms. "I'm truly sorry. I cannot make up for what has happened, but I hope to be a good son to you."

He drew Karah back to his side. "And the Three be my witness . . . I mean to see that there's *peace* within our borders from now on."

So much for omnipotence, he thought, feeling the weathered rancher's eyes on him . . . and feeling their approval. *Death is master even over the gods.*

He looked around: at the entourage standing at a respectful distance, at the gaping ranch hands, at the long honeycolored slopes beneath the evening sun. He was tired, and suspected he would be for a very long time. Olmya and the palace were coming, all too soon.

"Let's go in," he said, kneeling briefly and laying a jeweled feather from his hatbrim on the grave. "There's the business of life to attend to."

"I thought we'd come to the ending, where the heroes go home and all's well," Karah said with a quiet bitterness.

Bren took her hand. "There are no endings, only more beginnings," he said, willing strength from his palm to hers.

"No ending except this," she said, the tears falling from her cheeks to her mother's grave.

"Who knows?" he said, as they turned from the grave. "Perhaps that's a beginning, too."

MERCEDES LACKEY

The Hottest Fantasy Writer Today!

URBAN FANTASY

Knight of Ghosts and Shadows with Ellen Guon
Elves in L.A.? It would explain a lot, wouldn't it? Eric Banyon really needed a good cause to get his life in gear—now he's got one. With an elven prince he must raise an army to fight against the evil elf lord who seeks to conquer all of California.

Summoned to Tourney with Ellen Guon
Elves in San Francisco? Where else would an elf go when L.A. got too hot? All is well there with our elf-lord, his human companion and the mage who brought them all together—until it turns out that San Francisco is doomed to fall off the face of the continent.

Born to Run with Larry Dixon
There are elves out there. And more are coming. But even elves need money to survive in the "real" world. The good elves in South Carolina, intrigued by the thrills of stock car racing, are manufacturing new, light-weight engines (with, incidentally, very little "cold" iron); the bad elves run a kiddie-porn and snuff-film ring, with occasional forays into drugs. *Children in Peril—Elves to the Rescue.* (Book I of the SERRAted Edge series.)

Wheels of Fire with Mark Shepherd
Book II of the SERRAted Edge series.

When the Bough Breaks with Holly Lisle
Book III of the SERRAted Edge series.

HIGH FANTASY

Bardic Voices: The Lark & The Wren

Rune could be one of the greatest bards of her world, but the daughter of a tavern wench can't get much in the way of formal training. So one night she goes up to play for the Ghost of Skull Hill. She'll either fiddle till dawn to prove her skill as a bard—or die trying. . . .

The Robin and the Kestrel: Bardic Voices II

After the affairs recounted in *The Lark and The Wren*, Robin, a gypsy lass and bard, and Kestrel, semi-fugitive heir to a throne he does not want, have married their fortunes together and travel the open road, seeking their happiness where they may find it. This is their story. It is also the story of the Ghost of Skull Hill. Together, the Robin, the Kestrel, and the Ghost will foil a plot to drive all music forever from the land. . . .

Bardic Choices: A Cast of Corbies with Josepha Sherman

If I Pay Thee Not in Gold with Piers Anthony

A new hardcover quest fantasy, co-written by the creator of the "Xanth" series. A marvelous adult fantasy that examines the war between the sexes and the ethics of desire! Watch out for bad puns!

BARD'S TALE

Based on the bestselling computer game, *The Bard's Tale.*™

Castle of Deception with Josepha Sherman

Fortress of Frost and Fire with Ru Emerson

Prison of Souls with Mark Shepherd

Also by Mercedes Lackey:

Reap the Whirlwind with C.J. Cherryh

Part of the Sword of Knowledge series.

The Ship Who Searched with Anne McCaffrey

The Ship Who Sang is not alone!

Wing Commander: Freedom Flight with Ellen Guon
Based on the bestselling computer game, *Wing Commander.*™

Join the Mercedes Lackey national fan club! For information send an SASE (business-size) to Queen's Own, P.O. Box 43143, Upper Montclair, NJ 07043.

POUL ANDERSON

Poul Anderson is one of the most honored authors of our time. He has won seven Hugo Awards, three Nebula Awards, and the Gandalf Award for Achievement in Fantasy, among others. His most popular series include the Polesotechnic League/Terran Empire tales and the Time Patrol series. Here are fine books by Poul Anderson available through Baen Books:

FLANDRY • 72149-6 • $4.99 _____

THE HIGH CRUSADE • 72074-0 • $3.95 _____

OPERATION CHAOS • 72102-X • $3.99 _____

ORION SHALL RISE • 72090-2 • $4.99 _____

THREE HEARTS AND THREE LIONS • 72186-0 • $4.99 _____

THE PEOPLE OF THE WIND • 72164-X • $4.99 _____

THE BYWORLDER • 72178-X • $3.99 _____

THE GAME OF EMPIRE • 55959-1 • $3.50 _____

FIRE TIME • 65415-2 • $3.50 _____

AFTER DOOMSDAY • 65591-4 • $2.95 _____

THE BROKEN SWORD • 65382-2 • $2.95 _____

THE DEVIL'S GAME • 55995-8 • $4.99 _____

THE ENEMY STARS • 65339-3 • $2.95 _____

SEVEN CONQUESTS • 55914-1 • $2.95 _____

STRANGERS FROM EARTH • 65627-9 • $2.95 _____

If not available at your local bookstore, you can order all of Poul Anderson's books listed above with this order form. Check your choices and send the combined cover price/s to: Baen Books, Dept. BA, P.O. Box 1403, Riverdale, NY 10471.

Name _____

Address _____

City _____ State _____ Zip _____

GRAND ADVENTURE
IN GAME-BASED UNIVERSES

THE BARD'S TALE™

Join the Dark Elf Naitachal and his apprentices in Bardic magic as they explore the mysteries of the world of The Bard's Tale.

Castle of Deception
by Mercedes Lackey & Josepha Sherman
72125-9 * 320 pages * $5.99   _____

Fortress of Frost and Fire
by Mercedes Lackey & Ru Emerson
72162-3 * 304 pages * $5.99   _____

Prison of Souls
by Mercedes Lackey & Mark Shepherd
72193-3 * 352 pages * $5.99   _____

And watch for **The Chaos Gate** by Josepha Sherman coming in May 1994!

WING COMMANDER™

Fly with the best the Confederation of Earth has to offer against the ferocious catlike alien Kilrathi!

Freedom Flight
by Mercedes Lackey & Ellen Guon
72145-3 * 304 pages * $4.99   _____

End Run
by Christopher Stasheff & William R. Forstchen
72200-X * 320 pages * $4.99   _____

Fleet Action
by William R. Forstchen
72211-5 * 368 pages * $4.99   _____

STARFIRE™

See this strategy game come to explosive life in these grand space adventures!

Insurrection
by David Weber & Steve White
72024-4 * 416 pages * $4.99   _____

Crusade
by David Weber & Steve White
72111-9 * 432 pages * $4.99   _____

- -

If not available at your local bookstore, fill out this coupon and send a check or money order for the combined cover prices to Baen Books, Dept. BA, P.O. Box 1403, Riverdale, NY 10471.

NAME:_____

ADDRESS: _____

_____

I have enclosed a check or money order in the amount of $_____:

Paksenarrion, a simple sheepfarmer's daughter, yearns for a life of adventure and glory, such as the heroes in songs and story. At age seventeen she runs away from home to join a mercenary company, and begins her epic life . . .

ELIZABETH MOON

THE DEED OF PAKSENARRION

"This is the first work of high heroic fantasy I've seen, that has taken the work of Tolkien, assimilated it totally and deeply and absolutely, and produced something altogether new and yet incontestably based on the master. . . . This is the real thing. Worldbuilding in the grand tradition, background thought out to the last detail, by someone who knows absolutely whereof she speaks. . . . Her military knowledge is impressive, her picture of life in a mercenary company most convincing."—**Judith Tarr**

About the author: Elizabeth Moon joined the U.S. Marine Corps in 1968 and completed both Officers Candidate School and Basic School, reaching the rank of 1st Lieutenant during active duty. Her background in military training and discipline imbue The Deed of Paksenarrion *with a gritty realism that is all too rare in most current fantasy.*

"I thoroughly enjoyed *Deed of Paksenarrion*. A most engrossing highly readable work."
—Anne McCaffrey

"For once the promises are borne out. *Sheepfarmer's Daughter* is an advance in realism. . . . I can only say that I eagerly await whatever Elizabeth Moon chooses to write next."
—Taras Wolansky, *Lan's Lantern*

* * * * *

Volume One: Sheepfarmer's Daughter—Paks is trained as a mercenary, blooded, and introduced to the life of a soldier . . . and to the followers of Gird, the soldier's god.

Volume Two: Divided Allegiance—Paks leaves the Duke's company to follow the path of Gird alone—and on her lonely quests encounters the other sentient races of her world.

Volume Three: Oath of Gold—Paks the warrior must learn to live with Paks the human. She undertakes a holy quest for a lost elven prince that brings the gods' wrath down on her and tests her very limits.

* * * * *

These books are available at your local bookstore, or you can fill out the coupon and return it to Baen Books, at the address below.

SHEEPFARMER'S DAUGHTER • 65416-0 • 506 pp • $4.99 ____
DIVIDED ALLEGIANCE • 69786-2 • 528 pp • $3.95 ____
OATH OF GOLD • 69798-6 • 528 pp • $3.95 ____
or get all three volumes in one special trade paperback edition,
THE DEED OF PAKSENARRION•72104-6•1,040 pp•$15.00 ____

Please send the cover price to: Baen Books, Dept. BA, P.O. Box 1403, Riverdale, NY 10471.

Name_____

Address_____

City_____ State_____ Zip_____

PRAISE FOR
LOIS MCMASTER BUJOLD

What the critics say:

The Warrior's Apprentice: "Now here's a fun romp through the spaceways—not so much a space opera as space ballet.... it has all the 'right stuff.' A lot of thought and thoughtfulness stand behind the all-too-human characters. Enjoy this one, and look forward to the next."　　　　　—Dean Lambe, *SF Reviews*

"The pace is breathless, the characterization thoughtful and emotionally powerful, and the author's narrative technique and command of language compelling. Highly recommended."　　　　　—*Booklist*

Brothers in Arms: "... she gives it a geniune depth of character, while reveling in the wild turnings of her tale. ... Bujold is as audacious as her favorite hero, and as brilliantly (if sneakily) successful."　　　　　—*Locus*

"Miles Vorkosigan is such a great character that I'll read anything Lois wants to write about him. ... a book to re-read on cold rainy days."　　—Robert Coulson, *Comics Buyer's Guide*

Borders of Infinity: "Bujold's series hero Miles Vorkosigan may be a lord by birth and an admiral by rank, but a bone disease that has left him hobbled and in frequent pain has sensitized him to the suffering of outcasts in his very hierarchical era.... Playing off Miles's reserve and cleverness, Bujold draws outrageous and outlandish foils to color her high-minded adventures."　　　　　—*Publishers Weekly*

Falling Free: "In *Falling Free* Lois McMaster Bujold has written her fourth straight superb novel. ... How to break down a talent like Bujold's into analyzable components? Best not to try. Best to say 'Read, or you will be missing something extraordinary.'"　—Roland Green, *Chicago Sun-Times*

The Vor Game: "The chronicles of Miles Vorkosigan are far too witty to be literary junk food, but they rouse the kind of craving that makes popcorn magically vanish during a double feature."　　　　　—Faren Miller, *Locus*

MORE PRAISE FOR
LOIS MCMASTER BUJOLD

What the readers say:

"My copy of *Shards of Honor* is falling apart I've reread it so often.... I'll read whatever you write. You've certainly proved yourself a grand storyteller."

—Liesl Kolbe, Colorado Springs, CO

"I experience the stories of Miles Vorkosigan as almost viscerally uplifting.... But certainly, even the weightiest theme would have less impact than a cinder on snow were it not for a rousing good story, and good storytelling with it. This is the second thing I want to thank you for.... I suppose if you boiled down all I've said to its simplest expression, it would be that I immensely enjoy and admire your work. I submit that, as literature, your work raises the overall level of the science fiction genre, and spiritually, your work cannot avoid positively influencing all who read it."

—Glen Stonebraker, Gaithersburg, MD

" 'The Mountains of Mourning' [in *Borders of Infinity*] was one of the best-crafted, and simply best, works I'd ever read. When I finished it, I immediately turned back to the beginning and read it again, and I can't remember the last time I did that." —Betsy Bizot, Lisle, IL

"I can only hope that you will continue to write, so that I can continue to read (and of course buy) your books, for they make me laugh and cry and think ... rare indeed." —Steven Knott, Major, USAF

Send me these books:

Shards *of Honor* 72087-2 $5.99 ____
The Warrior's Apprentice 72066-X $4.99 ____
Ethan of Athos 65604-X $5.99 ____
Falling Free 65398-9 $4.99 ____
Brothers in Arms 69799-4 $5.99 ____
Borders of Infinity 69841-9 $4.99 ____
The Vor Game 72014-7 $4.99 ____
Barrayar 72083-X $4.99 ____
The Spirit Ring (hardcover) 72142-9 $17.00 ____
The Spirit Ring (paperback) 72188-7 $5.99 ____
Mirror Dance (hardcover) 72210-7 $21.00 ____

Lois McMaster Bujold:
Only from Baen Books

*If these books are not available at your local bookstore, just
check your choices above, fill out this coupon and send a
check or money order for the cover price to Baen Books,
Dept. BA, P.O. Box 1403, Riverdale, NY 10471.*

NAME: _____

ADDRESS: _____

I have enclosed a check or money order in the amount
of $ _____.